SUSAN BA

# THE HOUSEKEEPERS

Bathwick Hill▲

© Bathwick Hill Publishing LLP, 2020

Bath, United Kingdom

ISBN 978-1-9161350-3-1

Bathwickhill.com

Author: Susan Barrett

Artwork and Cover: Ali Tomlin

For Christina, who was nineteen in 1955

# Chapter One

Our fresh start would have had a different ending, if only we'd listened to the warning bells. Not that 'colourful history' appeared anywhere in the estate agents' coded details. (Translation: the scene of acts of unspeakable violence, baroque death or nasty murder resulting in permanent and awful haunting.) 'Massive potential' did though. So, the place was a dump. But by then we'd seen inside enough ruinously expensive holes to let that pass. Were accustomed to, even occasionally entertained by the *simple hacks* owners came up with to camouflage their bad taste and worse housekeeping. In one place, described as 'characterful', to divert attention from decades of damp, someone had thoughtfully set dressed the breakfast table with plastic croissants, gingham napkins, fake flowers in a vase.

Never mind the only places Bill and I had ever owned were new builds; pleasant properties, best described in just the three words: sterile, white and box, or that our idea of DIY was changing the light bulbs ourselves, of course we could tackle a 'real doer-upper.' Panicked to action by the bullish London property market of 2015, and because we really needed somewhere to live, we booked an immediate appointment to view.

Exactly what the property 'benefited from', 'comprised', 'boasted' quickly revealed itself on the threshold, with the forcing of the front door. Stepping over the surprisingly glossy junk mail piled up behind it on the mat, we followed the estate agent crabwise up a staircase, every step of which was stacked with broken things. An accurate write-up of what to expect on first and second floors, where we could do no more than look in at the dark entrances of small rooms stuffed with furniture. Even the bathtub brimming with clothes and shoes.

As if in viewing nothing much we hadn't seen quite enough, we negotiated our way back down to the semi-basement kitchen to inspect the abode of filthy formica, woodlice and the occasional orange slug tempted in by all that lovely rotten woodwork. Along with washing in a bath and sleeping in a bed, it seemed whoever lived here last wasn't too keen on cooking either.

Our rapid once-over ended with the 'wow factor' receptions on the raised ground floor. That featured in this house full of furniture just the one large black leather armchair. Continuing the hoarding theme however, it looked like, for years and years, no book, or magazine, or newspaper, flyer or leaflet, brought in here ever made it out again. Narrow paths between the piles of paper got me to that chair, grim and greasy and down on its heels as a street sleeper in a doorway. My husband meanwhile angled a floppy broadsheet he'd taken off the top of one of the stacks to catch what light he could through the grubby back window. And as if to umpire us from the centre line, the agent took up position by the tall doors that folded across to divide the two rooms. If you could have shifted them. Even this keen young man, you could tell, was somewhat disheartened by the small dank hovel he was supposed to be talking up.

Pretty much mute till now myself, I hailed Bill across the paper wastes: looks like we've tracked a reader to its nest.

Misunderstanding me, he called back: who knows what's been breeding in here – probably all sorts.

Allsorts are the worst, aren't they?

Eh?

Never mind, what's happening in the news where you are?

Catching my drift this time, he looked into the yellowed old newspaper in his hands: Vietnam, mostly. Oh, and The Beatles are top of the charts.

Groovy.

Picking up a second paper, wide as a bed sheet, he said: hang on, I think I actually remember this; says here we're at war with the Argies, over the Falklands.

Damn that Jeremy Clarkson and his comedy number plates, I lobbed back.

This verbal knock-up having gone straight over his head, the lad at the net called 'the clutter', then something about us seeing past it. We both chose instead to overlook him.

From where it had been put by, splayed over a chair arm branded by cigarette burns as if with the scars of self-harm, I picked up a vintage Penguin paperback, its cover illustration the rather lurid picture of a young couple kissing under a tree. Bill himself had by now moved on to examine the many random leavings scattered across the tops of the paper drifts. Overflowing ashtrays; a giant dried-up Quink inkbottle; elastic band ball; many biros; paperclip daisy chains. Delicately he replaced a pair of spectacles as they were: taking a dim view from their paper plinth. *What are these strangers doing here?* Suddenly self-conscious under the gaze of those glass eyes, careful not to lose the place, I put the book back as I found it.

Aware we were behaving with the sobriety of SOCO officers sifting through the evidence, wanting to lift the mood, I said: at least there's no call for the paper suit, the latex gloves.

Not having properly thought through the effect this would have on my fastidious husband, I followed this up with: no mould, no maggots, no corpses.

He let drop a sticky-tape dispenser.

Come on, Bill, it's office supplies and newspapers they hoarded not their own hair, or carrier bags full of rotting food.

You think, how about the strange smell?

We sampled the sweetish air that had a note of pineapple to it. Our estate agent did too.

Perhaps we should just be grateful it's not the usual loaf in a damp tea towel in a hot oven meant to mask any *nasty niffs*, I said in a silly put-on voice.

This hint of hysteria was probably the result of shallow breathing that, along with the odd pong, had cut down on my intake of oxygen. Ignoring Bill's raised eyebrow, I resumed the normal etiquette of the house hunter: poking about before passing judgement on the absent owner's weird lifestyle. On top of a blanket and coverless duvet muddled together in the chair's seat I'd noticed a Telegraph had been left folded to the crossword completed in firm green biro capitals. And down by the side there was a toaster, with single slice of very hard toast still poking out, electric kettle, teapot and many used mugs and plates full of crumbs and smears of dried-on jam. Also conveniently to hand, an old record player with a ziggurat all its own: of classical discs.

Crowded out of every other room, it was here, in this chair, that the recluse not only slept but also entertained and catered for themselves as well as – going by the barricaded bathroom – maybe even met other bodily needs.

If I wouldn't be pointing out to my husband the sleeping, or the putative weeing, I hoped the discovery of the little domestic tableau might make this seem less like the investigation of a crime scene.

Over here, I called.

Elbows in, my husband made his careful way down the thin goat tracks.

Taking a look, he said: how other people live their lives, eh?

Cosy, really, when you think about it: tea, toast and the Elgar cello concerto.

Really, I thought it was pretty grim. Going by the evidence of the newspaper archive, I reckoned the short-sighted, novel-reading, crossworder who lived here had done so, alone, for half a century. The last refuge of one of life's refugees, it had been in this fouled nest that all that time they kept obsessively abreast of events, while taking care to avoid the attention of the outside world. Despite conspicuous need, there was not a sniff of Social Service intervention about the place. No grab rails, no carers' clipboard with initialled rota and notes, no weekly pill organizer. If I couldn't know what were the circumstances behind the start of the shut-in's sad story I thought I did its last line. 'No forward chain' in the agents' details suggested they died here. And since that Telegraph was dated to six months back, probably in the autumn of last year.

My feeling was that she was a woman. Poor mad, sad, lonely, old bat.

# Chapter Two

How to describe the Celia of 1955, the year life went bung? Born just before the war, comfortably off in the Home Counties, as was normal for your times and class you're a bit of a prig and a snob. At nineteen, I don't like you much. But should remember it is because you are young that what you do and say can still make me cringe. Or want to reach across the years to give you a hug. Or a shake: I might feel sorry for you, you suffer, I know, but your sadness exasperates me. After days spent crying into teacups when you do finally get out of bed it's to drift about the living room. Just like any other dust mote trapped in the shafts of the low autumn sun, you revolve round and around within the thickets of too familiar furniture. The fern stands and the footstools and the fire screens and the many little drop leaf tables you've come home to. Eyes on your feet as they pass and re-pass down narrow trails that lead nowhere, you fail to notice the new sightline that's been opened up for you.

It's only when you're carried on slow indoor air to the window, feel its cool pane under your forehead, do you realise while you were away in the hospital someone must have arranged the removal of the vast Victorian chaise longue that stood here once, barricading the view. That this moment is of sparrows taking dust baths in the warm shadows under the lavender bushes, people passing down the street, white clouds in a blue sky. Because you lack the gumption, even if metaphorically, to smash through the glass and let back in sound and scent and colour, all remain unreal and unreachable as pictures projected on a screen. So life goes on out there without you, the spectator, while patiently you await the man riding to the rescue.

In the event, it's not a long vigil. The haunting elegy of the rag and bone man soon sounds from afar: 'iiiinnnnyyyyRAGBOOOOOOOOne!' It takes only a gesture from the captive at the window for your hero behind his clapped-out charger to present himself upon the doorstep, eager, ready and willing to free the damsel in distress from the heavy chains of her enchantment.

Over the few, giddy days of your liaison you'll discover the White Knight's real name is Mr Hubbard. The ever-so refined 'Ubbard himself chooses to address the maiden as 'mum', like some ancient parlour maid. In fact, your champion resembles the woman who once 'did' for granny, being similarly pursed of lip and cadaverously reedy, yet with the combined sugar tong delicacy and surprising sinewy strength of someone as used to handling bone china as lumping furniture to sweep beneath. Or humping it onto the flat bed of his cart to find its new, temporary home in a railway arch, under the sign of "Thos. Hubbard & Son".

Having worked his way through the movables, Hubbard's genteel rabidity turns next upon fixtures and fittings. When that source dries, to likely detritus turned out from the back of cupboards. To the very few things you actually like or would have been better advised to hang on to.

With now no rags or bones to throw him – the pram in the hall, of course, along with the furnishings from the top floor rooms are beyond your jurisdiction – understanding he's had all that's on offer here, without a backward glance, Hubbard's off over the horizon. Un-rescued, you remain. In watching him depart, however, your back is now turned upon a room culled of its contents. The only task your knight of the dreadful brown pinstripe suit, Ulster scarf and flat cap was successfully to perform. Though, evidently, shifting the lumber you've been lumbered with wasn't the correct stratagem for opening up a pathway for you out of these deep dark woods. Ugly and black as a blasted oak, that malevolent chaise, long planted on its spot, might have been rooted out and hauled away, along with, courtesy of Hubbard, the many other sticks of furniture, but simply clearing out this changeable old house was never going to empty it of its human history. For as it now appears, the owners of the banished furniture have put out little hooks to catch on and hold you fast in here. If their belongings had 'belonged' in a way you do not, blocked, baffled and bewildered still, it's you, so it seems, who may never leave the place.

# Chapter Three

If every sinister house story must begin with the wilful disregard of all the bad omens and horrid portents, of course we bought the dump.

I might as well have blamed spring sunlight for turning to powdered amber the dust and fag ash we stirred back to life in long shut up air, but to the irrational romantic – to me, in fact – it was actually the unadorned evidence of neglect and dereliction I fell for at first sight.

Even as we foraged down the dim green tunnel of the hall, kicking through the leaf litter of catalogues, property mags and flyers I succumbed to the allure of atrophy. Or as a Japanese connoisseur of ruin porn would have it: *haikyo*. Like in those photo essays by urban explorers who disturb the dreams of a long abandoned mansion or hospital or hotel, was entranced by the prospect of hacking my way onwards and upwards through the briars and brambles that clutched at the ankles on every stair tread. My enthusiasm for the viewing only keeping pace with the mounting tally of deal-breakers it discovered. Right up to the last: the cosy lair, where, half a minute before, the occupant might have put by her book, stubbed out her final fag, drunk down the last of her tea and, along with that slice of toast never buttered, popped off.

Surprising her in her absence felt like an intrusion, but necessary to breach the deep enchantment the house lay under for the half-century she was in possession. Just by squatting and accumulating, it seemed to me its careless custodian – whoever she may have been – was responsible for letting the place slip into the coma that had preserved something ineffable, irrecoverable, of the past in here. My only real consideration at the time, that if this sleeping beauty disguised as a tramp had held on, unloved and un-regarded, for someone to come along to lift the spell she slumbered under, mine must be the safe pair of hands into which this place, so delicately stalled in time, must drop.

Reaching for him across the top of that horrible old chair, I said to Bill: you know, this place *has* got massive potential.

He shot me a look of horror: you mean for a fire?

He'd had a point. In these rooms crammed with paper, the tale of the accident waiting to happen was told by the overflowing ashtrays and many burn holes. Equally eloquent of disaster averted was that the kettle and toaster, the record player too, along with a four bar electric fire, standing where the original Georgian fireplace would've been (was still, underneath the plasterboard?) were all of them multi-plugged into a dodgy-looking block adaptor.

But what probably should have frightened me off from the start was that we'd have to acquire from somewhere the sensitivity, and taste, as well as the cash, to do it up not just beautifully but fittingly as this rare property survival merited.

Regarding the taste: I'd watched the TV shows, hadn't I? As for the money, congratulating me on my vision, perking right up, the agent assured us a property of this vintage, so close to its 'original frame', at just under the mill, was 'sensibly priced.'

However sensibly priced, my husband didn't hide his preference for somewhere habitable to make a start on our new London lives.

I said: imagine the challenge it would be, the privilege, to take on somewhere so untouched as this. Who knows what we might find preserved underneath all the crap?

More crap? Actual crap?

Probably the least offensive hoard Bill could imagine digging up in here was nail clippings.

I thought: buried treasure.

# Chapter Four

As if it was not just their chattels they left behind them but buried within its very fabric their blood, skin and bones, nightly, the residents past reassert themselves, to whisper from the walls.

Having failed to put to flight the house ghosts in the purging of their possessions, you launch yourself into an even more thorough exorcism. As if unwinding the foot cloths and toe rags off a tramp after the grimy outer layers have been sloughed off, set to with the finer work of unpicking. Precisely obsessive, strip out every last scrap of the litter and dross that's been secreted deep within these old rooms by human hands. The paper and rags used to plug the gaps between floorboards, plaster and skirting board, windowpane and glazing bar.

Mostly torn from cheap magazines and newspapers, you'll discover this makeshift draft proofing often comes self-dated. From 1856 to nearly the present day the brief spasm of grubbing turns up a century's worth of yellow press cuttings.

'Missing woman found dead by river. Louis beats Walcott champ down twice. Bankers Optimistic.'

Cambridge-educated, with eyes ever-obedient to the printed word – what you saw, you read – and used to daily downing great draughts of information, at present you can tolerate only the tiniest sips of sense. So that, complete in themselves, like maxims, you find these snippets ideally suited to your reduced capacity. As for wanting to know whether her killer was ever caught, the champ came back to fight another day, their optimism was misplaced, you are as uninterested by the people in the stories as you are incurious about whomever it was squirrelled away this stale news in the first place. Like dirty feathers, letting them drop and settle all about you on the floor, your feet soon lost in airy nothings.

It's only noticing today's date, September 11th, looking back at you from a fragment of fifteen-year-old newspaper gouged out from the window frame that you consider the laggers themselves. Whose were the hands that were occupied this very day back in 1940 in sowing what you now as diligently unpick, Celia? Since it's "The Mail", you imagine a woman standing on this same spot, at this same window, stuffing.

Maybe she too watched and waited here for the worst to happen? Perfectly reasonable in her case since her bulletin comes direct from the Blitz, and this old square really caught a packet. Bending your knees, you wobble the softening edge of the horizontal fault line in the Georgian windowpane over an aspect that was radically altered by the bomb dropped on it. Of the terraced houses on the far side of the square *she* would have known, the five that took the direct hit are your own view of an overgrown bomb site. Violently opened up rooms with respectable wallpaper long exposed to view – birds and flowers grown grey under sunlight and rain. To your surprise you find yourself relieved the pane of glass you're currently looking through survived what the houses did not. It might mean she dodged that one at least.

That the fragile bit of newspaper dates from just four days after the start of the battle to annihilate London from the air suggests she hadn't yet learned to take shelter under a kitchen table in the basement at the first tuning up of the sirens. But, in the very thick of it, had instead tried to stop this old window from rattling with every blast of the raid that perhaps for her lent this particular day in September extra significance.

The linking of time past and time present in space gives you pause and as if you've been treading on her toes you take a step back from the window. Will the clues to the life you once lived here end up as just another dusty pellet the house coughed up or might your own antiquated tones some day pass directly into another's dreams?

Actually indifferent about your own legacy as you are unsentimental, by virtue of its tenacity alone, about pretty much anything inherited, 'Daily Mail woman' soon ends her days in this house as just more trash on the floor. Unlike your historian husband, you are no archivist.

Ten hours after William Bone closed the door on his comatose wife, he opens it on a scavenger, heel deep in shreds and tatters. The hunter, home from the hill – or back on the bus from South Ken – greets his bride with a nervous: "What, what, what? Been keeping yourself busy, I see!" Stranded amongst thousands of defunct words, seemingly incapable of uttering a syllable of your own, when you do find your tongue, his habitual geeing-up makes you brusquer with William than any keen young husband's homecoming surely merited:

"There's not a thing in the house to eat."

Keeping his tone carefully light, "Not even a single sausage?" he says.

In those useful hours the diligent housewife would be attendant upon her domestic duties, beleaguered by those dates, damn dates, you've lost all track of time so that the product of today's particular spasm of mad industriousness is, indeed, much mess and no supper.

"Well, then, what say I pop to the chippy?" suggests William, as if his disgracefully and hopelessly impractical new wife is deserving of just this treat after her very full day spent labouring over the clean slate.

Later, in unwrapping the battered cod and soggy malt vinegar chips, William, good as his word, went out again to buy for supper, you notice that the nails of your right hand are broken and quite black. Surprised to see this evidence of sustained purpose – yes, you think: my day has been very full indeed.

In the season of the furniture pogrom on returning from his day's business to ever emptier and more comfortless accommodation William never uttered a word of rebuke. Even now is too much of the gentleman to mention that letting go the nearly new Utility chair and sofa and the chenille living room curtains, shabby as they were, might have been a bad idea. It means, however, that another evening of domestic harmony must be passed under the eye of the street, Dr Bone seated in a deck chair unearthed from the final dumping ground of the coal cellar, his wife on a packing case.

Your husband has lit a small and smoky fire in the grate that isn't really needed this mild September evening but stands in for something lively between the two of you – like having a young pet, you think. And diligently you read books that in your case require not a page to be turned.

When the time comes round once more to prepare for bed, you gather up the newspaper you've been eating off, along with the wastepaper of history still strewn across the floor. Tipped onto the dying fire, yesterday's news emits a sharp and dispirited steam, whereas the sweepings of yesteryear are dry enough to catch at once. Briefly blazing before they settle as ashes and cinders, history's last hurrah makes an even more appalling pong than had the boiled vinegar.

# Chapter Five

I might have been grateful to the mad, sad, old bat for safeguarding my house from the rough improving hand of present taste and convenience all those years. Felt even a passing pang of sympathy for the wasted life that ensured this place slipped through the unsympathetic decades unnoticed and unchanged. Nevertheless, the first thing I did was to evict her. Chucking in the skip, the ugly black chair in which I imagined her squatting like a toad, or a spider at the middle of its complicated web. But even after I bagged and boxed up the rest of her stuff ready for disposal, my predecessor lingered on in the presence of her own particular smell.

To make sure to see her permanently off the premises, using the only likely implement to hand, a fish slice, I set about scurfing off the Hessian wall-coverings within which she seemed to have taken up permanent lodging as the odour of stale cigarettes, burnt toast, and pineapple. And when I finished scraping back this first layer, heel-deep in litter, just carried right on grubbing.

The timeline in domestic archaeology, just like any dig, going in reverse order, my excavations down through the wallpaper strata briefly laid bare each successive mood swing of fashion and economics the house was subject to these last couple of centuries. Hessian and woodchip, followed by murky flock wallpaper, painted thickly over yellow pigment, concealed magnolia and brown that in turn covered over long buried arsenic green and anaglypta. Disclosing only to destroy, I was not so much stripping out the historic context I fell in love with at first sight as liberating what must lie preserved beneath. Or so I told myself. Only pulling off the many layers of tramp's padding this old bag lady had clothed herself in on her long and perilous journey down the years in order to reveal the true aristocrat I knew she was all along.

My inadequate kitchen implement replaced by a hand steamer and a lad on loan from the main contractors, the eventual reward for all this fossicking was to strike my true buried treasure of authentic Georgian features and materials. Purbeck stone paving in the hall and precious Hogarthian hues in their original burgundy, sage green and stone on the walls. As if with the dropping of a last veil, my Regency Lovely was exposed at last in nothing more than her modest foundations. All that now remained hidden by those early nineteenth-century drawers, or so I thought, were her good bones. Lath and lime plaster, fortified with authentic horsehair and bare brick. Handmade. Naturally.

Soon after we received Listed Building Consent from the conservation officer down at the council, and what with the prospect of party-wall agreements ahead, I decided we really must make friends of the neighbours.

Leonard and Ryk, to the left of us, at the last minute couldn't make it for the proposed get-to-know-you drinks, so Bill and I greeted the couple on the right,

Greg and Debby, at our new old front door. The cause being to win neighbourly cooperation, actually forbearance, they were barely across the threshold and I was popping corks. Glasses hardly clinked, and pointing out the most thrilling of my 'finds' in the archaeological journey of the wallpapers: a rather marvellous scrap I'd excavated high up in the hall, the maker's mark, of Williams, Coopers and Boyle, *absolute dating* it to between 1802 and 1810. Glasses in hand, we next paused to admire the remarkably well-preserved panelling below the dado rail and the beautifully turned mahogany handrail and nineteen barley twist spindles of the first run of the staircase I'd sprung from beneath the easy-clean hardboard within which someone rational had boxed them. In the 1950s, I supposed, when the decorative was dumped in favour of function.

Only now allowing our guests out of the hallway and into the raised ground floor front, still, in eager-to-please mode, not letting them get a word in, I drew their attention to the elegant arched window, with the fault line running right through the handmade crown glass pane. Authenticating it as Georgian. To the exceptionally crisp ceiling mouldings, from which, in a labour of love and obsession that nearly killed me, I half joked, I'd already poulticed, then burned off an inch-thick accretion of multi-coloured paint jobs, ending up by taking a scalpel and a toothbrush to the detail.

I displayed hands that looked as if I'd spent the last month in picking oakum.

If I expected credit, I was getting none from Greg and Deb.

Bill came to my rescue, saying: you can probably tell, Abi's a bit overexcited about digging up the ancestors.

I took the hint to cool it and gesturing with my ruined hand toward the mutilated chimneybreast, said: sadly, the grave robbers got there first in the case of the fireplace.

All I got was crickets.

Giving it another go, I said: I guess our predecessor was to blame for that bit of vandalism?

As though she'd taken a giant dose of antidepressants, smiling vaguely, Debby stuck with 'no comment'; Greg, however, was off the blocks.

In nine years, I think I only saw the old bird a handful of times, and never to speak to, so, apart from the occasional blast of opera, haven't got a clue what she got up to in here.

By the state of the place, that'd mostly be hoarding, said Bill.

Raising my glass to indicate that I at least knew the value of misanthropy and inertia and gratified my hunch she was a woman was confirmed, I said: on the up-side, not touching a thing in here has knocked a good half-century off the journey we're about to set out on: to take this place back to exactly how it was in 1815, so I'll forgive her chucking the odd fireplace on a skip!

Bill toasted me back, I hoped not wholly ironically, saying: the fireplace we'll no doubt be spending a fortune replacing.

Although it was me who'd suggested this, it was to the 'other bloke', Greg responded: when you say *exactly* how it was, I take it you'll be putting in the usual mod cons?

Accepting the conversational baton, Bill was right back at him with the matey banter: even if Abi intends to turn back time in here, we'll definitely be having electricity, hot running water, who knows, even central heating.

Though this was a mild September evening, wrapping her arms around those weirdly wide shoulders of hers to suggest a chill in the air, Debby maundered inconsequentially: these tall rooms can be a nightmare, I mean the draughts…

I followed her husband's lead, by ignoring her. And, because I really didn't have a clue, hazarded: definitely central heating, but eco – I mean sustainable as well as unobtrusive – so something like trench or hybrid.

Misconstruing Greg's pained look as sympathetic interest, I enthused some more: before electricity was installed in here, newfangled gaslights replaced candles – getting rid of all the pipework, then patching up and re-plastering, was a real pain. So it'd be a shame, wouldn't it, to mutilate these poor old walls yet again just to install redundant radiators?

Absurdly, I patted a wall.

I see our role as curators rather than owners of this rather special place. The plan is to restore and conserve rather than renovate. You know, a bit of lifting and nipping and tucking so this venerable lady can face life in the twenty-first century looking refreshed rather than like she's had loads of *work* done.

If I thought I'd got past him that what this house would soon be undergoing would involve scalpels and fillers rather than pneumatic drills, this claptrap was enough to trigger Greg. Glancing off stage left, he said: I think Len and Ryk told us something similar before they started titivating their *old dear*. Still put us through two years of hell!

Debby got in: these old places aren't really designed for living in, though, are they?

The family mouthpiece himself scoffed: suffering through other people's *home improvements*!

The conversation really got going with a swing now we'd got on to how they were forced to endure months of chaos while Leonard and Ryk knocked their house about. But when Greg rounded off his list of grievances with the final insult that the householders moved out for the duration, I thought I could put a cap on it, saying: as it happens, we'll be staying put to fully share in the misery!

Neither Greg nor Debby reacting well to my attempt at humour, Bill generously helped me out with a bit of backfilling for the hole I was busily excavating for myself: like Abi says, these historic places come with a degree of responsibility, which is why, now Listed Building Consent's finally come through, she's taking a career break to project manage.

Best not to admit that until quite recently I thought LBC was only a radio station.

So she'll be on site the whole time to make sure the noise and dust is kept to the absolute minimum.

Before Greg could draw breath, I was right back at him with the enthusiasm: whatever this old house – or English Heritage – can chuck at me, I'm 'ard enough!

(English Heritage actually wasn't involved – at Grade Two the house being of insufficient architectural interest – but I hoped they got my point. I also happened to know that theirs wasn't listed.)

I was aware of trowelling on the northern grit but if Bill's vowels were the real thing my own adopted accent under stress was now thick enough to make you flinch. Clearly, it'd flummoxed Greg.

You've a background in the building trade, Gail?

Me? No! About a hundred years ago I qualified as a lawyer.

'Appen, replied Greg, hilariously.

I gritted my teeth and reminded myself we needed to keep him and his dull wife on side.

Bill and I both did, I said, giving my husband's arm a conspiratorial squeeze: but then I had one of those rushes of blood to the head and got a job as a researcher on a consumer journal, and after that, very short-lived, I was a researcher/presenter for a TV consumer show. I actually started to retrain as a teacher, before I discovered I don't like teenagers, but most recently I've been in-house lawyer for a small charity. As you've probably worked out I'm a bit of a professional schizophrenic or schizophrenic professional. You know: on with the next thing!

My accent had by now morphed into something straight off the hockey field. Toning it down, I concluded: anyway, with our relocation down south, the time felt right for a bit of work/life re-evaluation. You know.

Greg mock-confided in my husband: watch out, Bill. Woman wants a career break start picking out names and schools, mate.

Last in a long line of Badias and Roshinas, and Bilals known as Bill and Shayans who preferred to get Shay or Stan over Sharon, proud alumnus of a West Yorkshire comp, he bit his tongue. For which I was again grateful.

It was Debby, surprisingly sparked back to life, who stepped up to the plate, saying: because being a stay-at-home mum to three kids under eight is the easy option?

Like many an aggrieved spouse who mistook 'in public' as the ideal platform for battling out a festering domestic, she was evidently under the misapprehension that to prove its validity, gain sympathy, her side of things needed only a robust airing before witness. She shot me a look that I declined. If I wasn't much mistaken, here was a woman keen on making a connection. I might have been anxious to open up new networks as far as neighbourly good will went but as for new friends – even though we'd dropped off most of our old ones at the end of the A1 (M) – I wasn't bothered. In any case, as it turned out from here on this would be the Deg 'n' Grebby show.

With the same 'open air cover' sniping technique as his spouse, Greg swiftly got in his mirthful return salvo: the kids are great, of course, that's not to say if someone offered me a couple of quid on Ebay for 'em I wouldn't be tempted! 'S just if there'd been some warning she'd be chucking in the job to have them *before* we bought, arse end of 2007, bang at the top of the market, I might've decided supporting four dependants as well as a whacking great mortgage on just the one pay packet wasn't worth the postcode!

Aware the newly animate Stay At Home Mum was gearing up to come back at him, I piped up: that'll be a career, *not* a baby break. If I don't like teenagers, I really can't stand children!

(I think Deb got the message. I imagined I'd have been having quite a different conversation with Leonard and Ryk. I strongly suspected I'd have preferred it.)

Again joke-covertly, Greg said: listen, Bill, me old mate, never mind your *Grand Design* needing her hands-on project management skills, take no chances – hire a professional, get the wife back to some sort of gainful employment soon as.

Saying nothing, my own dear husband busied himself amongst us once more with the Prosecco. Greg quickly presented his glass for a refill, Debby sucked on a lemon. Before disappearing, never to return: I'll go and find another of these, Bill proposed, holding aloft the empty bottle as cover for his exit.

Unlike me, for whom social masochism – let's call it manners – would have its eventual reward, soon as we saw the back of them, in the laying bare of the particulars of their utter awfulness, Bill would no longer be arsed schmoozing the neighbours.

Picking up the pace, I invited Greg and 'the wife' to follow me for a quick tour of the upper storeys. And once they'd obediently inspected these, at a clip, marched them all the way down to the semi-derelict semi-basement, featuring the original-to-the-house dresser I'd spent a happy half-hour emptying of its stock of Angel Custard Powder, Ambrosia Creamed Rice, Pickering's Pie Fillings and Libby's Peaches – many with price labels still in shillings and pence.

Glancing around the cramped, smelly, subterranean lair, Greg indicated with his thumb through the party wall to the blokes next door, saying: size of the kitchen they've dug out for themselves down there: Tweedledum and Tweedledee. Talk about the Starship Enterprise, 's all floating modular units and touch screen controls. Fridge's smarter than me! Greg snorted, tickled to incredulity: would you believe they knocked through the rooms on the top floor, opened the place right up to the rafters, to make a 'media centre.' Bloody marvellous!

Debby, who appeared these last ten minutes off the Prosecco to be back on Prozac – seeing who'd she'd married perhaps she was – was roused to another burst of animation.

You should see their master suite, Abi, it's gorgeous…

Swiftly shutting her down, Greg said: ghastly: his 'n' his dressing rooms and a wet room that's all over black marble…

These lovely etched glass panels…

Done up like a Vegas chapel of rest.

Well, I think it's fabulous, said Debby, her flat tone belying the feeling.

Greg shot back: fabulously expensive! Don't get me wrong, I've absolutely no problem there – I mean *lovely couple*, threw the most fantastic housewarming do – just that's two serious incomes they've got to play with and, goes without saying, he said: no kids.

I settled for an enigmatic smile. Being cool with Ryk and Leonard for neighbours I presumed was meant to flag up an all-purpose open-mindedness towards us too: the mixed-race couple on the other side. Well, cheers for that, Greg, mate! What I actually took from this was that it wasn't the neighbours' life choices, or even the disruption of their renovation, that'd got right up Greg's nose so much as the ready cash they'd had to flash, extending outwards, downwards, sideways to create their one bedroom, two dressing room bachelor pad. Even if Greg was prepared to let pass that at least one of us was a native northerner, as well as brown, I suspected he wouldn't be cutting us any slack when he worked out we'd be spending an absolute bomb doing up this house. All the more reason not to mention Bill's big new job in financial services that had prompted our move south – if the law was bad enough, I knew from experience that banking was not nowadays a profession spoken of openly.

Not that Greg was fooled by my coy act. Greg knew a *lovely couple* when he saw one.

So then, Gail, never mind respectfully reinstating all the missing Georgian bits and bobs in the public rooms, taking care, obviously, to preserve those *poor old walls* – bastard actually flipped me air quotes – I imagine the serious construction work 'll be going on down here?

Lobbing one in subversively from the side-lines, as I was beginning to get was her method, Debby was again moved to mutiny.

Course they're going to put in a great big, modern kitchen. Why wouldn't they? I know I would.

Both neighbours looked expectantly to me.

Uh huh, I commented.

Debby was of course bang on the money. Restoring the public rooms to their full regency glory was indeed the plan, but I didn't actually intend us to live exactly like the Georgians. My very own fuck-off kitchen, installed in the massive rear extension we'd just got planning permission for, would be the model of modern living. Done up in gleaming white or possibly painted in a very dark grey – *Draughty Passage*, I was thinking – with brass and copper accessories and fittings.

As if he read my thoughts, Greg needled: with all the latest mod connery: the Quooker taps and spiralizers?

Oh, I think we all get that life's just too short to spiralize a courgette don't we, Greg? I said.

Debby smiled, I smiled.

Greg smiled: or wait for the kettle to boil?

Shame his smile wasn't quite robust enough to rearrange the rest of his face furniture.

Wishing they'd both of them just go now, in an unconscious replay of the estate agent's tour I smartly rounded things off by herding them back up to the reception rooms, where we began our lap of the house.

Looking appraisingly about himself, Greg said: seriously, though, Gail, central London house prices went up forty per cent the last two years, so, all I'm saying is, save yourself the hassle, love: take up Pilates, meet friends for coffee, you're still winning.

(Bought at the top of the market, did you, Greg, you big tease, you!)

We bared our teeth at each other and downed our glasses.

Gregory and Debora, the new neighbours I'd meant to charm into compliance before the wrecking ball was deployed, at last departed, leaving me only the solace of my bit of certified original wallpaper.

# Chapter Six

"IiinnnnyyyyRAGBOOOOOOOOOne!"

The pang you feel on hearing that familiar totter's alarum that heralds Mr Hubbard's arrival in the vicinity is made the sharper by the knowledge the cupboard wasn't quite bare. There *is* more in here you'd have preferred to see the back of. While recognising it was never an option to send off to their fate the tenants who, like its fixtures and fittings, came with the house.

Along with phrases like 'special treatment' and 'final solution', recent history has forever changed the meaning of 'living space', so that your mind winces from the idea of anyone claiming special rights over it. Unwanted furniture may be one thing, unwanted humans quite another. But, still, those inescapable lodgers! Even if one could ignore the pervasive olfactory prod of perpetually boiling cabbages, the McNamara's pram in the hall will always be there to ambush everyone who crosses the threshold. Sprung, lacquered, black, this monstrous contraption may well have dated to the reign of the last queen but one. To you it resembles nothing so much as an undertaker's carriage built for a dead baby.

It certainly does not escape Betty, your first Cambridge caller – almost the first caller of any description since you and William moved in here.

"Irish or blacks?" she robustly enquires.

Thinking it rather callous of her not to appreciate what the pram might represent for you, "Irish," you whisper, wishing you weren't bullied into openly branding the tenants as such, hoping you aren't overheard by little missus, as you envisage: listening in from her domain at the top of the stairs.

Betty remarks in her posh, carrying tones, "Breed like rabbits."

Hustling her along the hallway, you practically push the visitor into your own living quarters.

Not that these prove safer ground.

Lighting up, Betty sets off across bare boards in narrow expensive shoes, smoking furiously and appraising. Nervous as a cat you watch her go. Never mind the depressing evidence of the lodgers, your own accommodation equally does not find favour. Sucking on her cigarette, thirsty as a navvy, she manages on only the thin flute of her exhale, the wry tilt of her head, to disparage the deck chair, the packing case.

A married woman, with her own household, you think you really oughtn't to be bamboozled in it. But have no one to blame but yourself. Ever since you moved in here Betty has been angling to call on the invalid at home, until, for politeness' sake, you gave in and invited her.

Stalking some more on long scissoring legs: "Curtains?" she demands. Her sudden loud voice ricocheting back off the bare windowpane causes you to jump and squeak, "Hanging in shreds and tatters." With the single damning observation, "Dust," your husband's first fiancée in quick order next denounces the ceiling mouldings. You might have come up with a defence (in William's words) of their classical simplicity but she's already on to the next horror.

"Gaslights!"

Paused in her peregrinations by the regrettable wall brackets over the mantelpiece, his old flame now inspects the fire below it that you had the forethought to set and light in honour of her visit. Apparently not at all discomforted by the idea of the girl she was jilted for in her married bliss, she jokily remarks of the feeble blaze, "Love alone keeps one warm, eh, Celia?"

Self-consciousness rather than the fire has made you glow to your ear tips.

Easily browbeaten, as you are, if Betty hasn't worked out for herself by now what an open fireplace and extant gaslights signify, you aren't quite so ingenuous as to let slip that, along with furniture and curtains, you get by without electrical power in here. Not that your esoteric husband counts this an exiguity. When first you were shown over the house he had assumed there being no electricity installed was a selling point. The inventory of all that's wrong with it apparently at an end, rather than conforming to the usual mores of good form and common kindness, whatever was one's true opinion, and just congratulating the new house owner, being posh and intellectual Betty doesn't give a hoot about calling a spade a shovel, saying, "Frankly, m'dear, apart from the rather obvious dearth of ornamental clutter, the place reminds me of somewhere ghastly you'd go to visit granny." You yourself might not worship at the altar of history, so even if your return fire must be launched under the cover of counterfeit enthusiasm for old things, to have ascertained quite how divergent Betty and her Bill are in the important matter of *taste* supplies the ammunition:

"They might be shabby and old-fashioned but don't you find these rooms elegant? So I believe, in the evolution of the domestic interior, it's considered that the sublime point of harmony and symmetry was definitively achieved in the Regency era." Betty's having none of it. With that odd, distinctive gesture of hers of cocking her head, she fixes you with one eye, squawks, "As for the *gorgeousness of Georgian geometry*, or whatever it is, for goodness sake, what you and Bill need isn't an historic monument but a home. Buy yourselves some proper furniture, put up curtains and get rid of that hideous gamboge wallpaper!" Relieved she hasn't demanded to round off the house tour with an inspection of the domestic offices that in their appalling authenticity are beyond even William, you summon up some pep, saying, "The flock *is* repellent, you're quite right, actually I plan to paint over it in a more cheerful colour."

"Seal, darling, if you're truly fit enough for paintin' and decoratin', wouldn't it make a deal more sense to find some sort of employment to occupy yourself outside the home and get in a bloke for the whitin' of the sepulchre?"

The floor to ceiling swoop of her ciggie with which she mimics a professional paint job causes a great deal of fag ash to be flung about.

This allusion to your recent indisposition only ties your tongue, deepens your blush, but Betty's not paying attention to you. Shivering svelte shoulders up to elegant earlobes, she continues: "But as a matter of urgency, darling, replace the historical grate with a four bar that might do some harm – it's only been five minutes and I'm chilled through. I don't know how you stand it, really I don't, moonin' about in here."

"Honestly, I never feel the cold."

"Nonsense!" announces Betty, "It's as the tomb, and about as cheerful. What I propose is that you and I get out right this instant from under the eye of the oppressive wallpaper and go for a frothy coffee somewhere lovely and warm."

It comes as a surprise someone brusque as Betty might be sensitive to an atmosphere. But if you yourself too keenly know that feeling of being overlooked, the failure of the furniture and ancestor eviction makes *out there* seem impossible. Panicked by the prospect, unwisely you attempt to practise the subtle arts of bluff and feint.

"I'm afraid the only place I know of locally is a *caff* called "The Blue Kettle" – it has a giant kettle, painted blue, attached to the outside that gives out real steam – and apparently, not long ago there was a murder there."

"What fun!"

Really, you might have known better than to scare off Betty with horror stories. Being a sophisticate, she wouldn't bat an eyelid at frequenting the scene of a nasty murder. Should have guessed too she might actually prefer a greasy spoon to any nicer teashop on offer. Hailing from the land of Lawrence, Elizabeth Eleanor Seaton likely believed the only truly *valid* types were the social and intellectual elite and the labourer. As well as a proper blue stocking, being a knife and fork heiress, coming from an ugly town, an honourable place was no doubt reserved in Betty's universe for both the patrician and the prole – whom she most likely valued as *instinctual*. It's your own class: the mass of the bourgeoisie, happy at their 'brain' work behind desks in offices, she has no time for.

In desperation you add: "Looks to be frequented mostly by teds."

"Youth parading itself in sideburns and pink socks. No thank you!" Naturally, she'd take objection not to the toughs but the toughs' socks! Antithetical as she might be to an elegantly underdressed regency interior, Betty's sticking point would always be sartorial. Even you, whose entire wardrobe fitted into one small travelling case, and most of it selected and bought by Mother, can appreciate she's always perfectly turned out. Not that in any event socks carry the day. Underestimated at one's peril,

Betty has her own contrary alternative to the dubious charms of the teddy boys' teashop. As though she scrutinised best with her monocular vision which, given the impressive size and deviation of her nose, she well might, the visitor tilts her head at you and says, "Forget about smoking kettles round the corner, Seal, darling, I know just the place, deep in the very wickedest seam of the wicked West End, and *en route* we may discuss your views on the future." Momentarily confused, you ask, "*Food in a pill*, that sort of thing?"

Betty hoots.

"*Your* future, darling child."

"You mean employment?"

"Now you're back on your feet, what's needed is a little payin' job to stop the brain from goin' mouldy." Tossing her spent cig into the useless fire, she commands,

"Onward to the fleshpots!"

# Chapter Seven

We were now nearing the end of September and after weeks of Indian summer the weather had turned. Not that this was putting off the crowd at the cafe's outdoor tables. Stoically these soft southern jessies hunched over their patisserie as a cold wind whipped the froth right off their cappuccinos. An honorary northern hardnut, I myself took care to keep toasty warm inside with my mug and my bun. And I waited.

That Cara kept me waiting was no surprise. My newly local, old university friend specialised in being late, always had, always would. Cara owned time: she was its capricious mistress. She abused it; paid it no heed; did with it as she damn well pleased. It was because she was, as they say in my old stomping ground, a 'propa belta' – still, at thirty-nine, quite literally head-turningly beautiful – that not only was she able to keep getting away with this, but time actually came back for more of a kicking.

It would have been quite easy to despise or envy beautiful Cara, if the experience of being always surrounded by generous and obliging people who smile at you often hadn't made her rather sweet natured, smiley, and generous in her turn. Besides, as a phenomenon of fortunate genetics, she was of equal fascination to girls as well as boys. Cara was her own reward.

Sailing through university, she was let off essay deadlines, as by right given the best room in shared student houses and never, if she chose not to, bought her own dinner.

After graduating Cara was briefly one of those posh birds who fanny about in PR or Advertising for a while before Mr Someone or, more likely, the Hon. Somebody, comes along to provide just the right gilded perch to fly to. (He was called Alisdair, his dad was a baronet, if Scottish, and he was one of *those* bankers. According to our mutual friend Dimphna: a total merchant banker.) Comfortably cooped in her lovely double fronted, it remained only for her to fill its every storey with beautiful blonde chicks. Here, however, uncharacteristically, Cara proved less than perfect. She and Alisdair were married ten years before Fergus, the heir, was apparent. But seeing as prior to motherhood renovating and remodelling her house was our Cara's chosen field, two fabulously expensive interior design projects had nicely filled the interim. So this spur of the moment decision of mine to meet up with my old friend for a quick coffee was a way of getting free advice. (Anyway, this was what I said in my head to Greg.)

My second coffee sunk, intending to nip to the loo, I said to the waitress: excuse me, sorry, I'm supposed to be meeting a friend: tall, slim, long blonde hair, with one of those Buggery-boo pushchairs. Could you tell her I'll be back in a minute?

Even as the words dropped from my mouth I knew that in this neck of the woods my description wouldn't usefully narrow the field. Having anyway probably lost her at *excuse me*, the radgie mare looked back her incomprehension at me and carried on with her task of pushing crumbs off tables. Let alone not being trusted to identify Cara, even though I'd been sitting here half an hour, I doubted she'd easily recall me. Thirty-nine and blessed with a utility face, I'm invisible.

As it turned out, I should have guessed, I'd 've had plenty of time to visit the loo – to fit in a brief affair, indeed, while in there – Cara, as ever was, pitched up at just exactly the point I'd given up on her. Long accustomed to the impact she created, my gorgeous friend entered the cafe as a celebrity, the magic of her unexpectedly stupendous looks breezily declaring: look everyone, I'm here – you can begin!

Unlike Debby, you'd hesitate to slap the sad old SAHM label on our Cara – so effortlessly had she slipped into the yummy mummy aesthetic, pushing baby Fergus in his three-wheeled buggy was now an integral part of Cara's 'look'. You could just tell when the time came she'd ace the school run.

Conferring glamour upon the chosen mortal in attendance with a *sweetie, darling* kiss on each cheek, because she carried it off so beautifully like everyone else in her life I instantly ceded her the absolute right to treat me shabbily.

Sorry I'm late, Abs, she said on reflex. I presumed she had no idea whether or not she was and didn't much care – why would she? Still, she had the courtesy to follow this up with a line: Fergy did a huge poo just as we were leaving the house. Didn't you, darling? But enough of boring me and the infant phenomenon, how are *you*?

Well, tired. The house...

Tired – tell me about it! I had a rotten night with him, and I think the au pair's plotting her imminent defection.

Svetlana?

She corrected me: Svet actually ran for the hills ages ago, now it's the lovely Danica.

Danica?

Happens every time, soon as you get them doing things how you like them done, they're off again, back to Crovakia or Sloatia.

Said Cara, with the political science degree.

Noting my look: I know, I know, she said: poor loves. It's just that they, the huddled diaspora I mean, pitch up here all grateful and wide-eyed and two months later, and two stones heavier, they're back off to the fatherland in my Agent Provocateur.

Flashing me a ravishing smile she repeated her refrain: but you don't want to hear about all that...

Because I truly didn't, I took no chances and leapt in with my own news: like I was saying, work's started on the house at last.

Perhaps it was the grimly purposeful way in which I now opened up the big 'House File' I'd lugged along that made Cara balk.

Darling Abs: always one to go ever so slightly over the top when it came to mastering a brief.

A little stung, I said: all theory I'm afraid. But there *were* a couple of things I wanted to pick your brain about, being the expert.

Ignoring this shameless opening gambit, Cara had herself commenced a thorough cavity search of her huge, buckled, desirable tote.

I persevered: I was wondering, could you recommend a traditional blacksmith to repair the boot scraper? It's just a detail, I know, but it's original to the house.

Still seeking whatever it was: uh huh, uh huh, she said.

And, Cara, would you say Chesney's the one for repro fireplaces? I heard Stovax in Exeter is good too – or should we just bite the bullet and go reconditioned original?

…there you are!

She'd located the kid's Timmee Spillee drinking cup in one of the many dinky brown paper carriers with which she'd loaded young Fergus's sleek runabout. Although my friend had already kept me waiting for a scandalously long time she hadn't scrupled to dawdle at the deli next door to this very cafe for the laying-in of canapés.

Son settled with his drink and some olives – a scatter of black patent goat droppings with which to occupy and amuse the tot in chasing the shiny, salty things across the table top, she asked pleasantly: what was it you were you saying about your boot scraper?

Actually, Cara, what I'd really like your advice on is copying this amazing scrap of original wallpaper.

I placed my lit-up mobile between us: here's a photo, it's a bit out of focus…

Interrupted by the dozy waitress, by the time my friend ordered a fresh mint tea for herself and another *bol* of coffee for me, my third, we were back, somehow, on the subject of her revolting staff. At which point Cara discovered she was late for her next appointment. And I still hadn't managed to prise open her little black book (or little Blackberry) of recommended contractors and suppliers.

Strapping him in, she inquired of her wriggling infant: *chodźmy do kina*, Fergus?

To me, a mite defensively, she said: It's Polish for shall we go to the swings? We're not, but it makes him more cooperative.

We brushed cheeks.

Sorry to love you and leave you like this, honey, but now you've finally seen sense and come home, I mean back to London, and you'll be around during daylight hours, it'll be so much easier to meet up.

Giving me her devastating smile, she added, gnomically: you'll discover, once the men are off, doing whatever it is they do all day, it's a whole other world out there!

She made it sound like I'd joined a secret club. Perhaps I had: the mummies' coffee drinking, olive-shopping confederacy.

With that, together with her beautiful baby and tiny bags of oily goodies (presumably the *big* shop required the serious heft of a 4x4 and a willing Eastern European), out of the cafe door Cara wafted, pulling behind her the gaze of all those privileged to witness her passing. A light smatter of applause would not have been out of place...possibly a bar or two of walk-off music.

Dum da dum, da dum dum dubba dubba....

# Chapter Eight

The very wickedest seam of the wicked West End turns out to be "The Moka" on Frith Street. Seated up close to its steamy window, you drink coffee after frothy coffee, and Betty lectures you some more. Even as you nod across the table at her, the sleeve of your cardigan soon soaked with condensation, you know that amongst the other things you and your husband will be avoiding mentioning this evening will be that whilst he was at his work you stepped out with his old girlfriend.

Thinking back, it must have been in their graduating year that Elizabeth Seaton and he, Betty to her Bill, first became an item. I believe they appeared together in the "Footlights" review. "A Flash In The Cam" it was called – stupid pun. Tall, thin, disdainful Bet in a toga ornamenting a comic sketch about Nero. She handed him his fiddle, apparently. Of course, seeing as he had broken it off with her and taken up with you for the most sordid of silly, hole-in-the-corner, middle-class reasons, she was absolutely entitled to dismiss or despise the little tart who displaced her. Him too, of course. Though being a terrific intellectual snob, it was most probably the damage done to Bill Bone's brilliant career in academe by his unfortunate liaison with silly little Celia, rather than her own heart, that Betty most regretted. Presumably this was why, when he landed his job as *Curator, Medieval Texts*, she tracked him to his lair, down amongst the plaster casts in the basements of the Victoria and Albert Museum. Who knew, with *that* brain, Dr Bone might not make Director one day?

Anyway, since their rapprochement Betty had set herself the task of being enlightened and magnanimous with the fiancé stealer. The main prize might be somewhat tarnished by this unfortunate association with you but tucked in tight under Betty's chic, "French grey" wing, she might somehow cultivate at least the semblance of a proper consort for him, a rival worthy of her patronage.

Or as you then conceived she conceived it: Betty might yet make something of clever Bill's popsy.

Despite her threat that the purpose of this avid tête-à-tête over the Pyrex cups was to interrogate you further about finding a suitable job, Betty's so far stuck with her own brilliant career. So it transpires, since coming down she herself has been slaving *like a field black* (presumably one dressed by Dior, you ungraciously think) to launch a new literary magazine with some like-minded university chums. Having sunk her own cash, suitcases of it, into the Bloomsbury press, Betty's self-appointed role on "Sic" (as it were) is: Commissioning Editor, Verse.

I imagine this involved bossing women poets into uttering to order those poised screams of suicidal despair that were all the 'go' in those days.

The coffee drunk up, the evening drawing in, perhaps only now recalling the intended purpose of the outing, Betty cuts short the self-lionising to turn her focus fully upon her young companion:

"So, then, Seal, never mind paintin' the parlour, let's see about puttin' you properly to work."

Putting you 'to work' so it seems, means a bench might be found in the Bloomsbury manufactory, where the molten flow of words is rolled, tempered and ground to a cutting edge. But despite your promisingly elite – if truncated – academic credentials, as soon becomes apparent, oor Bet despairs of finding a proper use for you t'mill. For this brief confab has in fact uncovered what you secretly always suspected; that the best you have to offer is promise. The girl is promising, shows promise, promised great things. That was it. Perfectly enchanting attribute of untried youth: promise; far too airy and nebulous a quality for the steely questions real life would ask of it. Put promise to the point and, like the lovely soap bubble it is, having no substance or colour of its own but the glossy reflection of the outside world, just like that, it's popped.

It's quite dark on Frith Street by the time you part: Betty on rapid foot for her concisely modern abode, appropriate to the era furnished and fabric-ed throughout in Robin and Lucienne Day, located at the top of the Bloomsbury *works*, and you, far less willingly, for Leicester Square and a tube home north, to the Angel and that empty crowded house of yours.

Wending a solitary way through Soho you pass down streets that seem, thrillingly to one raised nicely in *urbs in horto*, to be populated exclusively by gangsters, spivs and their molls, Cockney costas, European refugees of tragic mien and the purveyors of filthy, delicious, foreign food. And prostitutes. So it transpires, lighting-up time in this wicked locale is cue for the tarts to report for duty. The stationary type advertising themselves by lamplight, under which they stand about in pairs to chat and give the eye to passing men, the ambulatory, you covertly observe, wearing berets and leading poodles. Perhaps this flaunting Frenchified rig is designed to provide the punters with a useful visual hint: the Continentals, having invented it, or so the English are led to believe, are best at sin? Following behind the flash of a particular pair of artificial silk legs most of the way around Soho Square, you entertain yourself in deciding whether she styled herself Gigi or Fifi. But having now got yourself into this shadowing malarky, less amusingly, must pause whenever the girl pauses, every fifty yards or so, to strategically let her little dog use a lamppost and allow for men to similarly exercise their natural proclivities, and approach. Allowing you plenty of opportunity on the halting return journey to Leicester Square to consider what might be the current formulation for contracting business with a client. *'Allo,'allo* perhaps?

Under the gaze of the moon, to the accompaniment only of the tread of your feet, you sing snatches of the old Cole Porter song, "Love for Sale", and wonder whether you yourself may be described still as *appetising* or, more aptly, *slightly soiled*.

# Chapter Nine

While at the cafe with, and waiting for Cara, the weather must have flipped from its earlier blustery preview of autumn back to nostalgic summer. Justified in holding their nerve, the people at the streetside tables were now tucking into their Panini. (Or Panino's, as chalked on the board.)

Li'l orphan Abi, I've probably always looked through windows into other peoples' perfect houses to imagine my improved life if only I lived there. And Islington, gorgeous and pristine under afternoon sun, did a fine job of reviving in me the imposter thrill of finding myself the new neighbour of these affluent and relaxed-looking older couples off out for *lunch: two courses, nineteen pounds,* who crossed paths with the mummies and their tots, homeward bound after their morning expedition for babyccinos. Babyccini?

Since it was now midday, I joined the beardy hipsters stood around an Ape van converted into a mobile street food stall that was parked up outside a pretty garden square. So many specifics, so much care taken, the assembling of my sandwich should by rights have been finished with a bow.

Going through the garden gates to eat it, I cut across the path of a hard-faced, pretty woman, in Stella McCartney pumps and Lululemon trackies, running circuits under the eye of this strapping bloke. Uniformed in black, arms crossed and thick thighs set apart, with her each completed perimeter of the garden, like some kind of sadistic gay Nazi guard, he twitched 'another' with his notional riding crop. Just a capricious toss of her high blond ponytail and off she'd trot.

I sat myself down on the grass with my gourmet snack amongst generations X Y & Z. Never alone with a phone, singly they sprawled in the sun to blissfully tickle the bellies of their palm pets.

Even if I was still, technically, a Londoner, I couldn't but feel a residual northern chippiness at all this show off affluence and on show leisure. Slap bang in the middle of what was once rightfully called the *working day*.

Never mind 'the men' about their mysterious business, however whoever might still be engaged in the getting of money, so it seemed, nowadays, not all of us were earning it nine till five. Cara was right, in the time I'd been away, tectonic plates had shifted – it was definitely a different daytime world out there. Different anyway to when I last regularly found myself out and about at a loose end during business hours. Rather than the carefree young, and young-again, in those days all you got were the slipshod or folk whose footwear was lined in fleece: retired, on benefits, or too lazy or depressed to lace up for the long round trip to the corner shop for tabs or milk for the cat. Foreign bread rolls, then correctly known as baguettes, were eaten by office workers at their desks, and as for al fresco dining, the clipped and clean-shaven youth of the times stood about on windy corners to scran their Coopland pies out of the bag. Pulled pork back then being something to do with AI. (Insemination not intelligence.)

Much like myself as a useless layabout student, the daytime folk were mostly underemployed fuckers, with no money. I did suspect however that this shift was not only down to my having attended a northern university but that, more significantly, all this was happening sometime last century. Even if other parts beyond Watford (Watford included) looked like the aftermath of the zombie apocalypse, so I'd observed whenever I emerged into daylight, blinking from behind a desk, these days every major city centre boasted its perpetually open bars and restaurants and coffee shops, its bustling gyms and glitzy department stores, hairdressers and nail bars. But while the local residents whole-heartedly embraced the concept of 24/7 retail therapy, work itself, not least the visible kind, as practised in these service and hospitality industries, sometime in the interim had become the province of other European nationals. With their perfect idiomatic English.

Pony-woman cantered by again and I decided that the German officer was more likely a Pole. Not a Nazi but her very own personal trainer. She must've been paying him quite a lot to put her through it I guessed. Like the topsy-turvy contract between sub and dom, where really it's the 'bottom' who has the upper hand in the relationship dynamic, and loves to tack up in bespoke gear, specialist humiliation in the nice ménage of a park came more expensive than what you got in a class down the gym. And by the evidence of her accessories as she cantered by: Withings Activité watch, Oakley sunnies, she liked a stage to flaunt it. Wealth. I speculated she was a Russian mafia man's moll, maintained in labels as his conspicuous consumer. Maybe Pavel doubled as a bodyguard?

In this neck of the woods, whatever the service: watching over them, sleeping with them, running their lovely homes, or their lovely children, it seemed the employers of those employees themselves likely came from somewhere else. As feasible Mateusz and Maria and Mahir were keeping Eastern European builders in business, digging out their mega basements, as society's wheels turning.

Whether as neighbours, employers or employees, for the beneficiaries of cosmopolitanism, easy enough to show proper tolerance toward the incomer. In my more recent experience of half a world away, so much harder for Mateusz, Maria or Mahir to integrate, even if you didn't want work picking cabbages or wiping old people's bums for the minimum wage, when it's them that takes the jobs that 're rightfully yours and you suspect them of stealing your social housing. And they've gone and turned your corner Spar into a *polski sklep* and that CofE church, long shut for business, into a centre for elderly Sikhs. Fuck's sake, my own in-laws resented the changes to the traditional character of their northern town. Their own parents having fled the Punjab for Dewsbury in 1947 when their close neighbours, recently made aware that they had reasons to hate and fear the people they grew up alongside, had torched the family compound.

As for the next generation and the one after that, far as Bill's cousins and their kids were concerned: the lot of 'em could booger right off, back to where they came from.

Out there, in the edge-lands, where inner city renewal is the gala opening of a new 99p Store, it's not so difficult to understand how hated are the shiny, heads-up people who look like they sailed through the recession and actually did rather well out of it, thanks. Talk about two nations, did the people in this garden have a clue how the rest of the country watched for a hard rain to come along and wash them away?

The same detested tribe of the well-propertied and feather-nested liberal elite to gain membership of which Bill and I had been only too eager to undergo the necessary rites and trials of initiation. Because in that other town, that other millennium, his and my motivation was to struggle free from the grip of our roots – working, him, chattering, me – betray our class and family expectations, turn our backs on a job in the media or the arts, a proper trade, to pursue careers in the law. We elected to put our hard noses to the grindstone to earn some real money. It was our fierce ambition to be allowed to work eighteen-hour days and skip lunch. To cheerfully moan about the sacrifice of another weekend and spend long haul flights in business class reading small print. A no-brainer really when, debt free and in demand, work was what got my generation of graduates into a nice clean office, and soon scaling the property ladder.

Just so, within months of qualifying, Bill and I left behind the last of our student dives for what was to be the first little flat of our own. Mortgage paid off in less than five years, it doubled in value in eight. The *who stole my cheese?!* years behind us, we began to look back fondly upon accommodation so minging it would in the common parlance make a pig blush. To regret a life we lived before we enthusiastically mounted the escalator that in those days swept you swiftly up to where you wanted to be (even if it did turn out to be more of a treadmill).

Careers launched, smugly grounded by our mortgages and marriages, whenever we original six university flatmates met up in one or other of our neatly-kept, well-maintained homes we'd gently reminisce about the joys of chaos and misrule. Unused to proprietorship, what adult rectitude we might have possessed anyway divided up almost to insignificance between the six of us, we'd behaved like the revolutionary mob revenging itself on the bourgeoisie, working in gleeful concert to reduce that Victorian villa we once cohabited, its contents too, into something like the 'after' pictures of a teenage house party shared on social media. Even if now slightly shamefaced at how we once ran amok, still it made us laugh to recall how we took it in turns to shut each other up in a wardrobe and send it crashing down the stairs. About cold kebabs for breakfast, cornflakes for tea. Or if you were particularly hardcore: ketamine, for both. A street sign for Cock Lane we smuggled into the living room. The smashed-up furniture – that cupboard – we snuck out into someone else's skip. Painting the living room black and covering its ceiling with luminous stars to make a rave room and, worse even than this cosmetic abuse, how our pogoing actually weakened the floor joists.

The looting and vandalizing days, like all other childish things, put behind us, for all of us responsible professionals that poor house had provided our necessary season of *rumspringa*.

True for me, certainly. At the start of the long summer vac, after a sensible year spent in the relative amenity of university halls, I couldn't wait to begin slumming it in my first ever student house share, shacked up with my hip and edgy new boyfriend. (At least that was what I gambled on him being.) Back in the day the teenage Bill looked like an indie (well, Indian) rock god: all cheekbones, sardonic lip and smouldering eyes. The rebel who ate no vegetables, hated his mum and dad and manufactured the perfect roll-up. The likely lad tipped for a first.

The only thing going for the nineteen-year-old me was that I knew I'd have to graft hard for what I wanted.

And I knew I wanted him.

He'd said, 'maybe we could hang out', next day I'd packed my kettle, single place setting, Habitat duvet, lied to the folks back home and moved in. My poster of David Beckham with his shirt off taped up next to his of Madonna: our cheerleaders looking down on us from the wall as we screwed, every day, all day, in what was once the respectable back parlour. We'd pushed the bed hard up against the French windows that opened onto the yard so that when the sun was right it shone directly in on us. Seeing there'd be no family holiday in the usual rented villa – it was the year the situation with Nico got intense – this was how I worked on my all-over tan that idle summer: lying naked on top of Bill's unwashed sheets in full view of the neighbours. And there we'd stop, smoking and talking and singing in the brief intervals between the sex sessions, till it was late enough to go out on the Toon. (See, there was a time you had to wait for back then.)

A couple of weeks into those lazy hazy days of summer love and squalor, I got up from our shag pit/sun lounger for a pee. Drugged on this occasion with heat and too much sleep, I was holding my hands under a running tap when a giant rat dashed across the floor and right over my foot. I screamed and a naked barbarian warrior wielding a snooker cue roared into the bathroom to defend me, his woman under attack. It was probably at that moment, for the first time, I got that he might even, actually, you know, love me back. Along with some other things those final two years of university taught me, like the art of the perfect roll-up, learning this about Bill meant I'd never be going home now. So, when the time came to disband our anarchist household, for each of us to go our separate ways, I stayed put. The two of us were all the family I needed, and all the shelter. And, honestly, I never felt an exile.

Before, suddenly, I had.

Dad dead, mum mad, and the family home long sold up, with now no one to hate, in fact nowhere not to go back to, when the relocation to London came up, it was me who argued for it. And, because he did love me, my husband agreed.

Made quite misty-eyed by the secret memory of those irresponsible days spent in bed with Bill, Beckham and Madonna, when sex could still be dirty and risky as well as make you laugh out loud, I found I was excited again by the prospect of us becoming the owners of an enviable house amongst streets and streets of other enviable houses. Or, as the agents' details had immortally phrased it: 'being located on a prestigious turning within fifteen minutes stroll of the many local amenities available on Upper Street.'

The sun went behind a cloud and, suddenly aware of time passing, I looked about myself. Another revolution the last twenty years witnessed was that back then the people fiddling with their phones would've found their hit and their diversion in smoking. The loud schoolgirl sitting next to me, cradling a shiny package that in the olden days might have been twenty of Silk Cut, was like, like: ….ok, darling, bye, bye bye!

It came as a shock to realise that the incomprehensible lingo she'd been talking into her phone and I'd been ignoring was English; it was me who spoke in foreign round here. I was the outsider. But if Bill and I had done it before, we could do it again: pull off that chameleon trick of matching ourselves to our surroundings. In fact I reckoned it'd be easy here, in this populous, prosperous place of all nations, to pass. By looking and sounding the same as them we might expect to live, unremarked, amongst this happy breed, these legion loafers in our new hood – or what I should probably now be calling: our *Endz*.

Gathering my possessions, I got stiffly to my feet and made my way back between the people, rapt and tender, checking out who liked them. If no one else in this little oasis in the city had anywhere else urgently to be I still had a day job to get back to.

# Chapter Ten

The perambulating stockings long left behind, anonymous amongst the urgent, homeward-hurrying crowds, it's only now that you regret further exploration of Soho's tantalising square mile of polyglot post-war depravity is not an excitement you'll likely be sharing with your inscrutable husband.

Months back, in the early spring, you remember, William had taken his new young wife on his idea of a London walk.

Pre-war guide book in hand, reading out information, that was, is and, if people like your husband had anything to do with it, always would be bang up to the minute, William whisked you first round St Paul's. After this gladdening tour of the Cathedral, you wandered hand in hand to find St Mary le Bow, also on Cheapside. Standing inside that blasted shell, you two looked back for that iconic view of St Paul's framed by the church's huge carved window that was violently emptied of its Medieval stained-glass that fateful night in May, 1941. As William informed you.

On what once was Wood Street, you next came across St Alban's of which, oddly (though, if you were going to put a positive spin on things, it wouldn't have looked a bit out of place in San Giminiano), only its tall tower alone remained. Monumental in its isolation, it pointed the way heavenward where, by way of high explosives, the body of the thousand-year-old church to which it'd once been joined had gone before. Heading south toward the river, William, sunk in gloom, now identified for his bride the ruin of the quaintly named St Andrew by the Wardrobe, before he turned back again for the massive and immutable touchstone of St Paul's, to find instead yet another ecumenical casualty of the Blitz. Its lid blown off, shorn of the medieval streets that must once have huddled up close to the protection of its walls, the lovely ruin of St Nicholas Cole Abbey appeared now to have stood always in these rough fields of waving grasses. Abandoned to willow herb and buddleia, golden ragwort, foxgloves and vetch, to you it looked tranquil and remote – and quite as romantic – as Wordsworth's Tintern Abbey. You liked also that thus opened up to the elements it could no longer hold that indefinable atmosphere of complacency and trapped self-regard, like the dowager's imprisoned fart, so often encountered within Anglican churches.

Brave men might have bolstered the resolve of a nation under threat, working to ensure Christopher's masterpiece, the sublime Cathedral, survived a targeted firebombing, but that so many other Wren churches were damaged or destroyed by human hand, and in the space of just a few years, you could tell was devastating to William. He'd known of course about the bomb damage but to witness at first hand those much-loved and familiar faces with their teeth kicked out, skulls caved in, made for a gloomy bus ride back to your newly-marrieds' digs.

Starting out cheerfully enough, that outing in search of Wren's masterpieces ended up moving William, a man you'd thought largely incapable of showing strong emotion, to the point of actual tears. But it now occurs to you that his sentimentality is not only reserved for the fate of churches. Or even for buildings you'd call 'historic'.

Thoughts keeping pace with your own hurrying feet, you recall how on that other homebound journey, to Balham, it had touched your husband to the quick to witness from the bus window how, 'safe as houses' having been made a meaningless maxim by the war, the population grown accustomed to the idea that nothing old is worth holding onto, bulldozers succeeded bombs. The City's tight medieval streetscape your slow double-decker to South London was navigating its way through, might largely have weathered the Great Fire, along with every other hazard in between, up to and including the *blitzkrieg*, only to succumb to the post-war mania for town-planning. So it seemed, fascism was not half as destructive as a socialist peace was turning out to be. (*Come back, Adolf, all is forgiven!*) For all you knew, William probably took equally to heart the demolition of those ancient slums as he did the stucco dropping off the front of a neglected Nash villa. Even the wilful sweeping away of something considered 'good' from the modern movement to make way for a bus garage you suspect might cause his shoulders to slump. Which explains why when walking down London streets, you've noticed William sometimes finds it hard to lift his head – for fear of what he might see or, worse, miss.

It's not as if you yourself don't care about the destruction of fine old buildings, only that according to your own practical philosophy: however well established, pruning and weeding will reinvigorate the garden. In a city tightly packed with its own history as this one, if the inhabitants of Londinium lamented their Roman amphitheatre burning down the Elizabethans got "The Globe". Which represented 'progress', didn't it? But it's perhaps because you don't imagine yourself as deserving of his sympathy as a damaged building, you find no comfort from this new appreciation of your husband's acute awareness of the fragility of things to waste or breakage or loss. Deriving for yourself instead only a bitter sort of satisfaction that Betty, who evidently has no time or affection for the obsolete and passed over, in this at least is not your rival.

# Chapter Eleven

Gone ten in the morning – the workforce yet to clock on, Bill off hours earlier for the big new, unmentionable job that's paying for all this – and I'm still messing about. Shirking when I might have been working. My putting off getting on with this morning's urgent task of sourcing paint shades mixed to genuine Georgian formulae, I blamed on no longer having the parenthesis of a commute at either side of it to define my working day's beginning and close. Though this wasn't the whole story. Being both my workplace and my work, 'home' itself now offered me no resort from the paralysing realisation that I was a really rubbish project manager. In the short time the contractors had been on the job the building schedule I'd supposedly taken charge of had already begun to slip disastrously backwards. Not forgetting the profligate spending upon herself this lovely indifferent mistress of a house of mine demanded day-to-day. And, as I was only too aware, this was our own, real money I was letting run through my fingers.

Fidgety with frustration that I was made involuntarily housebound by the lead contractor, Mr Casey (experienced in listed building work), I took my cold tea for a wander round the house. The works. Such as they were.

Another twenty minutes gone, my mug left forgotten on top of a sack of heritage lime mortar, and still no sign of Casey and whichever of his sunshine band of sons and nephews might, or might not, be swinging by this mid-morning, I ended up wandering into the front room, to wait and watch.

Even with the boost to our finances of Bill's pay hike, and the prospect of bonuses ahead, we could only ever have afforded to buy a Regency house in Islington because, apart from being a dump, it was located in this unkempt patchwork of a square. An imperfect quadrilateral composed inharmoniously of three parts Georgian to one Victorian, with ugly mid-twentieth-century inserts.

As for why our square was left incomplete, I'd discovered it was the original spec builder's intention, back in 1815, to kick-start a housing boom out here on the far reaches by flogging off his first-built houses at an attractively reduced rate to the less well-off willing to risk a dodgy new locale. The culmination of the elegant square, as advertised, being dependent upon these harbingers tempting in wealthier types to invest and so provide the forward finance to finish the job – which, because the truly fashionable refused the bait, it never was. Hence the Victorian terrace that made up the missing fourth side, erected on what probably till then consisted of some hovels and huts and sheep grazing. I guessed by the time these later nineteenth-century models with their trendy bay windows and gothic-style porches eventually went up the vanguard on the other three sides would've already been looking horribly passé.

A mere sixty years passed before a World War Two incendiary remade the

Victorian terrace again, as brickfields this time. At least it did the five houses that once stood directly opposite ours.

It must have been sometime between the late '40s and '50s the hole the bomb punched was in-filled by the ugly pre-fab Airey houses that today completed the square. Quite literally architectural stopgaps, featuring frames of prefabricated concrete columns reinforced with tubing recycled from the canvas tilt frames of military trucks, they'd been thrown up to accommodate the thousands made homeless by the war and weren't designed to outlast the century. Meaning the previous century.

When showing us round, the oversized tie knot assured us these temporary houses were due – overdue – for demolition and redevelopment by Islington Council. Another new outlook from this wonky old window that must help put us back into positive equity.

Thinking about the flux of history, I wondered what were the other comings and goings this window, like the constant eye of the house, had witnessed. Actually, now I looked, the latest slide in the show was even now passing under its astigmatic gaze. Dippy Debby, back from the school run, greeted the woman who jogged daily with her brown lab puppy. As she paced bouncily on the spot and it crapped on the curb, I rippled the watery fault line in the glass over them. Drowning the lot. Focus now narrowed to the glass itself, my eye was attracted to something on this side of the pane. Like the last jag of colour left stuck in the frame of a smashed stained-glass window, a Painted Lady butterfly illuminated an angle orange. Tangled and trussed by cobwebs, it struggled in its thin bonds. But on reaching to free it, I discovered dead brittle wings, animated only by the draught passing through the window's rotten glazing bars.

Mind still on the meaning of this trapped and trembling butterfly, the slam of *Casey Family Builders'* van door made me jump like it was me who'd been caught out. Speeding out into the hall, I was in time to open the door on Mr Casey, already launched, twinkling, into the day's excuses. 'Van broke down in Barking by Bow, would you believe it!'

Rather than delay him and his lads from cracking on a minute longer, I decided to hold my tongue. As I now knew, literally to my own cost, his line in banter or my own specialist subject: interesting house history, were guaranteed to keep us chatting on for hours over tea and biscuits.

In the event what put the kybosh on today's schedule was one or other of the nephews putting his foot through a rotten board in an attic room. Evidence of wet rot, so Mr C chirpily informed me; a serious leak in the roof that in his estimation must've been going on for some time. Any road, did I know, Georgian roof construction was particularly complicated, and prone to leakage? Added to which, the slates themselves were in a shocking state. Hardly surprising, so he assured me, seeing as how the jerry-builders who threw up these houses in the first place never expected them to outlast the century. Meaning the century before last. (Bugger me: these places were actually more obsolete than the bloody pre-fabs.) The only mercy, so he cheerfully informed me, was that some prannet hadn't gone and replaced the rotten Welsh slates with modern tiles too heavy for the structure of the house. In which case, I'd be looking at a world of pain.

The upshot of this lesson in dodgy building practices, ancient and modern, was that the roof would anyway now need replacing in its entirety – with new oak beams and conservation grade slate, natch. 'Absolute 'king nightmare', the old pro chortled, 'and none of it going to come cheap!'

If I'd imagined I'd awaken this house with my loving kiss, rather than opening her eyes and smiling her benevolence, this was beginning to feel more like Mary's creature had arisen vengeful from the slab to land a smack in the mouth.

# Chapter Twelve

Your improbable fairy godmother might have succeeded where Sir Lancelot failed, breaking you out of there, but it seems Betty's sympathetic magic is no match for the draw of 'home' after dark. Instinctive as an animal, you seek cover. And even if it is to the aroma of boiled brassicas; the dismal wet washing on the line; the pram in the hall that you return, you know yourself lucky to have a roof over your head, this place of your own. Or as close to calling it your own as is possible in this time of shortages.

In the increasingly urgent search for affordable accommodation in which to make your own start on life, having viewed dozens of places Hitler knocked about a bit or which poverty and neglect was in the process of quietly laying to ruin, this old house with its sitting tenants was a veritable *des res*. As opposed to damp and mice or major cracks and the showers of plaster shaken down on you every time you closed a door or forced open a window, a young couple with a baby on the way at the top of the stairs really weren't too much to put up with. Were they? Particularly not well-behaved lodgers, who never overstepped the terms of their tenancy, always paid the rent on time. Besides which, as William is always telling you, what you got in exchange for the inconvenience were these really *good proportions*. But however grateful you are for the shelter it offers, and the dimensions, you also know that you'll never truly feel 'at home' in this over-populated house.

Having stealthily negotiated the opening of the front door, the passage around that damn pram, you tiptoe across the cold dark burrow of the living room. Groping for matches, feeling for the gas tap, after a small explosion, and aggressive roar, the room is filled with startling white light. It lays the bare room barer. Very gently the pressure fails and the room goes back to black though for an instant after it burned out you seem to see it filled again with stuff. Not exactly furniture, but etched on your retinas the bulky forms of something left lying about. Adjusting themselves in time to the dark, rather than making sense of the incongruous thingamajigs that appear to be taking up floor space in here, your eyes instead grow accustomed to a spectral glow. The streetlamps in the square have made of the front window a parchment-yellow light box. Attracted to it like a moth, held in place there by bonds stout as gossamer, you stand and look out for ages. Here is William, head down, hurrying. Climbing the four steps to the front door, he glances up but does not see you, back to the dark room.

After weeks of waning warmth, this is the evening autumn proper comes to Islington. Not so much the season of mild regret for summer's passing as fierce anticipation of the winter to come, it slams in on a sudden north wind.

Quite unprepared for its sting, once the business of eating – off knees, with fingers – is done, as you sit on packing case and deckchair not mentioning things, you must huddle ever closer over that useless fire.

It's only now that a sharp wind blows and the sleet sets in, when you appreciate what every inhabitant of the house before you has each in their turn discovered and assiduously tried to deal with, using rags and newspaper. Your recent rout of the ancestors has succeeded only in reviving the drafts that groan and sigh from between floorboards, around window frames and shutters, come howling down the flue. You Bones could do with the insulation of history.

# Chapter Thirteen

My very stressed and taciturn husband was so late back from work, it was getting on for midnight by the time we finished our hungryhouse takeaway.

Seated uncomfortably thigh-to-thigh on the hard futon bed, eating off our knees while watching a small screen, rekindling happy thoughts of those early days of lack and want, I said: doesn't this remind you of living together in our first home?

The flat in Amstel?

Before that.

You mean that horrible student dive with the rodent problem? Wouldn't 've called it *home* exactly.

Why wasn't he, like me, recalling the sex and the laughs? Our young bodies. Cuddling closer, it was cold in here, I said: nevertheless, Bilal, the very first place we could call our own.

You mean it was the first place we bunked up together, along with twenty of our dearest friends.

There were six of us!

Yeah, the six that paid the rent. What you're misremembering through the bottom of that rosé-tinted glass of yours, petal, are the revolving boyfriends and girlfriends and the acquaintances of the boyfriends and girlfriends, dossing on the settee.

He raised his glass of the nice Waitrose Provencal rosé we were drinking.

(If little else, our taste in alcohol had matured.)

I had to laugh: ok, fair enough, that weird friend of Fran's, Micky Something, the early Harry Potter adopter, might've dossed for a couple of weeks in the cupboard under the stairs.

Yeah, we missed a trick there. I read an article in The Standard on the tube home about a 'room' to rent in Clapham that turned out to be just that: the glory hole. Five hundred quid a month, plus bills to share with the Hoover and the gas meter.

How about a garden shed in the corner of a living room advertised as a friendly flat share. To be fair, they had painted it pink and put up curtains.

Top trump you with a pop-up tent in a dining room.

We clinked glasses.

Camped out within these million pounds worth of decayed bricks and mortar, strange the mutual glow of self-satisfaction kindled by finding ourselves winners in the property-owning stakes.

Wonder who's living in it now? Bill said.

Can't imagine they'd have let it out to anyone, not up there.

Not the ironing board cupboard, daft booger: the student digs!

If the poor house is still standing, in that location you can bet it won't be students.

No, I reckon by now it'll have come up in the world, like us.

You mean: the hooligans that trashed the joint?

Bill laughed.

Thinking about the cosmetic and structural damage that subsequent owners probably cursed the unknown student delinquents for causing, it occurred to me that in my earlier speculation about the decades and the centuries that had passed under the wry watch of this house, I'd neglected to credit the humans who looked out from that fixed glass eye. It was they after all, who would have made sense of the show the world put on out there – on the other side of the windowpane.

D'you know, Bill, I'd actually love to find out who lived in this place before us. Might've been someone famous: a minor nineteenth-century woman poet or something.

Weirdly, I *do* know about a notable woman who lived here, or a notorious one, he added, sinisterly.

Wondering whether I really wanted to hear, tell me, I said.

Yeah, well, when I was round here one day with the surveyor, we surprised this seedy old bloke trying to get a gander through the window. Looked like Benny Hill, you know: gormless in a beret, wire specs and a flasher's mac, and a medal ribbon sewn on crooked. Says he's lived round the corner his whole life, is curious about the *For Sale* sign. Then he gets all aerated about this *bloody women's libber* who lived here, back in the day – the '60s I guess. Apparently, she was some sort of campaigner for legalised abortion or compulsory contraception. Something like that.

That 'notorious' of yours sounds like it was a poisoner.

You'd have preferred that?

Fuck, no!

Anyway, whatever she got up to in here, Benny took against her.

What was her name?

Bill looked askance: didn't ask. But she'll be there in the records somewhere, along with the rest of them: everyone who ever lived in this house.

\*

I went to sleep that night on the happy thought that: you never could tell, and a blue plaque *would* add value. So, then, tomorrow's effort might be gainfully spent in the systematic identification of every previous freeholder. Apart from the unlikely chance I'd find a murderer amongst their company, let alone a literary luminary, playing house historian holed up in the bedroom would not only distract me from buying more things online but keep me out of earshot of the cries of glee uttered by Casey and the gang as they uncovered yet another problem to be expensively put right.

# Chapter Fourteen

Naturally, even if at the time you had the words, you weren't about to confront the upstairs lodgers with any of the inconveniences you chafed under. Mrs McNamara is far too terrified of her young landlady for that. Terrified with a terror that's almost palpably hostile. This much is apparent each time you come back in through the front door and trigger the breathless silence that follows on as if from a scream, the sudden cessation of movement after an explosion that leaves behind it the impression that everything in the house is atremble still on invisible wires.

Some days, it's true, you do succeed in losing yourself in the quiet of another lonely afternoon. Lying reading in bed, forget the other woman, only for Mrs McNamara's chair to scrape softly on the floor above your head, for the flush of the lavatory your two households share. Making you nervous as quarry in your turn, aware that you too may be overheard.

Despite Mrs McNamara and you both being of a similar age, as well as having that other thing in common, because you *are* a bit of a prig, and shy, this mutual delicacy means that young housewives McNamara and Bone daily study to avoid each other, instead tiptoeing resentfully around the other's sensibilities.

But if you are equally skittish about acknowledging the other, nevertheless, in the standoff of the wives, I'm ashamed to admit you're happy to have the upper hand. Each Friday the upstairs tenant must present herself at the sector perimeter with money in a cheap envelope, *Doctor and Mrs Bone* in her best handwriting on the front, to pay their rent.

The first time she tapped on the door to the Bone's living quarters to deliver it, you called out in a little voice, "Who's there?" as if suspecting a burglar. Or a ghost.

After which debacle, in an effort to broker better relations between upstairs and down, you resolved that when next the woman called at the checkpoint with her envelope, it might be a friendly overture to invite her over the border for a small glass of something. A nicety observed by Gussie and Lally – maiden aunts of William's and landladies in that lodging house full of old ladies of reduced means off the Balham High Road that provided your emergency married digs – who saw off any potential embarrassment about receiving your money into their genteel hands by making sure to get their emolument in first.

But on the following Friday, when you opened the door to the lodger at the appointed hour, the woman bobbed a reflex curtsey and, unused to acting the grown-up, you went and bobbed one back.

Sherry and an arrowroot biscuit hadn't felt appropriate under the circumstances.

Ever since this diplomatic debacle there had seemed no alternative but for a state of cold war to exist between you.

Truthfully, though, this stalemate is confined to the working week and daylight hours. As the clock strikes six and masculine tread is heard once more upon the front doorstep, the self-imposed pall of silence and restraint you two women have been scurrying about beneath is lifted by the return of 'the men'. Who, having not the least idea about the lengths their wives put themselves through pretending to deny each other's existence, bring with them the relief of noise.

Even in this, however, you can't but be resentful of the lodgers sharing the house with you. For while William treads lightly in his brogues, Mr McNamara never thinks to remove his hobnailed boots at the end of his working day. It irks you too that, even if he could have been prevailed upon to go about in his stockinged feet, being a large man, lusty in his ablutions after labour, keen on the "Light Programme" of an evening, unlike his timidly forceful missus, there really is no ignoring his presence in the upstairs flat. More galling still, you suspect cockiness. That this lack of inhibition comes from his having calculated, correctly, young Doc and Mrs Bone will for a while yet be needing that little bit extra he pays for the one large and two very small rooms, shared bathroom and landing kitchenette (with use of copper and garden clothesline) they have as their share of the accommodation.

A couple of months married, one in his early twenties, the other still a teenager, it's true, certainly, that even if it is old, even if it is in Islington, it's only because of its sitting tenants William and you could stretch to buying an entire house. So you endure, telling yourself that, save for Friday afternoons, you wives really have no choice but to continue to make yourselves invisible to each other.

An unwished-for situation that worked pretty well: from the spring when William and you took over the house, until the late summer of that year, when the inevitable happened and the two McNamaras became three. A little addition at the top of the stairs you feared would inevitably end the uneasy truce you two spent the last few months in brokering. For if your every cough and sneeze only served to remind the other woman that there was someone else in the house with her, she must be quiet, how much harder must it be to keep a kid under the radar? In the event though, somehow, its mother managed it. Even to the point that when you do hear the baby crying, it can still catch you painfully unaware. Really, if it wasn't for the nappies, always a-flap in the narrow back garden, or the pram parked out front for its regular morning airing, you might almost convince yourself it is a phantom baby that dwells in the upstairs flat.

# Chapter Fifteen

As someone who could recall the days back when facts were expensive to find and information hard to get, it truly was amazing nowadays what you could discover for free, or a small fee, sitting on a futon in a bedsitting room. The only drawback being that not all of it was to be trusted and by sheer volume it flattered to deceive that your every question had an answer, or that that answer was correct.

Nevertheless, using government and heritage sites, it hadn't taken too much time and effort to track down the householder who appeared on the first deeds, or indenture, that related to our house. Dash m'wig, George Benbowe was the name of this gentleman (there was no mention of a Mrs Benbowe in the documents) and his profession was physician.

But what of the rest of them?

Well, after George had come George, followed by George, then George, William, Victoria, Edward, George again, Edward (briefly), George, and finally, eternally, Elizabeth.

All right, I cheated. But as the morning wore on I began to realise that, if this time-travelling galleon of mine had, indubitably, sailed under the flags of all those royals, the ship's company would, at best, only ever exist for me as a list of names, sexes, ages (at time of census) and familial relationships, plus the profession of each head of household. As for those who never even made it onto the official crew lists: the residents, lodgers, servants, renters and sub-renters who died, or were born, or moved on, in the decade between censuses, they'd simply have to stay anonymous. Nevertheless, while sovereigns came and went and history happened, it was this obscure lot who had undertaken to sail the vessel safely down the centuries to deliver it to Bilal (m) and Abigail (f), ASIAN/INDIAN, SOLICITOR, BRITISH/WHITE, DILETTANTE, for however many years before the mast we had signed up for. So even if I could know little of my predecessors, still I saluted them as comrades. Starting with my own George, who'd had the vision to buy in the first place and ending with *Mrs Canute*, who'd done such a very fine job of holding back the tide of change in here these last fifty years, alongside everyone else who came between, even the wreckers and vandals, all were deserving of acknowledgment for getting her through, battered by the winds of time and fortune, but not broken. Just as it would be for other hands to take over the wheel for the next stage of her perilous journey once Bill and I surrendered command. Their personalities in paint and paper layered on over the colours we once nailed to the mast. A stubborn scrap of early 21st-century wallpaper, a dab of Annie Sloan original chalk paint, perhaps, all that'd be left of us when we too were dead and gone and equally long forgotten. Which jolly thought prompted the realisation that the house itself might be something of an oracle, I might have already picked up cryptic clues about the lives and times of those who'd previously moved in their moveables, put up their pictures in this much lived-in house. For if walls had no mouths to speak of what and whom they'd witnessed, the marks that people made upon them, personal as hand stencils in ancient caves, might yet tell a more human story than could the account of names and dates and professions.

Having spent weeks in painstakingly stripping out the evidence of their existence, in reversing the process, putting back the padding, as it were, I convinced myself it might be possible, if only in my head, to piece together something of my predecessors from the tell-tale traces of decor and damage the house had harboured all along.

To start at the beginning, or rather my end point, it occurred to me that my own George the First, Mr Benbowe, was most likely responsible for the earliest wallpaper that was to be the last bit of decoration I uncovered high up in the hallway. Half an hour's virtual dumpster diving in the Georgian underworld, courtesy of the web, led me to speculate wildly about this single, professional gentleman who'd had the nerve, or foresight, to buy a house on this unfinished square, in darkest North London. With its rough open ground for cruising just across the way. Was my own unmarried, tasteful, extravagant George Benbowe, *chewser* of new-fangled wallpaper, a male lady; an indorser; a buggeranto?

After Admiral Benbowe quit his post, at least according to what I'd peeled back from the walls, things proceeded pretty much shipshape and Bristol fashion. But if this first leg was set fair, steady as she goes, as I now knew, having already charted what she was to weather over the course of that perilous two-hundred-year voyage, it was not always to be plain sailing for my *Flying Dutchman*. Storms lay ahead.

Or, more appropriately, since the London property racket was ever thus: an un-funfair roller coaster ride of ups and downs.

The earliest and most precipitous dip followed from that first run of Georges – the clue to this tipping point that would transform my house from desirable to decidedly down at heel, manifesting itself in the layer of crumbling lino we ripped up in the hall. Sandwiched between the horrible carpet foisted on us with the house and the original Georgian stone flags we happily inherited, this late-Victorian lino had released a miasma of ancient mildew and smell of mice that for hours after left in the back of the throat the sour taste of hard times. The same-era locks fitted to every door suggested to me that around this time the place was run as a common lodging house. Living hugger-mugger behind every clumsily secured door – not hooligan students but the working poor. Seamstresses going blind over buttonholes in the freezing little rooms at the very top of the house. Day labourers bunking together in our bedsitting room on the first floor. A dozen peaky, barefoot kids consigned to the basement. I imagined them sleeping in their rags in front of a cold kitchen range to be roused for early-morning bread, scrape and a jam jar of sweet tea and sent out shivering down the Liverpool Road for some begging and nicking by the female Fagin – the one who made her rent by whatever nefarious means she might – and to whom I assigned 'the front best' on the raised ground floor.

To back up this fancy, I had a look at the LSE's interactive *Poverty Map* for London streets compiled by late nineteenth-century social reformer and practical statistician, Charles Booth. Sure enough, this Islington square, at Class C, coloured light blue, signified inhabitants with: *Intermittent earning. 18s to 21s per week for a moderate family. The victims of competition and on them falls with particular severity the weight of recurrent depressions of trade. Labourers, poorer artisans and street sellers. This irregularity of employment may show itself in the week or in the year: stevedores and waterside porters may secure only one of two days' work in a week, whereas labourers in the building trades may get only eight or nine months in a year.*

If providing no sort of corroboration for my imagined life of this house, it nevertheless confirmed to me that, at this time, our square was indeed the haunt of the transient, barely respectable and intermittently desperate.

With the next sickening swoop of the roller coaster, I hoped to have detected an upward trajectory. Could the Edwardian cast-iron fireplace surrounds that were removed from the two top bedrooms and, in a rare bit of economic prudence, sold off by me on Gumtree, suggest that after a renovation job the house reverted once more to single occupancy? That servants, rather than impecunious piece workers, were once more in residence under the eaves. Certainly, as I now thought, the William Morris flowers I found growing still in the dark at the back of a cupboard were evidence of an early-twentieth-century upswing.

Quite another tale was told, however, by what had preceded their complicated vegetable sprawl: Deco papers, seemingly designed expressly to refute the previous generation's gentle preference for Art and Nature. Dating from the era when peace broke out after the war to end all wars, the machine-made repetition of their angular design to me nicely echoed the tattoo beat of the young people's feet that pounded out every last bit of residual *dulce et decorum* in here. Under the shadow cast by the last conflict, with an eye to the gathering storm clouds of the next, theirs being a serious age, the young folk of the young century refused to take it seriously. But instead they rolled back the rugs and danced like demons in the *piano nobile*, to leave forever after recorded in my wide oak boards the thousand pockmarks of their drumming heels.

In tribute to these heedless hedonists, I found an original recording of *Taint No Sin To Dance Around In Your Bones* on YouTube and cut my own lunatic shapes to it across this same floor.

Gaiety blazed but briefly. After that little upturn the next stomach-dropping descent would take this house rushing slap bang into the second world war of the century. In quick time loud deco geometry was muffled by the bilious boiled greens and boot-leather browns that were next in line to cover the walls. But even though, as I knew, a bomb went off just across the way, weirdly, this significant marker in world history went, so it seemed, unrecorded in the fabric of the place – or not that I noticed in my excavations. Miraculously, even the wavy windowpane directly facing it survived the blast.

A bit of a cliché, but the Second World War brought to mind Vera Lynn for my next musical evocation. I managed to avoid *We'll Meet Again*, finding instead a more bittersweet, less deliberately lachrymose romantic song by the forces' sweetheart to play out the era. That Lovely Weekend perfectly capturing the heartbreakingly plucky pragmatism of young couples severed by the turning wheel of indifferent world history.

I might not have discovered anything that spoke directly of the impact of this war on the house, but it wasn't difficult to retrospectively identify the signs of renewed tough times once it ended: in a return to multiple occupancy. The evidence of housing shortages, when families must double up, persisted in the capped-off tangle of gas pipes in the walls that once supplied the cooker at the top of the second half flight of stairs that, as I'd told Greg, it'd been such a hassle to strip out.

A note displayed in the front window back then perhaps, reading: *No Irish, no blacks, no dogs?*

Out of a sense of solidarity – I guessed, with or without the notice, a '50s version of Bill and me would have been turned away on the doorstep – I found Lord Kitchener's jaunty calypso *London Is The Place For Me* and played it very loud.

Nevertheless a little depressed by this vision of the drab and narrow-minded post-war world, I recalled the fabulous *Festival of Britain* wallpaper we uncovered in the kitchen, all jaunty pots and pans and brightly coloured vegetables tied onto twine. To me its cheerful frivolity suggested the eye of a woman. Maybe it was the handyman husband of this same lady decorator who boxed in the staircase and hard-boarded over every one of the doors? Joining up the dots of that virtuous industry of his, I believed I now knew him by the ghostly geometry of the many little holes that were left behind once I prised out his tacks and brought to light once more those miraculously preserved six-panel doors. Had he done it to save her on the dusting: no housemaid for Mrs '50s housewife? And was it she who painted yellow distemper directly onto the frowsty green flock wallpaper in the living room? Thinking these brave New Britons, like the last lot of post-war rebels, were determined to shock the rents, I put on in tribute a quick burst of *Rock Around the Clock*.

But if the thought of them working their own transformation in here made me smile, I knew their hopeful choices for the future represented only the tiniest ascent before the last big drop brought me bang up to date with the very last resident of all. As I now suspected: Benny's proponent of 'free love'. Although, if she had indeed stormed the second half of the twentieth century in the cause with a grimace and a stick of dynamite, in all that time my militant feminist did nothing much within the house to assert herself. Frying pans and flying carrots, and a whacky yellow paint job were lost under her choice of woodchip and brown hessian with a nicotine wash that dated back to when time froze over in this house. Based on my time travelling voyage down through the decor, all through the '60s, '70s, '80s, '90s and 2,000s, right up until the present, she'd restricted herself to this same bland and unchanging diet of oatmeal and beige that would be my own starting point.

If this was difficult to reconcile with the one bit of anecdotal information – that she was a bit of a personality – we had on any of this house's many previous residents, I could find absolutely no record that my mysterious Ms Firebrand/Miss Armchair ever lived here.

According to the few documents I did manage to dig up – since they were embargoed for a century, sadly there'd be no relevant censuses to consult – from the mid-1950s the place was owned by Dr W. M. R. I de Chancy-Bone. It'd been from his Dubai-based son, I presumed, the less elaborately handled Bob Bone, that we bought.

Shipwrecked in her island chair set in a sea of chaos, the evidence, or lack of it, suggested she'd been marooned here as a lonely castaway. Amongst all the washed up stuff of hers we unceremoniously dumped, there was not a trace of Friday. No diaries, no photos, no love letters. The only item that hinted at a sentimental life was the novel she'd been in the middle of reading: *A Change in the Weather* by C Chance, with its handwritten dedication inside the flyleaf: *to ES with love, admiration and gratitude from CC. Thanks for the fleshpots!*

Even if Elgar would've been more appropriate to her memory, under the circs, it didn't really seem right to celebrate that sad scenario with music.

*

My roller coaster ride ended with a jolt by the bumpers of here and now; I saw that it was again late – and still no Bill.

The Casey clan having long ago left the building, taking my usual wander to check on progress, I was newly aware that on entering each room someone else exited it. No more than that. No rattling chains, no mysteriously appearing bloodstains. Not so much as the whisk of a silk skirt disappearing around a doorframe. I hesitate to use the word *possession*, with its intimations of haunting, but it did seem best to sum up the uncanny feeling I had that many eyes looked back at me from the walls.

In seeking out the personalities of everyone who ever lived here or, more accurately, constructing them out of wallpaper, I wondered whether I hadn't so much ticked them off a list as invited them back in here behind the wobbly window. I might have warmed to my first George, was indeed quite happy to imagine this fey gentleman supping his dish of chocolate with me, but, apart from the forgotten and forgetful dancers, was less inclined to entertain the rest of them, jostling at my elbow. In particular, I feared the footfall of the grim Victorian gangmaster, in her elastic-sided boots, patrolling the hardwearing hallway lino in wait for the ragamuffins return with their haul of stolen pocket watches and handkerchiefs.

Confined to our bedsitting room, waiting for Bill to come home and ask me about my day spent pursuing predecessors, I felt the hairs tingle on the back of my neck with the sense of them. Everyone who ever lived in this house.

# Chapter Sixteen

With William gladly departed once more for the calm of his desk at the Museum, the moment's come once more for you to take up your lookout at the living room window. Having allowed yourself to be swept along by the unstoppable force of Betty right out of life's waiting room, no single pressing reason presents itself to leave it this morning. Or at least you're yet to come up with one – although it's always a possibility that you might think of something to go out for tomorrow.

Standing there, becalmed and to your mind no doubt rather tragic, it amuses you to imagine that from the street you must look like the captain's wife, waiting on good news, without much expectation that this was what the tide would be bringing you.

It might have been minutes or hours later that the sound of Mrs McNamara's tentative footsteps down the stairs brings you back to yourself. Back to this room. On the other side of the partition wall, from the hall, comes a soft clucking as Mrs McN loads up her pram. Shortly followed by her effortful descent with it down the four steps that bring her out onto the front path and under your gaze. Along with baby and a shopping basket she has their wireless battery, wedged into the pram's carrying tray. She's probably off out to get it refilled at "Pettits' Hardware". As the woman proceeds down the front path you step back from the window, out of her line of sight.

When she is safely down the road, *good*, you think: an hour at least to yourself. And improve the next couple of minutes of blessed solitude bending and straightening your knees to wobble the watermarked pane over the view of the bomb-damaged fourth side of the square. You wonder whether that other watcher, "The Daily Mail" reader, did the same. With a nod of her head, did she quake and shake to its foundations the solid Victorian terrace of houses she'd have known? Portent for what The Luftwaffe's bombs would soon be doing for real. Though that violently remodelled view is no longer exactly what you see from here. In the years following the war's end from ruination has come renewal: the urban eyesore is now wholly the territory of the grubby children from the flats on the Liverpool Road. Who, having requisitioned the old bomb site as their adventure playground, act out unchecked their own orgiastic rites of destruction there. Goodness knows you've watched them from this vantage point often enough, going about their business of de-reclamation. Little savages, they slip in and out by their secret trails between the willow herb and buddleia growing out of rubble, getting up to mischief within the unsafe shelter of tottering brickwork. Building bonfires in bedrooms, piddling in drawing rooms. One couldn't help but be impressed by their enthusiasm to the task; they go about their work with a will, as if it were not only their mad pleasure to destroy what little remained intact but their dogged duty also.

Your eyes now quickly find out a little group of hooligans. Heedless little ragamuffins, they are wheeling with their arms outstretched, doing their imitations of *Spitfires* and *Messerschmitts*. From the window you can see them in their consequence-free dogfights making the sounds of bombs dropping and planes screaming.

What larks! Having themselves missed out on it, for these kids war was no more than the name of a game they play. Whereas for you it remains **The War**!

Or *Woah!* as we Londoners fondly referred back to it.

Born just before the hostilities, your own in-between generation might not have played any very active part in the making of this recent bit of world history, but surely were its inheritors. Landed not only with the clearing up to do, and pay for; in addition, it's your lot's legacy to endure the vivid recollections of those lucky invitees who had been old enough to take part in the main event.

Oh yes, as they never tired of recalling, one's parents had experienced tremendous things: the firework displays put on nightly, the romance of the blackout, the vivid understanding of what truly mattered! Actually knowing these reflex heroes and heroines of their times, as you did, one might very well have come away with the impression that Europe burned chiefly to confirm in England and the English those twin national vices of always following orders, and saving string.

Even during the actual duration, should you have the temerity to bemoan your own dreary lot, Mother was quick to berate and correct: *how dare you, Celia!*

According to her, while Hitler nightly rained down Armageddon from the skies, young girls, little older than yourself, still arrived at their central London offices not only on time but unfailingly cheerful and, despite little sleep and no hot water – this last was very 'Mother' – smartly dressed.

How she herself could know this for a certainty was beyond you since you two sat out the hostilities in the Home Counties. (That red glow over there, on the horizon, was close as you were going to get to London burning, the occasional explosive offloaded harmlessly in a field by some homeward-headed bomber after a raid, your nearest brush with annihilation.) In fact, when prompted, the most miraculous example Mother could personally come up with in illustration of spunk on your own *home front* was that, even in the worst of it, milk bottles still regularly turned up on doorsteps.

Those milk bottles really stood for something. In Hertfordshire the sun came up, you had another cup of tea, and carried on. Mother's lesson being, you supposed, not so much that war is hell as that when everything one has known and trusted as immutable might at any minute be swept away, deranged, damaged, it's the commonplace, the whistling delivery boy negotiating rubble on his bike, the strawberry jam on the tea table, even if it's mostly carrot, that quickly becomes remarkable, and so all the more cherishable. Half the battle won, in fact. So it was that Mother offered up the little sacrifices prescribed by this ersatz version of ordinary life as doing 'our bit'. *Business as usual,* the bulwark behind which she took shelter from the horrid truth that violent things really did happen to regular folk just like you.

On other home fronts, far from the Home Counties, where they had not even the vast inertia of everyday life to cling to, a neighbour might spit at you in the street and bullyboys in armbands had licence to throw your grand piano down the stairs, chuck your typewriter out of the window. A yellow star to signal your difference all the clue the thugs needed to know it was you they hated.

By such small signifiers as yellow stars or waking again to milk bottles on doorsteps, one's fate was known. Condemned, spared.

In the face of that larger misery how, indeed, dare you, Celia, dismiss those little pledges of the proper permanence and order of things? While you yourself still had a future to look forward to, presume to find in them no consolation for the violent thing that had come out of the blue to smash up your own little world: the loss of Daddy?

Once the final curtain was rung down on the adults' big 'show' the spectators were turned out into the flat reality of everyday, spoiled. (Isn't that always the way: you enter via splendidly carpeted staircases, through Aztec palace or Egyptian temple, only to exit down some concrete steps onto a side alley that smells of piss?)

Hardly surprising then if not just for your generation, but all concerned, peace turned out something of the damp squib. The noble principal of *fair shares for all* they put us through might have got us through but that was soon enough devalued, remember, to the bloody awful, interminable National Loaf, Government Cheddar, and everyone being down to the last one of everything to wear? To the victor the spoils! Years and years of this, with not much prospect of more, or new.

True, to show, however briefly, happy days were here again they reintroduced oranges and bananas; threw some parties. As the sun at last began to go down on the Empire, to bestir in the nation that sense of self-pride it'd probably last experienced back in 1851, when half the globe was painted pink, put on a festival, with a new concert hall thrown in.

Neither side of the generational divide was particularly convinced, as I recall. Even if united at this time in wanting to see an end put at least to scarcities and privations, with all that once made their own lives precarious, exciting, important safely put behind them, hardly surprisingly, the previous generation found they preferred the splendid view of where they'd been rather than where they were bound. As seen through time's distorting lens, their past was mythical. For you, Celia, not having properly shared in their marvellous adventure: history was history. And believing anyway that we never learn from it, as someone on whose behalf a war was fought and won, you declined that unsought inheritance of guilt and gratitude, resisted remembering what tragedies or what triumphs befell which people on what day, and, to your credit, looked instead with clear and level gaze to an as yet unrealised future. Even if the main consideration would be what weapons might be deployed to destroy it in the 'next one', this was your world now. So while the parents gave thanks for something that had ceased to exist, their kids preferred the possibilities of the yet to be imagined, the still to come.

It might appear unfamiliar and strange, it might be only **The Bomb** in prospect, but 'tomorrow' has the virtue of being always novel, always perfectible. In time, this fag end land of rationing and ruination itself must cede to the birth of the new order. A modern, scientific world of ease and utility, perhaps, in which all would live in their own labour-saving homes in clean as a whistle, sootless cities lit by electric suns, with faster-than-sound travel, fuelled by energy from the A-bomb. Although as someone who came of age in the pinched and parsimonious fifties – poor you! – the innovation you're most keen for someone to get on with inventing at this time, is the affluent society. The new Welfare State might be a wonderful and worthy advancement but it's an end to the current code of holding back and behaving well that you long for more than anything. Being callow, you crave the stuff you used just the once, then threw away; desire all the bright, shiny, delicious, pretty, useless, material things you've never had. New clobber; new food; new fun!

It was only unfortunate for William Bone that, growing up so much mired in the past, his wife was quite so mad on living in the future. To a man who gave up on a history fellowship only to, relief all round, land himself a job in a museum, I imagine discovering this defect in you – even above the fact you can't cook and don't clean – must've come as the worse let down.

Again your reverie is interrupted by the tenant; returned from her expedition to the shops. Have you really wasted a whole hour revisiting the bloody war, Celia?

Stealthy and alert, like prey that's spotted the predator, you once again retreat deeper into the room.

Leaving the pram on the front path, along with her shopping, little Mrs McN lugs up the front steps the now heavy acid battery, careful not to spill. Lumping these inside the door, she trots back to retrieve the pram and its sleeping occupant. Tenacious as an ant struggling to manoeuvre a big, shiny black beetle backwards into the nest, she pulls the pram up those four steep steps and hefts it over the threshold. When she closes the front door, the sound from the street is shut off so that interior noises once more take centre stage. Through the thin dividing wall you listen to her park up, then heavily ascend the stairs to their flat, hauling up first the radio battery and her shopping basket, clumping back down them again to retrieve the baby. What a palaver, you tell yourself: just getting indoors.

Once more the hen-like crooning as she lifts the baby out of its pram. Awake now, its thin and querulous wail strikes up. Hungry, you suppose.

Hushing and soothing as she goes, Mrs McNamara hurries her protesting infant back up to their quarters.

You fail to consider that she is perhaps as conscious as you yourself about that loud, rude noise in this quiet and watchful house.

# Chapter Seventeen

When we first moved into this house I personified it, her, as an eccentric aristocrat: a frothy fizzy flight of fancy women out of a restoration comedy. In the process of re-attaching the flesh to her 'good bones', my dear revenant had latterly taken on the demeanour, at least she had in my head, of the last resident: watchful, suspicious of my motives, resistant to change. Maybe this was why, rather than just being the frustrating if foreseeable problems associated with the restoration of a very old property, I attributed the most recent run of setbacks to her digging her heels in, if not the evidence of an active ill will directed at me, who'd breathed life into her. Not to mention the cash sunk. Instead of the exasperating, if hardly preferable, notion that what I had here was an adorable, profligate mistress, keen on pearls, I endlessly indulged, every new bit of overspend had begun to feel more like the endless subbing of a needy and not very likeable but, nevertheless, resentful relation, with a grubby gambling problem.

Of course I knew the anima of the house was just the construct of an overheated imagination, whereas the contractors, unfortunately, were all too real. And, for now, present.

My morning so far had kicked off with yet another of those frustratingly issueless conversations with Mr Casey: his tight-lipped response to my latest apparently unworkable revision to the latest revision, a long drawn out *ffffff* of scepticism. As for my plan to discuss with the waiting sparks, definitively, where all the electrical points were to be sited, his passing remark that the last time he used the fascias I loved it had been in an old people's home was enough to send me fuming back to my garret.

As I was beginning to realise, in this man's world I was nobbut a daft woman. Or, down here, a bit of a cupid stunt.

Having spent the next hour in furious displacement activity, researching online the perfect toilet roll holder: one hundred and eighty quid seemed extraordinarily expensive, but there you go; it was French. I gave up and put the kettle on.

With my tray of carefully annotated teas, I located jolly Casey Snr and the lads literally looking into the latest money pit: the mud and rubble that constituted our, as it happened, authentically Georgian non-foundations. Eventual site of my fabulous kitchen, with brass knobs on.

Still holding my tray, I too leaned in, asking: should it be quite so wet?

Big Mike Casey, an unabashed four sugars man, restricted himself to a chuckle: my experience, love, wet's rarely yer problem in a Georgian house. Plenty wetter'n this un an' the original lime plaster still in perfect nick. That's the secret see, when they're not mucked about with, left to their own devices like, these places c'n breathe. Wet's only yer issue when some prannet goes and puts in a damp-proof course, concretes over the floor, uses water-resistant render on the walls. Like I say, it's then yer going to get moisture running right up to the first-floor rooms. Nah, what you want to worry about here is no pammets.

There should be pammets?

When we takes up yer stone floor slabs, pammets is what we wants to find.

All of us – me, Casey and the lads, looked again into the excavations in search of pammets. (Momentarily, I wondered whether pammets were related to prannets.)

Mr Casey put us out of our misery, saying: floor bricks. See, with yer bricks laid direct on the ground with open joints any moisture can dry up frough the floor slabs no problem. Any road, it's having no proper pammets you got yer plaster coming away somefing shocking.

All of a sudden, he dived forward into the pit to retrieve something.

Wiping the muck off what he'd disinterred with his horny thumb, thrusting it under my nose, he said: you're interested in old fings; what d'you make of that, then?

In rapidly backing away from a fold of skin clearly marked by pores, I missed my footing and, appropriately enough, spilled half their mugs of *slosh* down my front.

How they laughed.

Watch yerself!

Nuffin' to be afraid of, love, 's just an old baby's shoe.

I now saw that this was indeed the remains of a tiny pig leather shoe, or slipper, the grain where the bristles grew pricked out by dirt. Its sole was gone, rotted away, but the ankle strap remained fastened across the upper by a tiny white button. Tickled by my discomfort, Mr Casey said: build old as this one you expect to find stuff buried: cat skeletons, horseshoes, even onions. Mostly it's boots an' shoes though.

An' messages under the wallpaper, volunteered Dean, a weak, no sugars, guy.

Messages? I asked, my mind, horribly, supplying the suffix: *from the dead.*

Yeah, some old-time labourer writes their name or somefink filthy for the next one ter read when 'e comes to strip it dahn again. An' we find the fings what they frew away: clay pipes, beer bottles, pie tins, fag packets; all kinds a rubbish.

Warmed to this theme and apparently wanting to get one up on pie tins, Andy (nephew, day-labourer, two sugars, with) chipped in: I've worked in 'ouses where someone's died an' left behind a trace of theirself. See, a body what's decomposed on a floor leaves its outline. Specially oak floorboards, any hardwood, really. On a good one you can see the mark of the legs, where the 'ead went. You can even tell how large the person was, whether it was a man or a woman. It just sorta lays there, like their shadow or somefing.

I tried not to speculate what might be the tell-tale signs that someone had lain dead and undiscovered for some time in an armchair. And what that might smell like: overripe pineapple, perhaps? They would know.

You don't think the shoe's evidence of something sinister?

Laughing all the harder, Mr Casey said: didn't come attached to nuffing, love. Least, not what I noticed!

We all looked again into the muddy pit.

Michael junior (two, weak, without) piped up: stuff we find mostly we just bung!

Soon after my history lesson, they were packed up and gone on their merry way, leaving me the remains of the child's shoe as my souvenir of this day's particular distraction from getting the sod on with it. Along with the empty mugs, I carried it up to the squat we called our bedroom to show Bill when he got back from work. Whenever that might be. Whatever Casey might say about it being an everyday discovery, as I learned from my ancestor quest, the physical evidence of human habitation rather haunted the imagination, and with its still-buttoned strap, tangibly suggestive of the shape of the child's foot it once enfolded, the little thing was disconcertingly corporeal. There really was something potent about the worn apparel upon which dead humans have left their shape.

Maybe this was why – though I knew the house was deserted – when I went into the bathroom to bin my tampon, I took care to shut and securely fasten behind me this sole still-lockable door. Even though this too was unnecessary, when I finished, I pulled the chain. The sound of gallons of water sent crashing down from its cast-iron Victorian cistern lending me courage. Soon as the plumbing abated, however, like a listening presence, the vast and unnatural quiet of the afternoon house settled once more as if in wait for me on the other side of the bathroom door. Unusually for this hour, when the reassuringly ordinary racket of Debby's kids would normally reassert itself, the house next door was silent too. As the tomb, I thought, before I could stop myself.

Without even noticing, I'd come to depend on the pre-school pandemonium from the neighbours before Casey and Co. tipped up; the teatime showdown at the end of each day that filled the void left by their prompt departure. The sound of sibling rivalry from garden or playroom or, at the very least, the background ruckus of kiddie telly turned up too loud, together with a bit of parental yelling, always there when I needed it to calm my jangled nerves.

From what felt like the last living cell of a blackened, abandoned hive I sent my ears on a tentative aural investigation of the partitioned off spaces above and below me; picking up from behind the perpetual white background noise of traffic a faint wailing. I guessed it was little what's-his-name, the next-door baby. I'd already encountered Debby's older two: Kitty and Teddy, but the baby remained a somewhat shadowy little fellow. Encouraged by this sound of everyday life, I ventured out from the loo onto the open wastes of the half landing.

All too abruptly, the baby's cry ceased.

Without stopping to think - the sound of that wailing or, much more troubling, the quivering silence that immediately followed on from it was quite enough to induce panic - I bolted into our bedsitting room to be met by the winking button eye of that shoe. Tipping out the red-soled skyscrapers from their suitably sized box, with trembling fingertips I picked up the slimy bit of skin that had itself once held a foot and made myself tuck it in with the monogrammed tissue in which the stupid expensive shoes came swathed. Then carried the lot held out before me down the stairs, through the blasted hole of a kitchen and out into the back garden.

Very aware of the tall houses to left and right overlooking me, I hoped my mad little ceremony was not being watched and judged. I reckoned I could count on Leonard and Ryk having left already for their weekend cottage on the Suffolk coast and the continued silence from the other side suggested Debby and her kids too were away from home. But I was still very aware that the small white oblong box, placed next to the same-size hole I was digging with a plasterer's bucket trowel picked up en route, made it look very like I was conducting a baby's burial.

Feeling distinctly shifty, wanting to get this over with, as I continued to gouge between the roots of the winter flowering jasmine, the only plant that thrived in this sour earth, from sheer force of habit I nevertheless separated out any sherds I turned up, making a little pile of my domestic finds. I even took the time to wipe the soil off crockery that looked interesting, including parts of a large plate, decorated with a hand-painted design, quite possibly Georgian.

Fifteen minutes later, picking up the cardboard box to lower it into the cold clay, it'd surprised me how light the thing was. I had to reassure myself it was just the remains of a tiny shoe and tissue paper in there – nothing more solid or substantial.

I dumped the soil back onto the shoebox's white lid, firmed it over with my foot and scattered the dug-up bits of glass and pottery, like votary offerings, over the top of the little mound.

Then I stood in the deep and narrow trough of our back garden for that customary moment with my head bowed. Idiotic, I knew, but the dead baby's shoe seemed to demand this sober moment of contemplation.

Once I'd held my muddy hands for a long time under the comfort of warm running water, since I was anyway standing at the sink – me, with my big comedy boobs – I got round at last to washing up that day's many mugs.

# Chapter Eighteen

Mrs McNamara and baby safely and silently installed in their upstairs room, you resume your sentry post. Over in the bomb site a knot of miniature ne'er-do-wells, probably no more than five or six years old, are now stolidly engaged in throwing half bricks at some piece of shrapnel they evidently take for a UXB. If it is, and they manage to make it go off, they'll most probably succeed in finishing the demolition job the Third Reich already made a start on. Actually finding their giddy licence to lay further waste to the wasteland rather refreshing, you refrain from rapping a warning on the windowpane to the bomb squad. You'll extend to the kids the courtesy of letting them decide for once how things turn out. Even if that should be bang bang.

Besides, seeing that from the wreckage of the bombed-out houses a playground arose, a *tabula rasa* must only hasten the replacement of *boys' town* itself by the next new thing.

With more than a hundred thousand buildings destroyed or damaged beyond repair, the demolition of just these five to you represents the possibility of personal liberation. Inured as you are to living under a regime of centralised bureaucracy, planning by the state means that, whether by the kids or the council, the sooner this particular plot is cleared, the quicker it'll be ready for redevelopment. Progress! Even if ugly and inharmonious, new houses going up across the way hold out the hope that, along with the rest of the dispossessed and chronically overcrowded, the upstairs tenants themselves must eventually get the chance of somewhere municipal to move to. Both young couples shall have a place to truly call their own.

This thought brings with it a rush of sudden rapture you probably last experienced looking out at this overgrown and neglected bomb site when it was beautiful with orange-yellow flowers. Soon after that epiphany you were admitted to a hospital ward; and following your discharge from that temporary underworld found refuge in another. Hid your head in the safe solitude of this enclosure, and tried to forget. But even when you recognised the hiding place was a trap, spat out the soporific seed and tried to find your way back 'out top', still this cold and narrow space drew you back and held you close.

Now standing at the window, seeing not the husks of houses and scruffy boys playing war but marigolds, however hard it may be to imagine it, stuck as you are in winter, you know that spring is waiting under the surface, ready to come again.

The difficult passage between winter and spring, death and life, demanding a rite, it comes to you that you Bones having become, appropriately, proverbially, chilled through in here, a housewarming party will not only be apt, but, unlike that furtive festival of your wedding, in publicly embracing this place as your married home it will rededicate you and William as a couple.

But how to subtly suggest to him that all it might take for you two to begin again, better, might be to perform before witnesses a ceremonial of colour and light?

Practising the wiles of the wily wife, you startle your husband, home from his work, with a pleasantry.

"Hello, dear, good day at the museum?" Caught off guard, William forgoes his habitual, *what, what, what.*

"Oh, you know."

Anxious not to let him disappear off down this conversational *cul de sac*, you disconcertingly remark, "There's a lot to be said for divestment, don't you think?" Perhaps suspecting his wife has, somehow, identified something else to winkle out of your stark and comfortless accommodation, he casts a rapid, assaying glance about himself, saying, "But maybe a limit?"

With a merry laugh, you say, "I was looking at the place through Betty's eyes: she thoroughly approved of 'the dearth of ornamental clutter.' Did I mention she called?"

"No, I don't think…"

If this somewhat edited and stale report has the virtue of being true, believing that any proposal made by his ex-girlfriend will be more acceptable to William than one coming from his still-wife, you resort now to outright lies.

"Said we simply must throw a housewarming do to show off the perfect proportions, gracious dimensions of these rooms, as well as, of course, our good luck and very fine judgement at acquiring them!"

"Just like Betty to take charge," says William, still looking nervous. Gesturing about yourself, you brightly say, "If we *are* to throw a housewarming party, rather prescient of me, wasn't it, chucking out the heirlooms? I mean these acres of empty space do evoke the new page."

As if any sudden movement of his might properly set off this new excitable wife, William lets his jacket slip off the ends of his arms and onto the floor. You move across the room to drape it tidily over the back of his deck chair, saying, "The only thing of which Betty did not approve was the greenery-yallery papers these rooms are done up in."

Calculating your best bet for getting past him what's next in line for the execution block is to keep on riding the stalking horse of Betty, add: "Suggested we cheaply cover over the stuck-in-the-murk flock with a cheerful paint job: a sunny yellow or a sky blue. On the whole I prefer yellow to blue. Or even an orange." Pink of cheek, bright of eye, breathless with lying, on you tinkle: "Or yellow. Or a yellowy orange."

What you have in your mind, of course, is the blazing glory of marigolds.

"So, what, what, what d'you say, William, shall we turn a bright new, yellow page in here with a party?" William may well be surprised by this sudden enthusiasm for something he first proposed months back when you two first moved in here to begin upon connubial bliss that, being fat, self-conscious and morose, you vetoed. Knowing, if he hates any kind of change, he does love a shindig, you light the touch paper and stand back:

"I know, just the thing: you could invent a lovely yellow cocktail to match the new walls."

# Chapter Nineteen

At the conclusion of today's 'site meeting', picking my way back up through builders' crap piled on every step had recalled my first tricky encounter with this staircase; then cluttered up with broken and abandoned stuff. Like other foolhardy explorers who lost heart at various stages of the ascent, their expired remains, as I should have recognised, represented grim mile markers to the summit. Unlike them, I decided this time to abandon the climb, save myself.

\*

I surprised my dear friend, Dimphna outside her flat, engaged this chilly morning in the laborious process of opening up the front door. By the look of her: stripped of makeup, slicked back hair, slack trackie bottoms, an oversized anorak and a sports bag, my old college chum had been making the most of her sacrosanct day out of the office down at the pool.

Not a little put out, she asked: will I put the kettle on?

We proceeded along the narrow passage that led to her back kitchen. Seeming to soak up all the light and air, the thick row of dark dead coats hanging along one wall forced us into single file. From behind she was rigid and austere as an old umbrella.

Because Dimphna herself was chronically cold, her house was kept permanently too hot; the kitchen was tropical. Coming from the windy street into this overheated room, even she was feeling it. Half woman, half umbrella, in pulling off her waterproof outerwear, as if putting herself up on thin arms, her big head supported on its pole body was momentarily hidden beneath this canopy.

Emerging from the anorak, she disclosed a floppy t-shirt that advised me: *similes are, like, metaphors.*

I smiled: good swim? How was the experience for you: cold as ice, or like a tidal wave of pleasure?

For once she failed to quickly pick up on my verbal tease, saying: I'd go for *feckin' annoying*. What is it about men and their competitiveness? There am I, mindin' me own business, ploughin' me lonely furrow in the modest middle lane, only for some wanker to give us a good kickin' thrashin' his way past. Keep the bitch in her rightful place, y'understand? An', wouldn't you jus' know it, then he goes an' slows up to catch his breath. Didn't I just turn it up a notch; leave him standing?

Bet you did, I said, wondering where she found the energy. Perhaps sheer bloody-mindedness was the fuel that powered Dimphna Bean.

She went on: what does the fekker himself do then but move one across to the fast lane? If you can't beat the arsey bitch at her own game, simple: promote yourself! Spent the last fifteen minutes lapping your man on the inside. Nearly killed me. Doubt the bastard noticed.

What *is* it about men and their competitiveness, Dimp?

We both laughed, I relaxed.

She asked again: will I be putting the kettle on? Don't know about you, but I've a throat on me.

Dimp opened up the fridge and looked into it. Along with all the bottles of booze, some vitamin pills and half of a black avocado on a plate were briefly put on show. Evidently this wasn't one of her stuffing, then hurling phases. Catching me snooping, Dimphna slammed shut the fridge door, saying: whadda you know, no milk. Will you take your tea without?

I couldn't stop myself: whatever you're having, without, I'll have. What'll that leave: a lovely mug of hot water?

As always, whenever I attempted to bring up her size or weight, however obliquely, or that she'd spent these last two decades in diligently alternating between purging and starving herself to death, my friend went on the defensive.

I shall be takin' a tisane for my digestion, which you're quite welcome to also.

Many calories in a *tisane*?

Expect not. On a diet, are yer?

I let it drop. From long experience, when challenged, I knew that Dimp would spin some ridiculous story about her *digestive problems* and her chronic bad circulation. The treatment of which involved the soles of her feet being massaged by her latest wonderful alternative guru, somewhere off Harley Street. (Expensive as you like because, aside from the basic necessities of life, like calories, our Dimphna never stinted herself.)

Once she'd slopped boiling water onto a couple of bags of fat-free hedge trimmings, my thin friend lowered her bony arse onto the well-padded chair across the kitchen table from me, pushed across my mug and got in my punishment.

You're most welcome ter turn up here without so much as a text, doll.

If that's a problem…?

I made as if to leave. (Now I lived only twenty minutes' drive away, couldn't I just tip up on a friend's doorstep for a chat and a cup of tea?)

Guan, yourself, she said.

Her hand on my arm to stay me, a quizzical smile on the peaky, pixieish little face I still remembered as having more life to it, less nose. I noticed the teeth too that, most probably out of perversity, she'd never had *work* done on. Never mind the increasingly self-conscious *Norn Iron* accent she'd strategically lost, then found again (I guessed it was useful for unnerving her posh clients), I thought that nowadays it was her teeth that really gave her away. My friend Dimphna Philomena Constance Bean JP had unavoidably working-class Irish teeth; ill-formed, small and grey. Or was this just down to the effects of regular gargling with stomach acid?

Resuming my seat, I said: just fancied some human company that wasn't connected with the building trade for a change was all.

Choosin' between sample paint pots an' ordering bespoke wallpaper not as intellectually stimulating as you thought it'd be when you chucked in your latest career, eh?

Even if she'd come perilously close to the mark, actually not enjoying being bullied and patronised – I had enough of that from the Caseys – I told her: surprising as this may sound, Dimp, managing the restoration of a listed house *is* work. In fact, apart from the help my law's been in negotiating with the LA, you'd be surprised the expertise that goes into sourcing materials and matching heritage paints.

I was pretty sure the shade she'd used in this kitchen, her hallway too, and the living room, was magnolia. For a woman, I really got the irony, with a *big* personality, to me her unimaginative decor manifested a deep-seated self-doubt. This kitchen for example, like every other room, was low-lit, personality-free and sparsely equipped with dull, utilitarian furniture. The depressingly neutral, unloved and un-loveable stuff you might expect to come with a rental property. Maybe this was why, whenever I came up to London on business, or to visit family (what I had left of it) and we planned a get-together, she'd always suggest meeting somewhere else. Anywhere, in fact, but her home.

Meeting her eye, I said: aside from the pursuit of pigment, my time being more my own means I can properly catch up with the people I haven't seen half enough of these last few years. Speaking of which, I met Cara for coffee the other day.

Having forgiven me my dig, just as I forgave hers, my acerbic, funny, damaged friend was off and running again: coffee with Cara, eh? How long she keep you hangin'?

An hour? She's the excuse of spawn now, of course.

Dimphna snorted: an' let's not be forgettin' a house full a staff! Never ceases to amuse me the lovely Cara most probably puts her perfect feckin' existence down to good life choices whereas we, her dearest friends, know it's beauty, pure and simple, that's the charm. And money.

Dimphna Bean! I leave the two of you alone together in London for eighteen years and look what happens. Weren't we three bessie mates at university?

Unlikely as it seemed at the time, it was true. Palling up, I'd been the dull, dependable one mediating from the middle between the Belfast toughie and the beautiful bit of posh totty. For a second I wondered whether it was the impossible attempt to keep up with size six-to-eight Cara that'd set Dimp off on her long course of self-destruction.

Both of us took a sip from our steaming mugs of wee-yellow tincture and Dimphna, with a sigh of a gratification no longer delayed, efficiently lit up.

I said: I guess you can't really hold being practically perfect against her, and the money isn't her fault.

Taking a greedy drag on her cigarette: where would the fun be in that?

Only too aware – along with the fags, and alcohol – of Dimp's taste for gossip and character assassination, now we'd hit our stride in the dissing of a mutual friend, against my better judgement, I fed the beast another titbit.

You know, don't you, Fergus's first language is Polish?

Dimphna guffawed into her 'tea', delighted, as I knew she would be.

How posh 'n mixed up is that, growin' up more at home with the servants than your own mammy and daddy? Poor wee, Polish, dote.

Don't feel too sorry for Fergus, the lad's got public school, Oxbridge and The Cabinet written through him to the core.

Now y're suckin' diesel!

Even though the injured third party – usually that'd be my husband – wasn't here to be offended, falling into my usual role as conciliator, I felt obliged to dial things back a bit.

To be fair, young Fergy the fogey's a nice enough kid, and Cara's so clearly in her element. Wouldn't you just know it: ripely fecund suits our girl.

Sitting across from her now, as I had just the other day from glossily golden Cara, Dimphna looked like she was turning into leather and sticks before my eyes. Sepulchral through her veil of smoke, as though she'd heard this thought, she cackled: shame on me, fer the nasty, dried-up, ole witch that I am.

I laughed too but in my even-handedness was aware I'd gone and snuffed out the spark we'd managed to kindle between us.

Because I wanted, needed, to stay on here a bit longer, at least until we arrived at an hour when, since I'd quit smoking, she could legitimately offer me the other of her little indulgences: a proper drink, I'd have to come up with a new topic, fast. Our conversation might naturally have turned to what we did on our holidays, had I not happened to know that Dimp never went away. Ever. No, for Dimphna it was holidaying at home that provided the welcome break. Two restful weeks of no working lunches, no dinners with clients in a restaurant. And when her little recess, dedicated to excessive exercise, self-denial, Chardonnay and cigs, was up, she'd once more paint her eye sockets and cheeks that were grown downy as a grey peach, wind her bones in expensively tailored fabric, and become again what she was: the very model of a successful city lawyer. Driven, ruthless, a little bit crazy.

As for me, rather than a holiday, quite apart from a major life refit, I was having a new house, or a new old house this year. Or, come to that, the way costs were escalating, forever.

I needn't have worried, despite a powerful preoccupation with her own life, Dimp'd always had an almost psychic ability to sniff out anything awry in mine, even at a remove of two hundred plus miles and, unlike me, she didn't pussyfoot around.

Going straight for the jugular: so, how's the money pit?

Good! I said, taken aback. And, despite the gung-ho routine about finding it all fantastically rewarding, actually wanting a bit of sympathy quickly amended this to: terrible! I swear our builders are literally 'aving a larf, Dimp! Every fuckin' day there's something new that'll add yet more weeks to the schedule and thousands to the budget. The buggers informed me only yesterday all the partition walls are built of 'place' bricks. Know what they are?

She shook her head.

From what I understand: equal parts clay and ash; one touch and the lot come tumbling down. Least they do if Mr Casey has anything to do with it.

Dimp evidently neither knew, nor cared, about bodged building techniques, but there was now no stopping me.

We've got the lot, Dimp, wet rot, dry rot, woodworm...

Ringworm.

I carried on regardless: I mean, no proper sodding foundations, structure's built straight onto bare earth and nineteenth-century builders' rubble.

Least it's historic rubble, eh?

Pretending humorous exasperation, I said: all we can hope for is the dry rot'll cancel out the wet rot.

I really should have remembered, as well as to all known foodstuffs, Dimphna was whinge intolerant.

Your dream house's turning out more of the nightmare? she said, squinting speculatively at me from out of her wreathing cigarette smoke.

The outer bony carapace might look brittle, and fragile, as a seahorse's, but lord she was tough on the inside.

Unexpectedly, Dimp reached out her hand, the knuckles gnawed rough and red, to take hold of mine.

But that's not all that's been buggin' you, is it? Give it up, doll, it's that husband o' yours?

I was aware she'd have much preferred to commiserate with me over a glass or two if it was my husband I wanted a moan about. Had managed to make me admit that leaving my job and moving cities for him, like some trailing *traditional bride*, had proved to be the huge mistake she'd warned me of. But even if I was hungry for her concern, I wasn't going to open up to her about my marriage.

Truly, Dimp, whatever it is that's stressing me, it's definitely not Bill. We're fine.

Sure so, but there's something.

And, somehow, what I'd been suppressing all along popped out of my mouth: if you must know, there's a presence in the house.

Even though I was appalled at myself for voicing it, I couldn't help but be a bit gratified to see I'd surprised her.

What d'you mean *a presence*?

Something supernatural.

She snorted: you're getting your knickers in a twist over banshees 'n pookas?

I've always been fascinated by social history, right?

You have?

Well, anyway, since I started researching into the previous inhabitants of the house, I seem to have dug them up, or at least encouraged them back in.

Put a Santa hat on it and call it Randal!

Too quickly, I protested: Dimp, when I know for sure there's no one else in the house with me, I've heard things, weird things.

Yeah?

Knowing that to wring any sympathy for my imaginary squatters would take more than their mere *presence*, I cooked up causation behind some random noises, saying: a chair being moved in a room overhead, something heavy thrown or falling down the stairs. Ok?

Dimphna, anyway unimpressed by this guff, said: as one raised in the magical realm of the *sidhe*, you can take it from me, doll, all that's bollix. The house is just a big ol' house, the things that go bump in the night are just things. I mean, like you say, the walls tumblin' down, the rotten floors cavin' in.

I gave it one last shot: how about there's always this smell of boiling cabbage and wet washing?

To which Dimp had her ready response: 'tis well known, the smell of sulphur means trouble wid your drains, just like any unexplained 'cold spots' are what we rationalists call drafts.

I'm sure you're right, course you are, I said, still for some reason withholding the incontrovertible sound of a baby crying somewhere in an empty house.

Your nerves gettin' to you, what with the pressure you've been under, perfectly understandable if you're feelin' vulnerable, a bit isolated – chucking your job, relocating hundreds of miles across the country for your feller, she said, one-handedly tamping out her spent fag in the scorched scallop shell she used as an ashtray, making it spin on its axis.

Wanting to hurt her back for dismissing my baseless and irrational fears, I squeezed the bloodless claw I was holding a bit too hard. Her bones felt snappable as a bundle of dried twigs. Snatching it away from me, tenderly as she might an injured bird, she held it to her chest.

Somewhat ashamed of myself, I said: sorry, there's nothing of you nowadays. No insulation.

Reaching across the table, I attempted to give the withered skin of her upper arm an illustrative pinch. Dimp jerked away from my wounding touch.

Meaning?

I lost my nerve: just saying, every time I see you these days, Dimp, you seem...a little frailer...

Under the pressure of her challenging eye, I dried. When I extended my hand to retake hers, she made sure to keep it out of range, pretending to consult her watch.

Isn't it high old time you were getting back to your dodgy builders and your strange phenomena? Away wid yer, now! she said, humorously. Meaning it.

Yeah, back to all that, I replied, carefully non-committal. If I totally got that unexplained cold spots *were* commonly known as drafts and cabbagey smells meant bad drains, I couldn't help but wish I might stay a little longer in that overheated kitchen, talking with someone with no imagination, who called a lusty bollix on 'all that'.

*

By the time I got home my bladder was bursting with her lime flower fucking tisane. Dimphna never let anyone into her toilet, shrine to the strict observances of her own cruel religion. Creeping out of my own loo, this time without flushing so as to avoid the notice of the builders, still bashing about somewhere down below, I snuck into our bedsitting room to consult my mood boards. Bugger Dimp: playing about with my paint pots, swatches and samples, if not hugely constructive, at least worked as a displacement activity. Perfect for banishing the bigger and more pressing issue of those tumbling walls, collapsing floors and intrusive past inhabitants.

Determined as I was to leave my own mark upon an already well-worked canvas, looking again at my timid palette it concerned me that Bill and I would be judged in retrospect for our own failings on the decorating front.

Rather than that our lasting memorial over the coming good times and the bad in this house would be the currently in-vogue equivalent of all-over magnolia (most likely some variation on grey), I wondered should I be channelling those few ancestors who'd actually got it right? For example, follow the bold example of the nasty fluffy wallpaper in the front reception room that someone painted over in crazy yellow distemper.

Caught between hessian and flock, I vividly recalled the moment that fragile wafer of gold leaf appeared as quickly as it disappeared. I'd been halfway up a ladder, fish slice idle by my side, as it caught and kindled in the late summer sunlight. Even if, as I liked to believe, this was the handiwork of my lively 1950s housewife, of all the decorative choices I uncovered it came closest to the carnival of colour I knew the Georgians favoured.

With a similar sense of epiphany, it now came to me where and how I might bring together my first and last accidental arbiters of taste. I'd preserve in situ – under Perspex? – Gorgeous George's scrap of wallpaper, but hang the reproduction hand blocked papers based on his original in the front living room, printed up in her authentically regency King's Yellow.

# Chapter Twenty

Up a ladder, paintbrush in hand, if your enthusiastic decorating technique might fairly be dismissed as *slobbering over*, you prefer to think of your efforts as pragmatic. Not being bothered to strip back or burn off first, the distemper you mixed up in a pail to be as close as yellow comes to gold is laid on thick as butter over patterned wall coverings and paintwork alike. In this, as in most areas of your life, Celia, you are a bit of a cheerful skimmer over surfaces.

For the sake of a happy home life, William sensibly chooses to steer this course too. While you whistle and slather, he turns a blind eye on the slapdash handiwork, a deaf ear to the tuneless tooting and diplomatically bends his studious head over his own careful preparations for the housewarming party. Fastidious over his potions and lotions, happily diverted in perfecting his latest *patented pharmaceutical cocktail*: "The Age of Marigold", you speculate that Dr Bill Bone doesn't suit him half so well as *The Right Rev. William Bone, amateur chemist,* might or, since he's a Medievalist, *Brother Will, the ascetic alchemist monk.*

As for you, jaded as you believe yourself to be, dressed in one of his old school shirts, unwashed hair fastened up behind with a pencil, you don't look old enough to be drinking the gin-based concoction he's contentedly mixing.

Apart from the cocktails, William has laid in a couple of crates of brown ales – for any socialists amongst the guests, you presume – and some Indian tonic water and two bottles of "Wincarnis". You guess that should the supplies of "Virol", concentrated orange juice and "Delrosa Syrup" give out prematurely, they'll do equally well as mixers: the more conventional *Win* and the *It* to accompany any surplus gin.

Naturally, there are no lemons: none to be had down the Chapel market, love. No ice either. But this lack is of no account, even with a blaze going in the elegant inadequate grate, it's freezing in here.

Along with the drinkables, William has wisely put himself in sole charge of the eatables: devilled eggs, celery sticks, their gutters clogged by cream cheese, "Ritzes" with salmon paste, liver paté and – this, as I believe, being a nursery delicacy passed down the generations, nanny to nanny, in family Bone – "Marmite" marbled through with best butter (or, in these still straitened times, best margarine). These delicacies William has divided between the two big blue meat plates that somehow escaped your pogroms. Depicting an oriental scene, so your husband carefully explained, the platters are Middlesbrough, late Georgian: the subject, probably the tomb of the Emperor Acreb at Secundra. The sideboard upon which drinks and party food are displayed he has cleverly contrived from a door supported by a couple of packing cases, the whole shebang covered over with a red damask curtain. A length of purple velvet picked up from the same jumble sale has been thrown over the deck chair; a cushion and a bit of brocade disguise the packing case. And he's dotted tall candles about the place, to drip fittingly. If he truly abhors electric light, you assume William perceives gaslight to be almost equally anachronistic to a Georgian setting. Certainly candlelight brings out the glamour of these two grand-ish rooms – whilst usefully forgiving their emptiness, your own imperfect decorating efforts and the greasy film of black dust an open coal fire unceasingly manufactures to coat the lot.

Examining the overall effect – the dimness of the lighting helps – you have to admit William's succeeded rather brilliantly in suggesting the sumptuous on no budget. Never mind asserting your own resurgent personality in yellow paint, by loading every rift with ore your resourceful husband has smuggled back not only good taste but some comfort into these elegantly laid bare rooms.

Excited by the prospect of what will be the first party in your first proper marital abode, you dismount your ladder to work your own rapid revamp. Although applying a bit of Vaseline to eyebrows, brushing hair and changing into your one 'good' outfit, unfortunately for you, isn't going to be quite so magically transformative. It is, after all, the hideous, semi-fitted brown wool suit, with a three-quarters length sleeve Mother bought you to *go away* in after the wedding into which you slip. Quietly good quality, so she assured her daughter if, undoubtedly, a suitable costume for three March days in a private hotel at Frinton, less so for a knees-up in N1 you think. Zipping up, you discover the 'good suit' is semi-fitted no longer. Its short jacket hangs loose and the waistband of the skirt must be bunched up and fastened behind with a big nappy pin. Your brief flowering season already passed, the bud has bloomed, blown and rapidly gone over. And all in the first few months of married life. But you are nothing if not defiant: so what if it makes you look like someone's loyal secretary, since you have nothing else to wear this will have to do! Gazing into the mirror over the bedroom fireplace at the pale, large-eyed face that looks back, well as you are able by the dim light of the oil lamp, you pin up your long greasy hair into an approximation of a French pleat and draw on lipstick. The only stick you possess – a saccharine hue called "Stormy Pink" – failing to add either sophistication or sex appeal to your look.

Your tentative re-entry into the glamorous party room discovers William sorting through his bebop collection: some discs of Gillespie and Thelonius Monk and Bird Parker, of course. For Dr Bone, home is where the 78s are and, contrarily for him, in this regard William is not a trad man.

"'Round Midnight" strikes up in darkly brown and blue notes as you look at this stranger, your husband, and wonder if he remembers what was playing in his keeping room the night you met.

It was "Embraceable You."

Self-conscious in that hideous honeymoon suit, you execute a self-mocking whirl about for the husband's approval.

"Don't I know you from somewhere?" he says, moving closer so he can rest his hands on the jutting panniers that are now your hips: "Ah, now I remember, you were that Annatto Maker in here just now, dressed in rags, mixing up the arsenic and trisulphide pigment."

Because William laughs you do too.

Contained within his arms, his face on a level with your own (you're taking care to keep your knees bent), you have some difficulty in breathing. Hard to remember the last time you two were so easy with each other. Ages since you laughed together. Longer still that he found you embraceable.

After Frinton there seemed to have been so few opportunities. At dear Gussie and Lally's, in an atmosphere of potpourri and camphor balls, the thought of doing 'it' – even if legitimately – in the comfy, squeaky bed provided by those two, very nice maiden ladies, who surely still held that uncovered table legs were obscene, was enough to put a crimp on spontaneity. And quite soon after William and you got out from under the hundred eyes of peacock tail feathers displayed in art vases, had some privacy at last to make a real go of marriage, the accident happened. After that you told yourself it must be from a sense of delicacy and fear of hurting you that he continued to hold himself back. Besides, your female plumbing having first off made you fat and moody then thin and mad, you were so fundamentally altered from the carefree girl he met at a party that it was in fact perfectly reasonable he'd gone off you.

"You might have made a thorough pig's ear of applying it, but that 'King's Yellow' of yours is pretty spot on," William whispers, his warm breath making a pink silk purse of your own, "Apart from, presumably, not being toxic, I'd go as far as to say: authentically regency."

If it was your intention painting over the parlour in this hopeful yellow to put the nihilistic and divesting phases behind you, it's gratifying nevertheless to have got this right in his eyes. And – most encouragingly – his compliment is even an historical one.

Emboldened, you put your arms around your husband's neck, and to the wonderful "Blue Note" recording, quite un-fussily, you begin to smooch around the floor together. At five-eight William isn't short but, catching sight of the united reflection as it wobbles across the black mirror of the un-curtained window, as far as you are concerned those two inches between you make you look like a bone and sinew racehorse and he the ludicrous little perching jockey. But if it is remarkable that the window with the fault running through it should have withstood the wartime bomb, maybe even more so that something fragile as mutual affection, let alone attraction between the unequally yoked pair it now reflects, might somehow have survived the first dreadful months of your contrary coupling.

Then the music runs out.

He doesn't let go at once, but stands awhile, still holding you close, so that your breath mingles. His sweet from tasting cocktails – just as it had been on the night of that other party – yours salty with snaffled "Marmite".

Will he kiss you now, deeply, tenderly, as on that other night?

It is Betty Seaton's prompt and, somehow, peremptory ring on the doorbell that puts a stop to finding out. Breaking reluctantly free of your husband to answer it, the door opens upon his old girlfriend, striking a "Harper's Bazaar" attitude with cigarette holder. Eyes done up like butterfly wings, she's made herself extra exotic with a close-fitting turban made out of pink feathers.

"Betty. What a surprising hat!"

"Seal, darling!"

You lean to kiss cheeks with her, taking care not to disorder her slick plumage.

You only realise she has a man in tow when, showy as a matador, she whisks aside the skirts of her coat to flourish forth her prize bull on a lower step:

"May I present Rrroberto from the BBC!"

A couple of decades older than she he is dressed with appropriate dignity though his neat face topiary: beard and moustache, trimmed and shaved in such a way so as to rather obscenely emphasise blue and nakedly fleshy cheeks, lends Betty's BBC man a dangerous and lascivious look.

No wonder she's overexcited.

Introducing yourself, "Celia Bone," you say, reaching past her for an awkwardly off-kilter handshake; yours fitting his like a child's hand going into a large leather glove.

"Cecilia," he repeats, holding on too long. By adding that second 'c' and making both of them pointy as a pair of stilettos, he confers a sharp Continental sophistication you much prefer to the wet-eyed, amorphous blubber of Betty's 'Seal'.

"Manzotti, Roberto."

"Pleased to meet you, Signor Manzotti."

Excited by her new foreign friend, made extra expressive by bejewelled eyes and pink plumage: "*Conte*, in point of fact, Seal, darling," corrects Betty, tossing off a high little laugh and batting her butterflies.

"*Conte* Manzotti," you re-shake the rigid hand, adding, "Presumably from somewhere in Italy, prior to the BBC?"

"You *are* a funny duck, I didn't mean to suggest he was born at Alexandra Palace! No, Rrroberto is from Rrroma, aren't you *caro mio*?" Then, sotto voce: "Television; 'Talks'. Useful to know."

As if there was some doubt for whom, with a pointed red fingernail she harpoons her hostess in the breastbone.

Having now gained the top step, Roberto stands shoulder to shoulder with Betty, or rather shoulder to satirical chin, for the sexy beast has revealed himself to be a *toro pequeño*, or Italian equivalent, and Betty about the same height as you. (An observation that briefly makes you consider if William's proclivity was for tall girls, and Betty's for splendid physical superiority over her mates.)

Now that introductions all round have been effected, twice, casting about for something to say whilst their hostess gets around to actually inviting them in over the threshold, Betty paralysingly remarks: "So glad to see you're up to makin' the effort again, Seal, darling." Pinching a lapel between finger and thumb, she inspects the hideous costume: "quite good quality, and the Y-line silhouette's very '*this season*'."

The scraggy brown hen is rescued from having to come up with any reply to the peacock's condescension by the sudden look of horrified surprise that flashes over her face. Having assumed this must be connected to something you have said or done, you only now notice the series of thuds going off behind you. Turning to look, you find Mrs McNamara lying sprawled in a grotesque pile-up of limbs at the foot of the stairs. Themselves witness to the entire dramatic descent, Betty and her pocket Italian are quick to push past that bloody pram to reach her.

The hoopla has brought William too shooting out into the hall, but on seeing your tumbling tenant he hesitates to approach: little bare legs flung akimbo by the fall, the woman is showing off half a yard of thin white thigh and a bit of knicker. You, meanwhile, rattle off a round of stupid, belligerent questions: *was she all right, how on earth did it happen?* Ungenerously fuming the while that most probably William will have to abandon the party before it's even got going to run to the phone box on the high street and call for her doctor or an ambulance.

Making absolutely no effort to rise or right her dress, Mrs McNamara utters through pale lips: "Everso sorry, Doctor Bone, Missus Bone. Don't know what come over me."

"No need to apologise," you say, thinking she has every reason – stupid, secretive woman, creeping around the place like that, prying.

"Must've come over faint or summat," she says fretfully, the while looking over to where, haloed by the candlelit room at their backs, William, Betty and Roberto from Rome stand forming a chorus of concern at a discreet distance. You think to yourself: *but that's not quite true, is it?* Contrary as it seems, there is something in her sly, sidelong glance that suggests this fall was no accident. Rather, the woman has contrived for some reason in this overly dramatic way to draw attention.

"Showin' me drawers, causin' a palava in front of your party guests," she says, plucking ineffectually at the hem of her skirt.

Her face that was white as a dead fish is now quite florid – you are appalled to see she's begun to cry.

Disliking mess, and scenes, William slips away to fetch a candelabrum, the better to illuminate the scene. Passing it over to you, to your horror, he ushers away the first two guests, leaving you in sole charge of the situation.

The smell of alcohol strong on her breath as you lean over, trying to arrange her more decently and comfortably, Mrs McNamara confides in a rush, "My hubby'll murder me!"

Startled, you wonder whether the well-behaved tenants were engaged in a drunken domestic brawl that ended either with the wife being flung or flinging herself down the stairs. Had she meant to appeal for protection from her brute of a husband by, literally, throwing herself at your feet?

Threatening as is the following thunder of his boots down those same stairs, McNamara in person turns out to be as un-homicidal – and sober – as a justice of the peace.

"I come a cropper, Pat," says his little missus.

Looking up at her man from under drooping eyelids, she hiccups then giggles at herself.

With the world-weariness of nineteen you conclude that, rather than fleeing domestic brutality, the women is indeed only half-cut.

With an 'oops-a-daisy,' easily as he might shift a sack of spuds, if more tenderly, muscly McNamara hoists his limp little wife back onto her two feet. She remains rather saggy but can just about bear her own weight and doesn't seem to be in too much pain. If anything, you think, she's oddly loose limbed and lightheaded after her fugue. Probably the gin helped.

Briskly, addressing him over her little blonde head, you say, "There now, no bones broken thank goodness – she won't be needing a doctor."

Both McNamaras glance away at the door to the party room from behind which Betty's excited, querulous tones can be heard, interspersed by William's measured baritone.

"No, sure so, missus," says he, in a courteous whisper, "there'll be no call to disturb yer man."

Only now do you understand their confusion over William's honorific and, bizarrely, perhaps also that the good doctor's name is 'Bone'.

Deciding not to correct the misapprehension:

"If not a doctor, is there anything else…?"

As well as flushed and unsteady on her feet, you notice the woman is bolder than normal. If being tipsy is in itself sufficient explanation for this, as well as the fall, nevertheless it continues to nag away that her reckless nosedive down the stairs was wholly calculated. Triggered for some reason by overhearing voices in the hall, with alcohol playing its part only in so far as it gave her the courage to take the leap down that dark well.

Secure now that they won't be taking up your offer, you say, more warmly, "If you're sure there's nothing?"

Quite jovial, Mr McNamara is preparing to escort his barelegged and inebriate wife back up the stairs:

"A nice, strong cup o' tea an' she'll be grand."

You could have sworn the man tipped you a wink.

You accompany them as far as the first landing. To light their further ascent into territory wholly McNamara, hold the dripping candelabrum high as he opens then closes the door to their bedsitting room. Along with light from their oil lamp, released from within is a snatch of "Jack Jackson's Round-up": a wireless programme you listened to with Mother. Both looking up from whatever worthy thing occupied your hands to smile across the hearthrug at each other over the occasional input from that imaginary radio cat Tiddles.

Such an ordinary, homely, sound, you almost envy them the "Light Service" and that nice cup of restorative tea.

# Chapter Twenty-one

Most afternoons now, I sought cups of tea and company that in any other circumstances I'd have made efforts to avoid.

Round about four – once the Caseys knocked off and it turned crepuscular – when I should have been using my time more wisely: hoovering up the dust of ages shaken daily from this old structure, studying ways to claw back the runaway budget, I instead regularly escaped my own uneasy house to instead practise being a better, more sympathetic, listener round at Debby's. Whatever my first judgement of her might have been, and admittedly it hadn't shifted far, as my place became far too quiet, cold and uncomfortable for me to remain alone in it, the schools having by now kicked out, so hers was sufficiently noisy and alive with rampaging children to provide me with the refuge and solace from builders' chaos and an over-vivid imagination I craved.

For all I knew, in her turn, Debby dismissed me as selfish and smug, whilst at the same time, without knowing it, unfulfilled. Nevertheless, even if belligerently childfree, after a long day banged up with her own appalling kids, I was a fellow grown-up to moan to.

Sitting across from me at her kitchen table, hands held strangely inexpressive in her lap while the two older ones, Kitty and Teddy, played merry hell and little whatsit, the baby, smashed up his toys in the play pen, she'd drone on in that flat, doped-up sounding voice of hers about how underappreciated she was. Like every other self-sacrificing, self-satisfied stay at home mummy I'd ever come across. She'd complain that to anyone who went out to work (having chucked in my latest career, I was thankfully exempt from this despised lot) she'd become a cipher, a non-person. No one took her seriously anymore. Although, apparently, her hard labour was of a higher value to society than whatever it was the gainfully employed got up to while she was busy raising her kids on their behalf.

She'd hypothesise whether catering, cleaning, laundering and childcare constituted the nonessentials of family life: its little 'luxuries', bearing in mind if she didn't provide for them it was about the measure of her privilege as a woman with kids to go out and earn the money to pay some other woman to. And still end up taking responsibility for 'all the emotional work' – whatever that was – as well as a greater share than their father of the organisational stuff that went into the running of the household. Then, having got all righteous about it, she'd tell me how bloody boring it was, being stuck at home with no status, identity or money of her own, and only the children to talk to.

Conversational protocol demanding we took turns, when it came to my go, good as gold, Debby smiled her strangely disconnected smile, even nodded along, as I went on, and on, about how these houses were built with no *effing* foundations –

while seated in the cramped and inconvenient kitchen, which, because she couldn't afford to, she'd never had to endure the stress of disastrously digging out.

I might have been a little more diplomatic over our extensive renovation plans were not my building woes the necessary cover for what really drove me out from my own house every afternoon. Yet another setback in my schedule of works, or hike in the already enormous budget, little more than a nuisance in the scheme of things as compared with the one, huge, burning topic deserving of sympathy: my crying baby. Preferring to evade what was really bothering me, and not being able to whine in tune with Debby's particular preoccupations, the problems with our 'works' were all I could trust myself as trade-off for her tea and bikkies.

It was to my surprise then, a week or two into our unlikely afternoon alliance, that I was to discover a genuine connection between Debora and me. Began to get that her flat delivery, together with a fair amount of knowing self-deprecation, concealed some mordant wit that might almost have passed as 'northern'. Debby could poke fun at herself for the lazy cow she, at least half-mockingly, acknowledged herself to be.

Early in her youth, so she unemotionally explained, she'd decided to be useless at cooking, cleaning and ironing. Why not, seeing that such strategic domestic disability had worked for generations of men? Their age-old secret, so she once told me, was to maintain that housework was a skill set that fell halfway between unknowably recondite and not worth knowing. Meaning they owned that measly line: *I can never do it how you want it, anyway.* Put simply, housework was beyond or beneath them.

Candidly, though, based on what I witnessed round at hers, never mind all the moany baloney about nobly toiling away on the home front, unappreciated and unpaid, along with the other *little luxuries*, minimal input was a policy this militant SAHM extended also to childcare.

(*Ape light*, as I thought she called her method – bringing to mind that street food van – that equally incomprehensibly turned out to be AP lite. From what I could make out, a chapter of the Attachment Parenting movement designed for the parent who couldn't be arsed.)

The only thing, apart from Greg, that could rouse Deb to vague spasms of animation I was to discover was the latest manifestation of *over-parenting* she'd just been alerted to by The Daily Mail online. She was surprisingly quick off the mark to condemn *helicopter parents*, or *tiger mothers*, or whichever else was the super-capable managing style of the moment. But if she hated how they made it look like it all had to be such hard work Deb was even more dismissive of the model pushed on social media that only showed family life as fun and photogenic. Specifically, Debby was riled to a state that for her approached high fret by those young showman dads who'd sneakily worked out how to monetise their own home time by using their baby like some sort of amusing glove puppet in their YouTube vids.

Instagrammable or imprintable, cute kittens doing the funniest things or clever chimps conditioned in the intensive rearing lab, raising kids nowadays – according to her – was all about the parents. Whereas, she informed me, if you were prepared to put up with the disapproval, had the confidence to leave kids to their own, un-photogenic and unimproved devices, stopped striving so hard to make them remarkable, they might have a shot at experiencing their own childhood in the moment and the imperfect world in which they were actually living it.

It was with grim glee she prophesised, a couple of years down the line, the babies would be demanding their own editorial cut, and fee, and the kids whose pictures were published without their informed consent on Facebook suing their parents for invasion of privacy. And that when society passed peak perfect parent, her own preferred style of off-grid, benign neglect – meaning regular inoculations of alcohol for mum and dirt for the sprogs – would be recognised as the only true and superior brand.

Even if all this was a theory based on a scientific study conducted only in her own brain and, from what I'd seen of them, her kids were horrible, I wasn't going to take issue – benign neglect, just neglect, having been standard back when I was a kid. Then again, maybe I turned out fine because to my knowledge there were in existence only ten photographs featuring me between my birth and the day I left home for university. As a child of the '70s, with no means for sharing around the very sketchy record of my ill-favoured and ill-tempered teenage years, I was never exposed to the brute mechanism for public shaming and correction that is social media. So I just took another biscuit, and agreed.

Along with housework and childcare, it was difficult to identify anything at all that Debby now, or at any time, had striven hard to be good at. Certainly, not her career. Or so she claimed. I thought, however, I heard some lurking pride when she told me she was last considered a proper person when she worked 'in publishing'. Needless to say, I could never make her admit to this. Putting on the comic self-deprecation, she presented herself as little more than the girl who at literary launches passed around the wine and Twiglets at the back of a bookshop. Which she, nevertheless, contrived to muck up. Though, in mitigation, as she pointed out, she had had the good sense only to spill wine on literary greats. Salman Rushdie even asked her out after she gave him a good soaking in warm Chablis.

I assumed this jokey downplaying was intended to shield her from the horrible truth that by having the kids she might just have, as it were, put all of her eggs in the wrong little baskets. So what? Instead of making a thumping success of her career, she plumped for motherhood and equally as effortlessly managed to make a bit of a balls-up of that. She might insist that the thought of going back 'out there' made her feel physically sick, but it seemed to me 'home' was the safe prison within which she'd made herself voluntarily hostage to the lot of them. All the while convincing herself it was she who'd pulled off the scam.

It was perhaps discerning the rather ruthless disingenuousness with which dozy Debby contrived to organise her life according to her own contrary methods, and convenience, that made me warm to her. As for Deb, for all I knew, she believed my sudden overture of friendship at the end of days spent mostly in the fractious company of babies and builders was founded upon us two, both of us educated woman, being starved of intelligent adult company.

Anyway, having come to regard these afternoon sessions of ours as something of a secret sisterhood, it came as a surprise when she suggested something sociable. Seeing as we'd had her and Greg 'round' to ours first I assumed she was just buckling beneath the cast-iron protocol of returning the favour. They owed us drinks. Whatever. But the invitation turned out to be for a proper grownup dinner party – or *dp*, as in another of her handy contractions of effort, she abbreviated it. Which meant there would not only be 'another couple' present, she'd be cracking open the oven.

I knew this sort of entertainment was a rare occurrence next door: I ought to be flattered. Though I couldn't say I was looking forward to it. In her usual self-disparaging form, Debby had told me that in her house dinner was usually announced by the smoke alarm.

# Chapter Twenty-two

Broaching the door to the party room you think it a pity that before taking the plunge you hadn't followed Mrs McN's example and already made a start on the hard liquor.

William, Betty and Roberto are grouped around the Victorian washbasin in which he has mixed up his new cocktail: yellow Flowers of Sulphur powder, a dash of orange juice concentrate, and gin. Lots of gin. Betty, you notice, is already well into her first cocktail and contrary conversational gambit:

"....dead in the water."

"Who drowned?" you ask, the spectre at the feast with her candelabrum. Beckoning you over, attentive William ladles a large measure of the lethal concoction into a jam jar, which he proffers:

"No one died, dear. Unlikely as it sounds, Betty was explaining to us all about the future of television."

The latest disc having played down, your husband slips off to put on another and give the machine a vigorous wind up. Betty, in her feathered cap, turns her unbearable, cockeyed, attention full upon you. Taking a gulp of Dutch courage, you manage to master your rising colour by considering how this imperious yet somewhat demented gesture gives her the look of a cockatoo on a perch.

"Personally, Seal, I couldn't care less what it is they chose to transmit – shan't be watchin'. 'S just that, as the presses have been so eager to warn us, now the age of lower class broadcastin' is upon us, if it doesn't shape up and compete on the same level as this new Commercial channel the BBC shall deserve its awful fate."

Given that her *innamorato* is employed by it, you are surprised to hear this grim prognosis for the Corporation. But maybe by association alone Betty is now an expert. Unruffled, Roberto anyway regards with detached amusement the very fine stitching of his handmade shoes and you yourself are saved from having to formulate any sensible response to the terrifying Betty by Charlie Parker. Talking loudly over "Ornithology", William bebops his way back to the group by the washbasin:

"What was it you were telling us, Bet: Auntie's too egalitarian or not egalitarian enough to survive the competition?"

"Billy Bone, you absolute swine!" Betty squawks, giving him a swift, familiar, delighted jab on the upper arm with her red talons. Saving his drink, he toasts her back.

Speaking as if exclusively to you, she says: "*He* perfectly well understands – as in my view should those ghastly creepin' cultural intercessors down at the *BeeBeeCee* – transmittin' opera and concerts and new plays to the masses is not just misplaced nonsense, it's positively harmful!"

Addressing her boyfriend, Betty inquires, delightfully, "N*on* è vero, sweetie?"

The sphinx-like Roberto only smiles and tops up his girl's drink.

Seeing as a jam jar would not have sat right in that immaculately manicured brown hand, you notice he has made sure to provide both himself and Betty with a cut glass tumbler. Two subtracted from the complement of six, given as a wedding present. Taking a distracted sip, Betty continues, "Plain as plain, when any attempt's made to popularise it really good art inevitably ends up damaged and debased. I mean to say, what kind of an abomination is *Ballet for Beginners*! So that their *all roll over before the onward march of one-size-fits-all culture* ends up servin' no one well, besides being not at all what the people want, or need."

"Well, then, why not put yourself in the shoes of the controller of the ABC telly company," says William, plainly enjoying himself. "And tell us, do, Betty, what it is 'the people' want and need?"

The discreet squeeze he now gives your arm sends an unexpected sex thrill right down to your fingertips.

Without a scintilla of self-doubt, or irony, so it seems, she answers, "As for the common man, that'd probably be not a million miles away from what he used to get from the music hall: a proper belly laugh, alongside somethin' sentimental and somethin' suggestive."

You imagine the McNamaras, up there in their bedsitting room, happily reconciled to another Saturday night in with their wireless, as precisely the types Betty would like to defend from the self-improvement peddlers.

"Keep 'em quiet with a song, a joke and bit of *double entendre*, eh?" teases William.

"Darlin', I didn't invent the class divide. All I'm sayin' is it should be robust, not bled white and emasculated by the namby-pamby-ists."

Moving his arm to lie lightly, thrillingly, along the back of your waist, William continues to bait Betty, who continues to take him seriously.

"In which case, what may the middlebrow telly viewer expect to entertain him, Madam Controller?"

"I should say, above all, it must be *nice* and undemandin'. Parlour games played by poofs and actresses between jobs and more of folks just like himself: *pictures from life*, I think they call it. Perhaps a weekly dramatization along the lines of "The Grove Family" – so I believe the preferred listening-in of our own dear Queen Mum."

Yourself the daughter of a bank manager, raised a royalist in Welwyn Garden, the drink and the music having gone to your head, you make what will be your only contribution to the grown-ups' debate. Speaking into that sudden silence particular to the ending of a disc, you boldly announce in the voice of Gran Grove, "Oo, er, I'm faint from the lack of nourishment!"

At first quite pleased with your impression, till the host goes and presses upon you the platter of liver paté, "Marmite" and potted salmon and you must blushingly confess you only meant it as a joke; are not at all hungry.

Betty and Bill observe you with an incomprehension that reveals, as well as far posher than the royals, quite how socially and intellectually superior they are to you. Of course, these two would know nothing of "The Groves". William selects Bird's "Loverman", you take a rescuing swig of drink, and Betty rests her case, "Since that awful man Muggeridge's always tellin' us television's here to stay, my advice for anyone considerin' a career in it: forget the *beeb*, the future is commercial. I've said as much to Roberto, haven't I *tesoro*?"

Smiling enigmatically, he ventures no opinion.

It seems to you most unlikely that the suave and silent Italian aristo has given much thought to the matter, or, despite his girlfriend's daft *pronunciamento*, ever will. Only to realise that none of this guff is aimed at Roberto. In fact, if you were only paying proper attention when Betty introduced her new friend in the media as *useful*, you might have understood this social commentary for what it is: appropriately, a commercial. Having already plumbed the shallows of your ambition at the café, your ready knowledge of popular catchphrases must only have confirmed to Betty that you are indeed eminently qualified to turn out gift schemes and leg shows, low comedy and domestic drama for the box.

Snorting, you once again draw to yourself the bemused notice of the grown-ups.

During the wait for more guests to arrive and the party to properly kick off, conversation between those two old sparring partners, Betty and her Bill, carries on with sprightly attack and swagger, thrust and parry. Between subjects numerous and various they skirmish, in all of which Betty is guaranteed to posit at least three outrageous opinions concerning her personal vision for a rebuilt England. (You suppose she believes it only right that the educated elite – meaning people like her and brilliant Dr Bone – should decide how the society of the future might best be shaped.) The seconds, you and Roberto, meanwhile stand about on the sidelines, as it were holding the jackets of the duellists. His silence, however, is attractively impenetrable, whereas yours merely tongue-tied.

Feeling miserably out of place at your own party – wrong clothes, nothing witty to contribute – you long for some kith and kin in your own corner. All this would be made more bearable if only Sheila – who had a huge girl-crush on you – or Phil, or Wendy, or even twinset and pearls Daphne, were here. To realise with a stab of panic you're disastrously late for the Michaelmas term. Then, remembering, imagine them all 'up' there without you: drinking cocoa made with mostly water, eating cinnamon toast or Garibaldi biscuits in someone else's room and, to make matters cosier still, the white fen mists pressing against the window. Cocooned in just thinking for a living, their own futures on hold, you wonder: do any of them spare an envious thought for you, absent after the long vac as a consequence, appropriately, of the indulgencies and sins you got up to during the last Lent term? The one that got away, embarked already upon real life: wearing lipstick, hosting soignée parties at which race records are played and alcohol drunk. Perhaps best they aren't to know this girl who must've once looked like someone who knew a thing or two about the world has learned to regret the nunnery.

As for William's invitees, apart from those of his own university contemporaries who've taken up London careers, it'd seemed only politic to ask along new colleagues from the Museum. Which means, both sorts being for the most part young, unmarried men, the party will only get going with a swing once the pubs turn out and they feel themselves sufficiently emboldened by beer to risk 'women'. Having, indeed, delayed their entrances, the young men might, nevertheless, have been disappointed by the woeful dearth of young females provided, had not their host brilliantly anticipated that even the earnest, intellectual and sexually naïve – as well as the drunken hearties – will have fun at a party if there's only enough free alcohol supplied. Under its influence, when they do put in an appearance, the assorted chaps soon enough knot themselves into little groups of competitive hilarity and, lacking witty repartee of their own, in the patent tones of Bluebottle, Bloodnok and Eccles, woo from afar those few stray girls William has been able to rustle up. No longer able for decorum's sake to ally yourself with the intended targets of the rival "Goon Show" impressionists, you think it sad that, and in not quite a year, you have gone from being a girl who just *might*, to off-limits. Chatting you up really isn't worth the catchphrases.

Because your husband too largely ignores you, Betty might be bonkers but, evidently, she's stimulating company, glumly, you reconcile yourself to drinking more than is wise – and door duty.

# Chapter Twenty-three

Always happy to be the bearer of bad news, on the night of the party Mr Casey informed me all the windows needed urgent attention. It might be possible to keep the original panes but even if we made good rather than replaced (subject to the conservation officer's approval of materials and suppliers, obvs), this would truly blow the latest revised budget clean out of the water.

As someone who once spent far too much (£200) on a pair of Marc Jacobs silk knickers, that were dry clean only, maybe because I myself hadn't earned the money I was squandering, for the first time in my adult life I knew the guilt of losing control over my spending.

Full of angst over this latest costly budgetary revision, it might have been wiser not to raise the windows with Bill just as we were about to set off for Deb's. I knew how stressed he was at work and that he most probably couldn't conceive a way he'd like less to unwind on a Saturday evening than at the neighbours. (Having his eyes poked out with a knitting needle perhaps?) But having triggered his entirely predictable response about my failure to get a grip on the project, stupidly I didn't hold back from being pissed off right back at him. Even if for me the shiny new house had lost its lustre, was actually a fabulous rust bucket, his suggesting the thing was tarnished made me scream that since it was him who said historic places came with extra responsibilities, shouldn't he give me some fucking credit for shouldering the lot!

Stony-faced, we made it the twenty or so yards to the house next door on the wings of this argument, bang on the appointed hour of seven.

Even without the builders' rubble, acro jacks and sacks, Deb and Greg's own weirdly mirror image front best was more bomb site than cosy refuge.

I handed over our wine bottle, as price of entry, to Greg. No sign of Debby, presumably off lugubriously slitting her wrists in the kitchen. On perusing the label and discovering we'd accidentally brought something he might consider decent he got busy with the corkscrew between weekend-trousered knees. Ignoring the shouty command of the word ornament balanced on the bookcase to: RELAX, I turned my attention upon the larking kids, who were leaping off the furniture, scoffing from the bowls of Hula Hoops and Kettle Chips. Thank goodness, we'd been spared the baby.

Desperate to put Greg off the scent of anything untoward between Bill and me: Kitty, Teddy! I over-brightly exclaimed.

As if he'd only just clocked them, Greg acknowledging his rioting progeny: kept 'em up, he strained: fuck knows why! Cork popped, raising his voice over the din and using all the right emphases, he barked: time for bed the pair of you. And *no* more messing – do you *hear* me!

Not in the least cowed, mini-madam raised her swift objections to this plan: snot fair, snot even my proper bedtime yet – and anyway I'm two years older than *him*.

She whacked her little brother between the shoulder blades, making his jaws snap.

Shoving her right back, he countered: anyway, poo face, mum said I could stay up specially to see my auntie Abi.

*Says you*, came back the young satirist.

Brought by this barb to the brink of tears, Teddy's best response was: she *did*!

Although undoubtedly nice to be appreciated, I thought I now got the reasoning behind the kids still being up and about when we'd been prompted to arrive.

Whenever I came over here of an afternoon, their mother, (underestimated at my peril, I'd learned), was sure to include me in some capacity in the kiddy-wrangling: supervising bath time; posting banana puree into the little 'un's gummy mouth; perjuring myself filling in reading and homework logs. Under the cover of giving me, as one of the childless, the priceless opportunity to hang with her *dd* and *ds* I rather suspected was lazy Debby's strategy for training me up to motherhood on the sly. Who knew, I might get so carried away with the joys of practical parenting I'd wrest the job from her all-too-willing hands?

The kids' tit-for-tat pushing having evolved into a full-on scrap, their father demonstrating he'd himself acquired, somehow, the parenting skills to defuse conflict by way of diversion, barked: Kitty, Teddy, how about you *both* let your auntie take you upstairs? You can show her your Sylvanian Families.

If I didn't enjoy having my strings pulled, especially not by remote control, I understood that Greg was after all only playing by house rules: pass the parenting buck. Keen anyway to maintain a little distance between myself and my grumpy husband, at least until the alcohol kicked in, I sportingly agreed that: yes, Kitty, Teddy, I'd love you to show me your...

The seven-year-old looked witheringly upon me, saying: Sylvanian Families stink like pink, it's all about Mattel's Pixel Chix Roomies' House. You can watch them race for the penthouse suite.

Perhaps taking pity, Teddy said: I'll show you my Barker Labrador Family if you like.

I didn't know you had a dog, dogs, Teddy?

The lad momentarily baffled, Kitty took the opportunity to give her brother another shove.

No longer paying attention to his progeny, Greg slugged wine into the men's deserving glasses, and collapsed next to Bill on the sofa with the satisfied eructation of a chap who's discharged his parental responsibilities for the evening. My own husband too, with a large bumper of wine in prospect – as well as a bit of uncomplicated male solidarity, even if from an insufferable prat – prepared to relax after his hard week.

Dismissed, I trailed obediently off on the heels of an excited Teddy, Kitty bringing up the rear.

We wended our way up to where the high-tide mark of family life had washed so as to ring the walls with a scum of discarded shoes, clothes and toys. Encountering for the first time the older kids' cold little top floor bedrooms, it came as a nasty surprise to realise that this house, the very replica of our own, didn't comfortably accommodate two human adults and three small children.

The housing equivalent of fur coat and no knickers, beyond the rather magnificent, show-off reception rooms, these Georgian places were really rather inconveniently arranged. Maybe this was because, like microcosms of the social divide, the upper and lower classes had lived cheek by jowl in them – with no effort expended in making congenial the basement rooms where the servants laboured and lodged or these upper bedrooms, occupied by lesser family members. As Debby pointed out, these old places weren't really designed for living in.

Kitty plugged herself into her computer and docilely I followed Teddy into his own little bedroom where, shovelling clear a space for myself on the sticky carpet, I squatted to examine plush-fur and plastic homunculi, which was what Sylvanian Families turned out to be. After I judged I'd put in sufficient time doing voices for toys I suggested the kids might like to start getting themselves ready for bed. Kitty having blanked me – presumably she was hot on the chase for the penthouse suite – I tailed Teddy back down a couple of half flights to supervise teeth-brushing. On entering the family bathroom I had to step over the heavy wet nappy left plonked in the middle of the floor – baleful evidence of his mercifully absent little brother.

Seating myself on the edge of the bath, rather than look at Teddy pee on the loo seat, I examined the child art stuck to the walls. Here was the universal kids' four-square house, with windows for eyes, door mouth and a plume of smoke, jaunty as a feather, stuck in the triangular hat/roof. A jolly boat jiggling on a sea of blue curls had *I love you Mumy* scrawled underneath. Nicely mounted and preserved behind clip-on Perspex, they were all scrupulously attributed and dated. And every one predated the birth of little whatsit, her last. With the older two off at school, I presumed he'd been Debby's high-risk gambit for guaranteeing another four-to-five years stretch of undisputed home time – at a pinch taking her right through to: *three kids under twelve*. (After which she could claim that teenagers actually needed you more.) The evidence of these pictures suggested to me also that her littlest stratagem had tipped the balance from coping, to really not. That this baby's birth marked the moment Debby gave her final twitch of competitive mummying, stopped displaying their artistic efforts and simply allowed the chaos to close over her head.

Safe in the belief a child still in Reception wouldn't shop me I now turned my attention to the bathroom cabinet, and was squinting at the label on a bottle of pills that looked very much like Valium…and, bugger me! was this Viagra…? when Teddy wandered off without pulling the chain.

Haven't you forgotten something, young man? I called after him in my special auntie's voice.

Teddy instantly belligerent, even a little offended at this from a rank amateur, turned his silent glare on me.

Somewhat lamely, I suggested: flushing? After you've….

Unfamiliar with the accepted euphemism current amongst Islington infants, I deliberated between *pissed, micturated* or *weed*, then just pulled the chain for him.

Back under the eaves Kitty was no longer seated in fierce concentration before the computer.

Where d'you suppose your sister could've got to? I remarked to Teddy. In loud and carrying voice, he answered me: probably off having sex with her boyfriend.

Where on earth had a child picked up something like that? Perhaps I shouldn't have trusted my indiscretion with the bathroom cabinet was safe with him.

Teddy now firmly announced: I'll look for her.

I grabbed his arm: no, I'll…

Shaking me off, using the same voice of masculine command he must have picked up from his dad, he said: *I* know where she is.

Ok then, I'll just…go downstairs, I said, defeated by the logic of a five-year-old.

I made good my escape before the even more terrifying Kitty was located and, horrors, the two of them demanded book reading or song singing before bedtime.

Really too high a price to pay for my afternoon skulking rights.

Back in the sitting room Greg and Bill looked to be getting on surprisingly well – the level in the wine bottle had gone down by a good four-fifths. Lifting his head as I entered Greg pleasantly enquired: wee, teeth and bed – all tick, tick, tickety boo?

Hating him more and more, I was right back at him with the quipping: snug as bugs!

He smiled out of dead eyes and I smiled back. Since he didn't offer me a drink from the bottle I'd brought, I poured my own, emptying it to the dregs.

I was aware that Greg was the kind of man who automatically sent out feelers to every female under forty-five who crossed his path: the law of averages guaranteeing some level of success – however vanishingly small in his case – must derive from a hundred per cent hit rate. Despite early promising indications that I aimed to please, having fairly quickly been disabused of this, as far as I was concerned Greg now wisely economised on charm.

Even if happy enough to no longer be considered worth flirting with, not loving being dismissed as a handy substitute mum to his brats, I lightly inquired: Debby still slaving over a hot oven, I presume?

And somehow recommended myself as secondary wife.

Sure, she'd welcome a hand, Gail.

Having passed on him, get me to a kitchen. Fuck 'em, I might as well go and have a drink and a moan with my pal, Deb.

Entering the humid bowels of her house I surprised the cook poised over a plastic tray of mini quiches, wire sieve in one hand, packet of icing sugar in the other.

Looking up, she said distractedly: they need a bit of spiffying up.

And you thought: icing sugar?

In the age-old gesture of the harassed woman she wiped a hand across her brow, leaving a silvery trail of sugar through a strand of front hair.

Honestly, Abi, cooking doesn't *get* any tougher than this!

I laughed, flicking at her Mallen streak with a damp dish cloth: if you feel the need, Debby, sprinkle on a bit of grated parmesan, then brown the lot under the grill for a couple of minutes. But first off, if you want them to look more basic, rough them up a bit – like Sarah Jessica Parker in that film of hers.

You mean Allison Pearson in her book? said Debby, in publishing.

I smiled: trust me, if you want to leave them wondering how it is *you* do it, you don't want your pastry too perfect. Classic giveaway.

Failing to find Parmesan amongst the brightly coloured packets and bottles and tubs that fell on her feet when she opened the door of her rammed fridge, Debby asked: remind me again, Abi, why I'm putting myself through this?

As I couldn't stop myself from thinking: *dp* spelled trouble.

# Chapter Twenty-four

The last of the guests to arrive – you have the impression his timing is deliberate – is one Reginald Penfold, a Museum colleague. Bluebottle in the flesh. So very like that famous Goon character indeed you actually wonder whether underneath his huge, brown demob mac he's wearing a Boy Scout uniform. He isn't, as transpires when he and you tangle on the threshold to remove it. The mac safely deposited on the marital bed, as though it were a bottle of something, the lad wordlessly presses upon his hostess a battered game of "Monopoly". Receiving it, you can't stop yourself from asking, "Best enjoyed chilled or at room temperature?"

A small cruelty, it assuages your own feeling of being out of place at your own party.

"Room temperature, I suppose," mutters he, with a duck of the head. And with that involuntary gesture you seem to witness the memory of the school bully's fist, and feel ashamed. Evidently suspecting this was the wrong answer to a trick question, Reggie meanwhile blinks rapidly behind his bins. Must this pretty young lady really be the rotten swine who *deaded* him? Properly repentant for having recalled his rotten school days for him you end up being kinder and more attentive to the growing lad than is perhaps strictly necessary, or advisable.

Encouraged to come out of himself by the attention of his hostess, it soon becomes apparent that Reggie really does regard "Monopoly" as quite as much of the social lubricant as the bottle might have been. Keen on facts, particularly military ones, he's soon confiding how, back in '41, the secret service approached the manufacturers of the game with a request to create a special edition that was to be distributed by fake charity groups to prisoners of war held by the Hun. To be hidden inside the box: maps, compasses, real money and other objects useful for escaping. You gather from this dissertation Reggie means subtly to intimate that an interest in spies and invisible ink is founded on his own recent experience of working in the 'service' of Her Majesty. All strictly hush hush, you understood.

Roberto, now sans date, who's loudly telling your husband to submit something to her magazine – for no cash, naturally – apparently twigs from your expression of frozen panic that you might need rescuing from the clutches of the secret service boy scout. Suddenly at your elbow, he suggests in his confiding way you show him over the 'ouse. Grateful to him for springing you, if painfully aware that this won't take very long, you whisk Betty's trophy off on the thrupenny tour.

Having looked briefly around the bedroom and opened the door on the bathroom, there's nowhere left to go but down to the horrid kitchen. Just as you suspected he might, (after all, you are a female voluntarily alone with him, a Latin, in a suggestively darkened room and, as no doubt Betty has already told him, you have something of a reputation to live down to), Roberto quickly puts the move on. Hardly missing a beat after you half-heartedly slap him on his denuded blue cheek, Roberto follows up this undignified grapple by unhurriedly withdrawing from the pocket of his well-cut blazer a lustrously expensive cigarette case. In a disconcertingly post-coital gesture he offers it to you and, his smokes likewise rejected, returned to perfect equanimity after the dreadful knockback of being given the bum's rush by a teenager done up as dowdy forty-five, segues so smoothly into amiable chat that you're the one left feeling wrong-footed.

Sparking up, he asks, "So, 'ow do you know Elisabetta?" Seeing no point in beating about the bush, you answer,

"She used to be engaged to my husband, you know, *fidanzata*."

Roberto takes a deeply speculative draw on his little cigar, forcing you to prattle foolishly, "I mean, I'm perfectly fine about it! It was never very serious – they got together when they were doing a skit, I mean to say a comic play, at university."

Still dedicated to his cigar, Roberto raises a sceptical eyebrow to hear this. Things are not arranged thus in Italy. Instead of trying to promote her love rival into some form of gainful, halfway decent job, courtesy of her new boyfriend, Roman Betty would have straight out poisoned your tea. Or *vino bianco*. No messing. Or perhaps he's considering how best to satisfy his own compromised honour.

"Funnily enough, it was all about Nero's home life," you babble some more, "So I believe, Betty played his wife. She handed him his violin while Rome burned...." then, seeing Roberto is no longer listening, attentively enquire: "But what about you? How did you two meet?"

"At a cocktail party," is all he can vouchsafe on the matter.

Along with you, having apparently lost interest in his date's former love life, Roberto takes up the candle you carried down here, the better to light his circuit of the subterranean offices. And as if he's never before seen the like, which he might well not, proceeds to examine the copper in its annex and the dreadful cast-iron range, abode of black beetles and ancient grease. You're bourgeois enough to hope he won't notice the mousetraps.

Roberto sniffs and asks, "Why is always this 'orrible smell in English 'ouses?"

"Well, at least in this one, we have no electrical supply, so town gas, coals and paraffin are what we have for light and heat. Or perhaps it's the damp that brings out the smell?"

What does he expect? It might be malodorous, not to mention deathly dark and freezing cold down here away from the fug of the party room, but this is Britain dammit – we cheerfully endure!

Like a hound scenting the air, fastidious Roberto lends his fine Roman nose to the matter: "But is not only the 'orrible smell – this place 'as, what you call it: a bit of an *hatmosphere*, no?"

Ducking the refuge of his manly embrace – nice try, matey, but still no cigar! – you squeak: "Don't know about an atmosphere, but it *has* got terrifically good proportions."

Giving up on the girl with the interesting reputation, as well as his smoke, Roberto flicks his dog-end into the stone butler's sink to sizzle unseen and toddles off back upstairs to find the more fascinating Betty.

Somewhat surprisingly before the evening's out Reggie Penfold's "Monopoly" prop does see service. Nicely oiled now, the deep drinkers and the deep-thinkers end their evening sitting amicably enough together over it on the floor, to play.

Betty's ringing response to Roberto's smooth bemusement upon witnessing the juvenile fun, is to say that: being riddled through with an unresolved love affair with the nursery, a party inevitably put people like us in mind of 'games'.

Since nothing more of them is thereafter seen or heard, you presume she and her count have taken themselves off home in disgust, appropriately enough neglecting to observe the polite child's: *thank you*. But in going to fetch the oil lamp from the bedroom you surprise them lying amorously entangled on the bed. Startled by her hostess bursting through the door, Betty arises from the nest coats, an intense pink flush in the middle of either cheek. With her snog-smeared lipstick and the feathers of the hat in disarray, thinking she looks as if she's just come from her latest triumph in the circus ring, you exit, sniggering.

# Chapter Twenty-five

Debby might have got away with her sleight of hand on the cooking front – discreetly bashed and bubbling straight from the grill, her quiches could've passed as homemade – if only she'd been as canny with the prepping of the guests. The male half of the *other couple* was a drip and the female not only 'hardworking local councillor' but, as was to quickly transpire, queen of the pass-agg slap down.

Already having complimented Deb on her 'fun' little quiches, Kate said through a mouthful of the stuff: till it bolted, we had kilos of rocket off the veggie patch this year, didn't we Ed?

Her consort obliged from the other side of the table: peppery!

This is from Lidl, said Debby, deadpan.

Good for you, Deb! It's a bit of an indulgence of mine, I know, but after a hard day at the office digging's such a stress buster and, of course, getting the kids involved means they've always loved their veggies.

Wearing her dozy knowing smile, Deb said: that's where I've been going wrong all these years; standing over them while they choke down some broccoli, saying, 'just a little bit or no computer.'

Shooting back a sympathetic look, humourless Kate responded: I'm actually full of admiration for anyone who chooses these days to be a caregiver fulltime – I just don't have the patience.

She managed to suggest that what she didn't have the patience for was sitting around at home all day picking her nose and scratching her arse.

I stole a glance at my friend, who, hands in lap, was back to doing her vacant Madonna.

We then talked a lot – or Kate the councillor did – about the imminent closure of the library, until the entry of the Lemon Chicken, not so much done, as done for, provided her next opportunity for a bit of micro aggression aimed at the hostess.

Because she was someone who always spoke with her mouth full, still on her first taste, Kate inquired: sorry, any salt, and pepper?

Rather than passing them I'd have thrown the bloody condiments at her head.

Failing to get a rise out of Deb, Kate turned her sights on me, asking: so, Abi, Bill, London must seem a bit standoffish after the north, unfriendly?

Getting in quick, Greg chortled: first few years down here I thought the only way you got inside a Londoner's home was if you were related or sex was on the cards.

For our benefit, really Bill's, Kate explained: you'll find we're actually all of us immigrants round here!

Rising to the challenge, I said: even if the first sight of the Tinsley Cooling towers – that was, till they went and blew them up – always gave me the kind of warm glow you only get when you're coming home, and I prefer a pint with a proper head on it, I'm actually a native Londoner, born and bred.

Her smile broadening even as her calculating eyes narrowed, Kate said sweetly: my mistake, where are you from, originally, in London?

Since neither Deb nor Bill looked like they were going to take her on, I checked my privilege: yes, present and correct, and patronised back for the lot of us.

Holland Park.

Although I'd intended this shorthand to reposition myself on Kate's mental map, it was Debby, surprisingly, who got in first, saying: I'm a West Londoner too.

I smiled at her: meaning we *are* as good as related.

And I played the sex card.

Ignoring her husband, my friend went on: in which case, I'm the poor relation; might've been in the Royal Borough of Kensington and Chelsea, but where I grew up was still just a grotty flat over a shop on the Golborne Road.

Intending to show solidarity with Deb, dammit, I succeeded in coming across as both evasive and apologetic.

Ok, ours *was* in a garden square but it was actually pretty run-down when my parents inherited in the '60s. I mean a stockbroker did live next door – complete with a furled umbrella and a bowler hat – but for most of my childhood a postman and his family rented the upstairs flat we let out. Actually my parents, most of our neighbours too, probably, would've identified as 'bohemian' back then. You know the sort of thing: cash poor, book rich; inherited their furniture, voted Labour.

Postmen and bohemians – not quite the demographic of those fabled Holland Park squares these days! said Ed.

Guess not. Most of the nonconformists, like my folks, were long ago priced out by the capitalists.

Summing up for us, Kate pronounced: gentrification.

Yeah, said Ed.

Not at all sorry to disabuse them: I'm afraid my eviction from the garden was mostly down to bad luck and dodgier decisions. After Nicholas, my brother, died in an accident, my parents split up, then my dad died and my mum went a bit barmy. Sold up and somehow managed to dispose of the considerable proceeds fixing the world. I mean she squandered the lot on various lost causes and pet projects of hers in Latin America.

I reckoned a dead brother, matrimonial breakup, followed by parental death, maternal crack-up and bankruptcy – even if I held back that the accidental death was by heroin overdose and the other a suicide – should have been enough dysfunction to successfully shift us right off topic.

But to be sure of wrapping the thing up, I risked an axiom: like the great John Lydon tells us: never trust a hippie!

Funny that, usually it's the artists get the blame, said Ed.

His mild disapproval semaphored by the wagging of his chin, he now recited that dirgey old ballad of urban evolution: after the rats move on, the artists move in, then come the hipsters, who attract the estate agents and developers...

Cutting him short: you're an artist yourself, Ed?

A maker. To be honest, though, Abi, since I was priced out of my loft the work's been put on hold.

Clearly meaning to affirm, somehow, that Ed and she were more casualties than culprits in the process of deracination, Kate confided to the table: gentrification's a crime against the community we're really struggling with round here.

Cat amongst these gently grieving turtledoves, my husband said: Yeah? There's places I know would have your hand off for an independent cafe that employs the local youth and bakes its own cakes.

Quick off the mark, Greg got in: just so long as it isn't trying to flog me bowls of overpriced Shreddies!

Ok, but even that's got to be better than rows of shuttered shops, Cash Converters and a fortified offie, hasn't it?

This provocation coming from the mouth of a true son of the north, the rest of them probably credited with knowing a thing or two about shiteholes, Bill was let off more lightly than me: posh as fuck of Holland Park.

All matey warmth, Ed said: surely Bill! But it's really not just about some bougie cake shops, or me losing my workspace to a tattoo-sleeved prat in a beard and rolled up trousers, what you have to object to is the class cleansing, right? The atomisation. For the ordinary folk to stay put and, like you say, benefit from local jobs and amenities, we need social and affordable housing. I mean...

It's a crying shame how the real people who've lived and worked here generations are forced out by incomers, interrupted Kate.

This was her hobbyhorse and she meant to ride it.

I held myself back from pointing out as advance incomers – them with the pretty pink house round the corner with the mimosa tree out front – they'd done rather better out of insanely rising London house prices these last twenty years than those of us who unwisely limited our buying and selling of property to north of the M25.

Heels down, knees gripped, Kate said: I can tell you, Abi, Bill, it's an ongoing battle for us on the council trying to preserve the traditional character of 'old Islington'. Keeping it authentic!

Authentic? I spluttered.

(Must have been those notional quotation marks with which Ed respectfully cupped his *ordinary folk* and she her *real* people. Weren't we all 'real', even the middle classes?)

It's not like the latest wave of the white and wealthy are any less *authentic*. I've been researching everyone who lived in our house…

Any mass murderers…?

I persisted through Greg's buttonholing hilarity: the original 'original residents' were the metropolitan professional elite, just like us in fact.

Kate really didn't like to hear this about herself.

Abi, you should know Islington is rated the fourteenth most deprived borough in London.

Alongside claiming immigrant status, I guessed this made her feel better about living in her pink house.

All I'm saying is, Kate, what comes around goes around – I mean gentrification's just what happens whenever a previously 'nice' area down on its luck gets the reputation for being a 'vibrant community'. So cafes open, crack dens close, people notice the housing stock is actually rather desirable, move in and start converting the multi-occupancy places back into family homes. Bob's your uncle: property prices go up.

You're a social historian, right? asked Ed.

Greg was happy to disabuse him: on a career break from…what was it, Gale?

Taking the opportunity to grab back the conversational reins, quite hot now, Kate was back at me: what about areas that were never desirable places to live, Abi? What about Leytonstone, Walthamstow; Chingford for god's sake?

Greg said: I heard there's been the first sighting of a fixed-gear bike in Dagenham.

Chewing on a wasp, Kate continued undeterred: I'm just saying, before the *whole* of London simply becomes unaffordable, shouldn't we be putting in place a proper housing strategy?

I gave it my best shot: it's anecdotal, I know, but from looking into the microcosm of our house on this square, the makeup of a city isn't really down to social policy or planning so much as history happening. The big unavoidable, often unforeseeable, events – I dunno, like plagues or enormous population growth, industries expanding and declining, the world economy booming and busting, and wars, of course. Stuff we can have no control over but must react to as humans have always done: by relocating where we perceive it's safer or cheaper or a more pleasant place to live, or just where the work is. I'm not saying it's wrong or right, just that's what happens – over and over again – black or white, rich or poor, urban or suburban, one ghetto gets exchanged for another. Only variation is, nowadays people are as likely to move countries as postcodes.

Again I looked about me, before concluding: and, I don't doubt, in time the particular housing bubble we're all living in will itself burst.

More like a barrage balloon, said Greg.

Bill added cheerfully: so I guess, like Abi says, we should be making the most of the ironic breakfast cereal shops and the barbers offering hand-grooming down the high street before the ice caps melt and we have to gather our loved ones and run for the hills.

Amazingly, Kate swallowed down her wasp. I assumed, like Ed, she was giving my husband extra credit for not being quite as hideously white and middle-class as the rest of us. More real. Whatever. We then discussed climate change, terrorist attack, mass migration, over-population, pollution, reality TV. Because that was the job of people like us: talking about how things only got worse.

We rounded off the meal with fruit salad in a light syrup straight out of the 1970s. A taste evocation that in the innocence of its comforting retro vibe succeeded in shifting us off the topic of the ominous times we were living in.

We had the most wonderful fruit this summer in Umbria – lovely local figs and peaches, said Kate.

Ed reminisced on cue: from the *mercato*.

Mouth full, Kate added, sibilantly: delicious.

Rented this fantastic villa in the hills outside Siena, said Ed.

Greg now entertained us a while with his views on Europe and Europeans.

Not in favour.

We managed, nevertheless, to keep things pleasant up until Deb brought out the cheese board.

Turning her palm to it, Kate said: I don't do dairy.

Oh, sorry, I think there was probably cream in the quiches.

Definitely Parmesan, and isn't pastry meant to have butter in it? I said.

I find soya marge works well as a substitute, said Kate, nicely demonstrating she somehow found time in her busy schedule, fighting the cuts, defending the weak, to make her own vegan-friendly pastry from scratch.

High on her pyre, she smiled down the superior smile of the martyr upon the little, misguided people with their torches, and said: actually, you can never trust what they put in processed food.

Taking a less combative line than I might have, cleverly, slyly, our hostess at last got in her revenge. Putting out there the sure-fire topic of schools: *private or state?*

she switched off and sat back.

We were a good five minutes into the special pleading and posturing before our fellow guests must have twigged Bill and my lack of encyclopaedic knowledge of league tables or bitter sense of grievance meant no children. At which point the evening ran off the well-oiled tracks of dinner table conversation, derailed by the unspoken question: misfortune or – far, far worse – design?

Wearily, I geared myself up for my usual response to the inevitable query: *neither of us felt the need to bump up Bill's mother's already impressive grandchild tally. So, no, Kate, Ed, we only have sex for pleasure.* A formula I'd been honing these last ten years that worked every time to shut the questioner up. Or, if I was particularly narked: *children? Oh, we did,* – sad face – *the council just kept taking them away.* In the event we were spared having to account for our reproductive choices, amusingly, by the arrival of the kids, who claimed we were making too much noise. Practised crashers, Teddy and Kitty without further ado drew up chairs and tucked into the cheese.

Kitty, already quite the little food snob at seven, settling herself at the table, enquired: which cretin nosed the Brie?

I may have thought, didn't dare mention, Kitty, alone, nicely encapsulated why one should never have children, though Teddy ran her a close second.

Judging by their weary resignation, I was guessing Greg and Debby's every attempt at a kid-free evening ended up sabotaged something like this.

It was by now one thirty in the morning and I was desperate for my own wee, teeth and bed.

# Chapter Twenty-six

*It's already well after two ack emma*, as punctilious master Reginald Penfold no doubt would phrase it, by the time William and you have waved goodbye to the last of the guests and you get your husband into bed. Side by side, on your backs, both Bones stark awake, it's only when the ceiling passes by a second time you know for sure you've drunk too much. You guess your husband can't sleep for some other reason – apart from that once, you've never known him to get legless or, or for that matter, lecherous.

Hard to imagine there once was a time – and recently – when finding yourself under the covers with a man after a 'do' would have been deliciously thrilling. Now that you have licence to be here – a *Marriage Licence* no less – lying alongside William feels as erotically uncharged as bunking with a girl.

Since you know he too is awake, you ask into the eyeless dark, "What did you think of Betty's new television friend?"

"Signor Eyetie?"

"He's a *conte* in point of fact."

William comes back quick-as-a-flash: "Thought as much the first moment I laid eyes on the fellow."

"Then you won't be a bit surprised to hear I discovered him having his wicked way with her on this very bed."

Inebriation and insecurity over the old girlfriend mean you can't resist prodding for signs of jealousy. After all, he spent most of the evening talking to her. Not that your husband seems in the least disconcerted, saying,

"So everything they say about Italians and animal magnetism turns out to be true, whereas I, plainly, belong to the stereotype of the British gent." William adopts a deliberately donnish tone:

"As her accepted *young man*, bitch wouldn't even submit to what, in my day, was described as 'deep kissing'."

You match his dusty intonation:

"Couldn't swear they were in full-on *flagrante delicto* on top of the coats, but there was definitely some form of frottage going on *below the waist*. You should have seen her bright pink cheeks – matched her hat, beautifully."

William laughs.

If he relishes jokes – particularly word play – being far too self-deprecatingly English, and well-brought-up, to guffaw at his own, and insufficiently unbuttoned to often laugh outright at another's witticisms, you reckon this means a point up to you, one down to Betty.

Laughter in the dark sounding, as it does: intimate, perhaps it will still be possible you think to salvage something from the mood candlelight and jazz ignited, however briefly, before Betty's arrival put the dampeners on. Risking your instinct, you snuggle into William's side. He shifts his arm so you can rest your head more comfortably on the soft spot just below the shoulder bone. Curtains closed against the wild night it is so black in here that, though you can't properly see him, you are close enough to smell the spicy aroma of his underarm hair released by the spreading warmth of two bodies under the bedclothes.

The rumble of his voice now passing through his chest direct into your jaw, William goes on easily to say, "I thought the hat was actual hair she dyed pink – you never know what these smart, sophisticated types will get up to next." Awkwardly reaching his free arm across his body to find his wife's head, he ruffles her hair: "Much prefer mouse."

"Thank you. I suppose."

Nevertheless, this is going better than expected: William and you are dissecting the other people at the party, aren't you? Which is something proper married people did. Even so, if you're going to do the other thing married couples got up to in bed, you know you are going to have to turn friendly banter and hair ruffling into amorousness. He might be indifferent to news of Betty's dalliance but, more to the point, having largely neglected you most of the evening, can William be spurred to sexual possessiveness by the idea that in other men's eyes the new young wife is still considered fanciable?

"Regarding Roberto the rake, I've something to confess," you say.

"Eh?"

"Swine invented a transparent excuse to lure me down to the basement, then tried it on with me in the dark."

"I say: two girls in one night – how very Latin Lothario!"

Even if you had not made it crystal clear that luring you down there, then putting on the aphrodisiac frighteners, quite literally, wasn't worth the candle, it's disappointing, nevertheless, that your husband does not consider Roberto a dangerous love rival. In fact he chuckles at the thought.

"For a great girl such as yourself, my darling, being something of the charm bracelet Adonis, I'm supposing a Roberto with romance on the brain was not too hard to fight off?"

A little hurt by that 'great', you have another shot at it: "Well, not too, I suppose, but I *did* get on like an absolute house on fire with that nice museum chum of yours."

Still with amusement in his voice: "You surely can't mean Pvt. Reginald Penfold, ex National Serviceman, IC bogs and drains?"

Knowing the man in question, William's delighted incredulity at this blatant calumny should really have come as no surprise.

"I did notice the lad *monopolised* you most of the evening."

Still a little chastened, you choose not to laugh at the quip, saying, "Rather harsh, William, considering he's supposed to be a friend of yours?"

"More of a colleague. Penfold's actually a pretty decent historian, particularly solid on his late-century gothic revival."

Perturbed to hear that he's sobered right down now, it seems your misguided stratagem for spurring your husband to reckless abandon has succeeded only in dispelling the mood of easy amiability you equally accidentally managed to foster.

Realising words have failed, heart thumping, you decide to just shut up and kiss him. But shifting your weight to make your move William takes as his opportunity to withdraw the arm you've been lying on. Giving it a vigorous rub, he says, "A good evening, wouldn't you say, dear? Despite all the sexual shenanigans sadly passing me by!"

And here you are: lying next to him in a bed, stark naked but for a pair of flannel jimjams, ready, willing and legal!

But just a dry peck and you turn your backs on each other for sleep. And with that gesture your husband of seven months seems to snuff out the last of the candles, lift the needle off the 78. For him and you, evidently, before it properly got going, the party's already over.

You are woken briefly later this same morning, though still very early, by the noise of someone vomiting. Lavishly. Lying listening, it's possible to tell she is trying to do so discreetly but the retching noises coming from the lav you share on the half landing are unmistakeable: the inevitable comedown from having herself drunk too much at her party for one.

It's now light enough, just, to make out the two cut glass tumblers on the mantelshelf that Betty and Roberto must have left there when they took to this bed. The noises off cease in time and, on the edge of sleep, it pops into your mind that the flamboyantly pink Elizabeth Seaton was the girl who burned while Romeo fiddled. Comforted by the knowledge that from now on you would be at least a little better fireproofed against Bill Bone's old flame you drift off.

# Chapter Twenty-seven

A very little time after we departed Debby's with air kisses all round and assurances we'd had a simply super time, back in our own freezing cold and filthy building site, I remarked to my husband: that was ghastly. I mean, as like, us coomin' from the friendly north.

'Ave tha niver befoah read a Boowker prize shortlist, lass? It were an *Islington* dinner party atta all: invite folk over for a barney, chuck in some food.

Yeah, tossers.

(This, though I'd spent much of the evening insisting how very alike we all were. Come to that, so had Kate. Although, I guessed, even if she championed them, she'd never number herself amongst the 'ordinary'.)

Arms wrapped around each other, giggling, we tottered up to our squat on the first floor. If nothing else, Deb's evening had the doubtful distinction of being so dire that it'd got Bill and me laughing together again – silly co-conspirators against the rest of 'em.

Apart from being gorgeous, what made me fancy my husband was that he made me laugh. And his accent. Maybe this was why, at a booze-up in that no-nonsense northern town, when he jokingly glowered 'lass, I mun 'ave thee', quite soon after, he had. (His dick in my mouth and I didn't even know his surname.) The next morning, a little proud, a little disapproving of myself, alongside the other new university experiences in my schoolgirl's lockable diary I entered 'one-night stand'. In all humility I thought he thought, and I agreed, he owed me nothing more. Who knows, if he hadn't made the schoolboy error of holding out that straw I was so quick to clutch, there might have been the end to it. But even if Dimphna still regularly smelt a rut in our relationship, because I had, in the twenty years since that night we'd never really been apart.

Our united front against the pseuds having made us gentle with each other, forgiving and supportive, I wanted to keep going this mood of confederacy and mutual consolation. Pushing open the door to our room, I said: I don't think I've come across anyone who could rant on quite so earnestly about bloody rocket.

Bill put on Kate's lazy, nasal delivery: I mean, once you've grown your own you never go back to shop-bought, do you?

Whatever happened to water that, you know, actually tastes of *water*?

He smiled: I dunno.

I flicked on the bedside light, and surveying our comfortless accommodation, Bill said, drolly: if I'd known it'd be like this when I accepted that promotion and huge pay rise.

I'm sorry.

Last time I slept in the same place I kept my food was back in the days you'd still 've given Madonna one.

I was there, remember, Bill?

He put his arm around me: I do.

Working together efficiently we opened out the futon into a bed, made it up, and began to strip off. No longer subject to the benefit of next-door's central heating, and the warming effect of a bottle and a half of red wine on the vascular system having dissipated, it was baltic. Already in bed, Bill hadn't removed his beanie. Pulling my 'sleeping jumper' over pyjamas, rolling on my pink cashmere socks, rashly, I decided that we could risk turning up the fan heater to its highest setting.

Since moving into this last functioning room we'd made do with a single working power point for every one of our electrical needs: not only light and heat but also my laptop, the printer, the kettle and the iron and the incessantly humming mini fridge. I could still smile to think that not only had we replicated the chaotic and cramped living conditions of the last occupant in her den – all the necessities of life kept conveniently close to hand – but also her bent for arson. With each of our electrical appliances fighting for its place along the same six gang extension lead I'd already found out the hard way that some permutations were just too much for our elderly and temperamental fuse box. By a process of trial and error it transpired the various computations of plugging and unplugging meant that if I wanted a cup of tea while ironing by artificial light I had to choose between catching up with Homes Under the Hammer on the laptop, and staying warm. No competition some might say but the diurnal rhythm of my day was becoming dangerously dependent upon the sad stay-at-home's constant boon and companion of daytime telly.

Having gratefully hit the bed into which, just like everywhere else, the grit of ages, like sand at a picnic, had somehow insinuated itself, I was to discover that the fan heater/table lamp combo, together with a laptop and two iPhones on charge, were a joule too far for that overworked socket. As by the dropping of a theatrical fire curtain at the end of the second act, we were plunged into noiseless dark.

His voice unnaturally loud in the enforced blackout: bloody 'ell! Bill said.

Fucking fuse box, I unnecessarily declared, willing him to volunteer to be the one to do something about it, because *doing something about it* meant leaving this uncomfortable, if by now comparatively warm, bed, locating the torch by touch alone, then going back down all those dancers to the basement to reset the blown fuse. Taking care en route to skirt building materials and debris and avoid any missing floorboards. Eyeless, sensing no stirrings of intent coming from his side of the mattress, I said: we could just leave it …

Yeah.

Evidently Bill was quite as un-keen to venture downstairs into the muddy hole

— though his disinclination was no doubt entirely rational.

Shut off from every source of light — even those nightlights of the modern age: the ever-watchful red 'standby' eyes of electrical devices — it was pitchy black in here. As authentically an eighteenth-century experience of the night as I could have wished, with nary a historically accurate beeswax taper to hand, never mind the frigging torch, to pierce the gloom. Myself unseen, I smiled dopily in the dark. Even if I could have laid my hands on them, I happened to know the only candles we had in the house were scented ones in glass tumblers titled *Rain Under Shadows* and *Feu de Joie*.

Likewise, the ambient sounds I'd been ignoring in here had on the instant reverted to pre-industrial. Now we'd stopped talking and the background whirr of the fan heater, the refrain of the fridge was silenced, nature commanded centre stage. The storm I'd barely registered was really blowing a gale out there — quite hard enough to part the flimsy curtains over my beautiful, rotten, sash windows. I seemed to remember something about how sound waves travel at night making noises louder. And as though in confirmation of this thought the wind currently blindsiding our house appeared to scale it up a couple of notches. Under its slap, like a ship driven hard under full sail in heavy seas, I felt the place yaw and pitch beneath me. More evidence, or so I hoped, of the remarkable flexibility of the soft, slow-drying lime mortar from which these Georgian places were largely constructed. Or, alternatively, of quite how drunk I was. As the curtains opened and closed over the inescapable sodium orange hue generated by the always awake modern world, I realised that it was not in fact the perfect sable of thickest pre-twentieth-century night in here, merely murky. Feeling queasy, I clung on to my side of the bed and watched the flitting spectres of the windows, concentrated on the noises of the storm tearing through the rigging, and told myself that it was just an illusion, or down to Physics, that objects and sounds are transformed by the dark. The bulky thing looming with menace in the corner of the room was only Bill's shrouded shirts and suits hanging on their rack; the murmur I could detect in the lulls in the storm nothing more sinister than the occasional car whooshing down a wet street.

The soporific influence of alcohol and a late dinner eventually smothering these stray night thoughts, I was drifting off to sleep when the ship shuddering particularly heavily under the onslaught startled me back to alertness. Evidently, it had wakened Bill too.

Did you hear that?

I listened hard, but it was impossible to distinguish anything apart from the creaking of the sheets under stress, the lash of the rain, the thud of each broadsiding billow.

Is it a baby crying? I whispered. My jaw was clenched so hard I could feel my pulse in my fillings.

Close beside me, now bolt upright, Bill's orange-lit face was angled acutely with listening.

Not sure, was all he said.

Galvanised by a jolt of adrenalin, flailing with blind hands around the floor on my side of the bed, trying to locate the torch, I repeated: shit, shit, shit

Literally powerless: unable, with the flick of a switch, to defend ourselves with the banal, corner to corner, wash of electric light against whoever or whatever it might be on the other side of the door, cravenly I positioned Bill's body as a shield between me and it.

He gave a tremendous start, and I was so keyed up I screamed.

In stygian tones, Bill said: that sound, my dear, is the creak of the rope they 'ung her by.

You bastard!

My unfortunate response to the relief of tension was to whack my husband.

Ow! What was that in aid of?

Putting in my head all that stuff about the *notorious people* who used to live here.

Never did. Did I?

Going on about murderers.

That was you, you numpty!

Bill actually guffawed.

You weren't really frit were you? he said, arm around my shoulders. Shrugging it off, how I now regretted sharing with him my feeling about 'the others'.

You shouldn't joke about things like that, Bill. Look, I know it's stupid but I really do feel something bad happened here.

Abi, in a house old as this one, I can absolutely, positively guarantee you shit's happened. You should know that, the amount of research you've done.

Despite his mild dig, still nervous I might be overheard, I whispered back: maybe somebody died.

Just as likely several people were born.

Nothing like looking at the bigger picture for taking the hysteria out of history, I knew, but shouldn't he, of all people, be sensitive to the fact I had personal experience when it came to the shit happening in your own home? I was glad though I hadn't let slip I thought it was a child that died.

Instead I said: well, it could've been a burglar.

My money's on a ghost – nothing left in here worth tekkin'.

I whacked him again. Not hard.

Gerrof!

Finding his winey lips in the gloom, I kissed him, said: how about it?

Socks on or off?

Both laughing, we pulled the duvet up over our heads and under the cover of that black night, to the accompaniment of the unbridled storm, had the same kind of mad-crazy irresponsible sex like we did when we fucked each other in a freezing cold and squalid bedroom after a party.

# Chapter Twenty-eight

"Tea?" William cheerily proposes. "Won't take long – water in the kettle's probably still quite hot from my shave."

"Oh, you needn't bother about me. I'll get up and make myself one in a minute."

His clean-on, Monday morning shirt, dingy as it is, seems to you to give off its own light in the semi-gloom of the bedroom.

"If you're quite sure?"

William pulls on the first of his socks with an effortful grunt.

Every one of his socks is too tight for him – his wife really should have known better than to put them on a shilling hot wash, along with the shirts. Not that this bothers someone amenable as William. Like so many people from privileged backgrounds he is inured to drafts, inedible food, uncomfortable beds and ill-fitting clothes. As observed from the outside it is hard, indeed, to slip a cigarette paper between the Spartan upbringing of the boy sent to Eton then Cambridge and the one who ended up in a reformatory school followed by clink. Both ate and slept at regular hours and did what they were told by the beaks, or had what was coming to them. And upon release, for both, things must have looked pretty cushy on civvy street. William himself remains grateful, delighted, taken aback, to discover the comforts and conveniences of life outside an all-male institution.

Finished working both cardboard socks onto his feet, he is now putting on his indestructible, ten-year-old, handmade, naturally, leather brogues. Feeling you too ought to show a leg, you stir under the covers.

"No need to get up yet, you lie back and rest."

Sometimes it is the very equability of this thoroughly decent, hardworking and solicitous husband of yours that feeds the devil in you:

"I don't need rest – when will everyone realise I'm fine. Strong as a horse!"

Shoelaces double knotted, "'Course you are," says William, jumping up from the bed, the near prospect of escape, no doubt, lending him extra vim, "just thought you might prefer to stay where you were, in the warm. I know I should, given half a chance!"

Cheerfully hefting his navy surplus duffle, heavy as a sack of coal, onto his shoulders he kisses you lightly on the forehead before he ventures once more into the working world, taking his usual care to close the front door quietly upon himself as he sets out there.

His ever-considerate leave to stay in bed chafes. Even if, this being Monday, when you should by rights be preparing to haul the dirty washing to the launderette, you would much prefer to just lie here all day reading and ignoring mealtimes in hat, gloves and cardigan – as you sometimes did on cold term time weekends, pretending to be ill with womanly muscular turbulence. Actually in this instance fed up to the back teeth with being feeble and female, you throw back the blankets and scramble into thin dressing gown and slippers and set off for the first expedition of the morning to the dreaded kitchen. Pausing only at the top of the steps to the semi-basement to listen out for signs of life. Apart from the common ground of the entrance hall, lavvy and bathroom you share with the tenants, and you use like a thief, the kitchen is the most likely place to encounter Mrs McNamara. And this being washday, she might even now be heating the copper for her own laundering. No expensive round trips to the slip-slopping machines at the "Go Gay Laundromat" on the Essex Road for her.

Since there's silence from below you take your chances. In the kitchen you discover your very thoughtful husband has already made up the unwieldy range, stuffing it with enough coke to keep it hot for hours yet. Should you fancy one, you might even draw a morning bath – if it weren't for all that pumping.

Unfortunate that for you, Celia, initiation into mid-twentieth-century middle-class housewifery fell into that unlucky interval left between the departure of the last maid of all work in her little white cap and the arrival of the labour-saving device. The coming innovations of the "Ascot" water heater, electric oven, automatic washing machine and mangle, fridge and vacuum cleaner and iron, toaster, and electric kettle.

If only you'd been born a little later, who's to know, living life 'electrically' might have kept even young housewife Bone content in a kitchen. In 1955, however, because this one is cold, cramped, fetid, dark, sordid, insalubrious, awful, abominable – Roberto is not wrong – you cannot wait to escape it.

Shivering, you tip tealeaves from the pot William made earlier straight into the waste bucket kept behind its modesty curtain under the sink. Where they splatter onto potato peelings, many half-eaten celery sticks and Roberto's sodden cigar butt. In the cardboard box for non-compostables is more trash from the housewarming party: two broken glass tumblers (leaving an even four) and the shards of a big party platter the hearties broke playing some form of ducks and drakes with it down the hall. (When you're wearing shoes, you must remember to bury them in the back garden, under the winter jasmine.) Having sniffed it to see if it's off, Saturday's milk is tipped into the little milk jug, the kettle now whistling, water poured over fresh leaves. Scraping some marg onto toast and shoving that onto a plate you hurry the breakfast tray back up to bed. Another half-hour under the covers and you'll definitely think about getting up. Relighting the bedside oil lamp, you pour out the first cup of the morning and open up your library book.

The sound of footsteps in the hall, followed soon after by the flinging open of the bedroom door, causes you slop tea all over your secret agent.

"I was just about to dress and get on with sorting the laundry," you say, shutting up the guilty book and from force of habit shoving its lurid tell-tale cover out of sight under the bedclothes.

Made rosy and bright of eye by the weather on the streets, William says, "Sorry to give you a fright, wasn't till I got to the bus stop that I remembered I promised your boyfriend, Penfold something."

William, a lumbering camel-coloured quadruped in his giant coat, goes down on hands and knees to search under the bed.

"'Emile Mâle, *L'Art religieux du XIIIe siècle en France*," he says, holding up a small, plain, leather-bound book. Another kiss lighted on his wife's forehead and he's off again, this time giving the front door a good slam on his way out.

Safe now to retrieve your own book, that has blood dripping from hearts on the cover, you snuggle back down with it.

The cold smokey aroma that hangs in the room, activated by moisture soaking into the fabric of William's hairy coat, tells you it's begun to drizzle out there. In Royale-les-Eaux, meanwhile, it's a sultry 3 a.m. and you're in the middle of a tricky game of roulette.

Taking a bite of toast you wonder what an avocado pear might taste like and why on earth you'd want to eat fruit dressed with French *vinaigrette*.

Somewhere else, distracting as an aimless fly trying to find its way out, the sound of footsteps and humming makes you lift your eyes from the page. Surprisingly noisy for such a slight woman, the lodger thumps past your bedroom door on her way down to the hall. Mrs McNamara's lack of inhibition you guess comes from having mistaken the good doctor's loud second exit for the signal she's been waiting on. Believing his missus has cleared out with her bags of washing, thinking herself now safe from notice, she's going about her weekday morning routine unrestrained by the usual creeping resentment. You even hear her settle baby with a song: "*When the valley's hushed and white with snow, 'tis here I'll be in sunshine or in shadow, oh Larry boy, oh Larry boy, I love you so...*"

Funny how just knowing their name makes a person real. The phantom becomes a baby boy.

Still singing, she opens the front door and, as she does every morning, humps the contraption over the threshold, down the four steps and out into the front garden. Except for fog or an east wind, whatever the weather baby must have his healthful airing. And if it's raining, as now, she'll just put up the hood and protect the blanket with the pram's shower-proof cover.

Plodding back up the stairs, she passes again within inches of your bedroom door, her thin voice accompanying her all the way back to their bedsitting room in the upstairs front.

Soon after you detect the squeak of bedsprings. Tucked up with a novel, the oil lamp casting its glow and the rain playing "Chop Sticks" to itself outside the curtained window, it makes you smile to know that little Mrs McNamara has just settled down for her own sly mid-morning kip.

All quiet from above, you return full attention to Mr Bond who is, coincidentally, even now sweeping his luxurious hotel bedroom for listening devices. Finding no bugs, he stows his .38 Colt under the pure Egyptian cotton pillow when something heavy falls above. Brought abruptly back to this dismal North London Monday midmorning, you push the breakfast tray off your legs to sit up and listen. There it is again. Cautious as a burglar, you slip out of bed to position yourself directly beneath the source of the noise. You distinctly hear the squeak of bedsprings, followed by another thump. The fourth landing brings plaster splattering down onto your upturned face. Wiping it away, you continue to look up as if it were possible to see through the ceiling the woman jumping repeatedly off her bed. Her final heavy sauté is accented by a sharp yelp of pain that's followed up by a mournful and prolonged keening. So near and so helpless is the cry, as if you were indeed in the same room together, you blurt out, "Are you all right?"

The instant cessation of any sound at all from above – though the air seems still to fizz with the sinister potentiality of radio silence – is perhaps intended to deny the presence of either lodger or landlady.

What exactly does she expect you to do, you think crossly: just to save her feelings keep up the pretence she is alone and unheard in the house until you let her off the hook by contriving a suitably sleuth-like exit and convincing later 're-entry'?

Having anyway already shown your hand, it seems the only way to end this childish standoff is boldly to follow up on your blurted-out enquiry.

Quite aggrieved at having been put in this ludicrous position, you call up to the ceiling, "Are you in need of help?"

Still no reply from overhead – the stupid woman has smashed your lovely solitude with her pitiful crying, only to clam up.

Feeling far from compassionate, actually wanting to punish her, you say in a clear and carrying voice, "I'll be up in a minute."

To maintain landlady-like rectitude you consider throwing on some clothes but decide instead to just belt your dressing gown a little tighter.

Even with loins metaphorically girt, however, you must still make a conscious effort to pass the notional point, just beyond the shared bathroom and lavvy on the first half landing, that marks the buffer zone separating sectors McNamara from Bone. Treading cautiously in slippers within the neutral territory of the second landing, you negotiate the checkpoint Charlie of the gas stove, retie the dressing gown belt and, before you can think better, knock twice.

"Come in."

You're met not by guns trained in your direction but the desperate gaze of a wild, wounded animal, cornered in its lair. Unsure what to do next (even as she radiates vulnerability, she looks as if she might bite), you hesitate, saying, "Sorry to intrude," adding, disingenuously, "I thought there might have been an accident."

Plain enough you both know this for a bluff.

The tenant stays as she is: quite still, curled up against the head of an immense brass bed that's pushed up against the far wall. Determined not to be intimidated, you manoeuvre around the clotheshorse draped with her baby's boil-washed nappies, a card table and two chairs piled with more folded laundry. Arriving at the bed your toe hits the dirty nappies' covered pail kept underneath. It rings dully.

Mrs McNamara drops her eyes. Her backing down like this gives you the nerve to challenge more directly:

"I was concerned you'd had another fall."

Having read your fair share of rubbishy novels concerning teenage parlour maids 'in trouble' when you should have been helping Mother around the house, rather than simply the result of too much to drink, you now know for sure, or believe you do, how the early-morning vomiting is connected to this spate of throwing herself off and down things. Still not meeting your eyes, the woman begins roughly to chafe her ankle, commenting, "Must've strained it."

Preparing to retreat, "You *do* seem accident prone," you say, appalled to hear Mother's bossy voice – as used to keep the butcher up to the mark.

Looking sullenly up from her ankle, perhaps riled to insolence by the patronising tone, she says, "Sorry I woke you, Mrs Bone." Flustered, you smooth down the front of your dressing gown:

"Whatever gave you that idea? I was reading."

A loftily peevish defence that came all too easily: when you lived at home the sole guarantee of being left to your own devices behind a closed bedroom door. Whether Shelley, or Clem Yore, *Hail to thee, blithe spirit*, or Barry the cowboy: *redheaded riding fool, snake-fast and hog-wild in the saddle who forgets his shy cowboy's ways when he finds Molly Murry and goes in for some prime love-making....* it had the added merit of usually being the truth.

Nevertheless, she's succeeded in making you furtive and fifteen again. And all down to high-handedness: barging in here in high dudgeon and a dressing gown.

Attempting to shrug off that familiar feeling of sulky disgrace, you gesture a swift, unconvincing, consultation of your wrist, and tell your watch, "Is that the time, I really should be getting on with the washing."

It is, of course, really none of your concern if the woman punished and poisoned herself.

But as you prepare to leave she reaches across to catch hold of one trailing end of the dressing gown cord, saying: "I'm sure I never meant you to 'ear none of it."

Closely tethered, not caring to loom, either figuratively or physically, there seems no alternative but for dignity's sake to sit next to her on the high hard bed. Mrs McNamara, apart from having no shoes on, for jumping off the furniture purposes, is herself properly clothed for the time of day. She has on a nasty, fuzzy, bolero-type pink cardigan that she's contrived to dress herself in back-to-front. Tucked in tight under the waistband of her lumpy skirt you guess it's her intention to pass it off as one of those cute little short-sleeved, high-necked jumpers, worn, like the film stars do, over a push-up pointy brassiere. To make it more closely fitted, she's roughly tapered the side seams with black running stitch. Observing this tawdry bit of vanity makes you feel a little less uncomfortable about appearing in your perfectly respectable night attire at gone ten on a Monday morning.

"You really hurt yourself this time?" you ask.

"Didn't 'urt myself enough, did I?"

You two women snatch a look at each other now, both naked.

"You don't really mean that, do you?"

The bold hard face with which she meets your own has been put on to cover panicky fright.

"I swear I don' know what else ter do."

As she speaks, she tugs fretfully at the dressing gown belt, so you think unconsciously to reel you in.

"Nuffing seems ter work for me." Given her candour and her obvious distress it would be ridiculous to pretend you don't know exactly what she means.

"Well, from the little I know, falling or jumping rarely does – it's just an old wives' tale. Stories in books."

"I can't face the ovver..." Mrs McNamara starts to say before you bossily interrupt: "Gin only makes you drunk..."

"Findin' someone ter do it."

"Oh, I see."

She's so determined to be tough, yet at the same time out of her depth, you can't help but feel sorry for the woman. Less sharply, you say, "Would it be so terrible to go ahead and have it? You're a mother already, aren't you, and married, so, where's the harm?" Then, remembering your suspicions on the night of the party: "You and your husband are happy enough together?"

Sullenly, reluctantly, "We're in love," she says.

You knew this already, didn't you? Had seen the tender way he treated his wife when she took her tumble down the stairs. Her cow eyes.

"Unless it would be dangerous for you, I really don't understand the problem."

She shoots you another assessing look and you think she would be quite justified in telling you to mind your own beeswax. Even lump you one.

Instead she confides in an urgent rush, "Mum was down on my Pat from the off – very first time I brung 'im 'ome she called 'im *a bloody bog-trotter*!" She gives an unhappy laugh at the slight. "Didn't turn up at the church; didn't talk to me fer a 'ole month arter 'im and me was wed."

Since none of this seems to explain her dilemma, "I'm sorry," is all you can think to say.

"It's wiv 'im being foreign, see." Again and again, she weaves the belt through the fingers of her left hand: "N' *she's* me mum!"

"But you're reconciled?"

"'Ard not to: she lives right round the corner. So there'll be no 'iding it from 'er soon as it begins to show." Involuntarily, she glances down at her belly. "She allus said I'd 'ave too many: ten or twelve, straight off, like they do. The Irish. An' you know what men are, dontcha?"

Understanding this remark to be rhetorical you make no comment as to whether in your experience new husbands pester one for sex.

Jerking compulsively at the dressing gown belt, she reels you in closer: "An' 'im wiv his accent, me in the family way wiv anovver kiddie not yet a year, we'll never find nowhere decent to live when you an'," she hesitates a second before naming him, "Doctor Bone want us out."

Ah, here was the nub of it: you blush to think she overheard that *breed like rabbits* remark of Betty's. Against all justice, simply because William can afford the down payment on this house, his wife might casually determine the fate: the future happiness, or misery no less, not only of this woman and her husband but blameless babies into the bargain. Even if it should mean another year of the pram in the hall, a multiplication of the nappies, of course you won't throw the McNamaras onto the street.

"Naturally, Doctor Bone and I won't ask you to leave," you tell her, trying to sound properly benevolent.

"Fanks fer that, Mrs," she says, without apparent relief, or gratitude.

A bit miffed, you continue in a brisk no-nonsense tone: "I dare say, there's enough space up here to accommodate another baby." Then thinking back over those 'dozens', add: "In future, it's true, you'd be advised to take better care to prevent..." only to run out of steam: besides being a man, you guess Irish Pat's a Catholic. And who were you to be giving contraceptive advice? Someone for whom, if you were honest, birth control up till now was mostly a case of keeping your fingers, if not your legs, crossed.

She anyway rushes to take up where you left off: "That's exactly what I was finking: there *are* ways ter prevent it, nowadays, aren't there? Nice, safe, clean ways.

Like what you and Doctor Bone done..."

"Well, Doctor Bone and I *didn't* actually – that was rather the problem," you begin to say, embarrassed she might be referring to the sensible provisioning of oneself from the chemist's prior to *connexions*.

Suddenly confiding, she says, "It's the ovver what scares me rotten. There was this girl I knew went ter one, you know *a woman*," she shudders, "near enough did fer 'er. So I'd be everso grateful if 'e could jus arrange to 'elp me out, jus this once, like 'e done for you, down the 'ospital."

Letting go the dressing gown chord, she reaches out awful supplicating angel's hands. "I don't understand," you start to say, because, genuinely, you don't, then, all of a sudden, you know exactly what she means. Untethered, you launch yourself up and away from her, saying, "Silly, silly woman, my husband had *nothing* to do with my, my…it was an accident. A genuine accident!"

"I jus' fought, wiv 'im being a doctor…"

Since you are making very little sense, because there really is no sense to be made of any of it, you laugh. Saying through this rictus of mirth, "You know what the fucking funniest thing is?" Perhaps as surprised you knew that word as use it she snatches a quick look at you. "If he *had* been a proper doctor instead of just another useless sodding historian we'd never have got ourselves into this fine mess in the first place."

That she believed your miscarriage was an abortion, procured by your own husband, makes sense now of her bizarre behaviour on the night of the party. The gin on her breath: lingering evidence of an earlier, half-cocked attempt to try and drink her way to a termination gave her the Dutch courage to throw herself down the shadowy well of the staircase. And rather than any very serious attempt to rid herself of an inconvenient pregnancy, lying there, sprawled like a *papier-mâché* puppet with its strings cut, was her bravura appeal for Dr Bone's sympathetic and discreet medical intervention.

No wonder the woman hated you. So that you might continue to do nothing more constructive with your day than lie on your bed of luxury and read, rather than let it impinge on your cushy existence you'd contrived to correct your own reproductive slip-up with a planned medical termination.

Dejected, she mumbles, "I jus' reckoned, before it showed too bad, before Pat caught on…"

"Your husband doesn't know?"

Watchful again, she says, "It'd kill 'im stark dead, if 'e did. 'E dotes on Larry. Laurence." Speaking his name, involuntarily, she smiles: "Mum wanted Winston, but Pat wasn't keen, so I chose Larry; for Laurence Olivier in that film, you know the one: 'e's the king what defeats the fuckin' French."

In repeating back that word you understand she's holding out an olive branch.

"I think it's wonderful to name your son for someone noble like that: like pledging your faith in little Larry's future."

You meet her eyes, and for the first time in all your months of living under the same roof she gives you back her genuine smile. Pretty blue eyes and lovely teeth.

"That's right, tho, innit?" she says, "it's *'is* future I'm thinking of. I love 'im, I *do* – but the fought of anovver one, an' just months apart, it's too 'ard."

She gestures toward the clothes-horsed nappies and, as if in unintentional mimicry of the laundering process, rubs and writhes her hands together.

Then, looking across to the window, breaking the connection, remarks, "Rain's set in good 'n' proper now, if I don't get a shift on and fetch up 'is majesty, likely I'll find the l'il mite floatin' about in 'is pram, drownded in a puddle!"

You dare to give her ankle a pat, from which she flinches. It's the one she hurt.

"You shouldn't be putting any weight on that foot: let me go and get Larry for you."

Even as you make it you hope she'll turn down the offer; a real live baby in your arms for you is too hard.

"You're alright. 'E'd likely create if someone 'e don't know frem Adam come fer 'im."

It's true. Even living in close proximity with young Laurence from practically the day he came into the world, you've always made it a bit of a thing avoiding him. If you did happen, unexpectedly, to come across the two of them would dodge into your own quarters, closing the door quick. Little wonder she thought the landlady standoffish. A child hater.

"If you're sure, Missus McNamara?"

"Quite sure Missus Bone."

Two uncertain young women, neither more than twenty, you accept and acknowledge each other in the adopted dignity of your titles.

All emotion spent, stepping into run-down shoes she tries her hurt ankle and as if in premonition the frightened, defiant girl gives way to a battered defeated crone.

"Whatever happens, you can stay on in the flat. I promise."

With a weary, fatalistic smile, she says, "You never guess, do you?"

Knowing you never will, you say nothing.

She hobbles off to retrieve her roaring baby from his pram parked out in the rain.

*Susan Barrett*

# Chapter Twenty-nine

Its gurning mouth up-tilted to the sky to glug rain, the cement mixer parked in our tiny front garden was the only evidence that Casey woz 'ere. And might return. If not for many hours yet – it was still very early.

Peering out into the gloomy street, nevertheless, I checked my watch. It'd been two minutes. I'd resolved on five, but was compelled to turn around from the window early to again outface the empty room at my back.

What, or who, did I expect to confront?

*

Despite my husband's best efforts, the next couple of days following Debby's dinner party I wasn't aware, particularly, of negative vibes in the house. And, hard as I listened, hadn't heard the crying baby. Only to go out back with my rough sketches for the garden design and be confronted by the plasterer's trowel, still plunged stake-like into the very middle of my mawkish little burial mound under the winter jasmine.

I got it – really, I did – that the baleful presentiment of ill will the child's shoe had seemed to embody actually fed upon my own unease over this impossible bloody house. Looked at rationally, my nightmares were only practical and economic. But, oh dear, it was enough to spook me all over again, recalling the sick lurch I'd experienced at the unexpected weightlessness of the small white box I committed to earth; the feeling you get in the pit of your stomach when you realise you really have lost your keys; your phone; your mind.

Thinking it might be calming to do something practical with my hands, I gathered the broken shards of the platter left scattered in supplication over the top of the barrow, and took the lot back up to our bedroom with the idea of gluing the thing back together again – it did look Georgian after all.

But as yet another sheet of live plaster came crashing down to meet joists floriferous with *sepula lacrymans*, and three radios tuned to three different stations battled it out, door firmly closed against the pandemonium, rather than mending the plate I found myself instead, shameful, sweaty and a tiny bit frenzied, Googling everything I could find concerning children's shoes concealed in the fabric of a building. To my relief Mr Casey had been quite correct; such little tokens regularly turned up in old houses. Nothing sinister, they were used for hundreds of years as good luck charms. Offered up to a household deity either to protect against evil or correct barrenness amongst the females of the home. To halt anything wicked getting in, they were most often placed at 'weak' points of entry: over a door lintel, near a window, inside a chimney, under the rafters. There was no mention of where they should be located to best bestow fertility. It was generally agreed, however, to repel bad or attract good luck to a house, children's shoes were the most efficacious.

Knowing this, I might have considered exhumation and re-interment had not I decided instead to investigate whose might have been the last little foot my shoe charm once shod. Since, presumably, it was placed under the kitchen floor while the house was under construction, and appeared to have been already used before its rededication to the household gods, it seemed logical that this was a child of the first resident. Whose name, of course, I already knew – as well as the fact there was no mention of either a wife or children in the relevant parish records or census. Bachelor Benbowe was not who I was after. Somewhat encouraged by my next discovery that it had apparently been quite common to hide shoes in a house whenever an alteration was made, I was tempted to explore down a tributary that also ended up going nowhere. So it transpired, even if I had managed to pinpoint a date for the burial based on the style of the shoe – and from this deducing likely candidates – babies' button shoes like this one hadn't changed that much in style or manufacture between the late eighteenth and mid-twentieth centuries. My baby might have belonged to any generation between Georgian and Boomer.

And there I might have left it, had not my subsequent searches turned up an article in The Guardian online that would revise my benign reading of babies' belongings, and worse, found under floors.

According to the couple in the feature (photo taken from below to make the facade behind their perturbed faces seem properly sinister) a notorious Victorian serial child killer once lived in their recently purchased north London home. From where she ran her cottage industry of taking in then disposing of unwanted kids. As the concerned couple were to discover, there'd been stories in the press at the time of her conviction for murder that her little victims likely ran into dozens. Speculation some might still lie buried in the gardens or under the floorboards of the many Islington addresses, including their own, between which she flitted during the decades she was active in the child-disposal business.

Because it's my nature to look too deeply, to carry on stripping back when I might have been better advised to stop before I did real harm, I spent the rest of the evening, and well into the night, researching the horrible history of this homespun trade. As it seemed to me, the rather inevitable outcome of the 1834 Poor Law Amendment Act that, by removing any financial obligation from the fathers of illegitimate children, condemned women to bear all the shame and stigma of a child born out of wedlock while removing what little financial support they might once have had in law. The numbers of unmaintained, unmaintainable, infants thus boosted by that popular bit of policy-making stimulating in its turn an unregulated and covert business opportunity. In those days before adoption was formalised, desperate women for whom it was impossible to support an illegitimate baby on a single working girl's wage might answer one of the many ads then placed in the personal columns of the newspapers. Something reassuring, along the lines of: *A kindly widow with a little family of her own, and a moderate allowance from her late husband's friends, would be glad to accept the charge of a young child. Age no object. No objection if sickly.* To the girl 'in trouble', driven mad with anxiety: the answer to her prayers. A closer reading of the terms these professional bad fortune-feeders offered, of only a few shillings a week, plus one set of new clothes for the infant, or a handy, one-off payment of some pounds, should have raised doubts. That weekly stipend, and even the reassuringly large-sounding lifetime fee, were equally inadequate sums for raising a child to maturity. You had to wonder, indeed, whether those who went ahead and applied to these motherly matrons trusted, even as they handed over their life savings, or persisted in scraping together the regular pittance they paid, they really had found a workable way of providing for their baby's continued wellbeing? This being a racket that rather inevitably favoured the greedy and unscrupulous, how many appreciated what was implicit behind the wording? Simple, brutal, economics dictated this financial model only worked if the contract of service agreed was kept short term. On the miserly amounts asked by the baby farmer, to turn a profit she must let, or encourage, the little lambs she took in fairly quickly to perish.

Likely as not, in quick succession that set of babies' clothes asked for ending up in the pawnshop and the bastard in the ground. Having the double advantage of freeing up another berth in the con woman's crib while, if she omitted to tell her, ensuring continued payment by the mum for the rearing of her dead baby.

In most cases plain neglect did the job of keeping down the census. I was to discover, indeed, in the perverse estimation of a professional *child minder* (*No objection if sickly*) it was not the bonny, fit and thriving baby she valued highest, as on the restricted diet of watered down sour milk, arrowroot and corn flour provided he might take many tedious weeks to succumb. And if the little nuisance was going to take his time about the business of dying, sedatives such as laudanum, chlorodyne or paregoric came expensive. Best business practice therefore favoured the puny, ailing infants of two months and younger, who most rapidly and efficiently earned their wings – hence the sobriquet of *angel makers* with which the unkind of their kind were labelled.

Around two in the morning – and still no sign of my husband – I came across a contemporary account of what the police found when they kicked down the door to one busy professional *dying room*. Flies laying their eggs in the weeping sores of the many little starving babies left to die on their befouled rags.

Scandalous as they were becoming, society itself seemed largely to have turned an indifferent eye to the nastier actualities of this expedient and expanding industry. By the end of the 1890s, when the small business lady round the corner was trading, the yearly output of dead babies from front rooms ran into hundreds. And should there be opposition from the attending doctor to oblige with the no-questions-asked issuing of yet another death certificate, the tiny corpse was bundled up and smuggled out to be left under a bridge, on an ash pile for the sweepers to find, in a gutter or on a doorstep. Or, perhaps, just consigned to the convenient space between the pammets.

Most horrifying of all, when her renewable resources didn't just obligingly succumb to the effects of malnutrition, or galloping diarrhoea, or thrush, or impetigo, some angel makers gave Mother Nature a helping shove. The particular evil bitch whose case history it was that set me off down this nasty byway in the problematic matter of pesky female fertility through the ages herself economised on effort and outgoings by killing outright at least a couple of the babies she took off those ruined girls' hands.

According to the newspaper article, after drowning them in the kitchen sink, she disposed of her 'foster' kids' bodies by wrapping them up as newspaper parcels tied tight with dressmaking tape, conveying them down to the Thames in a Gladstone bag, and flinging them in.

Inconveniently for her, two of these unfortunates washed up and were thereafter retrieved. It was by the tapes she bound them with, cut from a roll discovered in her house, that they eventually hanged her. As it were.

*

Coming up for air again after my plunge back into these cold dark waters I ended up trawling through most of the night, I became aware that in the time I'd been watching out for Bill's homecoming in my dressing gown, the coal black sky had taken on the grey of wet ashes.

I looked at my watch. It was a full ten minutes since I last surveyed the empty room behind me.

Still no ugly old woman in her elastic-sided boots, Gladstone bag in hand. Deposited all across my wide oak floorboards, no infants, crying and dying in their own crap.

*

Before I saw it, I heard the throaty diesel rumble of a black cab approaching through the rain. Bill at long last.

The cab parked up but kept its engine idling. Believing myself to be fully justified, and not at all out of my mind after my sleepless night, my husband wasn't even through the front door when I launched my attack: fuck it, Bill!

Having just worked twenty hours out of the last twenty-four, he was on the edge of nervous exhaustion.

Hello to you too, pet, he said, closing the front door on the waiting cab.

You don't have the faintest idea, do you, what it's like for me, spending the night awake, listening out?

I warned you it was going to be a late one.

134

Weary as he sounded, I was taking no prisoners: you said 'late', not 'out all fucking night'!

It's what I signed up to – you knew that. You know that, he said, all the fight gone out of him. He tried to take the hand I childishly withheld: ok, I should've rung, but by the time the shit really hit the fan I didn't want to risk waking you just to say don't wait up.

So it turns out, as per bloody usual, I wasn't. Asleep.

What can I say?

Continuing to beat a man already down not making me feel good about myself, and needing his sympathy rather than his contrition, stupidly I showed my own weakness: I'm sorry, it's just, you know, I hate it, being alone here at night, jumping at my shadow.

Tired as he was, Bill couldn't keep himself from smiling.

You're not still going on about a presence, are you? Admiral Benbowe rattling his coffee cup.

Feeling foolish, I bit back: don't you laugh at me, Bill! I get, totally, that the past is full of shit, as you put it. But when you sincerely feel something horrible's happened right where you live, that isn't much of a comfort.

Abi, you know plenty of people actually choose, pay over the odds even, to live somewhere with a nasty history. I dunno: in converted lunatic asylums; sanatoriums for the incurable; the execution chambers in creepy old prisons. You're just going to have to leave off thinking places somehow retain the memory of the horrible things that might've happened in them and get over yourself.

Just because you can't pick up on it, doesn't mean it's nothing.

So, then, as a rational bloody bloke, I have to be punished for not being as attuned to old shoes as you are?

His using the shoe against me – confession of an unguarded moment – made me grateful I'd so far managed to hold back on introducing more horrific deposits hidden away under floorboards. But I was so angry with him for insinuating that my very real fear came down to no more than whacky female intuition, it was a near thing.

Instead, I said: stupid of me, I know, to expect understanding from someone with troubles of his own: out there in the real fucking world of schmoozing the boss and all-night drinking sessions!

Can you stop swearing?

Bill was extra polite himself and – as if my mentioning that other world of his had catapulted him back there – carefully southern-sounding.

Since I do have to get back to, as you call it, *the real world*, to earn the money you're so good at spending, if you'll excuse me I really need to have a wash and a shave.

Leaving me standing there, furious, with nowhere of my own to be, Bill trudged up the stairs to our makeshift accommodation.

I might have picked my moment better. After working through the night, he'd taken the dreaded *magic roundabout*: a taxi from the office that waited for you rumbling on the street while you showered and changed, to be greeted by my irrational vituperations on the front doorstep.

By the time he clattered back down the stairs in a fresh shirt, looking like death and smelling of sweat and deodorant (no shower as we currently didn't have one), I was feeling properly guilty for laying the extra burden of woman on the verge of a nervous breakdown on him.

Taking his hand, I said: you should know by now, Bill, I only ever expect the worst, but you're quite right, it's irrational.

That's the spirit.

I looked askance.

Sorry, you know what I mean.

I stroked his rough cheek from which he'd just scraped the beginnings of his sexy bandit beard that nowadays had some new grey in it, and kissed him. Not even having had the time to brush his teeth, his breath was rank.

He said: I shouldn't have been flippant – but, Abi, just because bad things happened in your past doesn't make it inevitable they will again and, even if they do, anticipating disaster does nothing to prevent it.

Bill put his arm around me, and I was touched that he acknowledged my own fucked up history might have informed my present fucked up behaviour.

Here's a thought, he said: if you must go jumping at shadows, imagine it's that daft bird with hairy legs and no bra of Benny's.

He smiled. I smiled. We embraced.

Breakfast?

Bill consulted his watch: a quick coffee?

I can expect you back at a reasonable hour this evening?

My husband looked defeated.

I'm supposed to go out with clients for drinks after work, but I'll do my best to cut it short. They owe me.

He gave me an apologetic grimace

I'll order in something nice. Round here the world's our lobster. D'you fancy a Thai or there's an interesting-sounding Anatolian restaurant that delivers?

We could always go out, said my husband, demonstrating he was quite as keen as me to get away from this place.

*

It was now just before seven and the wet, grey washing the day had hung up in the sky looked to be about as cheerful as it would get. Shivering in my dressing gown on the doorstep to wave him off for another twelve hours' slog, the cab with windows lit up orange looked to me like the cosy option.

Without a backward look, he was off, leaving me once more to the house spirits and this too too solid cement mixer in the front garden, symbol of my failure as a project manager, a wife.

# Chapter Thirty

The rain has really set in in earnest now: jangling musically down the drains, drumming its bebop beat on the dustbin lids, tapping out a syncopated rhythm against windowpanes. Chilled through – Mrs McNamara's quarters are quite as bleak as your own – still in gown and slippers, you creep back into bed for the briefest of brief warm-ups. You promise yourself just a few minutes more under the covers before you do something constructive with what's left of the short, grey day. Yes, quite soon now, you'll get yourself dressed, heat some soup for lunch then brave the cold and the wet for the laundromat. Or *laundrymart*, as the affectedly well-spoken woman who sold the little packets of powder and gave you change for the machines referred to it.

The couple of minutes back between the sheets duly lengthen into a couple of hours during which you must have slept, because you dreamed.

It's midnight in the basement. Strong moonlight casts the bars at the window as an elongated grid of shadows on the floor before the sink. Like being in a prisoner's cell, or a lunatic's, you think in the dream. Stepping into the squashed square of moonlight, automatically you repeat the action of this morning and reach behind the curtain for the waste pail. Your blind hand finding instead something squat and solid: a Gladstone bag, baleful in its potentiality. Not wanting to touch, you give the thing an exploratory poke with a toe and set rocking something solid within. But when you make yourself pick it up to look inside it's lighter than you might expect, and quite empty.

Startling awake, the hair at your temples is soaked through with tears and you discover that in the time you've been asleep the world's already begun to put up shutters. It must be late afternoon and nothing achieved! If your hard-working husband isn't to catch you out in bed for the second time today you must get up and dressed in a hurry. Shivering out of pyjamas and dressing gown and back into the same stale clothes you had on yesterday, you fling back the curtains onto a grainy grey that, never having lifted sufficiently to signal day was risen, is already thickening back into night. At least the rain's let up.

Not having passed this day in shopping and cleaning and laundering, to have his dinner piping on the table would obviously constitute a domestic comfort too far for you, the bad wife. But even if the home he returns to is unswept, unwarmed, ungarnished, you nevertheless manage, hurriedly, to pull a comb across your greasy head and make up the living room fire. So that, if not perfectly groomed to gaily receive him, you are at least decently dressed and actively engaged in the homecoming rites of welcome when the master of the house bursts back through the door.

As if returned from Antarctic exploration, with stiff and clumsy hands the conquering hero throws back his hood, unwinds his college scarf, and stamps some life back into feet encased in sodden brogues:

"What, what, what?"

In the act of striking it, you break the match.

Evidently William's giant duffle hadn't thoroughly dried out under the influence of the V&A's vaguely chugging radiators; he's drooping under the cold, dead weight of it.

Chucking the useless match into the unlit coals, you strike a wifely pose and enquire: "Good day at the pole? Reggie Penfold liked the book?"

Momentarily baffled, invariably civilised, he picks the second of these greetings, to respond to, saying, "Oh, yes, doted on it. Asked after you."

"Did he?" "Quite the fan there," William says, coming close enough to proffer an uxorious peck. His breath is visible and his duffel has smuggled in on its hairs that smoky outdoors smell of wet London streets:

"Very keen on you paying a call on his mother. Or 'The Matriarch', as he calls her – apparently, they live nearby: just around the corner in fact. Poor old bird's riddled with arthritis and desperate for company."

"Don't imagine I'd be much of a comfort to the elderly."

Once again you have succeeded in making him uncomfortable with this spiteful behaviour over which you seem to exercise no restraint.

His conversational opening having died the death, William removes the evening paper, his pipe and matches from the pocket of his coat. You watch with polite interest as he drapes it over the back of the deck chair to drip and thaw. He now makes a show of rubbing some warmth back into his hands, and this displacement activity exhausted, tries another conversational gambit:

"Goodness! But it's cold in here – I don't know how you stand it all day."

"I spend most of it in bed."

"Quite understandable if you aren't yet quite back up to the mark."

The look of concern he shoots you is guaranteed to bring out the worst.

In a brittle, bright voice, you say, "I'm feeling perfectly fine, thank you, dear, quite tip-top in fact – it was just the weather being so rotten I didn't fancy getting up."

Sensible man, he makes no comment.

Having yourself doggedly un-invented purpose, what chance does William's kindly dart of concern stand against the massive bulwark of your own, now habitual, resistance to finding meaning, or pleasure, in doing anything much?

You run trippingly on to say, "I *do* have firm plans for tomorrow, as it happens." Adding in the same, ridiculously blasé vein that hurts you even as you mean it to punish him, "Mother wrote to suggest a bit of Christmas shopping 'in Town', and treating me to lunch after. So, funnily enough, I shall be improving the shining hour in the consolation of the elderly."

While busying himself in coaxing the fire to life, so as not to have to meet the challenge of your eyes, William says, "Something nice for you to look forward to."

"Let's not get too carried away with all the fun I shall be having – you know Mother."

# Chapter Thirty-one

Bill was right, obviously: however uncanny the vibe, you couldn't forever associate 'home' with some past gruesomeness. Nevertheless, forget the blue plaque I'd imagined embellishing the front of this house, I reckoned it'd still be a useful service to the unwary if they put up black plaques to the infamous. I mean you can bet your bottom dollar no estate agent after his/her commission is voluntarily going to flag up that kind of useful information in the interests of full disclosure. But, however sensibly priced, you'd surely prefer to know that the top floor flat on mundane Cranley Gardens, Muswell Hill you're viewing was where Dennis Nilsen, serial killer and practical cannibal, once blocked the drains in disposing of decoy KFC alongside other, human, body bits? Wouldn't you?

Imagine Googling that address, number twenty-three to be precise, and coming across those details, after you exchanged.

No need with the Wests' place, Fred and Rosie's. Seems it wasn't only me that believed a place retained something of the horror that happened within its walls – to thoroughly cleanse Cromwell Street of its terrible associations, and deter ghouls, their Gloucester charnel house was razed to the ground, its very bricks thereafter reduced to a powder that was buried deep in an undisclosed location.

Without the black plaque in place of course I could never know for sure whether with all that digging and delving of mine I'd discovered a murderous old bitch once traded from this address. But what I had accidentally done was to accessorise with elasticated boots and a Gladstone bag the malevolent presence my helpful husband had already put at the end *of the rope they 'ung 'er by.*

*

Not an hour since Bill stepped back into his waiting cab and working life, needing something to distract me from this lunacy, I actually made a start on piecing back together the broken platter I'd dug up in the garden. Meanwhile, as I painstakingly reassembled and glued, the larger work of deconstruction carried on apace outside my closed door.

In the few weeks they'd been on the job, almost heroically, the jolly Casey band had been turning up ruinous problem upon ruinous problem. And not just them: only yesterday, humourless Mr Pope, our conservation officer down at the council, had taken it upon himself to explain how the Georgians constructed houses – quickly and cheaply seemed best to sum the thing up. As he informed me, being not so hard as a modern one the soft red brick from which these houses were built was particularly susceptible to weather erosion. I should also understand the tuck pointing used by the Georgian jerry-builder who threw up our house was a technique intended to disguise damaged or cheap bricks: the geometric exactness of the tucked ribbon joint covering up any irregularities. Bad news for me, as our degraded and fragile facade must be urgently addressed. Replicating the original building technique of course. And since, if new tuck-pointing is carried out inexpertly in patches, the results can be visually disastrous, as well as extremely expensive to rectify, this was a job – weren't they all? – best tackled by a specialist contractor, and wholesale.

Apart from being shoddily constructed in the first place, lack of maintenance these last forty years or more meant my regency darling was in truth a rackety whore: raddled, ravaged, rotten to the core.

This building project having turned into a campaign to overtake the galloping decay every new procedure laid bare, it occurred to me just how appropriately visceral was that phrase: *to gut*, as used to describe a house restoration. Far, far beyond the gentle art of undressing, brutal surgery seemed the only way forward now, with each incision inevitably demanding an ever-deeper cut. So that while I, cloistered with my plate, pointlessly endeavoured to reassemble, restore, revive, on the other side of the door the builders noisily hacked out, gouged and amputated. Never mind revealing her in her underwear, my tall thin beauty was being taken right back to sinew, bone and gristle, and daily haemorrhaging the input of cash I pumped in. All in the cause of saving the patient, or so Mr Casey reassured me. No way round it, really, love.

I glanced up from my mosaic work to the ubiquitous *Keep Calm and Carry On!* poster we bought for our last house. Even if it felt like it, it wasn't as if we were in the middle of an actual war but, clearly, I should take note. Try not to flinch as yet another stretch of mouldering brickwork or chunk of ceiling plaster came tumbling down. Endeavour to feel no pain when more nicks were accidentally put in that once miraculously preserved newel post. Stop mourning missing marble fireplace surrounds.

What was the beauty of symmetry to me after all, really? As for crumbling dentil work, rotten sash windows, broken boot scrapers, they were only 'things', as I told myself: stuff inherited from the past that I'd clung to out of sentiment, and upon which, because they seemed somehow to exult me, I'd conferred a special worth and significance. As if by some weird retrospective magic my fixing the past would guarantee the future.

I decided the particular ailment I was suffering was *anemoia*, meaning nostalgia for a time you never knew. Or maybe my malaise came closer to what you experience at the ending of a disastrous love affair. Recovery from either demanding that I let go my all-too-personal relationship with this house and just *carry on*. For the sake of my sanity, I must blank her outrageous demands and instead reconcile myself to a more pragmatic partnership with close fitting joinery and perfect, machine-made replacement windowpanes, conducted against a featureless canvas of newly plastered walls. Who knew, my frustration, fury, despair toward the love object that spurned me spent, along with everything else the builders stripped out, perhaps the malice I associated with this place might likewise end up in a skip? In erasing all memory of itself the house and I, both, could start afresh. And, who knows, I might even salvage from the demented harridan I'd become the woman for whom Bill rejected family, heritage, class, religion to marry. For above and beyond what any house could ever be to me, the orphan runaway, I knew that my husband was my real and only refuge.

*

That evening, still raining, I texted Bill: *CU 2nite 4 sage & pumpkin risotto, salad & rather nice Orville.*

I hoped the vagaries of predictive text would make my message come across more like love, less like nagging.

# Chapter Thirty-two

Dinner done with and, down to his skilled ministrations alone, the fire now blazing merrily, like Bathsheba and Gabriel Oak, if less chatty, Dr Bone and his wife settle on either side of the domestic hearth for another long evening 'at home'.

Pipe in mouth, William concentrates hard on the reading matter he holds up close to his face, like a defensive screen. Given the welcome the poor chap habitually receives, it'd be a hard heart that denied him this tried and trusted everyman's retreat into silence and his own thoughts. On the distaff side of the hearth, you, meanwhile, get on with your weaving – or, rather, do battle with the shawl begun months back. Like one of those issueless struggles of the Great War, as you knit then unravel, so the battle lines of inexpert stitches advance and retreat, advance and retreat. To the point that when the hour comes round again for bed the baby shawl is no bigger than it was at the start of the evening's long campaign. Still, it's kept your hands busy. The domestic clacking of the needles nicely substituting for any inconsequential chitchat that might have nudged its way in around the side of hubby's book.

Knitting and nattering, nattering and knitting.

You consider what might constitute the proper subject matter for a wife: *The price of fish nowadays! Shouldn't we get a dear little white pug like the Weanse's had? What are the chances, do you suppose, that we're in for another pea-souper this winter...?* Noticing his furtive sideways glance at the rhomboid of knitting that twitches like a dying thing at the end of those stabbing needles, on the spur of the instant, you resolve that if he and you are to succeed in punching a hole in this veil that hangs, heavy, damp and muffling as any smog between you, neither sniping nor domestic banter are up to the task. To get through to him, right now, you must say something bracingly loud, brutal and quite possibly tasteless.

"I thought I might as well give it a last mighty push. Finish the damn thing off!"

Heart pounding, you flourish the shoddy bit of handicraft under his nose.

"Hmm?" he ventures, startled to wariness.

"As it happens, it might yet serve – I discovered only today the tenants are expecting again. I should imagine, though, that Mr and Mrs McNamara wouldn't think this fit to wrap their baby in!" You hold the cobwebby thing to the firelight, the better to show up the many dropped stitches and runs, the better to force him into acknowledging it:

"What d'you think, William, would a newborn drop through a ladder and throttle itself on a loose thread?"

Hardly surprisingly, William struggles to find any appropriate response to this challenge.

Wishing it might be easier to penetrate the couple of centuries of good breeding that have gone into your husband's making, you say, "She's only a month or two gone, so it'll be a while yet before she'll be needing it."

"Uh huh," says your husband.

"Yes, due sometime in late July." It's only now in calculating the date that its significance hits you like a blow. Taking a deep and steadying breath, you nevertheless persist.

"Poor thing, she was worried we'd throw them on the mercy of the parish, but I've told her, after the baby comes, they can stay on – that's all right, isn't it?" Relieved to find himself back on firm-ish ground, William is quick to endorse whatever his wife has to say on the uncontroversial matter of tenancy agreements.

"Fine by me, dear, whatever you think best."

But you're not done. Having managed to smuggle into the room this unborn baby, proxy for that other dead baby – your own – that seems always to be bobbing about unacknowledged in the stupid fug of good manners that hangs deeply between you two, you have no intention of letting him politely usher it out again.

"We had a chat, her and me, I mean she and I, quite a heart to heart – mostly about her concerns for the future. Come to think of it, apropos of what exactly it is I get up to all day; how I pass my wilfully wasted daylight hours, this one at least I mostly spent in finding out how the other half, or at least the other half of the house, lives."

"Well, there's a turn-up," is William's quick, humorous response, "I had the impression you didn't particularly get on – you know what they say: never a good idea two women sharing a house!"

You are a little taken aback that he might have noticed what till now you believed to be a successfully covert campaign of attrition conducted between yourself and your foe at the top of the stairs. Have you underestimated Dr Bone's capacity to engage with what occurred on the other side of his book?

Supposing there have been numerous other examples of this phenomenon in olden times for him to draw upon in comparison, you say, "Actually, more like two enemy countries that share a common border. But probably much the same as in international diplomacy, once you get to know the other side, to understand they're human after all, and have the same basic wants and needs as oneself, it gets so much less simple to just hate, or fear them."

"The cold war is over," summarises William, as ever elegantly, bringing the simile bang up to date.

"Quite. I wouldn't go so far as to say that on the strength of one chat Mrs McNamara and I have discovered we're sisters under the skin. Nothing so trite. Nice as she may be, a woman like that's never going to be a close friend, it's simply that she herself is real to me in a way she wasn't before. And now she's pregnant again, and so very soon after the last one, I feel we should help them out. It shouldn't be too difficult to fit the new baby in here somewhere, should it?"

"So long as it's a very small one."

Pleased that they might have got somewhere at last, however obliquely, you are gracious enough to forgive him the joke.

William indicates with his pipe stem the bit of discarded knitting: "I'm sure they'll appreciate the gesture."

"Seeing as we ourselves shall never need it."

This is brutal. Unadorned. You meant it to be, though the hard and unembellished truth of what you've just said has the effect of shocking you, as well as him, to silence.

I believe those two sad young people in that moment each embodied within the empty shawl laid across its mother's lap the baby that never was. The spectre of something substantial enough to have, nevertheless, crushed the hopes and plans of both.

It is William, at last, who puts an end to this painful interval, saying, "That's all sorted then, and to everyone's mutual satisfaction."

Well aware of what has already been risked, wanting to push this far as it might go, however that might hurt, you take courage and persevere: "When things have got off to a bad start, sometimes it's a good idea to begin again, don't you think, William?" Determined not to let him wrap this up with another of his cheery aphorisms, voice trembling because it's so hard for you to put into words, you say, "I mean: set aside the obsolete patterns relationships fall into for fear of causing offence or hurt, so as to talk honestly and openly." Having pushed so hard, you lose your nerve and stupidly throw the thing away.

"Well, it seemed to work well enough for little Mrs McNamara and me!"

"Amazing what a bit of *détente* can achieve, isn't it?"

Slapping his hands on both thighs, levering himself purposefully out of his deck chair, your husband proposes, "Bed?"

Though it is hard to tell for sure whether, somehow, your appeal has succeeded in getting beneath William's gentlemanly crust to that part of him you know, or at least suspect, is vulnerable and tender, fine-tuned as you most certainly are to any hint of a sexual invitation from him, like a couple of spent matches points of warmth glow in either cheek.

According to the usual night-time routine, you venture down into the dreaded kitchen to wash up while William goes about turning off the gas lights and banking up with more coals the stuttering fire in preparation for the morning. Thus, properly and efficiently battened down for the night, you remove upstairs to the bedroom. And bed.

The curtains pulled tight once more across the filthy weather, you wonder if William guesses they've hardly been open today.

Before he gets in under the covers, measured in everything, he takes agonising care over folding his trousers before he hangs them over the footboard, together with his shirt, ready for tomorrow's use.

Nervous and self-conscious before him because you believe your body is so changed, leaving your own clothes where they drop you struggle out of nakedness into pyjamas and, gazelle-like, leap beneath the bedclothes of the frigid bed. By the time William has on his own pyjamas, buttoned to the collar, you've been lying expectantly tensed in it a good five minutes.

Easing in beside his wife, he asks, politely, "Lights out, or do you want to knit on a while?"

"Oh, I think lights out. Don't you?"

You can't stop your voice from shaking.

William turns down the oil lamp and the two of you lie, side by side, not quite touching at shoulder and hip. A chilly knight and his lady raised up on a hard catafalque that centuries have kept always together, perpetually apart.

There is a silence, a pause, between you that, to you, feels....electric.

Hot as if you ran a temperature: "Brr," you go.

"We could do with a good, thick eiderdown quilt now the weather's really taken a turn, don't you think?" your husband responds in the dark. "I could ask my ma to send us one down from Great Dishcloth."

*Great Dishcloth* is the joke, pet name for the ancestral pile, more properly Great Dixcleaux, meaning tenth descendent of Claude in ye olde French, or some such nonsense, anyway pronounced Disclue. By my calculation it was London that was 'up', but in Bone family parlance, Dixcleaux took geographical precedence over everywhere.

So aware of him, you ache to close that quarter-inch gap, but having learned from the failed overture on the night of the party that the first move best belonged to the knight, resist.

When he himself breaks through the exclusion zone, reaching across a heavy gauntlet to bump your arm in a cordial gesture of 'goodnight', nevertheless you are quick to follow up: putting a hand over his to draw it toward your breast. Suavely your husband continues the action, bringing your clumsily joined hands out from under the inadequate blanket, surrogate for that other thick eiderdown quilt you spoiled by bleeding all over it.

150

Having planted a courteous kiss on the back of your hand he replaces it on the top of the bedclothes, lightly, tidily, decidedly, as he might a dropped glove on the chest that stands in the hall.

And with this one casual gesture of denial it seems to you your absent-minded, amiable and compliant husband declares his steely resolve against the restarting of your marriage.

No longer a mother, and now never will be; having declined to be anything like a proper wife to him, perhaps it's only fair he rejects the part of husband. But if both of you refuse the rôles assigned to each, it seems to you that while you reach out to him as another human being in need of consolation and comfort, he chooses to punish and shut you down.

Unfailing patience and good humour might be the civilised way of handling this un-self-willed state of affairs in which you find yourselves but railing and screaming to you seem more honest. If the customary handful of dirt has already been thrown on to it, rather than just allow indifference or inertia to now shut up the tomb, with your bad-tempered displays of frustration you are at least trying to keep this young marriage alive.

As for Dr William Bone: nothing so messy as an expressed emotion. Celibacy and slippery denial masquerading as politesse are the strategies he adopts to turn life back once more into a semblance of what he had planned and came so close to achieving: the existence of the contented bachelor don, had not the accelerated outcome of one drunken evening's debauch shackled him to the bride who failed to deliver the goods upon which the bad bargain was struck. Just the excuse he now needed, it seems, to hold you to account for robbing him of either of those futures. As far as William is concerned: you're on your own, Celia, in this marriage bed.

Protected from passion, conflict or any hint of human kindness by that courtly self-constraint, your husband turns his back for sleep. Tomorrow after all is just another working day of the week and clever Dr Bone must get his rest. As for you, there's the prospect of that shopping trip with Mother.

# Chapter Thirty-three

Taking good care to keep my ankles high off a floor awash with trolling toddlers, as daylight ebbed, I found myself taking refuge once again in what had become my natural constituency and setting: in a kitchen with pre-schoolers and their educated, slightly stir-crazy, career-break mums. The only variation to my sad existence was that rather than escaping next door it was to Cara's enormous shiny-white, split-level, broken-plan concept kitchen that I homed this teatime.

Long inured to having a houseful: friends, neighbours, people popping in, I guessed it was largely a class thing that my friend could preside over the pullulating mass with such consummate calm and grace. Whether it was a background of boarding school, as was Cara's case, or growing up in the thick of a Mumbai slum didn't make many odds: very rich, or very poor, being subject to throng and hubbub from an early age, so it seemed, broke one forever of the bourgeois habituation of needing, wanting or even expecting to be alone.

People, people always; there'd been a time when I couldn't have imagined anything worse.

This particular afternoon my popular posh friend was hosting a pre-Christmas Gift Fair: one of those splendid dos organised to raise charitable funds for which ladies of good addresses throw open their three-to-four reception rooms, plus conservatory, to entrepreneurial ladies to sell to other ladies of good addresses things they didn't want or need. Again, not my bag – quite literally, not – as I was already in possession of a 'bag for life', hand crafted from an old maize sack in a South African women's prison. And neither did I care to *create my own Christmas bauble* for £10 at the 'painting station'.

It was just *sport-shopping*, I realised: just consumerism – and all in a good cause – but since it was the diversion of life and busyness I craved; in the circs, pretty bloody ideal.

Waiting patiently my turn with her at the kitchen island, I listened in as a couple of Cara's Bébéyoga! friends disparaged the parental skills of another who'd just left the premises.

Perched on my high chair, it seemed to me that if those famous bitches Martin Amis and Tibor Fischer had had a good run, theirs was as nothing to the poisonous sniping as practised by high-functioning mothers. Even the unpleasantness tweeted between Taylor Swift and Katy Perry, or Kanye and…almost anyone, failed to compete in these stakes. Why was it, I wondered, that bright, sprogged-up professional women were so very hungry to congregate together, and yet were so very hostile and unforgiving towards each other when they did?

As for the competitive over-sharing…with looks of rapt fascination they'd conduct these quick-fire exchanges that were at the same time both monumentally dull and hair-raisingly yucky. And this lot of co-commiserators didn't just tell each other about the potty-training traumas, they had the photos ready on their iPhones.

I reckoned they must all of them have been secretly looking forward to the end of maternity leave, when they might flee the dog-eat-dog world of mothering for their restful jobs back in high finance, the upper echelons of the media and the law. With a live-in nanny, possibly in a uniform, with gloves, to take the strain of the eighteen-hour days they were gratefully out the door.

It made me consider, also, that the mother's ransom Debby'd have to find to pay a woman to replace her was probably higher than she could ever hope to earn, spilling wine and cobbling together press releases.

\*

Came the hour, at long last, when all good infants must depart the party for Bedfordshire (Barnes, actually), I was finally able to separate out my friend from the horde. Seeing my need, bless her, Cara joined me on my island, with an open bottle and two glasses.

At last someone who isn't in the throes of weaning, she said, gracefully pretending exasperation.

We chinked glasses.

It having slipped my mind she was herself a mother, I launched in, chortling: one more emergency caesarean or projectile vomiting anecdote and I'd have committed matricide!

Cara gave me back a tight little smile. Unstoppable in my slightly hysterical, quickly tipsy state I asked: I probably don't want to know, but what is cradle crap?

You mean cradle *cap*, Cara said, it's thickened skin on the scalp that turns scaly, then flakes off – all babies get it.

Cara, after what I've been reading up on recently, you really wouldn't want to hear what I was imagining!

She did laugh, but I could tell she was finding me hard work and really no fun. And I'd been so counting on the restorative effect of this glass of something chilled and alcoholic, plus a receptive ear.

Tellingly, Cara swivelled away from me, the better to keep an eye on her own fleecy-headed honey chile (no cradle cap there) as he chased around the kitchen with her minute new Filipino. (The former Eastern Block supply must have dried, or perhaps his mother had worked out that *Chodźmy do kina, Fergoos!* meant: *let's go to the flicks, Fergus!*) I should definitely have taken the hint I'd outstayed my welcome when she instructed the manny – her underwear, presumably, was safe from him – to take the baby up for his bath, and didn't offer me a top-up. Soon after, she mentioned having to make a start on dinner. But, still, because I knew I could count on Cara being far too well brought up to throw me out on my ear, I kept my perch and toyed with my now empty glass. Being a bit clever about it, I reckoned I could cling on like this till Alisdair got home. So, when next Cara attempted to wind up my visit, I lobbed in a topic we both still had in common. Good as gold, she gave up her contact numbers for *little men* and *lovely suppliers*. I even made a show of scribbling down some of her recommendations.

But when she helpfully advised me to source all floor and wall tiles direct from Italy, or Portugal, thereby cutting out the middle man (like all rich people Cara was fierce about pulling off such teeny, weeny little economies in their huge expenditures – *thank heavens Tamsin won a music scholarship to Beneden, the stabling there for her polo pony is ruinous!*), I was forced to admit I'd already ordered all ours from the little, overpriced, tile shop round the corner.

Cara, clocking a lack of proper commitment on my part, snapped shut her own big *House* file.

My last-ditch attempt at delay was to appeal: Cara, darling, sweetheart, you don't understand, I need help! If I'm going to be able to afford Imperial Apiary wallpaper, at two hundred and forty quid the roll, you're really going to have to explain to me how to make massive savings!

A little mollified, she said: mmm, pricey. Mind you, I hate that one 'feature wall' solution.

Still keeping it light, I said: it's not just about me cutting down on my wallpaper habit, Cara, it's the basic structural work, I mean the really boring stuff, like the roof and the windows and the brickwork, that's taking me disastrously over budget. Forget *feature walls*, at this rate we'll be going down Homebase for the papers and paint and B&Q for the discounted plastic bath suite!

Gosh, that's a shame – last time we met you seemed so determined to get every period detail perfect. Pages and pages of research, I seem to remember! Never out of the Soane Museum archive.

Oh that, that was all *wallpaper*! I mean cover for not having a bloody clue. I don't know how you do it: veteran of not one, but two, immaculate makeovers.

I may not have sounded it but I was completely sincere; Cara nevertheless looked at me like I was some kind of idiot.

It's not rocket science, is it, honey?

To me it is: rocket science to Mars.

Darling, I had no idea.

She returned to her big book.

Look, she said: I've got a couple of contacts for really good project managers you could....

Coming up with something diversionary fast – even if I was only pretending to take her advice, I knew I wasn't going to be able to admit to Bill we needed to bring in a professional to finish the job – I said: the one positive in all this, Cara, is the time off work has given me the chance to think. You know, really think about what it is I want to do with my life?

(Yes, on just the one glass of wine, I succumbed to the high rising terminal.)

I carried on: you know I've always been fascinated by social history.

Have you?

Yes, well, anyway, I've decided to write a book: a partly historical novel, about the restoration of a regency house that turns out to be haunted. Not just haunted, what I mean is that this disturbing thing that once happened there is somehow summoned back by the woman who's doing the restoration. I don't know: either she triggers it in some way or is just super sensitive. Anyway, something evil's seeped into the fabric of the place and once it's unstopped it begins to make itself felt in the present day.

All she said was: you're writing a book?

I soldiered on: I got the idea from a newspaper article about these people who bought a house just like ours to do up, then found out this 'angel maker', I mean this child murderer, once lived there.

(I might myself have only just have come up with this book malarky, but I was warming to it.)

Terribly Victorian gothic – you'd love it!

Actually, Abi, I don't think I would.

Although there was no one else in the room, she lowered her voice: I'm pregnant, you see – just had my three-month scan. Everything's fine as far as they can tell, but I'm still feeling a bit vulnerable. You know, after all the trouble we had conceiving the first time, so, if you wouldn't mind...?

Alisdair arrived back soon after, accompanied by an old university friend he'd met at the station and brought along with him: would I like to join them for dinner – the more the merrier; plenty of food in the fridge, wine in the cellar?

Somewhat chastened by Cara's good grace in the face of my thumping great foot in mouth, I took my leave with the excuse that I'd promised Bill I'd be back, was cooking something special.

\*

Till my own husband did or did not come home, since my stomach thought my throat was cut, nothing for it but to forget about the risotto I promised him, summon the speed-dial pizza, crack open the 'nice Orvieto' and catch up on another episode of Hundred Grand House. Huh!

# Chapter Thirty-four

Soon as she arrives, next morning, in a honker, from your lurking spot by the window you watch Mother pay off the driver, fail, as usual, to tip the man, and ascend the four steps to the front door. Where she pauses to touch up her face with a dab of powder and straighten her gloves. Geared up and ready to give battle she beats her tattoo.

"I'm presuming you received the jam I sent – lovely homemade greengage – and the scarf, because I heard absolutely nothing back, Celia."

Before she's even across the threshold, Mother has launched already into her opening salvo.

"Yes, sorry, I did. Thank you."

"And the cake?"

"The cake too – William thought it the best Dundee he ever tasted."

He hadn't, but this remark has got you down the hall and into your quarters where Mother, who isn't blind, straight away spots her daughter's next offence: yellow walls.

"Foul colour!"

"William says it's authentically Georgian." Not listening, glancing rapidly about herself, in short order Mother pinpoints the other improvements you've made in here, demanding, "Where on earth did all the furniture go?"

"Oh, that: to a bad home, I suppose. It was hideous, so I got rid of it," you reply, dependably petulant.

"What do you mean, you *got rid of it?*"

"Some I threw away, the rest went to the rag and bone man."

Installed now in the slummocky deck chair, itself the faded memento of some long-passed Edwardian summer, to keep her where she is, put a stop to an inventory of what else might have gone missing since last she called, you press on her an overfilled cup of coffee. Not that any of this will immobilise her tongue.

"Celia, really! I call that rash, it might have been old-fashioned but it was perfectly serviceable and I can tell you young lady when Daddy and I first set up home together we'd have been thrilled with so much as a...." Sensing from the quiver in her voice that this way danger lay, adroitly you head her off, saying, "I know one should be eternally grateful for the little we do receive, and it's probably a horrible case of throwing the baby out with the bath water, but after what happened with the chaise longue, I couldn't seem to stand the sight of any of it..." Because Mother identifies this allusion to the miscarriage as an attempt to wrest the emotional high ground your tactic works a treat. Never to be underestimated, she now deploys her own blocking technique.

"And no darling William either!"

Dismay over the missing furniture is, after all, as nothing compared to the absent son-in-law. Something she might well have anticipated: having taken the nine-fifteen train to King's Cross expressly to avoid commuters on their way to their offices, by the time she docked in Islington Dr Bone will long ago have cast off for points southwest.

To Mother: just another bitter pill.

If Mrs McNamara's mum believed her Irish Pat beneath her, your own dear mama cherishes quite the opposite opinion of the son-in-law. As for the disgrace of those enforced nuptials, in her view William was the innocent, and injured, party. Duped and fatefully fascinated by her disreputable daughter's unnatural proclivity for *the doings of the farmyard*, as Mother termed it, the normal balance of his mind disturbed by drink, in her view it is only because he is so very honourable that William stepped up to neutralise the very tricky situation of which you were the author. In Mother's estimation Dr Bone is not only deserving of considerable credit for having defused her daughter, made her safe by matrimony, she's additionally in his debt for rescuing her own reputation into the bargain. And not a moment too soon. As she wrote on your return from honeymoon: 'I was so ashamed Tuesday last at Mrs Parry's bridge evening. Firstly, having to tell them you'd come down from Cambridge early to be married, then when the baby was due. Celia, as you may imagine, they can all count!'

The clue that the new mother-in-law, Marjorie, herself shares much the same low opinion of the girl who damaged her boy's morals and career prospects is that she wept to witness the necessary washing in public of grubby linen that was symbolically enacted in that hastily arranged wedding ceremony. Consistent, if for nothing else, in lowering the tone, letting the side down, it came as no surprise to you that you hadn't passed muster with the in-laws. Even now, barely ten minutes into Mother's visit, and you've already put your foot in it with your own, and only, parent: offering a lump for her coffee. Compounding the original offence with the offhand remark, "Remember the notice that went up in the window of the grocer's after the war: 'Paper bags provided, supply own sugar'!"

Like the necessary bit of grit in the oyster that brings forth pearls, mentioning sugar in conjunction with the war does a fine job of triggering the hurt tears already formed, waiting only to be sprung. Beautifully equipped in commanding the tragic role, having long since accepted she's governed by an unlucky star, Mother has you well trained in invoking her exceptional destiny to suffer. With sudden, theatrical gesture putting her cup from her as though you'd offered to poison rather than sweeten it, magnificent in her misery, she reproves, "Celia, you know perfectly well Daddy had a sweet tooth, yet you choose today, *of all days*, to hark on about it!"

After all the years you lived together have you learned nothing? If you were only a little smarter at looking behind this plan of Mother's to come up to town, you might have been alerted to the date and so have anticipated that on this *of all days*, her great grief would be hair-triggered. Alas, you hadn't.

(One had to be remarkably nimble to avoid setting Mother off.)

All because your father, her husband, was on this very date *Killed In The War* and thus could no longer indulge that famously sweet tooth of his.

In reality, Daddy was run over by a bus, crossing The Strand, but since the crucial circumstance of his stepping out unwisely had been the reduced visibility of the blackout, he was ever after described by her as having been killed not *during* but *in* the war. Or, more flashily, in the Blitz. Mother's small but telling distinction in prepositions not only making retrospective sense of the world and its unpredictable workings but lending his death, her loss, that little extra added dash of historical resonance.

But if it's cruel to, however obliquely, recall his death on this, the anniversary, perhaps more unforgivable still that you yourself have forgotten all about it.

It might have been to preserve your own memories of him – precious few, you were only five when he died – that you had taught yourself not to look back and wonder how life might have turned out differently with – for all you knew – a father's moderating influence. So successful in fact have you been over the intervening years in erasing the special import of December 3rd from your own memory that every time it comes around again, and you do remember, it's a fresh shock. As for Mother, with little else in life to divert her, she herself prefers to dwell mostly there, in the lovely, wallowy past, appropriating, reinventing and recycling memory for her own exquisite purposes. But having inadvertently bred up in you an early instinct to preserve and defend what was most deeply felt, you arrived at the conclusion – all your own – that an emotion requiring witnesses made it inauthentic and so remain stubbornly dry-eyed at the implied heartbreak of the sugar lump. Thus, provoking even more abandoned outbursts. Even if the right to grief remains hers first, his death principally part of her own uniquely interesting and tragic biography, her daughter's unnatural refusal now, or, indeed, ever, to cry in front of her, even to talk about him much, Mother can only conceive as evidence of a particular coldness.

Rather typically of someone who herself lacked empathy, she attempts to explain to her obdurate daughter what it is to feel.

"Imagine losing *your* own dear husband," she commands, giving a useful hint, "then you might begin to understand what it is to be quite broken-hearted."

Saying this, she puts her hand to her chest to assess how her own exemplarily un-calloused organ is holding up.

Long experience of playing the part of both prompt and audience to the grand tragedienne means you know enough of this scenario to understand Mother isn't after pity, pity not being what the weak may offer those with the upper hand. And so you try to look very contrite indeed, and say nothing. As one who appreciates Jane Austen for her deadly accurate sniping from the side-lines, in Mother's complaint you hear the echo of silly Mrs Musgrove's unchallenged assertion, *My sore throats, you know, are always worse than anyone's.*

Just as for the powerless Anne Elliot, you must make do with the subtle satisfaction of the watchful corner demon.

Forgiven, barely, you are on the very point of leaving the house, practically out of the front door, when Mother encounters – how could she not? – the McNamara perambulator and for the second occasion since her arrival – this time not even uttering – her unfeeling daughter causes her to shed pearly tears.

Still in the hallway, halted by that blasted pram, she revisits the tragedy suffered by a widow of only thirty-five, mother to a sole, recalcitrant child, now condemned never to know the solace due a grandmother.

After allowing herself these few additional minutes of sustained grief, perhaps realising she's already behindhand with her promised treat, Mother pulls herself together: "I meant this day out at the shops to be such a happy one!" she says, applying her hanky.

Squelching over mushy leaves, you set off smartly down the High Road to hail a cab.

Mother was taken as a child by a favourite aunt to Gamages Department Store to witness a miniature lake with toy boats floating on it. A glimpse into paradise she was never to forget. With its every retelling, indeed, growing only the more special. Thereafter the magic of Christmas for Mother was to be found only in Holborn, at Gamages and, despite its lights, never, ever, on Oxford Street.

Having already had that unscheduled holdup at the point of departure, instead of shopping first, you two ladies proceed directly to the department store's restaurant for luncheon.

Reporting early, you are soon seated by the restaurant maître d' at a *very nice* table with a good view of The Circus. Mother, extra garrulous, excitable and satisfied after her two lovely cries, barely touches her poached salmon. You have the cheese omelette with peas, and a side plate of bread and marg. Made ravenous by all that unexpressed ire and grief, in another display of unfeeling, without tasting a thing, you wolf the lot.

Both choose the tinned peaches and cream to follow. On sampling it, "Mock!" says Mother, in a carrying whisper. "You'd have thought Gamages might have done us a little better."

In those years the cream you got, remember, was still mostly made from

---

vigorously whipping together flour, sugar and margarine.

Not having had much of the real thing, you prefer the substitute: less rich, less cloying.

After luncheon, with lost time still to make up, it's straight to the first floor: *ladieswear, lingerie and hosiery* for you. Mother is insistent you are fitted for proper corsetry. Perhaps she has still in mind the blooming, ballooning, blushing bride who just half a year since she waved off on the Frinton train. Obediently, you stand in the dressing room behind velvet curtains that don't quite close while heavy duty elasticated stuff is draped about your shrinking form. Mother on her gilt chair meanwhile approves the trussing.

"Nothing like a 'really good foundation'! I always say it's the quality of the undergarment that guarantees the success of the overall 'look'." Conspiring now with the elderly woman knelt painfully at her feet, she comments, pleasantly, "Girls nowadays have no posture, you agree? Always slouching about the place, sitting with their knees akimbo, their shoulders sloped."

Mother, with legs correctly crossed at the ankle, sits a little straighter on her gold princess chair. You childishly curve your spine, hollow your chest.

"Laugh in my face all you like young lady, but in my day we knew what it was to be feminine." The recent promotion from daughter to wife having removed the remit of the sharp corrective slap across the back of the legs, Mother must vent her displeasure for your cheek elsewhere. There being no one else conveniently to hand, she chooses the crouching shop woman to take it out on, commanding, "For goodness sake, stop fumbling do, and give it a really good yank!"

The woman, who probably needed to hang onto this job, redoubles her efforts the better to restrain the scooped hips, doorknob breasts and concave tummy.

The sharp words substitute for the slap rather well you think: in both cases Mother can claim to have been driven to it in the first place (you've only yourself to blame), and its tonic application leaves her feeling fine.

In your experience of frustrated women (having lived for years in close proximity to one) when bright, pretty, undereducated wives and mothers used to getting it all their own way reached that *certain age*, recognising the sex card's already been played and the children all gone off to make their own lives or marriages, and with nothing much else up their sleeves by way of self-expression, or useful occupation outside the domestic sphere, they either gave way gracefully to the coming generation, took to lavender and faded tastefully into the furniture, or they commanded centre stage. And an unchecked tendency to triumph over the weak and voiceless made them indomitable. Inimitable. Just so, since her husband's death, and no corrective hand on the reins, rather early on in her new career as noble relict, Mother remade herself as a female force in her own right and reckoning.

Susan Barrett

Even as the nervous old woman sticks pins into your flesh, you resolve you will take care to furnish yourself with sufficient interests, skills and projects all your own, with or without the man, or the kiddies.

I'm pleased to say that, even then, you had no intention of ending up either the monstrous matriarch or one of those women made meaningless just with the passage of time, who brood on minute old injustices over the washing up, remote and alone in the kitchen.

The delivery of the finished item arranged, purchases paid for, (the cash and invoice still in those days sent via overhead brass tube and compressed air to the cashier's cage, with change and receipt returned by the same ingenious contraption), you calculate she won't today insist on revisiting that repository of her most magical memories; site of infant delight: the shop's toy department. Quite enough tears for one day! Meaning you must only survive another couple of floors before it'll be high time for Mother to catch the train back to Welwyn.

Almost done in *hats and headpieces* (Mother has the fun of a funeral in prospect) there is however a last minor misunderstanding, prompted by you mentioning that William hardly talks to you in the evenings, much preferring the company of his books. Whatever you might be attempting to say about the man you never should have married, Mother is determined not to hear it.

Appalled in a black cloche with cockerel's feathers: "Celia," she snaps, "if you only knew the times, even after all these years, I've been sitting before the fire of an evening and I've looked up expecting to see Daddy, sitting opposite me, smiling back, only to find his empty chair...."

What can you possibly have to complain about? William might be silent (and sainted), but at least you have the consolation that behind his book he isn't dead.

Realising you're on a hiding to nothing, you try to look very guilty indeed: safer, certainly, than having that conversation about the state of your marriage.

Mother and daughter part on good terms in The Circus as, with a wave of the hand, off she sets for the cab rank and home. On watching her departing back, you can see the day out in London has put a new spring in her step. Grief's uninhibited expression and shopping did that for Mother.

Back home, you lie down with a cold compress across your eyes to soothe a thumping head. Your early Christmas present from Mother sitting up smartly beside you on the bed is a 'proper', lady's handbag, solid and shiny as a glacé chestnut. Your own spoils from the shopping expedition are William's presents: a fountain pen and a boxed set of three handkerchiefs embroidered with each of his five initials.

Such a disappointment that although post-war department stores were at last

162

full of stuff you could buy, there was still nothing in them you might actually want to own. And walking over their thickly carpeted floors made your legs ache. And they were unbearably hot and overcrowded.

Having grown used to your own company and these chilly, bare-boarded rooms, you find you prefer asceticism and the company of the other ghosts.

# Chapter Thirty-five

If I was the virgin land in which he negligently planted his flag, Bill was my interactive sex map and manual. All through that first summer together I negotiated the terra incognita of his boy topography, making my own routes as I went, seeing off the ghosts of my predecessors. Bill, you see, had history whereas my dirty little sex secret was that my 'number' was one. And he was it: my *numero unico*. But I expected, hoped, then as now, I'd remain stuck forevermore on that comfortable, unfashionable single digit.

From the moment I first saw him love bit me hard. True, he was beautiful, clever too, and funny and, like me, a bit of an overachiever, but perhaps I loved him best for the ways in which he was so different from me. So different from everyone I knew.

I grew up amongst people who valued music, art, literature; his family watched their massive colour telly from multiple settees with the protective plastic left on. He was raised in a terrace of back-to-backs; I was born in a garden. His lot were angry grafters; mine free spirits. With lots of springy hair, keen on shagging, agitprop and arguing.

Despite the impression I might have given, it wasn't like my parents were poor just that most of our friends and neighbours at the time – not the postman – made something of a virtue out of having few material possessions or crap ones. (Our telly was black and white and kept inconveniently on top of a bookshelf.) But we *were* snobs. The grown-ups might not have been competitive about consumer durables – in this case: not the stockbrokers – but they sure cared about the size of their commissions. Every kid on our block knew what a Play For Today was worth – I mean its kudos quotient as well as what appeared on the cheque. My earliest memories of going to sleep of a light summer evening was to the furious clatter coming from open back bedroom windows of electric typewriters or early pcs – the staccato sound of a TLS article doing battle across the garden square with a sketch for Not the Nine O'Clock News.

Inverse snobbery can be a cruel ideology under which to live though. I got my first stolen toke on a joint at the age of seven and none of my inoculations. At eleven, my brother Nicholas, Nico, was packed off to the Comp, talking posh and wearing broken sandals and canvas shorts passed down from our father.

Coming from that kind of privilege, understandable, perhaps, why I gratefully adopted Bill's straightforward trajectory for my loadstar. When you've tried the alternatives you know, believe me, it's stability, predictability, dull dependability that will see you through the storms of life. Although you might understand also that these solid attributes can be the braver life choices.

What my wayward upbringing mostly taught me was that peace of mind came through the study of rules and principles that didn't change. (I *did* love rules.) It was only when I made it as a no-nonsense solicitor in that down-to-earth town that I discovered long habituation to turmoil meant this dependable existence I'd striven so hard to achieve could seem pallid, bland, somehow unsatisfying. I was bored to death by the hard-won certainty of my life. Fettered by the foundations I so carefully laid, oppressed by the walls I put up. Maybe this was why I could never stick long to any particular career? But if I found that letting go my chaotic past and cleaving to the northern rock Bill represented wasn't a cure for my addiction to existential angst or splashy self-dramatization, what kept him and me solid as houses in the early years was fear.

If, as I knew, Bill had absolutely no artistic pretentions; was a stranger to introspection and overthinking it then patently, I was none of these things. Neither did he prize imagination over facts, and he knew where he was going, how he intended to get there. Whereas, I did not. But even after I got to know him for the dear kind man he was, still it worried me there might be danger in his difference. So that what had attracted me to him in the first place once we were a couple also kept me successfully on the edge of my seat, adrenalin pumping, imagining terrible scenarios.

As far as I was concerned, it could only be a matter of time before he saw through to the mess-up I was on the inside and left me. Until that was, one very cold morning a couple of years after we married, I grabbed his thick trench coat to wear on the walk to work. Digging my hands into the pockets expecting gloves I discovered amulets instead: tactile fetishes designed to give pleasure. For a finger to fit itself to: an acorn cup and a small stone with a hole in it. A crunchy little pinecone and a weighty coin, both delightful in their contrasting hand feel. And there was something small and smooth that warmed to the touch my blind fingers didn't recognise. Cheating with a look, I saw the single heart-shaped earring of translucent orange amber — suckable as a caramel, and as easily cracked — that'd disappeared from my dressing table a month since.

It was by these small secret tells: evidence of a sentimental interior life I'm ashamed to say I hadn't credited him with, that I truly began to trust my own warm but breakable heart to Bill's hands. If he couldn't fix me, I knew he loved me.

# Chapter Thirty-six

Husband and wife, Dr and Mrs William Bone, make a well-matched pair: both of an age, similarly educated, fit and physically attractive, and they share the same values as well as a taste for the right sort of jazz. (And, even if grim-faced, both sides showed up to bestow their blessings upon their hastily mounted nuptials). You can't help but wonder, however, whether it is the other young woman living in this house who is the well-married one.

In their cold, cramped and inconvenient living quarters at the top of the stairs, it seems to you that she and her husband have achieved that fine balance between give and take, mutual needs answered, and tolerant understanding offered that made for a happy partnership. More important, clear as day, her Pat loves and desires his wife. This you know from the fiddly little mock pearl buttons on that fitted back-to-front cardigan of hers. Buttons that before he left for his work on the black stuff he must've taken the time to fasten, every one. The virtuous industry represented in the doing up of buttons she couldn't reach not only an expression of his love but the need to cherish and touch her also.

Yet, how precariously balanced is marital happiness?

Inexperienced as you are, hard nut that she is, it's not so difficult to understand why, as the precursor of 'too many', the upstairs tenant fears this pregnancy. For the woman at the top of the stairs the servitude of un-moderated maternity means a remorseless debasement of body and soul, an erosion of self that'll see her careworn, misshapen and old before her time. Inevitably, unavoidably the remorseless multiplication of the shitty nappies would be what finally did for her. And by turning a loving husband into an enemy or a predatory monster, tip the odds against love and content.

For him also, a wife exhausted and overwhelmed by many babies born close together, and a working wage spread too thin to provide for the little dependable comforts of life, might wreck the relationship between man and woman.

Even without the sentence of hard labour, not so impossible to imagine that for your own sort an unplanned pregnancy could ruin lives.

Day shutting up shop early, as it does at this time of the year, by four all is quiet in the square. Quiet as the tomb from above too. Your unexpected heart-to-heart hasn't freed Mrs McNamara to sing out loud to her baby. Her customary self-consciousness, or a new appreciation that it is anyway ineffectual, seems also to have put a stop to her downing more gin or throwing herself off the furniture. But having shared a house with her these last few months you anticipate before long the enamel pans will be once more set a-clashing. Like clockwork, she'll be out on her kitchen landing, making culinary preparations prior to her husband's homecoming.

167

Being midweek, nothing special. But she'll, somehow, still see to it he has something hot and tasty for his tea. And when pay day Friday comes round, using the three functioning gas rings on the stove top and the hard-to-light oven, her man will find his reward at the end of another working week in roast mutton, roast potatoes, cabbage (of course) and mint sauce, and for 'afters' a nice bit of tart or that suet and raisin pudding they for some reason called "drowned baby". The one you boiled forever in a bag and steamed up the windows. You have the grace to be ashamed that from your position of superiority you had mocked her for it. Little wifey going about her mysterious domestic routines and rituals, shopping and cleaning and laundering and caring for the baby, yet still striving always to have his dinner on the table, ready and waiting. Even if hackneyed, you can understand that there might be a sort of nobility to it. You, whose only satisfaction in food preparation was the restful paring and paring away of potatoes. So very diligent in this, horrified by the wastage implicit in those unstrung potato pearls, Mother largely let you off kitchen duties. So you never learned.

Unlucky husband of a lazy wife, William must call at the chippy for his evening meal, or go hungry.

Here at last comes the dependable domestic clamour from the top of the stairs. A solidarity you never could have imagined, it is a comfort to know she is here in the house with you, another living human soul.

If only you'd had the courage to go up there, interrupt the pan bashing, just talk to her. Despite what you said to William, you and she might have learned to put aside your self-identification as wives – fecund and barren, domesticated and impractical, landlady and tenant – and just be friends.

Women's lives so varied, with talents and duties so diverse, that there's no meaningful measure or test with which to compare ourselves: one against the other. You only know that she inhabits this house, her life, in a way that you, going ghost-like within it, do not.

To what end are the many hours you've spent in here? Every weekday morning William ventures out hopefully into the mysterious material world of work whereas you pass your days sequestered within the domestic sphere.

Even if it still makes me want to shake some sense into you, of course millions of couples lived so then. He went out and worked for money, the wife, meanwhile, found her daily satisfaction in keeping the cosy nest to which her happy husband homed each evening. Though, looking back, this married model of the '50s and '60s seems to me now no more than a mass nostalgia trip. Poor women had always worked outside the home, wealthier ones employed domestic servants, but for a society that still craved a return to stability after the war housework came to be considered not only normal, the proper expression of womanhood, but vitally necessary also to the wellbeing of family and community. Upon the bulwark of their orderliness, industry, decency rested the hope and expectation that the nation's housewives would turn back the clock to a better time that never was.

Unfeminine, unfeeling, perverse you of course had set about editing every imperative for wifely pride and purpose within the home, by chucking out the furniture. Contrary to every sort of married wisdom of the times, conspired with Mr Hubbard to make damn sure no surface remained upon which you may lay a rectifying hand. So that in passing vaguely from room to room you may not even dignify your wanderings by carrying a duster. Even if you wanted to, you may neither polish, whiten, cleanse or repair.

Liberation from the domestic treadmill might at the time have constituted a perverse kind of victory – get thee behind me "Milton", "Brasso", "Vim" and "Omo"! Certainly, it was your bitter pleasure to humiliate and degrade the holy sepulchres that came with the house. Swiftly, ruthlessly, thoughtlessly directing the rag and bone man, along with his idiot lad, to haul away on his 'orse 'n' cart every ornament or appurtenance orphaned by the passage of taste and time.

But if you enjoyed a sense of achievement in systematically working your way from the basement kitchen right up to the notional iron curtain on the stair, where your bloc found its limit at the McNamara gas stove, condemning as you went, this energetic break for freedom ultimately was an act of nullity and denial. Because symbolically freeing yourself from that unsought women's realm in which you found yourself stranded did not inspire you to grab hold of your own put aside life and get on with living it for yourself, Celia. In breaking the polishing pact, you have yourself ensured your only pursuit is self-absorption in an empty room.

And though you might have felt your spirits lift with every sentence handed down, thinking back about all the stuff you gladly sent off upon the tumbril for that journey of no return now causes you only guilt. Perhaps it bothers you on some subconscious level to consider that those passed over, voiceless relics, long confined in sunless rooms might epitomize a female heritage upon which you have consciously trampled. You might never have appropriated as your own the women's lives the furniture stood in for, but it makes you sad to now consider the concatenation of hours, days, months, the useless years spent dusting, wiping, polishing these things that ended up tossed unceremoniously onto the back of a totter's cart. Every piece of it knelt to by the generations of women that came before you: the female servants, wives, mothers, virgin daughters, maiden aunts and poor relations. But no matter the effort they sunk in, because of you, and your renunciation of all that, those lifetimes wasted in genuflection before the furniture will go un-memorialised. By not even so much as the lacquer someone spent her days in fussily rubbing off a Benares brass coal scuttle; the over-sharpened blade of a paring knife may they be remembered: the anonymous housekeepers.

Retaining most poignantly the frequent touch of women's hands, it is the kitchen equipment in particular that most makes you regret the ruthlessness with which you disposed of the lot of it. The sundry pots and pans and soup tureens, vast enough for turtles to swim in, the divers antiquated kitchen implements with handles to turn that set in intricate motion parts with which to cut or crush or crimp – the uses for which one could only guess at. (Making flowers from cucumbers, de-boning hares?)

To think: women's work, repeated day after day in identical form, decade to decade, century after century; getting nowhere, producing nothing memorable of themselves, nothing lasting, nothing new. No wonder it makes you sad.

# Chapter Thirty-seven

The kitchen TV tuned to Get Squiggling, mercifully with the sound turned down, I found it soothing to watch her, seated across from me at the table, taking so much care over sweeping into a neat pile today's breakfast toast crumbs. After another horrible morning spent in evading Mr C. and his belligerent brick hammer, apathy and gentle ineptitude were exactly what I needed. And in contrast to Cara's clinical kitchen, which, indeed, mimicked a brightly lit and immaculate operating theatre – complete with surgical grade knives – I was only too happy to fester here, in a comfortably soporific fug, where the usual muck and mechanics of family life were very much on show. Also unlike Cara, Deb never seemed to have other mums from the school gates and their kids round. Until her own children drove me away, or Greg – if not my own husband – got back from work, shameless in my need, I knew I could count on hanging out here, not saying much, for hours on end.

Waiting for the kettle to boil, I now observed Deb emptying the dishwasher and considered that the horrible truth about housework was, quite literally, it was never done. Round in circles it went, never completely achieved, because ultimately it remained unachievable to complete. No wonder women turned homicidal if someone went and wilfully walked over their freshly washed kitchen floor, slept between their laundered sheets, spent twenty minutes gobbling down something it took an hour to cook, and dirtied the bloody plates. Again.

Never having done much of it myself, being privy to housework these last few weeks – even if this self-elected housewife, fierce in the assertion of her right to respect, pottered to very little purpose – I thought I could now better appreciate the hidden rhythms and revisions in the life of a house during weekday daylight hours. Not that I was ever going to mistake as worthwhile a life measured out week in, week out, by washing and cooking and cleaning. For those of us who, like me, practically and personally had no time for ordinary housework, we found our reward instead in inventing other, more esoteric, ways to work in the home and garden beautiful.

Consider the satisfaction of the executive type getting sweaty in his holey jumper, chopping wood to feed the vastly expensive Harrie Leenders wood burner in the weekend cottage he could have, should have, paid the odd job bloke down the pub to do. The divine indulgence, the expense! of packing the larder shelves with your own hand-labelled jars and bottles of produce from garden and hedgerow.

And unlike the fugitive achievements of renewal and replenishment as witnessed round at Debby's, having its fixed end point and an achieved outcome, what I'd been getting up to most recently on the domestic front – so I believed – was worthy of the sort of public prestige you were never going to get for your lovely line of sheets blowing in the breeze. However privately satisfying that might be.

I did not consider the plunging of my hands into filthy water, the burning of them with Nitromors dull drudgery. Or as menial those painstaking hours I spent genuflecting to the ceiling, picking away at the mouldings with my sacramental scalpel. Quite the opposite, so I believed the sore wrist and chronic stiff neck I gave myself were worthy of respect: because by these wounds got by my hard labour, Bill and I might transcend the ordinary status of just living in a house to achieve 'lifestyle'. A transubstantiation I imagined that would thereafter make housework – the standard, repetitive stuff – into something more like the observance of sacred rite and ritual.

Everything made perfect, Bill and I would devote ourselves to the polishing of the granite worktops in the kitchen, to the fragrant beeswaxing of the 'good' furniture in the lounge. Both would beatifically minister, with shining evangelist eyes, to the enviable shrine of our own making. (All that investment, financial and personal, wouldn't you treat your house like a temple?)

Still, since living inside a house meant also sleeping on and under linen, wearing clothes, eating food (sometimes even cooking it), I'd be kidding myself if I believed I'd be the one to tackle the associated dirt, dust and mess day-to-day living generated. Fairly soon after we saw the back of the builders I assumed I'd be getting a cleaner in – meaning, a woman – to deal with the loo, the flip-top bin, the sticky kitchen floor and all the rest.

Then Debby went and ruined my private musing upon the status of work in the home, offering me a domestic treat.

Would you like to get the baby up from his nap?

Always a possibility but on balance, since I'd only just sat down, in fact: no, I wouldn't. But because she never objected to me dropping in on her to disturb that precious bit of quiet time she had to herself when, as she described it, she 'put him down', said: love to.


With the curtains closed it was surprisingly dark in the little top-floor bedroom under the dormer and, far from the steamy kitchen, so cold I thought a window had been left open.

Wary of startling him into wakeful paroxysms of rage and fear at being confronted with a face that was not his mother's looming at him out of the dark, tentatively, across creaking boards, I approached the kid's cot.

Silent in the icy gloom, that tough, watchful little boy was lying perfectly still and alert. Eyes open wide, he looked unflinchingly back up at me. Not for the first time I thought there was something not quite human about this baby.

Hello in there: it's only me, your auntie Abi.

Reaching down into the cot to pick up the unwieldy, unyielding little body I was met by the biscuity smell of unwashed blanket, the hint of wee. His little red hands were cold as ice, cheeks shiny with some slick bodily secretion that had dried on – tears, saliva, snot?

Overcoming my vague revulsion to holding him close, I descended the many stairs that would deliver him back into the arms of his mother as if I was carrying a weighty, if fragile, package full of shit. Judging by the pulpy warmth of his nappy, perhaps I was.

Back in the fuggy kitchen Debby held out arms hungry for the baby she'd been separated from an hour.

Hello, there, little man, she said, smoothing his frowsty bed head.

She kissed his slimed face and as if her touch turned him back into being a human baby he began to struggle and whine to be free of her. Arching his back, turning his face away from her greedy lips, with an imperious arm he indicated the screen alive with silent colour. Debby settled him on his beanbag in front of Cbeebies; turned up the volume.

Bik bik, the little tyro bid his mum, settling himself back magnificently.

(Aww, just like his dear old dad!)

Putting a biscuit into either hand, a backup on his knee, Debby said: there you go, Buggerlugs.

I was dismayed to see they were from the packet of lemon Duchy Originals I'd brought round.

Son settled, his mum had her phone out fast.

You're not going to Instagram that, are you, Deb?

She gave a little snort: you must be joking – I didn't even wipe his face! Believe me, you're never going to see a kid in an uncoordinated outfit, much less one with a snotty nose on one of those lovely mummy accounts. Twenty-four seven, from the moment of their birth, they're curating and narrating their perfect kids' perfect existence. I mean, *literally*, from birth: legs freshly waxed and spray tanned for the 'crowning' shot, right up til the selfie handover, can't afford to relax their very high standards for a single second.

Useful for obituaries, though, I commented.

Yeah, said Debby: in the future it'll be the mourners who see the dead person's whole life flashing before their eyes.

Exhausted by her outburst, she took her usual slumping place opposite me at the kitchen table.

I am the influencer of precisely one follower: my mum. Luckily for me she doesn't expect much. The last time I made her proud, the last time I was really good at something, I was probably fourteen, she said.

Fourteen, seriously? Good at what – puberty?

Hardly! I was a champion swimmer. Talk of the Olympics, no less. Like that was ever going to happen!

(With a jolt, I realised that somewhere, at the back of my head, I'd known this.)

Deb, where did you go to school?

Holland Park Comp. Why?

We were at school together!

Were we?

Yeah, I was the maths nerd in the year below; you were the girl who brought back all the cups. The inspirational one we were always having to clap in assembly.

Wow, she said: this is like falling into some kind of freaky time vortex.

Quite excited by the coincidence, I said: you know the first time we met, I mean met again, I thought you had these fantastic shoulders. You know: wide. Strong.

Shrugging them, Debby dumped more tea into my mug, saying: but then was then and now is now.

I thought how weird it was that in differently informing the past the present gave it additional meaning. Or vice versa. But most of all it made me sad that when Debby last tried to be brilliant at something she nearly succeeded.

# Chapter Thirty-eight

Chased out of their playground by official wreckers, the bomb site kids are put to shame by the scale and efficiency of the destruction currently taking place over the way. Their moment come, the hollow houses of the Victorian terrace quickly fell, not to UXBs but the simple yet massively more effective method of hauling down any still-standing brickwork using chains and a tractor. After which the council workmen went noisily to work in their new made brick quarry to excavate an even bigger hole for themselves. A hole that will before long be filled in again with pre-fabricated houses for homeless families to move into. However, in just the last couple of days the violent shifting of the scenery out there has already altered utterly the habitual view framed for you by the front window: something beautiful has emerged to improve the interval between destruction and renewal.

As if with the sweeping aside of a curtain, the trees and shrubs that must have been there all along, growing in the rear gardens of the bomb-damaged houses, are put on show. It won't be long before they'll be lost again, cut down or hidden behind the new buildings. Gone, but for remembrance.

Because this hastily erected emergency housing isn't designed to last, you think you'll very likely be living here still to witness the next hectic revision of the view, when the pre-fabs themselves will be replaced by something more permanent and likewise themselves soon forgotten.

As if looking over your own shoulder you gaze across at this secret strip of urban forest while in your mind's eye still see the bomb-damaged houses and, with a sensation of flying or falling, what's to come. Is it the past that haunts the present here or the present the past? To which category do you yourself belong?

Although they've stood in ruins for years the crashing facades have released the smell left behind after a firebombing. A cloud of masonry dust hangs over the now silent square like a pall of something burnt and dead.

# Chapter Thirty-nine

Decades of consultations (literally) during which they actually considered listing the slums over the way – fuck's sake! – followed by more delays over testing for the possible presence of blue asbestos in the structures, before Kate and her cronies on the council finally pulled their fingers out and sanctioned demolition.

I knew exactly what was going to fill in the hole they made sweeping away the pre-fabs because I'd already checked out the successful proposals down at the local library – before it was closed, to improve my service. After all the usual argy-bargying over the importance of the redevelopment being in architectural sympathy with its surroundings, final planning permission received was for a mixture of, as they styled it, *vernacular* private homes and some smaller, 'affordable' housing. (Set at eighty per cent of the local market rent, affordable to whom exactly, Kate?)

Presumably to indicate they were fun, as well as affordable, these economy models were to be decked out in fascia panels of bright yellow, with functionless porticos stuck on.

As for the more expensive executive homes, from what I could work out the *in sympathy* part of the brief meant that they would retain the window lines of the anyway hugely undistinguished Victorian villas spared by the wartime bomb, with retro bays added to likewise feebly ape those originals to either side.

What I wouldn't have given to hear our dour conservation officer Pope's views on what he might regard as sympathetic to a predominately Georgian neighbourhood. I suspected it wouldn't come close to what I was actually going to have to look at.

Watching from the window of this raised ground floor room, I witnessed the first of the precast concrete slab walls to come crashing down. Hurrah, nevertheless! Half hidden, off to one side, I could also keep a useful eye from here on the woman who regularly encouraged her chocolate lab pup to crap on the pavement (presumably 80% cocoa solids in this locale) before she set off with it for their morning run. Unaware she was observed, when it'd finished doing its 'business', as usual she exited without bothering to place the steaming pile in the decoy orange nappy sack she took care to carry, tucked into the waistband of her jogging bottoms.

There'd be ructions from the man beside whose gleaming motor the offence had been committed. The man who happened to be Greg. A couple of days ago he'd resorted to posting a bad tempered little note on our square's WhatsApp group: *To the person, or persons* (how very legal*) who persist in allowing their dog to fowl* (sic) *the footpath on the north side would you please pick up and dispose of properly as this practice is both unhygienic and offensive.*

Bloody gun dogs: leaving half-dead pheasants about the place. Still, it amused me that Ms Fit should be the offender – judging by the leer he gave her every time she jogged perkily past, with 'Juicy' emblazoned across her bum, Greg fancied her rotten.

A masculine roar startled me back to myself. Evidently, on leaving his home, Greg had put his foot firmly down onto the coil of puppy crap, getting it all over the shoe he was now attempting to scrape clean on the kerb. Leonard and Ryk had come out to see what all the fuss was about.

With the smell of shit in my nostrils, myself unseen, I watched the bastard hop.

# Chapter Forty

If you, as they say, burned water, Bill Bone was considered quite the genius of domestic economy on his staircase. His Cambridge parties were legend. Bachelor Bill in his pomp had gained the enviable reputation for being capable of whipping up something nutritious and delicious – not to mention alcoholic – from practically nothing at all. In fact, it was largely down to him being able to contrive a decent cocktail on a tight budget that, in possibly the last act of your own volition, you slept with him and, as a direct consequence of which, you were married. In truth: the free choice of neither.

It was sampling his own toddler nephew's NHS orange juice that your soon-to-be husband first made the intriguing discovery the metallic-tasting concentrate that in those days came free from the baby clinic in brown medicine bottles with a screw cap made a perfect mixer with gin. This "NHS Destroyer", as he titled it, lubricating the memorable party he threw to celebrate the award of his PhD, at which the two of you were introduced.

At this time you were seeing the pompous boy who dragged you along: the boy who had high hopes of high jinx later on.

Dr Bone – the host – spent a good twenty minutes engaged in earnest debate with this chap, a real medic, identifying efficacious mixers newly available on the state: the possible sedative benefits of combining alcohol with cough drops; whether the addition of iron tonic worked as an improver of cheap red wine. That sort of thing.

Never mind what best went with what, not having much to say for yourself back then at parties – no need to make the conversational running when you're that rarest of rare birds at a Cambridge knees-up: a pretty girl, up for fun – you just stood about smiling and drinking. Besides, it'd seemed deliciously decadent to be getting gently plastered while simultaneously giving a kiddie scurvy. This Bill Bone was an absolute hoot, as well as a bit of a dish – rather like Dirk Bogarde in "A Doctor in the House."

Perhaps Mrs McNamara had thought so too; a contributing factor in her misidentification of him as someone at his ease in a white coat?

Suffice to say, both being well-oiled as well as well-fortified by sunshine vitamins, William's bedder caught you out the next morning, practically still engaged in the act of sexual intercourse.

That kindly woman, however, promised not to report the crime. Another of this Bill Bone's unexpected talents, so you were learning, was that he was indulged as a useless brain box by anyone who worked for a living. Like "General Motors" giving to a charity for distressed carriage horses, a patronage that seemed only to confirm that the tousle-haired young man you just bunked with was harmless. Quite soon after, however, you were to discover the newly doctored Bill Bone wasn't quite as quaintly obsolescent as he might've first appeared: you were expecting.

When you found out for sure what was 'wrong' with you, after a little initial difficulty locating it, at last managing to retrace your steps back to Bill Bone's set with those tidings of joy, fortuitously, you were to discover him still in the act of packing up his old school trunk for home: the one with all the pokerwork initials burned on the front. Being ticklish about perceptions of privilege, while at Cambridge he'd lopped off all but the last and shortest surname for everyday use and similarly abbreviated his forename to a monosyllable. Explaining your confusion over the Bill Bone you met at the party and the 'W', followed by many other initials, the last two of them hyphenated, that appeared on this trunk and the board at the bottom of his stairs.

By his blank reaction to the news you were bloody-well preggers, at first you could only assume that W M R I de C-B, as you now knew him, might be having trouble placing you – after all, you had barely been introduced, formally – before you realised he was more likely watching life as he'd been pleased to imagine it circle the plug hole before it disappeared forever down the drain.

Which, as far as the glittering prize of his fellowship was concerned, soon after proved to be the case. In the event the bedder taking pity on her young gentleman and keeping her word and her tongue was neither here nor there because your disappointed young man, the actual doc, did not and so higher authorities were informed. And back then in the dark ages the authorities took a predictably dim view of unmarried dons *doing it* with undergrads, especially female ones.

Self-determination wiped out by that alcohol-fuelled liaison and subsequent pregnancy, you both understood there was little option but to reorganise plans for a future, which, for you at least was at best, vaguely plotted. As for William, perhaps he believed that taking on a wife might at least be akin to providing oneself with a good cook general. In which case he was in for another big disappointment.

Anyway, in that era in which shame still worked all too well as the mechanism for social correction, this was a pickle that might only be put right with honour by matrimony. So you pursued the only safe and decent – and legal – course available to the girl of the time who'd jumped the gun, and soon after in haste and disgrace took to the veil, and orange blossom.

# Chapter Forty-one

I can feel the masonry dust in my eyeballs. I mean, I knew it'd be hard, but it's like living in...

A building site? Debby commented, topping up my tea.

Not having properly considered in whose joint I was currently sitting, I said: yeah, well, next time, I swear, I'm going to buy somewhere immaculate, spend the next twenty years trashing it, then move.

If she noticed the irony, Debby didn't hold it against me. Glancing around her shambolic kitchen, she said: Greg's talking about moving again: like you say, somewhere that's already had all the work done.

Would that make much financial sense, what with bloody stamp duty and...

Interrupting me, she said simply: it'd break my heart.

Rather than comment, I took the last of the Prince's biscuits I'd brought with me – even if I was feeling queasy I was also ravenous.

Debby went on lullingly, mournfully to say: what he doesn't understand is that this house isn't just mine, it's *me*.

If I'd believed women only chose to stay *at home* with the kids over going 'out' to work if they were depressed single parents living on benefits or, like Cara, incredibly rich and effortlessly sociable, spending so much time with Deb I now understood they could also be held there by the complexity of their own desires and needs. Or were simply made housebound by their fear of 'out there'. For whatever reason, voluntary or imposed, generations of women have identified themselves with and inhabited their homes in a way that men have not. Not so much the 'angel in the house' as its resident ghost. Maybe why stories of hauntings nearly always feature an isolated female in a building with an animus she herself has somehow fomented.

A bit disturbed by this thought, trying to make a joke of it, I said: you mean I've been killing myself single-handedly bringing up the neighbourhood, only for Greg and you to jump ship?

Well, you're half right: for him this house's always been more investment than home. Just the place he happens to leave from and come back to after work, and when he's not around not a thought in his head that for me and the kids life carries on.

Having no imagination, I could see that as far as Greg knew those were the exact same crumbs on the table, cold tea in the pot, as this morning's but, to be fair, she probably had about as much interest or curiosity in his busy day, lived in that other mysterious world. And they probably were the same crumbs.

When he *is* here, I mean when he has to be, on the weekends, he's either striding about issuing orders or hunkered down for hours behind a closed door, watching sport, waiting till he can be wholly himself again and relax: back at the office. D'you know, Abi, at the last Christmas party turned out they didn't even know he was a father?

Smiling vaguely at her silent son, transfixed as usual by the jiggle box, Deb went on: my life's meaning is being their mother. If ever I fantasise about turning back time, having another go, after a certain point I know I'm just going to have to replicate everything I did in my life, every choice I made, just to be sure of having the same kids.

Through a mouthful of biscuit, I said: meaning you always have to have sex with Greg. Three times.

There's that, she laughed.

I reached for another biscuit, my fourth, and Debby gave me a significant look. Thinking she was making a point about snatching the food from out of the mouth of her child, I said: sorry, just been so hungry recently.

She rested a light hand on my sleeve, saying: always starts like that for me, worse luck, never a spot of throwing up – just hitting the carbs.

What are you talking about?

You: being pregnant.

I'm not, I said, calm as anything, just been rushing around all morning, doing things in the house – you know, sourcing door furniture – and I forgot to have lunch.

Because, as I suspected, she didn't want to look me full in my lying face Debby actually got off her chair and started picking toys up off the floor to 'hidy' them away in the crockery cupboard.

Course you're not. Sorry. There was just something a bit broody in the way you looked at Sonny-Jim just now, she said, indicating the buddha of the beanbag.

Broody, I didn't think so! If I'd ever doubted it, recalling the too-intimate feel of him, heavy in my arms, the smell as I held him close, of milk and urine mixed, I knew for certain there wasn't a single maternal bone in my body.

# Chapter Forty-two

Freshly laundered by three days in Frinton, the scion yet to embark on his consolation prize career at the Museum, there'd been just the one invitation to visit family Bone in their mausoleum. The married couple were invited *up* to dear old "Dishcloth" for the weekend. Or, a *Saturday till Monday*, because, *don't cha know*, that's how long a weekend dragged itself out in the country? It was only when the Daimler, unstabled specially to meet the young people at the station, turned into the carriage sweep and pulled up at the solidly baronial front door that you properly came to grips with quite how grand was the family to which you were hitched. Confounding the hideous prospect you'd been imagining of three straight days of womanly confabs with the new ma-in-law over the kitchen table and the mending basket. Quite evidently Ma Bone does not darn and you suspect the only occasion she has cause to enter a kitchen is when the rural dean invites himself unexpectedly to luncheon and she must urgently discuss ways of extending the joint with Cook.

Just so, Ma with the secateurs and trug, leading with the splendid authority of her early-century monobosom an assortment pack of dogs, Fa chasing up the rear with his stick, received the young marrieds in the rose garden. Being rich, Marjorie laboured manually, and only out of doors.

By then in their late fifties, (though he'd already had time to fit in his stroke), apart from the thin scribble of blue blood veins over cheeks that'll come from cosying up too close to the cavernous grate in one draughty barn of a room or another, both the in-laws' faces wore the same preserved and glassy look of those who don't hold with the showing of feeling.

Meticulously welcoming, unfailingly gracious and cold they conducted the prodigal and wife indoors, to a library in which was set out on a deeply polished Jacobean dresser the restorative tray of refreshments customarily provided after the rigours of the train journey. Wood and wool sandwiches, coffee kept tepid in a silver flask that lent to it the taste of tarnished metal, dust in the sherry drunk from un-rinsed eighteenth-century lead crystal glasses.

"Yum! Eatables and drinkables," declared the undernourished lad, home for the school hols, "may I?"

The dogs according to length of leg having either jumped up on the furniture or thrown themselves down to pant at their feet, everyone tucked in.

When the men left the ladies to look at a prodigious old pike the gamekeeper had finally landed in Big Cock Pond, on best manners, you must withstand the full, evaluating scrutiny of mother-in-law. Coolly weighing you up in your civvies, (it was that honeymoon suit again), plainly she continued to find her daughter-in-law below par. Never having felt yourself to be in greater danger of making a loud, uncalled-for noise in a quiet place, you said something about washing your hands. And, knowing you must get away fast before you gave way to hysterics, stepping over the prone bodies of dogs, fled the scene. Despite this tactical exit you succeeded in further embarrassing yourself by tugging at a likely looking door at the very same moment it was opened from the inside by Fa Bone. He mumbling something incomprehensible out of a lopsided mouth as you fell awkwardly in over the threshold.

Little more than a flimsy afterthought, an addendum to the immemorial architecture, this bodge-up of a cloakroom had a grudging and temporary feel to it: one wall mostly comprised a blinded window – its seventeenth-century carved stone frame camouflaged by flowery wallpaper – the other was no more than a bit of wobbly partitioning. Seated behind its sticking door, it was evident that palsied pa had undershot the bowl, leaving behind himself, cupped by curled linoleum, a little pool of his patrician piddle at the pedestal foot.

Despite first impressions of old money and long entitlement it had buoyed you a bit that this smelly, ancient, awkwardly engineered lavatory summed up your new husband's world to a tee. The impulse to comfort; convenience; advance in the home beautiful was not only considered an unnecessary expense but condemned as vulgar.

No wonder William wasn't in the least bothered living as you did.

After Church – *thank you, vicar, lovely service* – and before Sunday lunch – *no more of the mashed swede for me, no, absolutely, thanks!* – the newly marrieds took themselves off for a wander in the family woods. Ending up in a dripping copse within sight of the house.

"I'm sorry, Celia," was all he said.

"I thought you liked it? Absolutely nothing works."

"Long training in repression of self, I'm afraid."

Having been made to feel thoroughly second rate, and always rising to a challenge, particularly if it involved risk – and sex – you pushed him hard up against an ancestral oak with the tight drum of your belly and kissed him correctively on the mouth.

"Steady on there," the new husband laughed, though you could tell he was warming to the idea.

"Another example of long training in repression of self?"

"Somehow, one just doesn't imagine doing it in Devon."

Determined not to concede to his upbringing, or your own for that matter, you kept him pinned: "If it helps, imagine we're somewhere else. Monaco?"

Giving his crinkly smile, William pulled away and pinched you on the cheek.

Shortly after, because you were now a sensible married couple after all, and this was Devon, you went back indoors for some tea with dog hairs floating on it that caught in your throat and made you snort liquid through your nose.

# Chapter Forty-three

Spiky as she was, Dimphna's company would be a welcome alternative to shirking my job at the building site down at, ironies, The Daily Grind. The café round the corner where, in return for light and heat and power for my laptop, every morning I drank endless cups of their expensive coffee and justified my presence alongside the other *McFreelancers*, 'working from home' or writing their novel, by pretending to pick up tips 'n' hints on the Georgian drawing room from Houzz, The Georgian Group and SPAB websites.

Though Dimp'd sounded less than totally delighted to hear from me, she agreed we could make a day of it. Even proposing I join her for her regular Friday swim, down at the pool, thrashing the blokes.

Not for Miss Bean the municipal baths, no, she patronised the swish and trendy new gym that occupied what was once an art deco cinema. But never mind the piped music, fluffy towels and eager-to-please staff in their little terry towelling shorts, clipboards at forty-five degrees, Dimphna was only too delighted to point out how unremittingly wanky it all was. A pool wasn't a proper pool, apparently, without a plaster floating in it, or worse. Stubbornly she straddled the divide between her defiant Irish working-class origins and her adopted persona of well-groomed London professional. She might have been the first of us to make it down here – a deliberate one in the eye, I always thought, for Bill, against whom, at least in career terms, she measured herself – but I couldn't but suspect it was all this straddling that hurt her so.

Breaststroking side-by-side, relentlessly setting our own pace, up and down the middle lane we cruised. I observed the other swimmers recoil as grim-faced my friend bore down upon them, cleaving the water like a gargoyle figurehead. She might as well have been flying the Jolly Roger. God help the man who tried to muscle his way past.

Done with our swim, we adjourned to the well-provisioned showers that, at least for me, having not had access to one for months, were really what I was here for. The ordinary, extraordinary, luxury of washing one's hair under running warm water!

Before she herself stripped down and showered my skinny pal was careful to close the cubicle door. Hard to see the point of this modesty since her fatigued spandex had been quite revealing enough: loose-lipped around the tops of shrunken thighs, unforgiving over deflated breast bags. In delightful contrast, the woman across from me left her door wide open. Big and black and triumphant in her naked flesh, I admired her as she slapped the busy piece of appearing and disappearing soap over her magnificent person, all the while singing. So proud, so unconscious of her splendid, sexy fat I thought: here is that rare thing: a woman who hasn't learned to hate and distrust her body. Then I saw quite how vigorously, aggressively even, she worked that soap; noticed it was to *the Lord* she was singing and it struck me that perhaps she'd been taught to think her body not ugly, but dirty – an ungodly object, deserving of punishment and mortification by extreme cleansing.

Showered, dressed and coiffed, Dimphna and I relocated to the nearest wine bar to pass what remained of the morning. Quite obviously neither of us wanted to return home yet. Though in her case she most probably dreaded the emptiness she'd find there.

Bringing over our second round of drinks, the waitress, perhaps to suggest that apart from alcohol a wide range of foods was also available, put down between us a complementary bowl of mixed olives. Provocatively, I made a point of offering these first to my friend. Picking one up between disdainfully tweezing fingers, Dimp nibbled off the flesh, said: mmm, delicious, then carefully placed the stone on the table and took a needy sip from her new glass. Naturally she was drinking. Smoking and drinking were her cover in social situations – they gave her a pretext; projected an illusion of joining in with normal life. In full war paint, balancing a glass, juggling a cig, Dimphna Bean could appear to be consummately at home, in charge. Not far beneath the surface, however, I thought the little Irish immigrant scamp might be heard still, screaming: *Look all yus bastards, I made it. Hard as it was, and cruel, I made myself fekken fit in!*

But if I knew to hold off from interrogating her personal failings and frailties, Dimphna herself was not so delicate.

Observing me as I tucked greedily into the olives, she remarked: who's it rattled your cage?

Momentarily taken aback, I grimaced a smile. Did she really not get that I might've just spent the morning doing drill expressly so I wouldn't have to think about what or who was troubling me?

No one, I mean there's nothing wrong with me, I said, an open and serene smile still affixed to my lying face.

Seriously doll, since, stands to reason – because you don't have one – it's not your job gettin' you down, is everything ok between you and your feller?

For Christ's sake, what is it with you, Dimphna? My relationship with Bill is fine.

She gave me that look known as old-fashioned.

I mean it's brilliant, absolutely fucking splendid!

Dimphna said: sure so.

This, coming from someone who to my knowledge had never had a relationship that outlasted the month. In fact I couldn't remember the last time she'd a bloke on the go; might even have suspected she was gay, if I hadn't happened to know that Dimphna wouldn't have seen any reason to keep that quiet – not while there remained an Irish person left in the world yet to be offended. Might, indeed, have suspected she was gay for me, if it wasn't plain from the moment she met him that her habitual antipathy towards my husband was based on jealousy. Of him, not me.

I was actually nervous she might nick him off me when I'd first introduced my friend, scary Dimp – back then, a fierce thirteen stones of gorgeous white flesh contained in ripped fish nets and bondage tartan mini skirt, the lot topped off by a bleached blonde back comb *up ta here* – to the beautiful, moody, boy with the super sharp brains I fancied. Instead of which they instantly recognised each other as rivals: wily escapees from the same school of low expectations and hard knocks, and as such mutual objects of comparison and challenge.

Toning it down, I said: honestly, we're fine. Long marriages are like long journeys, ya know, Dimp: sometimes it's the rough patches along the way that keep the going interesting.

All I'm sayin' is, must it be his route?

Dimp, if you'd, just occasionally, give Bill the benefit of the doubt, you'd know he does not and never has expected me to behave like some Punjabi bride, walking two paces behind. So even if we are having a bit of a difficult time that's mostly because I hardly see him.

Dimphna flicked the olive stone off the table onto the floor. We both watched it roll, gathering an unappetising grey fur coat of dust as it went.

Not copin' well in the fancy new job, eh?

(Damn her, Dimp always was a whizz at processing small print.)

Chilled as I was able, I replied: it's just he seems to feel the necessity to work these insane hours. You know, doesn't like to be seen to be the first one out the door.

*Presenteeism*, she said: no one wants the reputation for being a 'half-day Johnny', so they all hang on forever in the office, psyching each other out.

The working late I get, sort of, what I can't stand is him showing the clients a good time after hours, like some kind of corporate boy-geisha.

Ah, well, that's commonly known as: *the run-up to Christmas*.

I hope it *is* only bloody Christmas because on the rare occasions I do get to see him he's barely there.

I'll never get my hid round, out of all of us, t'was you got the first...and now you're the office widow?

I make my own choices, Dimp, always have. And I'm happy with them. I amended this to: *very* happy with them.

Good woman, she said, plainly unconvinced. She went on: so, what is it you're after choosin' to do: project-manage listed building renovations, is it?

Well aware that I was stepping into her trap, I blazoned it out.

As you'll no doubt be interested to hear, I've an idea for a book: a historical novel about a child killer.

A book now?

I had to wince. Must my friends flag up, and with quite such insouciant economy, that this might be only the latest in my, admittedly, long catalogue of grand schemes?

It's actually pretty gripping stuff. Horrible, but gripping. Bill's right behind the idea; thinks it's a winner and, since you ask, it's going really incredibly well.

If I couldn't seem to shut the fuck up, this was because I knew, sooner or later, she'd find me out. She always did.

Dimphna raised a sceptical eyebrow; evidently, I was boring her now.

Listen, d'you mind, Abi, I could kill for a fag?

Aware I'd just been let off lightly, I shrugged my consent. I hadn't known Dimphna for going on a quarter of a century not to get that smoking for her wasn't so much filthy habit as life support – a dependency that meant the last time she went to New York for work, she didn't travel by BA with the rest of her colleagues but flew Turkish Air, coach, which still allowed it.

We settled ourselves with the other down-and-outs, sucking on their fags at pavement tables in the freezing cold, but the prickly silence between us persisted. Attempting to find a less problematic topic of conversation than my choice of life partner and serial record for taking up then dropping careers, I said: did I tell you I saw Cara the other day?

I swear, didn't we have the exact same conversation the last time we met up?

Yes, and doesn't that tell you something about yourself?

She cocked an eyebrow.

Weren't we three practically inseparable at university and now we never manage to be in the same room?

Ask after me, did she?

Well, no.

Despite the gale blowing, having managed to light up Dimp snatched in a mighty lungful of vanishing smoke as though it were the heady aroma of new mown hay. I witnessed her tightly wound body relax.

On the out breath she said: ta be brutally honest wid you, doll, it's not like we have much in common these days. Last time I *was* in the same room I tell you, I was about ready to walk over hot coals to get away from her wee man.

Fergie?

Him too.

I had to laugh.

Little does he know, but young master McDiarmuid is soon enough going to have to look to his laurels: she's expecting again.

Leavin' you an' me wid only our careers and alcohol to validate our existence? she said in that clipped, clenched way smokers have.

In my case, as you pointed out, that'll just be the alcohol, I said, and smiled, glad that she and I were safely back on terms of complicity again. We toasted each other: I with the two-thirds full glass I'd carried out here, she with her nearly empty one.

The tacit truce between us shakily in place, Dimp said: the two of us against the attack of the mummies, eh? Then, speaking with the emphasis of the nearly pissed, added: yeah, personally I follow the helpful advice printed on the dishwasher pod wrappers.

I had to think a minute.

Keep well away from children?

Got it.

As if somehow this turn in the conversation had suggested a useful new angle on me, and my problematic life, with myopic intensity she scrutinised me across the table.

Y'*are* lookin' peeky, tho'. Different, somehow. Even if it's not your man, there's somethin' up wid you.

Though, briefly, my guts seemed to fill with scalding water, I said: not been sleeping too well recently is all.

(Was there really something about the way I looked – something that Debby, and now Dimp, had picked up on? True enough I was feeling like death warmed up, but that *was* most likely stress, and I really hadn't been sleeping well.)

Luckily, she hit upon the supernatural worries I'd spilled the last time we met to interrogate, saying: worryin' about the haunted house?

Worrying about the huge mortgage extension we've just taken out on the haunted house more likely!

Very carefully Dimp rolled the crumbling end of her fag around the edge of the ashtray to make an even point of it.

Since I'd rather she didn't attempt another stab at exactly what was making me squirm in my seat, I said: I don't know about you, but I'm feeling a bit drunk – two large glasses on an empty stomach, you know – an' I'm starving after all that exercise. So 're we going to have something to eat here, or what?

We both watched as she neatened and neatened the end of her cigarette.

Bloody smoking ban, she managed at last.

Trying to keep my shivering under control, casting around for the waitress, I said: look's very like it's eating in public they'll be banning next.

Because I calculated the best way to shift us off the subject of me was to bring up her own failings, I added: should suit you, that.

Never mind the mild inebriation, Dimp was back at me, sharp as a tack: they'll not be banning eating in public straight away, you'll see: they'll have designated troughing areas first, stuck out the back somewhere, phase it out that way, gradual like. My kinda venue: plenty a alcohol, no food.

She gave a mocking laugh.

I couldn't stop myself doing a double take – in all her years of self-starvation this throwaway line was the closest I'd ever heard her come to acknowledging it was her that had the problem. And I wondered: was it harder for the anorexic to *just say no* to food when every second shop on the high street's pushing it at you or, if heroin's your habit, be constantly on the hunt for something society has actually criminalised? Forbid yourself, as if it were poison, a substance fundamental to life or be forbidden the ingestion of something that will, absolutely, cause you harm?

Whatever, both were choices that, if you carried on making them, would do for you in the end.

# Chapter Forty-four

Being too drunk on heat-treated orange juice and gin to properly take note, the details of your first time remain vague. I do, however, remember clearly the last time William and you were to make love, Celia. It was a Saturday afternoon in the summer of 1955. By which time you're truly enormous, with two milk bottle legs and ten chipolata fingers. Heavy and uncomfortable, you are also restless, full of ticklish, unspent energy that seems to seethe under the skin, race in the blood.

Seeing that you're incapable of settling to anything, ever considerate, William rescues you from yourself: taking you out to The Empire, where "The Ladykillers" is playing. Being a matinée, it's still quite light and warm outside when you leave the cinema. Both lifted by the silliness of the film, you dawdle home, hand in sausage-fingered hand, down abandoned afternoon streets that smell of sun-baked dust, both whistling the minuet the thieves put on the gramophone whenever they pretend to be practising. On this same sunny afternoon, probably for the first time since you married, you feel your age: nineteen. And trust that youth alone, and its inherent need to be happy, to find joy in life, will mean everything shall work out fine for the doc and you.

But what awaits you back home, just as it did the very first time you opened the door on it, will soon enough put the dampeners back on that idea.

It was springtime when you moved in here and you'd been so relieved that – just in time before the baby came – you and William had found somewhere of your own to live. You brought nothing with you from the Balham digs, having nothing but a double bed to bring. Good and solid, made of wood, it was all you had in the world to start off married life together and, at the time, you'd believed, enough. Purchased from "Heals", delivered to the house before you took possession, as it transpired it was a good job you'd had only this. The day you took the cab all the way from South London and William staggered with his large wife over the threshold, it was to discover that the previous owners of the house for some unaccountable reason had left behind them every piece of furniture, every furbelow. Long uninterrupted accretion of at least a couple of generations of tight tidy wives and proud providing husbands, the place was packed to the gunnels and most of it old-fashioned, broken, or just plain hideous.

Thinking back, I realise it must have been the last in the line of housewives who lived here – I have in mind the watching wartime woman – who resolved she'd be the one to break free of the lot of it. Her house sold on – to you – no longer trapped by her trappings, clearing out, without having first cleared out, she just skipped lightly out from under and away. One couldn't very well blame her for that even if, as the next wife in line, she bequeathed you the dead hand of duty she escaped.

Sure enough, back from the flicks, that accumulated pressure of expectation and legacy is there to greet you. Smothered by the smell of dusty textiles and old polish, once more this place closes in over your head. Perhaps thinking his wife's sudden depression of spirits means she's fagged from the cinema outing, William suggests you take the weight off your feet. Certainly lightheaded, you kick off too-tight shoes and strip down to your petticoat to rest.

All these years later, I still regret that petticoat: green silk, trimmed with coffee-coloured lace, by then stretched tight as a drum. It was my prettiest item of clothing, and I'd saved up weeks to buy it for myself.

Since you have no intention of lying on the filthy old chaise that commands the spot before the front window in that nice petticoat, you trot obediently upstairs to the bed. Will joins you there and, grotesquely swollen as you are, curled up behind, this will be the last time William makes love to you.

Still spooning, his drowsing breath in your ear, sweaty where you touch, you get up needing a pee. On exiting the lavatory, rather than rejoin William on the bed, you carry on down the stairs to where light from the open living room door has spilt itself across the hall floor. Inside the room you find the evening sun has been busy spinning light into gold. The better to look out at an enchanted world you kneel up on the chaise, its old leather warmed by the sun, for once not unpleasant to the touch. And from within the embrasure of the window behold the wonder of marigolds. Set ablaze, the flowers have generously clothed in beauty the rucked-up rubble of the bombed-out houses. You wonder whether it was when they lost their windows to high explosives and could no longer see to disapprove that the first escapees crept from one neat, confining flower bed, eventually to run riot all across the whole bomb site. Like sap rising, again you feel that irrepressible urge to be young, happy and free. Green as this young marriage of yours is, at this moment you believe that William and you may succeed in pushing down roots between the tight-packed lives of the others who've been here before and in turn anchor yourselves in this old house.

You two would come through all right and be beautiful.

Kneeling there, the last of bright glory playing outside, you nod your head to ripple the seam in the window over the flowers. It's like shaking out, again and again, a cloth of gold.

Behind you, in the body of the room, you fancifully imagine that if the declining sun is orientated just right the fault in the glass will have projected itself on the far wall in a delicate wash of watery marigold light. But when you turn to look the sun has sunk too low in the sky to reach so deep. The jostling furniture is already lost in dingy shadows – it's gone back to being ugly in here, and chill. Shivering, you're overtaken by a particular revulsion for the nasty old chaise longue, its horsehair stuffing, like sad random pubes poking through the cracks in its black hide. Massive as it is, from the very day it was brought here on the back of a cart, sometime at the turn of the century, to be manhandled up the four front steps by strong blokes in hessian aprons, you imagine it's always lurked on this same spot. The dead possession of the dead, for you this monstrous piece of furniture epitomises the unwanted inheritance that came with the house. Putting your back into it, you attempt to heave the nasty belligerent thing out of the way of the window and the marigolds.

How bloody ironic, ironically bloody that, if not jumping from heights, or self-boiling and gin, an activity hackneyed as moving heavy furniture, on this occasion really did bring the thing off. Ironic, too, that because you are, as they describe it in the books, *displaying nesting behaviour*, trying to make the place your own, that you give it that vindictive push. And feel something 'go' inside. Nothing much: little as a suspender pinging free.

An hour later, after he's ran out to ring the doctor from the box on the high street, then for an ambulance, William must cut the saturated petticoat off you, wrap you in the eiderdown quilt and carry his bleeding bride back over the threshold.

# Chapter Forty-five

Lying awake next to my exhausted and smelly husband, victim of one too many *Treasure Chests*, the £100 a pop cocktail they served at Mahiki, I listened to him snore.

Is there anything quite so isolating, so provocatively self-satisfied sounding, just *so* fucking unfair, as your drunken husband snoring when, because he's sleeping, you can't?

The luminous green face of the alarm clock blinked 5:15.

Just another forty-five minutes and he'd be up and out again. Poor sod. Though, obviously, at this moment I hated him. Blamed him too – not just that by keeping me waiting up last night gave idle hands and furious brain work to do in my little upstairs cell, totting up dates, but also for providing the gamete that the congruence of those dates seemingly confirmed had merged with mine to make the zygote I was now incubating.

*

It was probably eight hours ago, around about the time I gave up expecting Bill home at a civilised hour, I let my signature pumpkin with crispy sage risotto burn onto the bottom of the pan, opened a bottle and thought about proving Deb and Dimp wrong.

Probably seven hours, and half a bottle down, since I realised the answers I was looking for might just lie in my big, project manager's book. The era of the lockable schoolgirl diary being long gone, the only dates I noted these days were the delivery of building materials or the arrival or departure of trades, so by linking something more *concrete* with it I thought I might perhaps work out not only the manifestly unmemorable event of last having sex with my husband but also, crucially, the date of my last period.

Haddaway! there it was: the red letter day on which I not only had the painters, but the plasterers in.

The very day they started work on the living room walls, and I nicked one of their bucket trowels to dig the hole for the baby's shoe, I'd scribbled a marginal reminder to myself in green biro: *tea bags, sugar, Tampax.*

A couple of weeks later the practicalities of the house restoration and my hidden hormonal history intersected again. My dashed off calculation for the costs of reproduction windows to replace the ones Mr Casey informed me were shot had, as I remembered, been the cause of the argument between Bill and me on the night of Debby's dinner party. The night of the storm, the blackout and the 'haunting', when having a bit of a fright in the middle of the night proved to be the all-natural alternative to Greg's stash of Viagra.

Five hours ago and, as Tess might say to Claudia: the scores now in, I looked up a web site sufficiently scientific to neutralise the unavoidable prognosis that when the adrenaline and the male and female sterol levels were running high that night, the luteinizing hormone was surging also, causing the release of an oocyte into the uterine tube, prior to fertilisation. In other words: a perfect storm of timing, opportunity, and negligence – too cold and drunk and horny to get out of bed to find my cap.

Even under the cover of a biology lesson, even trimming here and there, I couldn't make the relevant dates add up to any less than three weeks late. According to the NHS website I then consulted (the accepted house style here being cosily collegiate, an unsettling experience for the accidentally expectant) this meant I might already be seven weeks gone.

And so it was about three hours ago that the zygote became 'your baby'.

Against all the odds: my advanced age, together with the fact that in the last two months we'd probably only done it that once (which, by my calculation, put the chances of my conceiving in the region of immaculate), I was pregnant.

Me, who'd never knowingly felt broody.

If I hadn't felt so 'sick' about it, or simply – as I now realised – properly sick, I might even have had a grim, drunken, chuckle to myself. Back in my TV days a colleague and I had been having lunch at a street-side table when, on eying up a passing crocodile of nursery school tinies, dressed up in their tiny gingham smocks, she announced she'd come over all broody. Her Serbian boyfriend, the new one she didn't want to scare off, asked her what that word meant and, quick as a flash, she came up with: *Broody*, Andrej? it means a strong and independent woman.

The clock blinked 5:45, Bill snored.

In the countdown to now, this minute, it was only a couple of hours since, at about three in the morning, with the elaborate caution of the very drunk, he'd crept up the stairs to our bedsitting room. Finding me awake, agitated, and more than a little mortal myself, my husband had unfortunately misconstrued as further evidence I was incapable of going to sleep sober and alone in the house. We then circled again through the tired old exchange about my unfittedness to function as a rational adult.

It hadn't seemed the perfect moment to announce I was pregnant, probably. Dammit.

Sliding off the side of the futon, I slipped into my slippers and my dressing gown. Because the kettle was in this room and I didn't want to risk waking Bill with its clamorous boil, together with a mug into which I'd plonked a tea bag and some milk, I carried it down to the living room to plug in there.

Shivering, waiting for the kettle to boil, for the hundredth time I vacillated between thinking that at only thirty-nine this was a fucking disaster that before I'd had the chance of doing anything significant with it would ruin my life and, at nearly forty, this might well be my one and only shot at it.

I decided to drink my tea and think this through somewhere in the house Bill would never come looking for me – if I hadn't been able to tell him in the heat of last night's drunken acrimony I really couldn't bear to face him now under the sober light of morning. Bypassing our bedroom door, his even, unconcerned breathing going regular as oars through water behind it, I climbed with my brew to the very top of the house.

Opening the door on the little room under the mansard, my heart leapt into my throat. Just as it was the very first time we viewed the house, this abandoned room appeared in the half-light to be filled to the gunnels with furniture. But what propelled my panic into the thin cold air as a stifled scream was that amongst the other bulky forms, exactly where the cot would've stood at Debby's, something in the shadows squatted and grinned.

I only screamed the once, and it was more of a yelping gasp than the full-on banshee wail that might still have brought Bill running. Eyes now accustomed to winter's early morning gloom, I saw the leering homunculus was only the builders' Henry and what I'd mistaken for old furniture the paper-hanger's table, various ladders and planks, sacks of plaster and bundles of copper piping. I took a breath. Other than tripping in the dark over the trailing nose hose of the orange vacuum cleaner, there was no danger lurking up here in wait for me. All was perfectly mundane, explicable and solid enough.

I collapsed heavily on to an old chaise pushed up against the wall under the window, releasing little puffs of dust from its horsehair interior through rips in the upholstery that tainted my tea with must and mildew.

How was it possible that in all the months I'd lived here I'd never before noticed this substantial piece of furniture? It took up half the floor. Then it hit me that the most unsettling thing up here was not the changeling vacuum cleaner but the seat I was sitting on. Like the nervous girl who suddenly understands the hand she's been holding for reassurance in the haunted house, in the dark, cannot possibly be her boyfriend's, because it's his panicked voice calling to her from downstairs to *get out now!* I galloped back to our bed, back to Bill, as though I had devils on my tail. Heart still pounding, I calmed myself to the sound of my husband's indifferent snores.

His breath might stink of cigarette smoke and alcohol after another evening's schmoozing, he might be unconscious and incapable, but he was warm and real and he was most definitely breathing.

# Chapter Forty-six

After the procedure: *to clean you out down there*, they have the good sense to keep you well clear of the maternity ward, wheeling you instead into a long room of post-operative old ladies. This barrack being ruled over by a monstrous matron, whose obsession it is to put on the best possible parade for the daily inspections of her consultant commander-in-chief. Whenever his ward round is imminent the old dears are ordered to lie to attention, arms at their sides over the top of the bedclothes, and if asked a question reply only in the brisk affirmative.

Each morning, bed pans duly filled and emptied, the most junior of the staff measures, with a ruler, not only the width of the turn down on the top sheet but the precise distance between each bed, straightening and shifting accordingly.

Another of Matron's foibles is that whenever a bed is vacated, as they regularly are, the occupants of all the others must be rotated. As elderly lady after elderly lady is either discharged back home or, more likely, sent to her eternal home, so the next in line is promoted. Little by little advancing on her last resting place: the bed nearest the ward door. Aware the inevitable has come as pronounced by Major Gen. Matron, she mostly accepted her time was up and before too long meekly departed this mortal coil. But occasionally the next quivering Miss Gee to be bed-hopped a little closer to The Exit, and her ultimate destiny, although unresisting, starts up a lament. But resistance is futile, as all of you inmates know, for if one's ultimate fate is in The Almighty's hands Florence with her lamp has the casting vote round here. And Matron's convenience is not to be brooked.

In the bare fortnight you're to spend there, along with its blunt methods and common sense philosophy concerning the dead and the quick, this ward comes to represent the whole world to you.

Even within the camps, so I believe, people accepted that all life was encompassed within the monstrous workings of the regime, finding if not comfort in it, then a perverse sort of normality to hold on to.

When they thought you sufficiently recovered, Mr Blade (how appropriate), the consultant surgeon, scandalises the female boss by sitting on your nicely straightened coverlet. Patting your arm, he tells you that you are a sensible girl, that you'll soon come to terms with the knowledge it is unlikely now, impossible actually, to have children of your own. Nevertheless, you should be thankful that you're young and healthy and have your whole life ahead of you. On consulting his notes: seeing you've been to Cambridge, have probably read some books, he adjusts his spectacles and assures you that apart from being sensible you are a clever girl and so have a wealth of other choices. As he speaks all you can hold in your head is that you mustn't move your hand because Matron has expressly bidden you to place it over a worn patch in the coverlet – as if he'd have noticed or cared. Anyway, whatever he says, because you've been promoted to the bed nearest the door, you already know that one way or another you'll be making it out of here.

Just so, next day you are discharged.

When William comes to wheel you away, the little honeymoon case balanced on your knees, you make him turn the chair to take one last look back down the surgical ward for women. Although tempted, you think better of calling out to those who most likely aren't, like you, going to make it over the wire, the cheery, encouraging lie: "When all this is over, I'll meet you in Piccadilly for that pint!"

Home to Islington, where once again William hefts you up the steps and over the threshold. Only this time he must manoeuvre you around the new obstacle that in your absence has sprung up in the hall.

Settled in your nuptial, now sick bed, not having a clue what to do or say, he starts bringing you the endless cups of tea you weep into; the taste of salt in every one. It is in this bed that, for the first time, you'll hear the cry of Mrs McNamara's baby, born while you were away in the hospital, having your own emptied out. And it will be upon this same island that William will find you marooned each evening, just as he left you: still in pyjamas, the tears running unchecked down your face.

When William dares to share it with you, your five months husband will handle you in it as if you're mortally injured or in great pain. You aren't, but perhaps because he feels himself to blame, he has learned to be frightened of causing you further harm. And sealed up again, cauterised, by the physical assault of the miscarriage, you yourself are something of the nervous, re-made virgin.

Two young people who have not done 'it' – at least not wholly consciously – as anything other than expectant parents, and rarely as a married couple, being *in the family way* evidently was so intrinsic to you as husband and wife that now there is no baby you are doubtful and self-conscious with each other in this big marital bed as any maiden sweethearts who've never once sat down together un-chaperoned in the same room.

Never having properly practised how to talk to each other as people might who've had the luxury of getting to know each other first, mindful of what's unexpressed, now inexpressible, rather than confront your problems within what could have, should have been the intimate refuge of mutual comfort and consolation, night after night, dutifully you give each other a kiss of consolation that's like an apology and turn your backs for sleep.

Yet to become the rack upon which you torment yourselves, and each other, your shared bed is solely the childish resort of shut-eye and dreams.

One might say it was those two too solid pieces of furniture: the baleful implication of a chaste marriage bed; the intransigence of that inimical old chaise, that between them killed off tender first growth before it had its chance to properly take hold.

# Chapter Forty-seven

Gone ten in the morning – Bill had sloped off back to work, the Casey clan were once more merrily engaged in shaking the house to its non-existent foundations, and I'm getting on for a whole twelve hours further up the duff. Seven weeks, plus a day.

I need only to open up my laptop to find out what that meant: a millimetre of nail growth, the beginnings of eyelids, four chambers already fused into a beating heart, perhaps?

Wanting distraction, I went upstairs instead, to check out the mysterious appearing chaise. Maybe, somehow, it'd been put up in the small loft space by previous owners of the house, in which case the builders would have found it when they were checking on the leaking roof and moved it down into this top floor room to be stored with the rest of the stuff not currently in use.

Solid, filthy and black as the old armchair we discovered in the living room this ugly stepsister in its greasy pelt of worn and ripped leather, if not authentically evil by daylight, similarly made my skin crawl. I gave it a trial shove – it must have weighed a ton – and retreated. To encounter Casey himself on the landing. Feeling I'd been caught snooping in my own house, blushing, I said: just checking out progress up here.

And set myself up for another interesting talk on the extreme sketchiness of Georgian house construction. Did I know, f'instance, even when they started off building with a double brick depth at street level by these upper storeys the exterior walls were down to just the single? Funnily enough, even the party walls up here shared just the one brick. In his estimation, the additional half-brick of the back-to-back chimneybreasts of this house and next-door's was all that was providing lateral restraint. As I imagined it: two drunks, arms round shoulders, each relying on the other to stay upright. Laughing off my alarm, Casey assured me that what made this place so terrifyingly fragile and kept it standing was all down, once again, to the handmade building materials. The moveable timber-stud lath and lime plaster partition walls, the light fibrous plasterwork ceilings, most probably the bloody pammets. Anyway, in Mr Casey's expert opinion, any more rigidly braced and a building precariously poised as this one couldn't 've withstood a high wind. Make that a gust, he said, restricting himself to a chuckle.

Not wishing to dwell on the seemingly dire implications of all this, I blurted: I was going to ask you; the old leather chaise in there – could a couple of the lads tip it for me?

Giving me that look known as old-fashioned, he repeated: *leather chaise?* as though I'd made the thing up but, sure enough, later that day, when I dragged the rubbish bin out onto the pavement ready for collection, there it was: upended in the skip.

Putting out her own wheelie bin, Debby spotted me and came over.

Are you really throwing that out? You know it's old, don't you? Probably Victorian.

Could be Louis-fucking-Quinze for all I care.

Not like you, she said, leaning into the skip, the better to check the chaise out.

You could restore it.

It's yours, Deb, do what you like with it. Personally, I think the thing's hideous.

I made to retreat.

Not so fast you, you've been avoiding me and there's something we need to talk about, isn't there?

At this very moment Ms Fit put in an appearance with her own bin. Seeing that she'd probably engineered this 'chance' meeting of the neighbours, thinking on my feet, I pushed Debby back through my front door, slamming it shut behind us.

I haven't been avoiding you, I lied, and, somehow, from this she was able to deduce what I myself had only been considering seriously these last few hours.

I knew it! I can always tell. How many weeks along are you?

We *should* talk…

I was cut off by the sound of enthusiastic drilling coming from the basement.

But not here.

It wasn't just the impossibility of finding somewhere quiet in the house, still a little spooked by my experience with the nasty chaise, I was actually a bit afraid of giving voice to my news. Frightened, as they say, to 'go public', because it was my irrational notion that within this house something malignant might be stirred back to life if that information were spoken out loud.

She said: at mine?

The kids round here had already broken up for Christmas – the streets and tube were full of them – so I wasn't expecting her own house to be an oasis of silence and calm. But it appeared that her three had just been packed off to the monster-in-laws for the first few days of the holidays.

Seated on her collapsing sofa, she said: when did you find out?

Too earnest, I replied: three o'clock this morning.

When you did the pregnancy test?

Bright and breezy, though I wasn't feeling it, I said: haven't exactly done one yet, but the dates don't lie. So now I've just got to decide what to do.

Do?

You know: keep it, or not.

I might have been more sensitive to the fact that displayed on the mantle shelf were the tasteful black and white framed photos of her family: Deb, Greg, Kitty and Teddy prone on a fur rug. A three-quarters headshot of Kitty posed with hand supporting chin for extra winsomeness. Teddy, very sombre, holding his Sylvanian dog. The baby, as a newborn, tricked up, for some reason, in a pea pod outfit, his little round face the single pea emerging from the unzipped end.

Commendably neutral and un-judgemental, Deb said, obviously, that's got to be totally up to you and Bill to decide.

I haven't told Bill.

Now she looked shocked. I could almost see her processing the information that I hadn't thought to tell my husband about this pregnancy I'd already seriously considered terminating.

I know it's your body, and all that. But I *do* think you should involve Bill in this as soon as possible. It *is* his... I mean it's his decision too.

She laid a light, cool hand on my arm that felt like a brand.

Maybe I should confirm it first – you know, do a test. Perhaps there is no decision to be made.

We looked at each other in mute recognition of this fiction.

Then she said: do the test and talk to your husband.

# Chapter Forty-eight

The fierce old bird you occasionally see about the place, regularly drunk, often shouting, sometimes singing, passes by outside. An eminent Victorian – remember them? – packed into smelly black bombazine, she's hobbling fast in too-tight boots. Off out who knew where, carrying who knew what in that Gladstone bag she holds in a strong and mannish fist. Something sinister, you think. And maybe it's because the woman resembles the only abortionist you have yet to encounter – being you, in a book – it pops into your head exactly what is the urgent business she's going equipped for.

It was in Colette's short novel, "Gibriche" that you first read about old mère Gibriche. Expert, anxious, but not over-considerate, she performed the little procedure on her own daughter, Biche, or fittingly Doe. The day after, the big, chapped maternal hands must go again and again beneath the quilt to feel for the sudden gush of haemorrhaging blood. The delicate, trembling, large-eyed creature died under those brutal hands upon the blood-soaked mattress of her narrow bed, below a barred window.

As the disreputable toper disappears down the street, you speculate that if one had a pregnancy you wanted quietly rid of, it probably was now, just as it always has been, a badly kept secret who was the 'old wife' you sent for hereabouts to avail yourself of such timely interventions. You imagine that Mrs McNamara's friend: the one who was nearly 'done for', was attended by someone exactly like this old neighbour woman in her mourning black. Driven to it by shame or fear she'd been willing to risk even her own death or mutilation rather than the unthinkable: being left saddled with a baby she didn't want or couldn't keep.

*You never guess*, she'd said.

Watching the nasty old woman go, you think: why must it be guesswork?

In those far off, ignorant days, from the very first minute of being born girls, with bodies adapted specifically to the job, poor or rich – Queen Victoria had nine – most were subject to the tyranny of fertility. Trapped by the very trap set to catch your man, hoist with that same petard, pregnancy was the payoff to which malign nature had destined the female sex.

The only way to keep reliably safe from such little catastrophes, as far as you knew, was to live life as a nun, or a lesbian. Though these alternatives weren't for you, Celia. Even at the age of fifteen and the first visit from 'Auntie Flo' – further back than that: having agreed, enthusiastically, with Freddie Pierson that it might be more fun to play at doctors in the dark than take healthful outdoor exercise involving only tennis balls – you were primed. The incendiary set to go off, the accident waiting to happen.

It hadn't helped that in matters of the world, inevitably, literature was your only guide. Right up until your first lesson in sex as it was actually practised, most of what you knew, or believed you knew, concerning the carnal was gleaned from reading "Forever Amber" under the bed covers.

Mind you, seventy references to the sexual act itself, however coy, thirty-nine illegitimate pregnancies, seven abortions, and ten scenes of women undressing in front of men – you counted them – gave one a useful inkling of what was to come. Or so you trusted.

In your defence, it wasn't just the type of reference work Mother dismissed as 'servant girls" or just 'low' but a deeply sensitive appreciation of the finest works of English literature that encouraged you down the primrose path to inevitable ruination, gathering rosebuds. Persuaded you to take on trust that there was indeed not world enough, or time, to resist a fanciable chap.

Put simply, you were ever the sucker for the propaganda of male love poets. Though it wasn't only the boys who were to blame. When you probably should have stuck to Austen and good sense you read far too much of the Brontes. But in your girlish imagination safe consummation in marriage to that firm hand on the tiller man Mr Darcy just didn't compare to heartbreak with Heathcliffe.

Of course, as it turned out, all your guides were coy when it came to consequences – rather than those of Mr Marvell or rodgering Rochester, you'd actually have been better off appreciating the works of Marie Stopes.

Surprisingly, there was a girl at school, in the sixth, who – *quelle scandale!* – beat you to it; getting herself in trouble 'that way'. When she failed to turn up for the summer term it was let known that Angela had gone to a clinic in Switzerland for a 'little operation'. The English Literature 'A' Level class she did not rejoin was informed it was to have her appendix removed. Even those uninformed girls of the day weren't so easily fooled. Agog with horror: she was killing her baby (and how had a baby got there in the first place?), Angela's cautionary example had been quite enough to keep them (obviously, not you) on the straight and narrow. And, contrarily, rather than bleeding to death and pointing a moral, the prodigal herself returned later that month, sans 'appendix', practically fluent in French, sporting a lovely tan and adept at cracking an egg with one hand. To put the tin hat on it, she wasn't expected to sit her exams but proceeded straight to London to partake of the 'season' and snag for herself a suitable husband. Which she duly did.

The lesson you unwisely chose to draw from all this: *swine husks delicious, cancel fatted calf!*

Since the rewards of sin looked quite rewarding, hardly a huge surprise then that you too were 'caught out'.

You might have told yourself that if you'd only known how high the stakes you'd never have got into the game in the first place or, at least, not played your hand with quite so much devil-may-care, but with the cold, empty gambler's mood common to adolescents knew in your secret heart it was the risk wherein lay the thrill.

Besides, your hand had anyway turned out not quite the busted flush.

Although, to be sure, it might have been better – or more conventionally – timed, your life wasn't so much 'ruined' as inconvenienced. So rosily, indeed, had things turned out that you might just as well have set the whole thing up as a bluff, Mr Bond – the gamble had paid off: you were laughing. To all intents and purposes that old-as-the-hills feminine wile of the *surprise* pregnancy had worked to scoop the jackpot of a good man with prospects. And even supposing your aberrant female anatomy had performed its important primary function by having the baby, what need you ever know of nappies? First off, there'd have been nursemaids and nannies a-plenty to deal with all the associated beastliness of babies, and then a good school, far away, would've finished the job satisfactorily. Just like William's parents, apart from by calendar appointment, you'd rarely have had to encounter the kid. All the more leisure time for you!

As for the indelicate issue of 'too many' thereafter, people like you generally kept a better muzzle on fertility with cap or condom.

Or separate bedrooms might be deployed to put the stork off the scent. If you were properly posh, once the heir was secured: separate wings.

Not that William and you had need of any of the above precautions, the stork having flown the nest, never to return.

# Chapter Forty-nine

So, I'd taken the test and it'd turned out positive. Debby was right: I really must talk to my husband.

I didn't.

As if personally tasked with tallying them up for some great adjudicator in the sky, like every woman I knew, I was my own ready reckoner of my partner's faults and minor infractions. Even if we didn't shout, much, day to day, over the years we had learned to conduct the kind of argument without words that kept the resentment fizzing nicely. He always leaves the oil and vinegar out on the counter, you perpetually put them back in the cupboard, where they belong. And, surely, he might've learned by the age of thirty-nine how to completely set or clear a table. Or what a laundry basket is. So it goes on. But intimacy breeding hostility, such low-grade daily conflict is no more than the normal collateral of choosing to organise society into mated pairs that, thanks to advances in health and hygiene, nowadays may survive to cohabit for multiple decades.

Years and years of living together, eating together, sleeping together. All those conversations about what kind of loo rolls to buy, how his whistling along, every time, to the University Challenge theme music drives me up the wall, yet I couldn't bring myself to mention in passing that I was pregnant. Something so huge it seemed to block out daylight and at the same time tiny. At seven weeks and some days an embryo – not yet defined as a foetus – was the size of a blueberry. Apparently. But as another day passed, mentally I ticked it off, wondered what, fruit-size-wise, came next – and still I put off speaking to Bill. I did, however, supply his side of things, which was to blame and reproach. Useless, I knew, to blame and reproach him back but somehow getting all self-righteous (even if only in my head) helped overcome my own guilt for this reproductive fail. Because, he was right: an accidental pregnancy was exactly the kind of un-thought-through mess-up my family would make.

Illogically, insanely, it was actually easier to think my husband was pig-headed than admit to myself that I was afraid that by telling him about this impending fucking disaster I'd find the limits to our compatibility. Far as I was concerned, we'd mutually agreed on the terms of a partnership that did not include children – but did I really know that? Would Bill want a child; did he believe abortion was a crime, a sin?

Stalled in time, I made no arrangements, cancelled no plans, and still the days carried on regardless, counting down. My brain bruised by sadness and sleeplessness, I let them pass by in gentle, fuzzy-headed displacement activities. Whether watching magical property makeover shows or flicking through *Get-a-Life* mags, didn't much matter, just so long as I blocked that image, like out of a Ribena ad, of merrily dancing blueberries, all in a row. But even as I cycled between old editions of Homes Under The Hammer and riffling through pages bursting with the *comédie humaine* (or, as these publications apostrophise it: *Life! Death! Prizes!*), I knew, of course, I had to act. Sticking my head in the sand might work, to a point, with the house, but I understood this other matter wasn't just going to resolve itself.

Pretty damn quick I was either going to have to face up to what was really happening and keep it or, since I didn't like babies, or children, for its sake as much as my own, get on and terminate. Either way, it wasn't going to be a decision I could reach without talking to someone. The state I was in, this patently wasn't going to be Bill, not yet, which left the only other person in the world, apart from me, who knew.

Running round next door without my coat, I waited for ages, shivering on her doorstep, before I heard Deb on the other side of the door putting the chain on. She cracked it just wide enough to show a slice of her face, gaunt in the dimly lit hallway behind her. She'd been crying.

Sorry, not interested, never buy on the door, she said, closing it on me.

Although I couldn't see her, aware she was still standing there, like an idiot I waited on the doorstep for a few minutes, before calling self-consciously through the letterbox: come on, Deb, it's freezing out here.

Opening up, silently she led me into her front living room. Even though it was early afternoon, still light, the curtains were closed in here and there was a nasty, musty, sweet whiff of wine left standing in glasses.

Shifting some Sunday papers and other crud off the sofa so we could sit side by side, I said: what's up?

Nothing.

Up close I could smell the fresh alcohol on her breath.

Debby, is there anything I can do?

Explain about men to me.

Following on from the defeated, *nothing*, she said this with considerable venom and, as though pricked to action, began to lift up, then put down again, the many bottles standing in a semi-circle around her spot on the sofa. Finding one half-full, she sloshed red wine into a couple of the used glasses on the coffee table.

To men! she said, lifting her glass in an ironic kind of toast.

On automatic, I raised my own.

Sounding almost larky now: can't live with 'em, can't kill 'em and still hope to get away with it on a technicality.

Has Greg been cheating on you?

*Explain about men*, I was assuming, was about more than leaving the loo seat up.

Debora looked stagily askance at me.

Don't cha' already know all about it? Thought everyone did – it's been round the block like bloody wildfire – an' the funniest thing is: none of 'em's that surprised!

That cow with the chocolate lab? I blurted out, following up, equally ill advisedly: it's not Kate, is it?

Aware she was losing it, speaking very deliberately, she said: 's someone from the office. Been going on for months. Apparently.

Oh. I'm sorry...

She's twenty-four.

Having passed rapidly between catatonic, manic and, now, maudlin, Debby exhaled shakily, took a gulp from her wine glass and repeated lugubriously to the ceiling: twenty-fucking-four.

Rather than put my foot back in it, I decided to just let her take this wherever it was going. I was rather glad I did because, suddenly switching back to ferocious mode, she stormed: but she understands him, so that's all right then! 'Course she fucking *understands* him, why wouldn't she? Aren't the two of 'em united against the same enemy: the no-status, middle-aged house nag? I mean she's actually young enough to still hate her own mother but he, of course, even if the bastard's forty-fucking-four, 's only *too* delighted to go along with the idea that...

Taking another huge swig of wine, she carried on right where she left off.

...I'm the boring *adult* who's stopping them from just being, you know, young an' free and in lurve! You should see him – he's so full of the fucking joys of life he's started dressing like a teenager!

Tears welling, she swallowed juicily.

Not going to look so good in those jeans with the crotch cut out, is he? Wanker!

The wine glass she was waving about for emphasis back-spattered in sanguineous arcs all across the Sunday supplements.

I said: why don't I make you some black coffee and....

*I* don't understand! I fucking well understand the fucker's grown up enough to be responsible for three children of his own.

Debby glanced around her sitting room as though she expected to spot them amongst the clutter.

Bastard roped in his own mum so he could be sure they'd be away from the house when he announced he was leaving us.

She downed her wine.

Weird thing was, after I cried and we had a shouting match and he cried, d'you know what we did next?

Hoping she wouldn't tell me they had sex, I said nothing.

Bloody drove to the big Sainsbury's and spent a fucking fortune.

She was silent for a moment in contemplation.

Then he left. Odd, isn't it, the last thing you do together is stock up on supplies. Just him, me and the kids, like paranoid preppers hunkered down for the duration with all these multipack toiletries and food and booze – she gestured at the bottles massed around the sofa – which, as you see, has really helped me process the experience. Probably just cathartic for him, you know: like having a really satisfying shit. Eats, shits and leaves, she said, laughing bleakly.

\*

Over the next hour or so I managed to prise the empty wine glass from her hand, put the empties in the recycling and make a half-hearted attempt at degrunging the sitting room. Deb slept through it all.

It was dark outside, had been for ages. I turned on a few lamps and, checking my watch, realised my hour was imminent. Rather than face the West End, kind Mr John Lewis was sending Christmas – all of it – to my doorstep this year, and I needed to accept delivery. Shaking her awake, when I told her I really had to go, she looked blearily back up at me from her corner of the sofa.

Soon as I was out the door I suspected she'd be opening another bottle and hunkering down for the night in her crackly newspaper nest.

Trying to sound upbeat as well as conciliatory, I said: you know where I am if you need me, yes?

I'll be fine, she said, giving me back a watery smile.

You're sure?

Jus' one thing, Abi: what was it brought you round here today without putting on your coat?

Just the usual: a moan and a cup of tea.

D'you know what all this 's taught me?

For added emphasis she reached up from the sofa to grab my hand. Imagining this would be something more along the lines of: *all men are bastards*, what she actually said knocked me sideways.

The truth about kids, about sacrificing your own life to them, at the end of the day it's not worth it. They're not worth it.

As she spoke I noticed her eyes were fixed on the staged portraits of family harmony displayed on the mantelpiece.

I mean, what am I; what's the point of me? By the time you realise you've boxed yourself into that corner of being their mum it's too late, your confidence to be anything else, gone. So what's left of the person you once were, who you wanted to be? Nothing. All used up. The last time I amounted to anything I was at school, right? Tragic, eh?

Come on, you're more than that!

Because I couldn't for the life of me come up with anything more specific. Quite anxious to get away, I said: give me a ring, send an email, a text, a tweet, an emoji, just bang on the wall, and I'll be back in a flash.

I will. I mean; it's good to know you're there.

Right-o!

Quite apart from making my delivery timeslot, I urgently needed to get back to my own cold and deserted home the better to think this through.

# Chapter Fifty

Mrs McNamara has gone out to get her radio's acid accumulators topped up ready for their Christmas listening. The one and only time she's ever to entrust Larry to the lackadaisical care of the landlady. Easy enough for you to keep an occasional eye on the baby since his mother has parked him in his pram for his morning airing in the front garden, although today, rather than stand sentinel, you have chosen to sit in the deck chair and read. Hearing heavy footsteps passing along the passageway you assume that she's back already from the shops, laden down. Sure enough, when you glance out, the pram is empty. Surprised she didn't look in to relieve you of your watch you set off to the basement to make a pot of tea for you both. Hearing the kitchen water gushing into the stone butler's sink, expecting to find her already down there, you call, "Hello, you're back early, I was just going to..."

Larry is laid out on the kitchen table as someone, not his mother, bends over him removing his clothing.

You give a little scream: it's the ugly old toper in her old-fashioned black bombazine. Unfazed, she looks up from the baby she's still turning expertly around and about on a sheet of newspaper, as if she were preparing a joint for the oven, demands, "What you doin' in my 'ouse?"

"This is *my* house."

"No it ain't, lovey, and you knows it." The now naked Larry is making compulsive frog-like movements in the chill air, holding him down under the firm palm of one large hand she makes a fist with the other to threatening.

"Nah, clear orf out of if!"

Frightened as you are, you stand your ground, eyes on poor whimpering Larry, and in as commanding a voice as you can muster, you say, "Take your hands off that baby immediately!"

Amazingly, the woman steps back from the kitchen table.

"Oh, it's you is it?" she grudges, her tone now wheedling. "I 'ad a feelin' you'd want 'im back, stupid little cunt."

Seeing as the woman's quite mad, "I do," you say, "so you can just hand him over right now and we'll say no more about it."

Nasty again, she sneers, "You'll live to regret it, lovey – look at you, you won't manage. Believe me, 'e'll be better off like this. Less suffering for 'im, an' you, in the end."

In the same instant as you make a grab for Larry, with one swift, terrible, movement, none too gently the old woman sweeps him off the table, straight into the overflowing sink behind her. He's only submerged a second before, throwing yourself across the room to reach him, you plunge both arms up to the armpits into the freezing water to retrieve the baby. After a stuttering pause he begins to yell at the top of his lungs. Her coarse, reddened hands hanging at her sides, the woman is not in the least cowed.

"Suit yerself, deary, but if you're expecting that money back, you can think again 'cause that's all long spent. It don't come cheap the raising of the dear li'le mites."

Taking care to put some distance between yourself and the mad woman, not making any sudden moves, you say, "All I want is the baby back. Nothing more."

"Well, then, you got what you fuckin' come fer, dincha?"

The trembling, screaming, freezing baby held close, the water running off him, you hurry up the basement steps, along the hall, out of the front door, slap bang into his mother who's toiling up the garden path with the radio battery.

"Where you think you're going with Larry? An' why's he wet frough?"

Mrs McNamara abandons her battery to take the rigid baby into her own arms. As she soothes and cossets you garble something about an old hag in a long dress in the basement. On hearing this, without another word, she sets off at a rapid trot up the front steps.

Wet through and shivering fit to bust, you call after her distractedly, "I wouldn't go back in there, she's dangerous, evil, mad!"

"Nah, she wouldn't 'arm a fly."

You following just behind, she hurries Larry back through the front door, left ajar in your panic to get him away to safety, back along the passageway, back down the few steps that lead straight to the basement and the waiting child killer.

Empty, but for an old Gladstone bag left standing on the pile of newspapers on the table: mouth open wide; ready to receive.

"Didn't even stop long enough for 'er cup of tea," remarks Mrs McNamara, turning off the still-gushing taps.

"You know her?"

"Me nana. My grandmother."

Grabbing the rough kitchen towel, she lays Larry down on the table and, concentrated wholly on the wailing baby, competent as the old woman, turns him round and about while vigorously rubbing some warmth and colour back into him.

"Mum usually manages ter keep 'er indoors but she's a terrible one for wanderin'. Pass us anovver tale will ya?"

Expertly, deftly she uses the dry towel to swaddle him. Parcelled up tight the baby's roars cease. Looking into the pinched played out face, she says, "Dotes on Larry, she does."

"You're sure it was your nana?"

"Oh, it'll be 'er all right, Missus Bone. Seeing 'im in 'is pram, she couldn't 've 'elped 'erself. Couldn't resist pickin' 'im up for a little cuddle, an' findin' 'erself outside an open door she'll 'ave been in like Flynn."

"But she dumped him into freezing water."

"Working with wet fish all 'er life she's a thing about water tanks."

"And newspapers?"

"Yeah, that's the fish again. An' 'er bein' mute, like, she couldn't 've told you who she was."

"Mute?"

"Not a word out ov 'er since she took 'er funny turn ten years past, poor dear." Again she looks down into his little urchin's face. Wrapped up tight like a pea in a just popped pod, it's the only bit of him still visible.

"Anyhow, no 'arm done – apart from Larry's maybe caught 'is death, goin' out in the street soaked frough like that, and not a stitch on 'im."

Since the kid's mother seems to have transferred most of her maternal angst upon his rescuer, you let the matter drop. Best not to mention that you know the front door was shut tight and that this particular loopy old woman definitely had the faculty of speech.

Back in your own quarters you strip off your sopping clothes. Along with your cardigan, blouse, vest and brassiere what you do not remove is the sense of him, the intimacy of his weight in your arms, the feel of his live body against your own. Moving, breathing, crying. Even though you didn't find him in any way cute or appealing, weirdly, holding Larry close, you experienced such a fierce impulse to defend and protect you wonder whether this is what mother love is like. Loving so hard, made so vulnerable to their needs, what might a mother not give or do to keep her baby safe from any hurt or harm or pain?

To give him the best of her, to do right by not only him but the unborn one too, even the phantom 'too many' thereafter, it comes to you that the threat posed by the neighbourhood abortionist you seem somehow to have summoned or dredged up from your sub-conscious, wasn't to Larry but his mother. That this spectre was sent to you as a warning that your little upstairs neighbour, driven to it by love, was even now preparing to sacrifice herself to this last resort that terrified her. The immemorial solution to an unwanted pregnancy, conducted down a back street where hypocrisy conventionally took up residence; the necessary trade that, unwilling to break the habit of its bad old ways, society had made sure would carry on generating the wicked midwifes, the black guardian angels to do its dirty work.

Not being a chorus girl from the Paris of the *Belle Epoque*, having been brought up to be quite ordinary in half-timbered Hertfordshire, when you found yourself facing the same dilemma as Mrs McNamara, you might reasonably have suspected that a teller of tales of the rackety Parisian demi-monde really shouldn't be relied upon as a guide to life. Unwanted pregnancy being an everyday disaster that must on occasion befall even nice, well-spoken, middle-class girls, like you, should have had the wit to work out there probably was a solution, if still illegal, for the irresponsibly knocked up that fell between the expensive round trip up a mountain in Switzerland, and a dirty woman in a corset and black bombazine, poking about up there with a curtain ring shoved up a rubber tube.

A disgraced doctor, perhaps, willing to break the law for not too much cash and no questions asked or, for preference, a socially-minded, kind, crusading one? With a talent for staying out of plain sight. But if you absolutely knew for a certainty while it remained a felony, there was no *nice clean 'ospital* of Mrs McNamara's fantasy you're determined to somehow save her from the next-door Ma Gibriches.

Who's to know if you had not learned the lesson that abortion kills at Colette's knee and thought twice before running back up those college stairs in a blind panic you might have saved yourself.

# Chapter Fifty-one

If I hadn't had the conversation I was expecting to have when I popped round next door, without even putting on my coat, for her to have said, unprompted and out loud that kids weren't worth it, seemed, somehow, Delphic. Of all people, Debby had broken the mother's love conspiracy that claimed they were the best thing in your life. But her baffled resentment at what motherhood had both taken from and forced upon her was plain enough.

Whatever Greg might believe about the chafing bonds of parental responsibility with which she was so careful to fetter him, rather than imprisoning her husband, it had made Debby the warder of her own jail. However she might argue it – that home, family life, was her place of refuge – her fear of an open door made that clear. Debby – the Debby who'd once told me children were the meaning of her life – had helped to make my mind up. So, I wouldn't be waiting up tonight to have that overdue conversation with Bill because first thing in the morning I'd be booking myself in at the doctors. Fuck him and his opinion – whatever that might be – my body, my life, my choice.

Decision made, I took a sleeping pill. And soon as my head hit the pillow, dropped so swiftly into sleep I was like a stone falling into deep black water.

My dreams this night led me on a hallucinatory wander around my old childhood home. As is the way with dreams, each room I called in at on my way to the very top was nothing like and yet, still, I knew in my bones this was 'home'. I'd got all the way up to the eaves, to Nico's bedroom, and was looking down upon that scruffy shared garden when, startling back to the reality of rough boards beneath bare feet, I understood I'd gone for an actual wander in that other repository of dread, my current home.

Standing there, in this little attic room in Islington, its filthy eyes upon another scruffy square, my own blurred by tears, I said what must pass as a little prayer for Nicholas. Poor, beautiful, lost Nico, you didn't deserve that your lasting memorial might be to qualify our childhood home for a black plaque.

*

When my brother and I were growing up there in the late '70s, early '80s, it was all very low-key, very commune-y, *mi casa e su casa* on 'the square'. These still being the hangover years of the permissive society our parents and their friends weren't big on locks or such bourgeois nonsense as personal space. Or heavy parental responsibility, guidance, safeguarding. Semi-posh, semi-feral, under-parented and over-inquisitive, my brother and I went freely in and out at back doors. From the time I could toddle I was intimately acquainted with the interior of every house that backed onto the half-acre of communal garden. Could have told you where each and every family kept their peanut butter jar, their comics stash, and who had a Nintendo Entertainment System. And seeing that we were more likely to be fed – and at a sensible hour – in any of those other houses Nico and I were proper little regulars at every teatime table. When we clamoured, vaguely, the grown-ups chucked extra fish fingers in our direction and, sometimes, after Doctor Who, even bathed us – all together in the same tub, with a dash of Matey from the doll-shaped bottle. If they seemingly didn't distinguish us from their own this was possibly because Nico and I were most likely dressed in familiar items from the hand-me-downs that made their way on and off the backs of every child on the square. Or maybe they were just being kind.

One warm summer Nico and I got into the nightly habit of exploring together the airless, inward-looking world of the night gardens after dark. I must have been a peculiarly unimaginative child because when we made our way down through our own empty house and out of the kitchen door, I didn't wonder where mum and dad might have got to. Bare blind feet going over grass, trying to avoid the dog shit, we two small voyeurs in our pyjamas were attracted like moths to the lighted rear windows of the houses. Even though, as I say, we had perfect liberty to come and go as we pleased, we crept up close to look in on the lives of our near neighbours. I don't remember we ever caught out the families being anything other than normal, but perhaps that was the point. We'd just stand there, hand in hand, on the outside, in the dark: watching a mum slice a loaf, a dad read the paper.

Growing up like we did, Nico might have rebelled – swapped all the arty-fartyness of home, like me, for a sharp suit and haircut. Might have reckoned that working regular hours in the dependable job that earns the solid money with which you bought all the stuff you wanted was worth the hassle. But he hadn't.

The first time they hauled him back, elegantly wasted after a couple of months of living in a Deptford squat, soon as he'd eaten, had a shower, my brother reapplied the kohl around his eyes, pinched a bottle of wine, some cash, and disappeared back out there. He was sixteen. When their lad turned eighteen, nineteen, twenty, Stef and Adam, the parents, maintained the pretence they were cool. Told all their friends Nicholas still had plenty of time to get his act together, get himself off to art school. (It was their secret plan to wangle him a place on the foundation course at Central St Martins.) They simply could not seem to get it into their liberal heads that the only freedom Nico ever wanted they couldn't give him and the only thing he needed to express was a fascination with futility, and opiates his chosen medium.

I, meanwhile, studied facts and planned to get far, far away.

Nico turned twenty-one, twenty-two. Occasionally he'd still turn up with face and hands sunburnt from sleeping rough, itchy with the dermatitis brought on by body lice. Or perhaps this was just another side effect of heroin?

It was like helplessly watching a drowning man coming up for air only to sink back under, each time for a little longer, down a little deeper.

Years of this, then nothing. No mugging raids on the family finances; no calls from police stations; no sightings of beggars with maybe his hair, his limping walk.

I was well embarked on my sensible career, married to Bill with a mortgage and a good future ahead of us when, looking terrible, smelling worse, Nico pitched up on the parental doorstep. The phone call came: he's alive! I dropped everything, rushing down south to be there. A bath, new clothes and a sunny Sunday lunch: all of us round the kitchen table for once, crying; laughing; eating. Talking. The Priory was even discussed. I booked a week off work, and the following day he was gone again.

The next time Nicholas appeared out of the blue for however long it would take to shake them down, I ignored the call. Soon after Stef discovered my brother curled up on his childhood bed, in his old attic bedroom, dead. With his thumb in his mouth, she told me, the needle still in his groin.

Her and Adam's lives really imploded then. They swiftly separated after the inquest (verdict: dependence on drugs – who'd have guessed?). They'd been married nearly forty years so you'd have thought they were set for a whole life tariff but I guess in the end it was only Nico keeping them together. And since they no longer needed to maintain that familiar address for him to home to, sold the house for multiple millions. Not long after, Dad, Adam, jumped off Archway Bridge, landing in front of a Range Rover travelling along the southbound carriageway of Archway Road. The last time I saw Stef, before she took off to heal the world, Nico by proxy I suppose, she was living in a little over-stuffed Victorian railway worker's cottage in Battersea. She told me that day having Nicholas and me was the best thing she ever did with her life, her only true happiness and fulfilment. I hadn't believed her.

# Chapter Fifty-two

As he makes his slow approach up the steps to the front door, framed as you are by the window, it's impossible for you to ignore Penfold, or he you. There is no alternative but to acknowledge the lad's cheery salute – two fingers ludicrously raised to his beret – and open up.

*Enter Bluebottle, waits for applause. Not a sausage.*

He might insist he was just passing when he spotted you but it's plain that Reginald is burdened today by something greater even than that preposterous mac of his.

You offer tea, the lad following behind you all the way down to the kitchen to 'help' make it. Positioning himself at your elbow to watch you do the necessary he then trails you back upstairs, creepily close behind.

You requisition the packing case so that he must take the sad deck chair – it gives you some pleasure to notice his discomfort feeling the touch of his behind through its canvas upon his heels. A couple of sips of tea, and Penfold's big moment has arrived:

"I hope you won't think I'm presuming, Missus Bone but since Mother and I are quite close neighbours, it seemed only right that we should offer."

He eases the collar of his Macintosh that, like some sort of dingy tart-killer, he's kept buttoned to the chin.

You try to look interested.

"It was she herself, actually: the Matriarch," Reg pauses to chuckle at the witticism, "charged me with asking if there's anything she can do, anything at all, to help you?"

"Very nice of her to consider me, Reginald, however I don't know that I need any help, as such. But, please *do* thank her for the kind thought." Reggie lets squeak another puff of steam from under his too-tight collar:

"We just thought: with Doctor Bone not being around for much longer…"

"What do you mean, where's William going?"

Though, clearly, his intention was to cause consternation Reggie has the courtesy to blush a brighter red.

"Crumbs, have I just gone and let the cat out of the bag?"

"I don't know, have you?"

"Here's the thing: I happened to overhear that Doctor Bone, Bill, William, recently received his call-up papers for National Service…I say, I *do* feel awfully bad, being the bearer of bad tidings. I just assumed by now you'd know all about it."

Surer of his footing by the moment, he gives you no opportunity to respond to this news.

"To be honest, since he didn't put in his time before he went 'up', I was rather surprised to hear he got away with it as long as he has. I mean I just assumed he was a *Conchie* or C3."

*C3*, indeed: the cheeky little rat bag!

Thinking on your feet, having no idea whether this was true or not, you say, very sensibly, "My husband deferred his National Service to complete his first degree, then his doctorate."

"Of course. Naturally. That'll be it." And seeing as this was all going so swimmingly, Reggie confides in a glad rush: "Can't say I'd fancy it myself; a squaddie at his age! I can tell you, it can be a rather bloody experience: thrown in, willy nilly, with the other ranks...and some of those World War Two 'erks' that 're still knocking about can rather lay on the old *brasso, blanko and bull!*"

He's quite ecstatic at the thought of twenty-five-year-old William finding himself the 'old man' in barracks.

"I take it you hated your time as a Serviceman, Reginald?"

This sets him, quite literally, back on his heels. Hasn't the daft bint gathered from his easy grasp of the lingo, National Serviceman Penfold was thick with the lads?

"Well, I don't know about that. You might say my time in the Kate – I mean, Carney: *the army* – was what made a man of me." You do well to suppress your incredulity. Not quite understanding the purpose of his visit: the opportunity to gloat over William's misfortune, or your own ignorance of it? Not being much interested to find out, you stand, saying, "Thank you for your concern, Reg, I'm sure Bill will be delighted to have any advice you can share with him about dealing with the other ranks."

"Of course, anything at all for old Bill..."

Following his hostess's lead, as, being nicely brought up, you know he will, Reggie scrambles to his feet. Not an easy thing to do: get yourself up out of a deck chair while holding a half-drunk cup of tea.

Even as you make your move towards the door, it's painfully apparent quite how desperate the lad is to be let to stay on. The better to advance his cause as replacement prop and stay to the abandoned bride perhaps?

"As I say, it was *you* the Matriarch and I were more concerned about..." he says, extending more of that sleazy sympathy. "If there's anything the old lady and I can do, any service we can offer – as neighbours – whilst Bill's away from your side getting his knees brown in service of the Empire. Anything at all...?"

"Well, there is something I need urgent help with."

He gives his hungry dog look.

"Since, as you say, she's lived around here for centuries, and most probably what, or who, she doesn't know just isn't worth knowing..."

Reggie leans his face in closer, smiling.

"...perhaps you could ask your mother, the Matriarch, if she could let me have the address of a really sound, local abortionist?"

It probably isn't worth it, but this silly response does the trick of shifting Pvt. Penfold out of there *pronto quicko*.

*

If you think this evening's *What, what, what?* lacks conviction, William's follow on remark is flat out dejected.

"I had a bit of bad news today, dear."

You save him the agony, saying, brightly, "Your call-up? I already know all about it – that little twit Reggie Penfold was round here earlier, very eager to spill the beans." William does well not to betray his surprise that the cat is already truly out of the bag.

"The top and the bottom of it is, Celia, I've found the extent of the influence of my useful cousin in the Ministry: I'm to report to Islington Town Hall in the first week of the New Year. Then off to some camp somewhere for basic training, then probably overseas: Cyprus, Germany, Kenya, maybe Malaya..."

As it happened, poor William, it'd been Suez. But all that was still to come.

"Leaving me here to cope alone?"

"Shall you mind very much, Celia?" Because you are still stone-cold furious with him for having kept you in the dark, you don't hold back, saying, bright and cold, "Oh, I don't know, living on a Serviceman's wage while you're off getting shot at up the jungle might be just the impetus I need to stop moping about indoors all day and get myself a proper paying job. I mean the Queen's shilling isn't going to cover the mortgage on this place, is it?"

Given your vindictiveness, it's with admirable composure he replies, "Rather than getting a job, what I suggest is that you to go back to the University." He even manages a joke: "I mean, my being away bashing quads for two years is the perfect opportunity for you to finish your degree without distraction. It'd really be a crime not to make the most of that brain of yours."

"Till the hogben test, never flunked an exam."

Not picking up on this sour little jest, he continues, "As a graduate you'll be in a far superior position to find for yourself some sort of employment you might enjoy."

You have a brief glimpse of yourself: a happy girl in a quiet bookshop.

"But, William, if I'm at Cambridge and you off square bashing – I think you'll find's the expression – and being called *an 'orrible little man* by someone who left school for the army at fourteen, there'll still be the mortgage to pay..."

Rather quickly, he interjects: "We could sublet."

"Sublet?"

"Temporarily at least, we could let it to Betty. I happen to know she's having some trouble with the lease of that place of hers in Bloomsbury. Added to which, the poor old thing's been thrown over by her boyfriend: Bob the lothario."

"I see. My goodness, if you only got your call-up papers today, you really have been thinking hard and fast!"

Discomforted, he holds his tongue. Your own brain meanwhile is going like the clappers.

"But what'll become of the McNamaras?"

Hardly surprisingly, William is a little taken aback that the tenants should feature so near the top of your list of concerns:

"I suppose they can stay on. I don't imagine Betty will be needing the whole house to herself." He smiles: "Who's to know, having the labouring classes to hand, she might find them an interesting study."

"Don't poke fun at them, William, please." Giving a curt nod of compliance, he turns his back on you, so that you know what he is about to say is very hard for him to express directly. Maintaining the same measured and reasonable tone as always, not meeting your eye, he says:

"Actually, Celia, dear, my being property of Her Majesty's military forces might provide a pretty welcome opportunity for us to take stock. I think you'll agree you haven't had much self-determination in all this up till now. What with your mother putting the screws on. Mine too, truth be told. But given the.... unfortunate change in circumstances, this might be the moment to rethink our own situation. I don't mean to suggest that the baby, the notional baby as it turns out, was the only thing keeping us together, but since it no longer.... pertains, it seems only fair that for once it should be left up to you to decide."

"Decide what?"

For a 'clever girl' Celia, you're pretty dense.

"If you want a divorce, Celia, I'll give you one."

Preferring still to evade the particular notice of centre stage, even as he says this William crosses to the back room, putting more distance between you.

"You know I'm fond of you, Celia, dear. Always will be," he says, albeit to the fireplace. "What you've been through...it's only that, now you're no longer under any particular pressure to stay married to me, I feel the future should be left in your hands entirely." Perhaps thinking your continued silence suggests noncompliance, ever the gentleman, he continues to insist you take the prerogative, saying, "Please understand I mean to put you under absolutely no pressure either way. If you'd prefer, we can leave off deciding anything till I'm finished with the army, or the army's finished with me." He chuckles uneasily. "But, as I say, in the meantime I strongly recommend you complete your degree."

Because you can't seem to come up with anything sensible to say, you say nothing.

"If you're worried about securing a grant, my parents are only too happy to help out on the financial front."

So they too have already been consulted.

After a little pause you say, "I know I can be a bitch, but it wasn't just my fault things didn't work out for us, was it?" It is now that William says the most honest thing he ever will say to you in that room. You are grateful to him for it then. I am now:

"If you're a bitch, it's the way our being together has made me treat you that made you one. You deserve someone better, Celia. I mean that. "

With this last display of decency, as always keeping it friendly, William expedites the process of being free of you.

And you of him, of course.

# Chapter Fifty-three

At under eight weeks the procedure was still a simple, practically consequence-free (apart from the obvious) case of taking two rounds of pills at the surgery, with a couple of days in between. Apparently, you could expect a little discomfort but nothing too bad. Bit worse than period pains according to the literature but no one need be the wiser.

Simple. Efficient. Sorted.

What I had yet to organise was where I was going to spend the time between the two appointments. It needed to be somewhere comfortable and warm, with a sympathetic person on hand to help out with the practicalities. Obviously not home, not Bill. And plain enough, the state she was in, I couldn't ask my friend next door. Cara, too, being happily pregnant herself, clearly didn't fit the bill. Who was left that I could depend upon to be discreet, functioning and non-judgemental?

Even if she'd turned into something of a frenemy, and it was going to be very, very hard to stomach her *I knew it!* still she was someone I'd known all my adult life, could drive a car, and kept a warm house. A very warm house. And she wouldn't be in the least tempted to tell Bill.

*

I sat on her hard sofa and attempted to make out her expression in the gloom. Apart from too hot, Dimp's house was always sepulchral.

Just as I expected, she was solid.

So what's the deal?

Very concise and sensible myself, I set the thing out: drive me home from the surgery, put me up for the rest of the day. I won't expect you to fuss over me, nothing like that, just stay with me while....

You don't stop in the hospital?

She sounded flabbergasted.

No hospital, Dimp, just the doctor's.

Sure enough, but it's got ter smart, hasn't it?

Like I say, after the second pill they send you away with painkillers and antibiotics. That's it, really, until you go back for a scan to check every-thing's...shifted.

I wished I hadn't chosen that word.

We sat in silence for a diplomatic couple of minutes while I composed myself.

So you'll help me, give me somewhere to hang out?

What you sayin'? Sure, I will. 'Course I will. What are friends for? She hesitated a moment before blurting: all those years together you'd 've thought Bill and you might 've worked out by now how not to get up the spout.

I gave a weary smile, and thought: go on, then, bring it on. I should've known what to expect from my friend Dimphna Bean, the wee scally who used to shout out in the street to vex any passing nun: *try wearing a cap!*

But said: quite right, we have no excuse.

At least you know now you're not barren.

Though somewhat callous, this was true enough. A couple of generations of failsafe contraception would do that for you: break the causal link between fornication and procreation. Nevertheless, what she said brought home to me like nothing else, not even the little blue line, I really was pregnant. Taken aback by the unexpected strength of my feelings, I said: I'd rather not talk about it anymore. So how about you and me just sit here in silence a while, and drink ourselves stupid?

Will I go get the corkscrew?

Bless her. Dimp was always there for me.

We sat together in her impersonal sitting room and with studied concentration began to work our way through her supply.

When, exhausted and drunk, I fell asleep on her uncomfortable sofa she let me lie.

It must have been hours later that I came to in the semi-dark with her hovering over me.

Seeing that I was awake, briskly she asked: how y'doin' doll?

Absolutely spiffing: you?

After many moments of silence, she said, now you've slept on it, you're still sure?

Yep, reckon so. I mean, I have actually slept on it rather a lot – that's why I've got so little time left to get on and get the thing done. See, after nine weeks it's a surgical solution, I said, all rational and self-possessed.

Taking me by surprise, she asked: an' this is the right course?

Well, plainly. It'd be ridiculous for me to even think of having a baby now – I've got quite enough on my plate.

A house restoration?

Not just that, Dimp! I said, somewhat exasperated that she still didn't get it. Wasn't she the one who spent the last twenty years telling me Bill and I wouldn't last?

Then my most militant ally among the childfree suggested something in a very small voice that, quite simply, knocked me sideways.

If not now, Abi?

Because it was easier to make a joke of it than consider that – damn her – Dimp might have touched upon what was in my most secret heart, I laughed, and said: you re-found your religion?

In that instant I really worried that she had. When it came down to it Dimphna grew up a Catholic, in Ireland. Erstwhile resident of a country in which it was still illegal for the unmarried to obtain contraception, deep down might she still believe that the only justification for abortion was if it were the result of a rape or incest, or the kid was going to be born terribly handicapped – that, perversely, an accidental pregnancy was the fitting comeuppance for the careless, or immoral, or inadequate?

You're not turning judgemental on me?

Course not, forget it, Abi. Whatever you decide, you know I'll stand by you. No question. An', I swear, I'll never say a word to Bill.

She sounded sincere. I smiled miserably back at her.

I didn't like children. Never had. Children patently ruined your life. Look at miserable Debby. Look at Greg – the bastard. Look at my own parents. But what if the house restoration, my chucking in my latest job, my desperate book idea, were all of them substitutes for the most frightening, enormous thing I could possibly imagine doing with my life? Something I hadn't until this moment dared openly to admit even to myself. Because, sitting across from Dimp, I knew that what I really wanted, more than anything, was a baby. This baby.

Dimp, what am I doing? I haven't even told Bill I'm planning to abort his... I mean, I haven't even told him there is a...

Saying the word out loud was beyond me and before I could draw breath, I was overcome by a sob that tore its way out of my throat. Coming cautiously over to me, she held me tight as she could. Crooning, more Irish than ever, she said: I know, I know, an' I'm so sorry for you.

Though I could barely feel the weight of her, held in her awkward embrace, she was practically sitting in my lap.

I managed to get out between the wrenching: I'm the one that's sorry.

We remained in that fragile hold until she sighed and shifted and, aware she was finding it difficult to breathe, I loosened my grip on her narrow ribcage. We held hands for a few more minutes and then she disengaged to retreat to her end of the sofa.

Thing is, I've got nowhere proper to live and the way things are looking, probably no husband either.

Dimp put on the sidelight so that I could at last read her face.

Me teeth 've started dropping out, was all she said.

She leaned forward and pulled back the parchment flesh of her cheek to display her missing premolars and I had a horrible flashback of her reaching inside her mouth to pluck out the olive stone before casually putting it aside.

Smiling tightly she said: still, you win.

It must, I knew, have taken her just as much courage to show her own frailty as for me to confess I'd changed my mind about the abortion.

There's always a way forward you know, Abi. Might not look like it right now, but, believe me, whatever you decide to do, you'll think it was inevitable, and the right choice. People always do. As fer me, I'll not be growin' these back in a hurry, she said grinning gappily.

She reached across to give my hand a squeeze, said: so, it's decided, you'll have another go at being happy, willya?

I've still got to tell Bill.

Before I could start crying again, she got in: whatever it is you two decide, you've my blessin' -'s far as I'm concerned: go forth and fuckin' multiply if that's what you want.

You? Counselling indiscriminate spawning, I said, shaking my head in faux disbelief.

I'll be knitting no booties.

I know, I know: all that plastic paraphernalia, the conversations about breast pumps...

How I see it: if having kids makes a mockery of getting an education, squanders your talents, ruins your life, since you've enyway been doin' that yourself for years, where's the harm?

There was something reliable and comforting about Dimp's inability to sweeten the pill.

Dimp, does it have to be this hard?

No....yes.

We both cried for a bit. Quite a long time, actually – you wouldn't have guessed a woman her size had so much water in her.

It was now evening and because, as always nowadays, I was clamming hungry I speed-dialled Deliveroo, in fact I recklessly ordered two meals. Seated still on her sofa, the TV on in the background, we both wolfed our food. It might be fairer to say, since I was now officially eating for two, I wolfed whereas fastidious Dimp felined hers. Nevertheless, she put real, actual food in her mouth and chewed (and swallowed). I knew this, because whilst pretending to be fascinated by what was on the box, I watched her. And, while I cleared away, she didn't shoot straight off to the loo to stick two fingers down her throat.

From my experience of people who engaged in risky survival strategies, when challenged, even when it was plain to see it was their preferred mechanism for coping with life that was killing them, they'd always claim they were fine, everything was fine. They could handle it. What was my fucking problem anyway? So her showing me her gappy teeth made me think this might be the moment at long last for me to intervene in her long drawn out suicide attempt.

All I said was: you're eating.

An' that's strange?

Exasperated, I shot back: stop messing, Dimp. You know what I mean.

This time she didn't snark back, so I took a harder line: look at yourself, you're a skeleton.

As I might have expected, Dimp retaliated with a joke: It's not that I'm too thin, doll, I think you'll find that it's your eyes that are too fat.

What gave me the courage to persevere was the terrible truth that if I'd confronted Nico the last time I saw him – even if I didn't know it would be – I might have saved him.

Your teeth falling out is no joke, Dimp.

Am I laughing?

It's not something that's going to get sorted by crystals or aromatherapy or homeopathy. None of that New Age crap.

Guess not.

Feeling my advantage, I was ruthless: so this time you're going to have to get on top of your anorexia, or bulimia. Or whatever it is. No messing.

No messin', she dejectedly agreed.

Like you say: there's always a way forward.

She glanced up from her lap to meet my eyes, said: right-so.

*

Dimp made me up a bed on her hard and horrible sofa, and I slept better than I had for weeks. It was just about getting light when, on her way out to work, she woke me with a cup of tea – real tea, with milk in it. Her parting words: if it's a baby you and that husband of yours decide you want, go ahead. Don't look back and don't overthink it, just take the fucker by the horns. In me vast experience a the world, it's what people do when they've got it all and – don't ask me why, fer I haven't a clue – it seems to make 'em happy or, at least, they're so fekkin tired and strung-out it gets in the way of all the wanky whining about the meaning of life. So, then, drink your tea, wash your face and go talk to that husband of yours.

With that she was gone.

# Chapter Fifty-four

You'll soon enough be able to interrogate Betty in person over exactly how long she's been party to William's extensive plans for reorganising all your lives. The very next morning she turns up on the doorstep. Not caring to beat about the bush, you confront her before she's even had the chance to divest herself of coat, hat and gloves and complain about the cold, saying, "I hear you're in need of temporary refuge?"

Betty chooses to understand by this, from the boyfriend.

"Darlin', Roberto's behaved like an absolute heel."

"Other women?"

"Seal, sweetie, the Beeb's absolutely chocka with them, every second person in his department..."

"Talks?"

"*Talkin'* wasn't what was at issue...a little Miss Jones, a Miss Muldoone...I mean there's nothing concrete, just the distinct reek of fish."

"Betty, in his case I'd trust to your sense of smell – you know he even tried it on with me on the night of our party."

Betty has the very good grace to say, "Poor you!" Seeking within her handbag for her compact, she begins unselfconsciously to powder her wonky nose so that when she speaks it's through pursed lips, "Was he beastly?", she asks.

"Rather civilised, actually – after our grapple he offered me a cigarillo."

"To think, it was my plan to get you two together in a locked room so you and he might huddle up and thrash something out. On the work front, you understand!"

Pitched somewhere between a bark and a hoot, Betty gives her short cry of upper-class laughter.

"Wasn't intendin' to let you out of there till I knew you'd given in to him!"

"Hardly your lookout, Betty, Roberto turning out a rotter."

"To be perfectly honest with you, never mind the man, I was beginnin' to mistrust that title of his – what with all these Continental types that 've come crawlin' out of the woodwork since the war, claimin' they were done out of the ancestral silver, the family *castello*. Goodness, tho', he *was* a bit of a gorgeous gargoyle. No?" Finished dusting, she snaps shut her compact. "Forget him, I have!"

Simple as that it seems, she has.

"More aggravatin' even than the man question, darlin', half the staff of our little press have mutinied – can you believe intend to start a breakaway magazine..." Dipping deadly accurate into it again, Betty now withdraws a packet of fags from the yellow gape of her handbag. "…the rats! 'S to be called "Inc." or some such nonsense…" Sparking up, she sucks in smoke. "…this new magazine of theirs."

You do find it hilariously appropriate Betty has been toppled by a popular rising of the intelligentsia.

"But quite frankly m'dear, bugger the mag, bugger the man, my blasted Bloomsbury landlord is being a terrific bore over the leasehold of my little flat so the most pressin' of my problems will be puttin' a roof over my head at murderously short notice."

Betty crosses the floor, to flick ash into the fireplace.

"With William away at camp and me back at Cambridge, at least we should be able to help out on the homeless front."

Betty tries, not very successfully, to look surprised, saying, "Bill might have suggested in passin' my movin' in here…."

"Even though it's somewhere ghastly your granny might live?"

Betty flashes her smile: "One would have to rip out that ghastly fireplace, put up modern wall coverings, hang some curtains, of course, and I don't think I could survive this yellow of yours for long, Seal, but the place *has* potential."

"So, all's well that ends well?"

"Darlin'," she puts her hand on your arm, "I'm beyond grateful: puttin' up with Roberto, puttin' me up!

Embarrassed by the intimacy of her unexpected touch, you blurt, "Before you get too carried away with my generosity, I should warn you that the house doesn't come without strings."

She gives you her quizzical cockeyed look.

"William might not have mentioned: alongside the ghosts of all the residents past, in taking on this place, you'll also be inheriting some current ones: Mr and Mrs McNamara – you know, the ones with the pram? But them, I promise, you'll hardly notice."

"Seal, darling, what is it they say about beggars and choosers?" Dipping again into that handbag of hers, insouciantly as though it were ten bob, Betty plucks out a fifty-pound note. Presenting it, says, "Some key money for your trouble."

You flinch from the thing as though she meant you harm, saying, "No, honestly, Betty, I couldn't possibly!"

"Nonsense – least I can do."

You're beginning to agree: it *was* the least she could do. A good and obedient girl, you think you deserve reward for willingly going along with the arrangements the grown-ups made behind your back as if they were no more than circumstances falling fortuitously into place.

It then occurs to you that you yourself might manipulate the situation from the wings to your own ends. Betty, being fearless, would be bound to know the best man for the job.

"Please don't take this the wrong way, but do you have the address of a good, safe abortionist?"

Typically cool and organised, without a flicker, "Dear girl, is that all?" she says, plunging straight back into that miraculous handbag to spear her little address book. "As it happens, a Sommerville woman I know needed one in a hurry a couple of months back and I was able to help her out with a quite lovely chap that got struck off I was introduced to at a party. Terribly glammy and handsome! I think I have the address still."

Beadily, she consults the minute address book. Being fearless, as well as believing herself above the law, she's listed him under 'A' for abortionist. Now fishing for her notebook, using a tiny silver pencil with which a debutante might note her dance partners, she scribbles the glammy doc's details.

"I know I keep bangin' on about it, but after you've taken care of that other matter, what I advise is a job. Really, the only way a girl may be truly free, make her own choices in life, is to have her economic independence. We should think ourselves lucky that in this day and age we at last have the possibility of fulfillin' ourselves by somethin' other than 'the man'! In light of recent developments: *he* may come and go, but what you've built with the sweat of your brow is yours forever. Along with the room of one's own, dear, money's the thing."

Placing the note and the cash in your hand, Betty gives you quite the warmest look possible out of one gimlet eye. Rather than the cockatoo on its perch, you are surprised to discover in this mannerism the regard of the wise, grey stork.

Soon after her departure you venture upstairs with the money and the abortionist's address, along with a last-minute addition all your own.

You surprise her on the landing, occupied in warming the baby's milk in a pan on the stovetop. Because such a tremendous sum embarrasses you, very much less graciously than Betty you bestow the fifty-pound note by posting it into Mrs McNamara's pinny pocket, saying:

"Look, I hope you won't be offended, believe me, I'm in no position to judge, please, just take it."

Wiping off her hands, she retrieves the folded note and failing to comprehend so great a sum, asks, "What's this then?"

"Fifty pounds. It's a fifty-pound note," you lamely supply, "Enough, if that's what you want, to go ahead with the...you know: *the other*."

You push into her other hand the slip of paper, saying, "Here's the name and address of a proper doctor who'll make a clean, safe job of it."

The woman examines Betty's scrawl with the same incomprehension as she had the bank note.

You fully expect she'll do what you yourself did, what any well-brought-up girl would do: refuse it. In which case, you would press her to accept.

Nothing of the sort.

The money and the address still held loosely, she says only, "Fanks." Then indicates the sorry thing the landlady still holds, saying, "An' what's that in aid of?"

"It's a shawl I knitted – I suppose it's in aid of the baby," you say, then, blushing, appalled she might have misunderstood, blurt, "For Larry, I mean."

She looks so stony-faced you think: that's it, the woman's going to clock me one.

Instead she laughs.

"Gawd's sake!" she says, reaching out to steady herself on your arm, quite creased up with it, "I fought it were a floorclorf."

A little taken aback by the mirth, even a little affronted, you say, "It was only a gesture, I know I'm not much of a knitter...."

"You can say that again!" Taking pity, she pats the hand holding the shawl, saying, "It *were* a kind fought, though – that, an' the doctor's name." She turns the bank note over again, as if it were mythical, "An' all this money. But I won't be takin' none of 'em orf you. See, I've decided to keep it. End of the day, I'm a tough bleedin' bird – some'ow I'll cope." Then, less gung-ho: "It's only what we're bred to, arta all, innit?"

She was, undoubtedly, a tough bird. Tougher than you, certainly. Nevertheless, feeling that you are dismissed – after all the effort you put in – rather starchily, you say, "Well, then, everything's been resolved satisfactorily."

"G'warn! Like I say, it's very kind of you. An' all this money!"

Her hands not knowing what to do with it, she's rolled the note up into the long white cigarette she now offers back to you. You hold up your palm to her, as though in fact turning down a smoke, saying, "Do keep it – it'll be a help with all the extra expense you'll be put to with the new baby."

At this moment you understand that pleasure Betty must take for granted: the autonomy to pass it on that having one's own money gave.

"Oh, I don't know about that..."

"Really, honestly, missus McNamara, it'd please me."

To physically put some distance between you: demonstrate you have no intention of taking back the money, you say, "Shall we go and have a look upstairs to see about making a nice little nursery up there?"

Even though you've lived here seven months you have never once visited this little garret under the eaves. Just like your own quarters, you discover the abandoned room was left stuffed to the gunnels with furniture, though this lot is broken and quite useless; like the deformed or demented or elderly relations one hides out of sight, out of mind.

Looking around the place, as though trying to sell her on the idea, you say, "It'll need a good clear-out and a clean too, some new curtains and a lick of paint, but I'm sure your husband can take care of that and you'll still have plenty left over to buy whatever else you'll be needing for the new baby."

Having appraised the place, you two gravitate to its grubby little window. Shoulder to shoulder you both look down onto this unfamiliar aspect of the square. Running up to the full stop of the festivities the ugly new houses across the way have been going up fast. So fast Dr Bone must now keep his eyes averted as he hurries along the road to the bus stop each morning.

Noticing some falling flakes, you say, "Look, it's begun to snow."

"Snow in time for Christmas!" she says like a little girl.

Not looking at her: "Did you tell him yet?"

"Yeah."

"He's pleased?"

"Fit to bust." She gives you her lovely smile and, not sure that, stupidly, you aren't going to cry, you again present the baby shawl you're still holding, bunched up like a duster, saying, "Sure I can't tempt you with this?"

Though you'd meant it as a joke, this time the inadequate bit of knitting doesn't reduce her to unselfconscious giggles. Looking startled, she reaches out for it: "Yeah, a course..."

"Don't worry, I understand, it's really not fit to wrap a baby in!"

She smiles her relief.

Then, her face stiffening, she says: "My milk!"

With that she's haring back off down the stairs to rescue her boiled-over pan.

Using the pointed end of a shattered chair leg you prize up a floorboard in this little attic room that would be a nursery. The shawl packed tight into the space between the noggins, you hammer back the board with the heel of your shoe. And finally lay to rest the sole sorry souvenir of this most momentous year.

Back downstairs in your own bedroom, with the long kitchen scissors to hand, you climb on a chair the better to witness in the mirror above the fireplace the act you're about to commit. Slicing crossways, through your combed forward front hair, you make a short, Juliette Gréco fringe. Then, evenly as you can, you cut six inches off all the rest, to just below the ears. The cut hair splashes softly upon the floorboards in an exploded semi-circle of dark feathers.

In the street, the snow feathers are falling thickly too. Lying along the tops of their bare black branches, the trees in the square are made graphic; the forgiving, fluffy white quilt thrown over the building site has formed dimples and hillocks out of rubble.

When William gets home the whole square is made over as a peerless beauty mantled in white under a white moon, and his wife as Juliette.

# Chapter Fifty-five

I must have gone sleepwalking again because I found myself up in the little attic room, looking down. It'd begun to snow: a frosting of sparklers soon dotting the narrow slot of the square to complement the stars above it, bright and lively as phosphorescence in a dark sea. As I stood there the scene was swiftly turned monochrome. The trees became a steel etching and the half-built houses were made insubstantial, illusory, behind the veil of thickly falling snow.

This time I understood what I'd been brought up here to do: I must rescue someone. A child. A boy. To show me the portal through which I could reach him, the moon had helpfully painted the shadow of an elliptical window onto the floorboards. Visible through the broken board the nephew put his foot through many months ago, curled up between the noggins, I saw that there was something white lying here, forgotten. Levering up the splintered board, I reached down into the space for it and my hands closed around a bit of knitting: a baby's shawl. It came up so easy and light it was as if I held nothing.

In a startled reflex I flung out my hand, smacking it against the mattress where Bill's body should have been. The hair at my temples wet with tears.

According to the green light of the alarm clock it was now 4:00. A little panicky, I ventured downstairs to look out for a cab. Only to find him, standing in the wrecked, denuded front room, under a bare electric bulb. Maybe it was because I was still half-asleep, still disturbed by my dream, that the malignancy of this place was particularly active tonight.

It's been days, we have to talk, was all he said.

Yes, we must. We really must. But first we should go somewhere.

Bill glanced around himself, saying: isn't this exactly where we should talk?

As if to baffle and block what he believed would be my inevitable objections, speaking fast, he continued: instead of putting it straight back on the market we'll have to see the restoration through. It'll have to be done to a sufficient standard – wouldn't make financial sense otherwise – but maybe not quite as high spec and high tech as you wanted. As we intended. That way we can at least have a stab at getting the budget back on track and, who knows, even reduce the schedule a bit.

He took a couple of steps towards me.

You mean we should talk about the house? I don't give a stuff about the fucking house.

Bill halted halfway across the floor to me. He was shaking his head in disbelief.

I repeated: I don't give a stuff about this fucking house, about where we live, how we live. All I care about is you. You are the one, the only one, who can give me what I need. Bill…

I moved to close the gap between us but he backed away from me, rubbing his eyes.

Well, what I need is somewhere comfortable to come home to.

Little enough, I knew. I took another step towards him and this time he didn't retreat.

You agree, Abi, we have some decisions to make?

Absolutely.

Stupidly, it seemed to me that, somehow, I'd cleared the chasm that seemed inexorably to have been opening up between him and me ever since we moved in here. Without even having to speak it out loud, Bill, of course, understood me.

We *do* have choices to make: what to do about this house, the baby…

Baby?

I meant to tell you before, but you've been back so late recently and we haven't exactly been getting on, but, you're right, we really must talk.

Bill retreated another couple of steps.

We *must talk*, must we? Now!

He was shouting quite loudly.

There's still time to…. I mean: it's still a choice we can make together…

Can we? Isn't all that's expected of me is that I fall behind what you've already decided. Which mostly I do. With very little complaint. I envy you, actually, Abi, you're educated, qualified up to your eyeballs, and you have all these options: change your job, change your job again, stop work, renovate a Georgian house, have a baby…

Don't you see, that's what's so hard: being pulled in all these different directions, never knowing what's for the best…feeling guilty I've made the wrong choice, wasted an option….

Because that's what life owes you: self-fulfilment, happiness?

Isn't happiness what everyone's after?

Maybe it is. But from where I'm standing, what I'm working so hard to provide seems to be your entitlement to pick and choose from a great big buffet of what life might just have to offer you. And, Abi, whatever you have on your plate, you keep going back to the table.

Though his sudden rage was shocking, a small part of me was appalled to think he might be right.

Bill, it's this fucking house…

Holding up his hand, he said: can you stop swearing? For once. Stop.

By now I'd backed him hard up against the window.

Though I was standing square in front of him, he wouldn't even look me in the eyes.

So, let me understand, this house, that you *had* to have, has fallen short – but, what d'you know, that's all fine because a baby's just what's needed to fill the gap? I can't deal with this. I can't deal with you anymore.

That's really it then, is it: we're done, you and me? I risked, hoping to shock him into a denial. No answer. Still not looking at me.

Taking a breath, I said: ok, then, first thing, I'll ask Dimp if I can move in with her until I've worked out something more permanent.

If that's what you need to do.

Bill's immediate capitulation cracked my heart right through.

# Chapter Fifty-six

You might both have received an education in holding back, both knew how to endure, but the difference between you was that over time your bad and William's best behaviour had only increased. The nicer he was to the convalescent, the more forbearing, the more of a bitch you grew in your turn. At first tongue-tied, then vindictive, then ashamed of yourself, you'd found it impossible to honestly say what really lay at the bottom of your inexcusable treatment of a kind and patient husband. Ever since you first embarked upon that courtly dance of denial, however, you've probably been gearing up to the confrontation in which the sharp words would be replaced by the throwing of sharp objects.

It was on the liberating night of the hair-cutting incident, as I remember it, you two were having a nightcap (gin with "Floridix" – William was probably trying to put some flesh back on your bones), and as if none of the last year amounted to anything very much, William started to say to his wife, "The sexy *rive gauche* look suits you, dear, the young men of Cambridge better watch out..."

And off you went, just like that. Not stopping to think, as if it were a grenade, you launched the cut glass tumbler you've been drinking from straight at his head. Even as it left your hand you found relief from the tension that'd been building in you, probably ever since you stopped crying into teacups.

Given your height and your strong right arm, it was lucky William used the same evasive technique as he did for the hard words. Just in the nick, ducking out of its path. Meaning that the hurled tumbler smacked with considerable force square onto the pane in front of which, only a second before, he'd been standing. At the moment of impact it let off the noise of the most tremendous explosion – as if the window in that dramatic instant released the pent-up memory of the last missile it survived all those years before: the wartime bomb. Odder still, just after he sidestepped your googly, you could've sworn it wasn't your own startled face looking back at you from the polished black mirror of the window but quite another woman. Whoever she is, or was, or will be, like the noise of the bomb, so it seemed that glimpse of this unfamiliar face was released, or relived in the memory of the sharp blow upon the pane.

Although it hit home quite hard enough to shatter the window glass, extraordinarily it was the heavy tumbler that smashed into smithereens. The wedding present set of six now down to an un-useful and uneven three, quite detached, you thought at the time.

You should have known, even in the instant, what little chance stood this grand, futile gesture against generations of self-constraint. What chance, indeed, despite all the erratic tutorials learned at Mother's knee, against the deep, sustained polish of his bred-in good manners. In this William Bone would always be the victor.

Immediately after the tumbler struck home he went pale and quiet, and then he simply stepped over the broken shards splattered across the floor only to return with a dustpan and brush with which to sweep them up. In this too, any evidence of the struggle between you would be tidied away.

Unable to bear it, you took the dustpan from his hands, saying only, "I broke it, let me take care of it."

If there was a definitive moment in which the girl who believed in the promise of marigolds switched over to the one that wanted something different, something more, it was when I flung, with murderous intent, the glass tumbler at my husband's head. And gave him final permission to leave me.

# Chapter Fifty-seven

It is at the very moment I realise Bill is suggesting we're over, done, that the most extraordinary thing happens. As if I've just served an unplayable zinger across the room at him, my husband ducks and the window he's seconds before been standing in front of, divides neatly across the horizontal fault line. We both watch as, in slow motion, the bottom half of the old pane falls into the room and smashes into smithereens on the floor.

In furious disbelief Bill shouts: you threw something at me!

Bill, I swear I didn't.

Then what made it smash like that?

My first thought, I have to admit, is: a poltergeist.

Cracks have now opened in the masonry to either side of the big, arched window.

More fascinated than furious, Bill says: look at that! The whole front of the house must've dropped and the pressure put on the windowpane made it give way at its weakest point.

Christ, Bill, I think you're right! Bloody builders...

Abi, I don't think we're safe in here.

I'll just put on some clothes...

I mean we should get out *right* now!

Grabbing hold of my hand he pulls me out of the room and down the hall. But the pressure the collapsing house has put onto the lintel means the front door won't budge.

Wait here, I'll find something to lever it open. When I've done that, Abi, fast as you can, I want you to run. I think the whole house might be about to go.

Bill's soon back with the wrench he now uses to make a purchase hole in the doorframe. Levering hard, ripping apart its hard as iron two-hundred-year-old wood, he manages to force the door open the few inches needed for me to escape. As I run across the square, I'm so relieved to hear his footsteps coming after me.

We both look back at our house. If I envisage immediate collapse, that the poleaxed drunk would face-plant into the road with a dying roar, for now at least the sagging house remains standing.

We stand there in the snow, Bill shielding me, holding me, like he'll never let me go.

It's only a house, Abi. Only a house, he says.

# Chapter Fifty-eight

Another September. Could it really have been getting on for the sixtieth since I left? Familiar and unfamiliar, the marigold room of memory was now all done over in dirty brown hessian, there were curtains hanging at the beautiful window, even some furniture. Anyway, an armchair. But, stupidly, the change in here I really couldn't get my head around, was the electric. When she switched on the overhead lamp I nearly reflex-clapped.

Because I was not at all sure I was invited to stay, not liking to presume, I went instead for a bit of a wander around the tottering stacks of books and papers that made as much of an obstacle course in here as had the massed furniture of my day.

Across the paper wastes an old owl peered back out at me from a hole in a tree.

"You got rid of the old fireplace," I said.

"If one's to live in any comfort...."

"Still, it was rather elegant."

She cocked an eye at me – a gesture that I was chastened to realise I'd forgotten.

Taking the plunge, I said, "I was sorry to hear about Will, I mean Bill."

"Even, as they say: after a long illness, bravely born, it came as a shock."

"He and Daphne had a happy marriage?"

She sniffed a sniff but said nothing.

"Funnily enough, I always thought it'd be a monk's life for our Bill – you know, locked abstemiously in his cell, head bent over his learned tomes. Come to think of it, he was made to have children. And I wasn't – quite literally, not. A bit of a duffer in all the female camps." Attempting to leaven the atmosphere, I reached for our common cause: "I maintain it was the study of literature that made such a terrible wife of me. You know: cogitating rather than cooking. But when I was starting out no one ever wrote about clotheslines or extending the loaf, did they, so, I ask you, how was I to know about any of it?"

"Right till the end he did every scrap of the cooking."

"Good for him – a man of his generation! So, everything worked out for the best: Bill got family life and I my life's work." Ignoring my efforts to keep this light, sociable, she sucked on her teeth, "Congratulations, certainly, are due on the sterling success of your various campaigns. But if you must know, Bill was quite a bit upset by that book of yours."

"Which?"

"The paperback."

"You read it?" I said, genuinely surprised. Betty handed over a battered copy of my neophyte novel.

"For years people called him Dirk."

I turned the thing over in my hands. It was the edition with the cover I hated and, yes, I could see the artist had made the young man look like Dirk Bogarde in the Doctor film series.

"Did they? Why is it, I wonder, if you're a woman, and write about sex or kids, even feelings, people always assume it must be autobiographical?"

"Daphne upset herself over it too."

"Truly, I'm sorry to hear that, I am. All I can say is it was intended to be a look back from a more enlightened era at the dysfunctional sexual politics of the fifties."

"Bill never meant to be unkind."

"I know. Really, Betty, I don't hold any of it against him. All these years on I can see Mrs William de Chancy-Bone was as much at fault as the doctor. At nineteen, she was a prig, as well as a snob, and I don't think I like her much."

Betty surprised me by saying, "Well, I always thought you brave. A good, brave girl. And I apologise for making you blush."

"Not hard to do: you were so much more sophisticated than me, and posh."

"Actually, Seal, I may have been posh but I was kind."

"Yes, Betty, yes you were that, and I *do* appreciate you nagging me about getting a job was about my independence, my sanity too! And even if I was intimidated and horribly jealous, I always envied your ability to appear so cool in a corset and heels."

I'd managed to crack that gargoyle face of hers.

"Ghastly thought, suiting the fifties!"

I didn't say that, so little had they suited me, I had to wait for the '60s for the sexual revolution to catch up with me.

"I also have to thank you for dragging me out of here that day, you remember...?"

Finding a pen in my bag, I wrote an inscription in my young book. Reading it, she smiled and put it by.

We were silent for a while: two old women marooned amongst our memories and the accumulated rubbish of the last half-century.

"I was meaning to ask you about someone else that share's our past," I said at last.

"That awful, lurking little Penfold man?"

"God no! Is he still around?"

"Not your greatest fan – buttonholes me in the street to this day, asking after 'missus Bone'."

"It was actually our tenants in common: Mrs McNamara and her husband I was curious about." At mention of the McNamaras Betty's face softened.

"You knew of course she was one of the famous Barnsbury Smiths?"

I didn't.

"Well, let's say the acorn didn't roll far from the tree: quite soon after I took possession, she and Pat moved over the way, into one of the little houses on the other side of the square."

I crossed back to the window, she joined me.

"You can see it from here," she said, pointing it out.

Seeing the pre-fabs, remembered the bombed-out terrace, I found myself unconsciously bending my knees to shift the fault line in the window over these houses I hadn't stayed here long enough to see as new-builds, that were now suddenly old, like me. And it struck me that the seam in the glass was like the portal between then and now, and this house the still point in whirling time.

"Before they picked up sticks again and went off to live in one of those ghastly new towns she used to come over to char for me." Metaphorically, Betty's glance swept the room at our backs. "As you see: stuff seems rather to stick to me. Puts the fellows off like nobody's business: negotiating the labyrinth!" She hooted that laugh that in the last decades I found I'd also forgotten.

"Till she and Pat deserted me for Milton Shulman, or wherever it is, it was her alone standing between me and this total dereliction. Not just her, Pat turned out quite the handyman: panelled over the dreadful dust-trap doors, ripped out the ghastly fireplace. Did wonders in the kitchen too, though I wasn't so keen on his choice of wallpaper – all those vegetables on strings. Who'd have guessed an Irish navvy could be quite so flamboyant?"

It occurred to me that she hadn't touched a thing in this room – probably the whole house – since the McNamaras departed. Although I could not but be appalled that to her mind 'housework' was the exclusive province of those women she called 'chars', I was nevertheless impressed that, by the look of this place, these last sixty years she had resisted cleaning, washing, cooking. Although this was no doubt down to her class rather than her feminist principals.

"Did the McNamaras have any more children?"

"Just the two."

"Larry and…?"

"Barry."

"I'm glad to hear Pat worked out how to put on a condom."

Ignoring me, she said: still smiling around her cigarette at the memory, "She told me once, if she'd had a girl, she'd have called it Marie, after herself."

Myself, I was properly chastened that Betty should know something I never got close enough to find out: her name was Marie.

"You know it was actually she who got me involved in the abortion Bill in the first place so, funnily enough, you could say what began with an ordinary working-class woman was brought to its resolution by a son of the manse."

(What I didn't tell her – too precious – was that what I did for her, and for all those women who came after, was down to that good, brave girl, Marie McNamara. And that most likely if she hadn't inspired me to get on with what was to be my proper life, sixty years on I'd be the one still looking out from this window, still haunting the place.)

As if she'd been reading my thoughts, Betty said, "And all that while you were off, changing the world, here I stopped: poor passed-over thing!"

She squawked a laugh that turned into a smoker's cough.

Because she was a poor passed-over thing, and it was tragic, meaning to be kind, I said, "I came across a back copy of that first mag of yours the other day. "Sic" wasn't it?"

She cocked her head at the dreadful title.

"I was impressed to see you talked Bernard Levin and Kingsley Amis into contributing."

"Odd to think of those two tucked up between the same covers."

"Weren't we all going through our Marxist phase back then?"

"I certainly wasn't!"

"No, Betty, dear. Naturally *you* weren't."

She gestured at the dusty stacks homed around her chair, saying, "One continues to toil at the well of course but absolutely no one makes money from writing anymore. What I would call *literature* if not already dead is mortally injured." Taking a deep draw on her fag, speaking on the exhale, she said: "The bottom falling out of the knife and fork business didn't help the finances either – who nowadays puts a canteen of cutlery on their wedding list? Do they have lists?"

"For all I know they don't even use cutlery."

"All in all, I really let down Mrs Wolf – not only no money but I can't even call this room my own. But my poor Bill was so kind; letting me stay on here all these years. Even now that he's gone."

Settled companionably on either side of her horrible electric fire I stayed on a while, me perched on a paper stack, Betty rattling through her crossword in the chair.

We were enjoying then the last few, poignant days in which summer into autumn slips, as Emily Dickinson so nicely puts it, and I seemed to witness the very moment one season conceded to the next. Almost imperceptible, but real: there, it turned. The room grew cooler and more indistinct and in this long drawn out and melancholy twilight I considered the wife I once was, the doors I opened, the ones I didn't.

And my words echo...

# About the author

SUSAN BARRETT was born in London and has lived there all her life apart from a year spent in Sydney, working as a short-order cook, living with a Maori brother and sister rock musician and opera singer. In her twenties and thirties she worked in film and television production, and got a toe on the housing ladder. Then she left an interesting and lucrative career, with status, to have two children, at a stroke demoting herself to housewife, mother and insecurely employed scribbler. As it turned out, all the above invaluable research for novel writing. The Housekeepers is her third published novel.

picture: Kathryn Faulkner

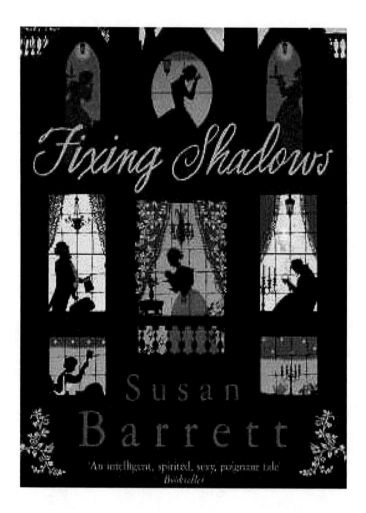

'An intelligent, spirited, sexy, poignant tale'
Bookseller

## FIXING SHADOWS

A star-crossed child is born at Fainhope Hall in 1873. For while the duchess is delivered of the infant upon whose head the fate of the Fainhope title and fortune rests, her governess, Miss Manilla, secretly gives birth to a baby of her own, illegitimate and destined for the workhouse. But the noble heir who will secure his mother's status is sickly, and does not survive the night, which the other, nameless boy thrives. And so a covert swap is arranged: the dead child for the living. The two women are locked into a pact that will seal their own fates, and that of the duchess's empire.

## THE INCONSTANT HUSBAND

When Patrick McKinley steps into her life through a window Rose Seaton's heart – primed to love by her mother and romantic novel habit – finds it's target. But dazzling though he undoubtedly is, this bohemian young artist is hardly the son-in-law her industrialist father has in mind. At a ball in honour of Queen Victorian's diamond jubilee, Patrick fatally ensnares her; now Rose must choose between the genteel tedium of home and home-grown suitors, and Patrick's quest after an ideal, artistic existence. Home doesn't stand a chance.